A Place
of Promise

THE KADE FAMILY SAGA

VOLUME 2

A Place of Promise

LAUREL MOURITSEN

STRATFORD
BOOKS

ISBN: 0-929753-08-9
The Kade Family Saga, Volume 2: A Place of Promise

Stratford Books
Eastern States Office
4808 37th Road North
Arlington, VA 22207

Stratford Books
Western States Office
P.O. Box 1371
Provo, UT 84603-1371

A Place of Promise
First printing: October, 2004

Printed in the United States of America

Dust jacket painting: *Nauvoo, Illinois, mid-1840s*, by Dan Thornton
Used by permission.

Portions of dialogue contained in this book are direct quotations from
actual historical figures as found in the seven-volume work, *History of
the Church*, by Joseph Smith.

Started reading 1/ /14
Finished " 1/25/14
24 chapters   Started reading
389 pages   8/18/18 Sat
               65419 SR 19 S.
               Wakarusa IN 46573-9707
               574-226-3207

Started 11/ 18/ Thur
              21

1,25 AM
      ended 12 pm Sun. Nov. 5, 2020
Started Vol. 2,   12 10/pm
reading

CHAPTER ONE

*I*t was cold. So bitterly cold that Elizabeth's breath frosted the
window as she stared out into the night. The angry shouts
coming from the street terrified her, and the light blazing from
a dozen torches scorched her eyes. In the gleam of the bobbing
and weaving torches, she saw dark shadows darting across
the yard.

"They're coming, Mama!" she cried. She turned from the
window just as the door to the cabin burst open with a sharp
crack and cold air rushed in. On its wing came half a dozen
men with torches flaring.

The intruders overturned furniture, smashed crystal and
china, jerked draperies from windows. Rough hands grabbed
at her. Elizabeth tried to dodge away, but her body moved like a
clock winding down. She screamed as one of the men cornered

her, his eyes wild and brutal. She twisted out of his reach, screaming, screaming, screaming . . .

Elizabeth awoke with a start. Sweat was pouring down her cheeks, and her legs were tangled in the bedclothes. The close darkness in the room felt suffocating. She gasped for breath, desperate to dispel the darkness and the ghostly nightmares. She scrambled from her bed and with shaking hands lighted the oil lamp on the nightstand, then turned up the flame until it drove the midnight shadows into the corners of the room. She cast a hasty glance at the window near her bed, afraid of seeing gleaming torches outside.

She hadn't experienced a nightmare like this one in over a year. She used to have them often, waking in the middle of the night with a scream on her lips and her nightgown soaking with perspiration. The Missouri persecutions still scarred her memories. But there were no torches now, no mob, and no angry shouts coming from the street. The only sound was her sisters' quiet breathing as they slept.

Elizabeth drew a shaky breath and turned down the lamp before its glowing light woke her sisters. She felt calmer now. She gathered enough courage to walk to the window and look out. A half-moon rode high in the sky, shedding a soft light onto the fields and gardens below. All seemed silent, still, and serene. Elizabeth pressed her nose against the pane. From her spot in the loft room, she could see half a dozen cabins nestled along the bend of the river, cozily wrapped in darkness. No demons rode abroad on the streets; no ghosts floated among the fields. The only specters lingering now existed solely in her mind, haunting her with fearful memories.

She wondered if James was ever tortured by such nightmares. Perhaps he had been too young to have many memories of their sufferings in Jackson County. Her brother had been only three-years-old when their father died and their mother sold the family farm and moved with Elizabeth and James to Missouri. In those days, the three of them had clung to each other for safety and support. But then her mother had met Christian Kade, and before Elizabeth could come to terms with the idea of having a stepfather disrupt the balance of their family circle, her mother had married him. She and James called him "father," but the name had never tasted sweet in Elizabeth's mouth. For Elizabeth, having Christian take the place of her natural father was another in a string of adversities she had suffered in Missouri.

She cast a last, quick glance out the window and then padded back to her bed. She lay under the blanket of moonlight, trying to dispel from her mind the last blurry remnants of her nightmare.

CHAPTER TWO

"That's it — secure the bandage now. Don't tie it too tightly." Dr. John C. Bennett stood back, allowing his young protégé to complete the dressing.

James Kade fumbled with the cloth bandage, and it was some seconds before the unruly ends yielded to his inexperienced fingers.

Dr. Bennett peered at the dressing James had just applied, and then addressed his patient. "That should take care of it, Brother Carter. Keep your arm immobile for the next few weeks and it should heal nicely."

"Thanks, Dr. Bennett. I appreciate it." Phineas Carter shook Bennett's hand, tipped his hat at James and then left the office.

The doctor began putting away the unused gauze and instruments.

"That was a nasty gash, wasn't it, Dr. Bennett?" James said, wincing as he recalled the ragged tear in Carter's forearm. It hadn't seemed to affect Bennett at all for the doctor had calmly sponged off the injury and deftly sewn the gash closed with a needle and coarse thread. Then he'd allowed James to bandage the wound. Twelve-year-old James had felt his heart beating wildly for fear of making a mistake as he wrapped layer after layer of cloth bandage around Brother Carter's forearm, and then finished it with a knot.

"A laceration of that type typically is. I've urged the men to take precautions when using those new mechanized grain reapers, but invariably I get a case like Brother Carter's once or twice a summer."

James nodded with understanding. He was familiar with the sharp vibrating blade on the horse-drawn reaper for he'd spent the last month working on a neighbor's farm, helping with the harvest. He earned twenty cents a day for his labors, which he was saving to buy an antler-handled pocketknife he'd seen in the window of the mercantile. The harvest was nearly in now, just in time for James to begin the fall term of common school.

"Farm-related accidents make up the biggest share of injuries during the summer months," Bennett was saying as he bent over the drawer where a collection of gleaming, odd-shaped instruments lay, lined in a row. "Yesterday I treated a fellow whose foot was nearly torn away. He'd gotten it tangled in the wheel of a moving hay wagon."

Bennett slammed the drawer with a bang that made James jump.

The doctor's office occupied the front portion of his small stone house near the river. It held a bed, two chairs, a table with a wash basin and pitcher resting on it, and the cabinet where Dr. Bennett stored his medical supplies. In addition to the front office, a second, smaller, adjoining room served as Bennett's personal office and doubled as a birthing and surgery room. As the physician narrated for James the procedure he'd performed on the patient's foot, he spoke in his usual rapid fashion, using his hands to embellish each point. His eyes were never still; they darted from one spot to another as he talked. His narrow brow, beaked nose, and black, beady, restless eyes gave him a hawk-like expression. He swooped about the office like a bird of prey, snatching into his claws a bottle of medicine or a roll of bandages.

Dr. Bennett was an acquaintance of James' father, Christian Kade. In one of their conversations together, Christian mentioned that James was interested in doctoring, and Bennett suggested that James visit him at his office. James had already been half a dozen times and on each occasion Bennett had talked with him about the practice of medicine. But he was surprised when the doctor invited him to wrap Brother Carter's arm today, even though Bennett had directed him every step of the way. In Brother Carter's hearing, Bennett had referred to him as "my young assistant," which made James' chest swell with pride.

"I'd better be going," James said reluctantly. "I still have chores to do at home."

"You may come tomorrow if you like," Bennett said, rinsing his hands in the wash basin.

James watched the water turn pink from the blood on Bennett's hands. "Thank you, sir. I'll do that. Good night, then."

Bennett grunted.

James jammed on his cap and started out of Bennett's office.

"James?"

"Yes, Dr. Bennett."

"You did fine, boy."

"Thank you, sir," he responded, elated by Bennett's word of praise. He shut the office door behind him and started home. Bennett had said he'd done fine. Fine! He happily kicked aside a pebble in his path, plunged his hands into his pockets, and began whistling a cheery tune.

Dr. Bennett occupied an existing stone house, but most of the Saints upon arriving in Nauvoo had erected rough log cabins like the one in which the Kades resided. The Kades' cabin consisted of two rooms separated by a log wall, and a second story loft. As James approached the house, he could see smoke curling out of the chimney on the slanted roof. The roof extended over the front of the cabin, creating a narrow covered porch. His mother's rockingchair held a position of honor on the porch; at the moment, it was claimed by his four-year-old sister, Roxana, who was rocking back and forth with her rag doll cradled in her arms.

The chair squeaked rhythmically as she rocked. James could hear her singing to her doll with the creaking of the chair as accompaniment. When she noticed James entering the yard, she bounded from the rocker and ran to meet him.

"James," she cawed. "Where have you been?"

James took her hand as they walked together to the house. "At Dr. Bennett's office."

"Are you sick?" Roxie asked.

"No. I was helping him."

"Effie is sick," said Roxie, holding out her doll for James to see. "She has an ouchy on her toe. Can you make it better?"

James paused to study the doll's cloth foot. A stitch had come loose and the rag stuffing was beginning to poke through.

"I think I can. But Effie will need stitches. Remember when you cut your ankle on a sharp rock and had to have stitches?"

Roxie bobbed her head. "I cried and cried."

"Yes, you did. Maybe if you hug Effie real tight while I put in the stitches, she won't cry."

Roxie pressed the doll to her chest. "James will take care of you, Effie," she crooned, "and the stitches won't hurt much."

James patted his sister's dark curls, then hurried into the house with Roxie at his heels.

"James, is that you?" his mother called. Lydia Kade stood at the fireplace, stirring their supper, which bubbled in an iron pot hanging from a hook in the hearth.

James went to his mother's side and sniffed at the contents in the pot. The hearty aroma of diced potatoes, carrots, and stew meat simmering in the broth sharpened his appetite. He patted his stomach in anticipation. At twelve, James was already as tall as his mother. And he was filling out. His shoulders were becoming broader, and his arms and chest more muscular.

"I expected you before now. Have you been at Dr. Bennett's office all this time?"

"Yes, Ma. He said I could come again tomorrow, too."

"You're not making a nuisance of yourself, are you?"

James shook his head quickly.

"Then, you may go — so long as you don't neglect your studies or your chores. Wash your hands for supper now." She turned her attention to Roxie who was explaining about her doll needing stitches.

Instead of going first to the pump to wash up for supper, James slipped into the adjoining room where his father's books were kept. Christian was still at the printing house where he assisted with the publishing of the Church-owned newspaper, the *Times and Seasons*. For the past several days he'd been talking with the brethren about the possibility of starting a secular newspaper in Nauvoo. James turned up the oil lamp then went to the shelf that held his father's books.

He bent closer so he could see the titles clearly. His father had collected a small library with topics ranging from poetry to economics. A well-worn volume of Thomas Paine's essays, printed lectures by Holmes and Emerson, Cooper's novel *The Last of the Mohicans* which James had read and reread eagerly, and Bancroft's *History of the United States from the Discovery of the Continent* occupied prominent places on the shelf. Classic Greek and Roman authors sat next to contemporary writers such as Cooper, Dickens, Hawthorne, and Irving. James' eye quickly moved through the familiar titles until he found what he was looking for. He pulled the bulky book from the shelf and flipped through the pages. A copy of *The People's Home Medicinal Library,* or a book similar to it, was common to every household where it could be referred to in the treatment of illness or injury. James read a piece on the treatment of lacerations. Then he snapped the book shut, consumed with a longing to know more about medicine, what caused illness and how best to treat it. He'd seen enough of suffering and death, even at his tender age, to know it on intimate terms. And he wanted to do something about it. Make a contribution. Have some small part in relieving the pain and misery of humankind. He returned the book to the shelf and stood staring at it for some time; then he turned down the lamp and left the room.

When supper was over, James' sisters cleared away the dishes while Lydia put two-month-old Zachary to bed. Christian settled in a chair to read his newspaper. James seized the opportunity to speak to his father in relative privacy. He pulled up a chair opposite him and sat down. Noise from the street filtered in through the open cabin door, left ajar to provide relief from the sultry summer heat.

Christian glanced up from his paper and smiled. "How did everything go today, James?"

"Fine, Pa. I finished all my chores and most of my studies."

"Most of your studies?" Christian's eyebrows rose a fraction of an inch.

"I promised Ma I'd get up early to finish what I didn't get done today."

"That's fine," Christian replied. He turned again to his paper.

"Pa?"

Christian looked up a second time.

"Can I ask you something?"

"Of course." Christian folded his newspaper and set it aside. "What is it, son?"

"I was wondering if you have any medical books packed away."

Christian scratched his chin, thinking about the question. "No, not any more. I used to have a couple of books, but they were destroyed when a mob broke into my cabin in Jackson County."

"Oh." James was visibly disappointed.

"I'm sorry, son."

"That's all right."

"But I'll tell you what we can do. I can borrow one for you. I'll ask Dr. Bennett. He should have some books you'd find interesting. I'm sure he wouldn't mind lending one or two to you."

"Do you think so, Pa? I've seen the books in his office. Rows of them. I hadn't dared touch them, though."

"I've a better idea. Why don't you ask him yourself the next time you're at his office?"

"If you think it would be all right."

"No harm in asking, James." Christian reached out and rumpled the boy's hair.

"Thanks, Pa."

"You appear to be quite serious about all of this. Have you thought about becoming a doctor?"

James nodded. "Yes, I have. I've thought about it a lot." He described his afternoon in Dr. Bennett's office, how Brother Carter had come in with a terrible cut on his arm after getting it caught in the reaping machine, and how Dr. Bennett had washed the wound and sewed it closed so that it looked to James almost as if nothing had ever happened. "He let me bandage it over. The only way people will be able to tell is by the scar it'll leave. Pa, I thought that was the most wonderful thing I'd ever seen done. To take a man's skin as torn and bloody as Brother Carter's was and make it well again was remarkable. I want to be able to do the same."

"Then that's what you should do. I'll help you in any way I can. Both your mother and I will."

"Do you think I could? I'm not quick and bright about things like Elizabeth. Maybe I couldn't learn what I need to know." James frowned as his confidence waned.

"Of course you can. You bandaged Brother Carter's arm today, didn't you?"

"Yes, I did, and Dr. Bennett said I did a fine job," James said with a surge of pride.

"There, you see. I believe you may have a natural bent for the profession."

"But I'd have to go away to school. There's not a school of medicine here in Nauvoo. That would cost money. And you and Ma need my help here."

"We can work out all those things in their own due time. Meanwhile, if you're sure this is the course you wish to pursue, perhaps you could apprentice with one of the doctors here in town. That way, when you are ready to start in the school of medicine you'll be amply prepared."

"That's exactly what I've been thinking."

"You'll be successful, James. I've every confidence in you."

"Thanks, Pa." James gave his father a hug.

"What is James to be so successful at?" Elizabeth approached them, her skirt swishing as she walked, and her long ringlets bouncing at her shoulders.

"Your brother is planning to become a physician," Christian told her.

"A physician! Aren't you a bit young for that, James?" Her voice was teasing, but her blue eyes betrayed a trace of sarcasm.

James shook off the sudden embarrassment her words caused him to feel. "Not right now, of course. But in time, yes, I'd like to become a doctor."

She shrugged. "I can think of more pleasant occupations."

James was surprised by his sister's belittling remarks. Although Elizabeth was two years his senior, they'd always shared a close camaraderie; lately, however, he'd noticed a shift in her attitude. Whereas once he had been able to talk with Elizabeth about anything and have in her an ally and friend, now she seemed to be growing distant and unapproachable. He studied her for a moment while she conversed with Christian, considering the differences between them. She was more witty and clever than he, and more adept in social situations; he was inclined to be reserved and serious-minded. James admired her spunk and her courage, as well as her quick mind. While he struggled to do well in school, she seemed able to grasp the essentials of any subject without much effort.

But Elizabeth had her weaknesses, too. She could often be stubborn and belligerent. And she occasionally exhibited selfishness and pride. James tended to forgive her more negative qualities for he knew that she carried scars from the past, manifested in frequent nightmares. James had heard her cry out in her sleep just the night before. She used to confide in him when she was tormented with haunting dreams, but now the only way he knew she was suffering was when he heard her restless moans in the middle of the night.

"While James is deciding his future, I have a request. Mama said to ask you if I may have a new bonnet for the church social this Saturday," Elizabeth said to her father.

"What's wrong with the bonnet you already have?"

"It's getting old and worn, Papa. I saw the most adorable straw bonnet in the mercantile the other day and I so had my heart set on it," Elizabeth pleaded. "It's not at all expensive, either. If you approve, then it's fine with Mama." Elizabeth teetered on her feet, awaiting her father's decision.

James frowned at his sister. He was well aware that their mother had agreed to the new bonnet only after Elizabeth's endless cajoling. He'd heard her badgering Lydia about it for the past week.

"All right, Elizabeth. Just be sure pride isn't overruling good judgment."

"Oh, it isn't, Papa. Thank you so much." Elizabeth flung her arms around Christian's neck. A moment later Roxana scampered over with her doll, and Millicent straggled after her. Both girls climbed their father's knee and snuggled into his lap. Two-year-old Milly laid her head against Christian's, her soft red curls splaying against his cheek.

James sighed. The private discussion with his father had come to an end. He borrowed Roxana's rag doll, and with a needle and coarse thread closed the hole in the doll's foot while Roxana anxiously looked on. When he'd completed the task to Roxie's satisfaction, he climbed the ladder to the loft that served as his bedroom. A pile of schoolbooks rested on the nightstand, put there by his mother for summer reading. He sat down, eyeing them with misgivings. The scene at Dr. Bennett's office that afternoon sparkled in his memory. He imagined himself working alongside the doctor, cleaning and stitching their patients' wounds. He smiled as the scene unfolded in his mind.

The sun felt warm and prickly on the back of James' neck as he hurried home from a morning of fishing at his favorite hole along the bank of the Mississippi. He whistled as he walked along Water Street, his fishing pole over his shoulder. He wasn't far from Joseph Smith's two-story log house; perhaps he'd catch a glimpse of the Prophet. Brother Joseph was often outside chopping wood or talking with some of the brethren. Occasionally he'd stop to play ball with the boys, or challenge them to a wresting match. James enjoyed listening to his sermons preached in the grove near the temple site. They filled him with a fire that warmed his soul for days afterwards.

James glanced at the Prophet's home as he walked by, but he couldn't spot Brother Joseph in the yard. When he reached his family's log dwelling, he pushed open the door and set his fishing pole on a chair near the window. A note lay on the table; his mother had taken the girls shopping. Probably for Elizabeth's new bonnet, James thought ruefully. He cut a slice of freshly baked bread left cooling on the window sill, smeared it with raspberry jam, and gobbled it down. Then he left the cabin, heading for Dr. Bennett's office.

Dr. John C. Bennett was one of the most respected men in Nauvoo. Not only was he a physician with a successful practice, but he was also mayor of the city and major general of the Nauvoo Legion. Bennett had come to Nauvoo the summer before, in 1840, and quickly became a trusted friend to Brother Joseph and the other Church leaders. He'd worked tirelessly to secure the city's charter and build up the town. When the Saints first came to Commerce, as it was then called, there was nothing but a few log cabins and a couple of stone houses set in a swampy mosquito-infested marsh. The Saints had turned that marshy bog into a thriving city.

It had not been easy establishing Nauvoo. After being driven out of Missouri, the Saints were destitute. James remembered well his own family's exodus from the state; they had left Far West with only the barest of necessities piled in a creaky old hay wagon. With no room in the wagon for them to ride, the family had made the cold and wearisome trek across Caldwell County on foot. James shivered, recalling the endless tramping over the frozen ground on feet numb with cold.

When they reached the Mississippi, they met several families of Saints making their way across the river into Quincy, Illinois. He vividly recalled seeing one little girl with rags tied on her feet for shoes, and a tattered blanket wrapped around her shoulders for a coat, starting across the ice-covered river. The rough ice bit through the rags on her feet; as she crossed the frozen river, she left a blood-streaked trail to mark her path.

Once they arrived in Quincy, they stayed with James' uncle and his family. James was grateful for his uncle's warm house and equally warm hospitality. While they rested and recuperated from their travel, his uncle helped them obtain a sturdy wagon and team of horses. James suspected he also gave Christian money and food, for when they pulled out of Quincy three months later, they were well supplied with both. By that time, the Saints were gathering in Commerce. The Prophet had just recently settled there himself after spending the previous five months unjustly incarcerated in the squalid jail at Liberty. The Saints were jubilant to see him once more, and his presence bolstered the morale of the people.

During the summer of 1839, as the Saints were pouring into Hancock County, many fell sick with fever. Brother Joseph was ill also, but after he regained his strength he went about the camp administering to the others. James heard it said that he miraculously healed a number of the Saints; some were made well on the spot under Brother Joseph's hand. James had no doubt that what he'd heard was true. As a young boy, he had been healed by the same priesthood power.

Under Joseph's leadership the city blossomed. The name was changed to Nauvoo, meaning "The City Beautiful." And it was beautiful, indeed. The city was situated on a high point of ground around which swept the mighty Father of Waters on three sides. East of the city stretched an expanse of prairie and woodland. Opposite Nauvoo, on the west bank of the river, spread the town of Montrose. James loved to sit on the river bank and watch the steamers chug into view. The Mississippi was alive with all kinds of river craft — steamers, keelboats, flatboats, and barges. Many visitors traveled by river to Nauvoo to see the Saints' growing city. Nauvoo was easily the most promising spot in all of Illinois. Almost 4,000 people resided there, from nearly all parts of the country and immigrants from Britain. Members of the Twelve Apostles had recently returned from their missions to Great Britain, bringing with them hundreds of converts.

Perhaps the most distinctive thing about Nauvoo was the temple that was being built there, on a rise that overlooked the city. The cornerstone had been set in place four months earlier, on the sixth of April, and construction was progressing at a steady pace. It was going to be a magnificent temple. At great sacrifice, the Saints were donating their time and money toward the building of it, but James knew the temple would be a blessing to them. Baptisms for the dead and other sacred ordinances would take place in this holy edifice. James had felt the spirit of the work already while laboring on the temple with his father. It was a calm, sweet spirit of assurance. He could hardly wait for the structure to be finished.

Though he had been in Nauvoo little more than a year, James loved the city. The sights and smells of building, the cultivated fields, the stores and shops, all of it elicited a tender contentment in his breast. At last the Saints had found a refuge, a place of peace. He retained only vague memories of his early home in Green County, Illinois; in Missouri, most of his young life was filled with the terrors and uncertainties of mob rule. He had seen his neighbors suffer abuse and persecution. That was the reason he wanted to become a doctor. As a physician he could alleviate some of their sufferings; nurse bruised bodies even if he was not able to repair shattered dreams. And Dr. Bennett was willing to help him.

Bennett welcomed James into his office, and during the afternoon when he was unoccupied with patients he talked with James about the practice of medicine. When James asked if he might borrow a few books, Bennett agreed to loan them. He even showed James how to set the broken arm of a young man who came to the office in need of the doctor's help. James' admiration for the doctor was unrestrained. He thought Bennett was the finest man he knew and he hoped some day to become just like him.

CHAPTER THREE

Elizabeth idly twisted a blonde curl around her finger. She'd rather have worn her hair parted and pulled to the back in a sleek bun, instead of hanging loose at her shoulders, but her mother said she was too young for such a style. Elizabeth didn't agree. She would be fourteen in another month, certainly old enough to dress her hair more fashionably. She imagined herself clothed in an emerald silk dress adorned with lace, ribbon bows, and puffy English sleeves. On her head she pictured a wide-brimmed bonnet trimmed with green ribbons. The image was more satisfying than the plain dress of checked gingham she wore.

"Miss Kade."

Her head jerked up. "Yes, Brother Bowers?"

"Can you provide the answer for us?"

Elizabeth's cheeks grew hot. She glanced across the room nervously. James, who was seated a few rows away, stared at her. "Um, what was the question, sir?"

"If you had been listening, instead of daydreaming, Miss Kade, you would have heard the question." The schoolmaster thrust her a sharp look. "Who can help Miss Kade with the answer?"

A couple of hands shot up. One of the boys in class answered the question to Brother Bowers' satisfaction.

Elizabeth frowned. She felt Brother Bowers had deliberately tried to embarrass her. Elizabeth wished she were elsewhere — anywhere but in this stuffy old classroom talking about a dead civilization.

"Psst, Elizabeth."

Elizabeth twisted in her seat. Sarah Rogers, a girl near Elizabeth's own age, slipped a folded piece of paper under the desk to her. Elizabeth took the paper from Sarah's hand and hid it in the folds of her skirt. She waited until Brother Bowers' back was turned and then she quickly opened the note. On the paper was a drawing Sarah had made of the schoolmaster. The figure resembled a scarecrow complete with a lumpy body, arms and legs bent at haphazard angles, and a pile of school books balanced on his straw-stuffed head.

Elizabeth giggled. She couldn't help it; the picture was comical.

"Miss Kade?"

"Yes, sir?" Elizabeth answered quickly.

The schoolmaster marched to the bench where Elizabeth sat. He was tall and spare, with long arms and legs. He had a sharp, angular face and iron gray hair, and eyes that had no place in them for mirth. He paused directly in front of Elizabeth. "Is there something humorous you would like to share with the class?" he asked sternly.

"Humorous, sir? No, sir," Elizabeth replied. She scrunched up the note into a tight ball. "I don't know what you mean."

"May I have a look at that?" The schoolmaster pointed to the wad of paper clutched in Elizabeth's fist.

"It's nothing. Really. Just notes I was taking on the lesson. I was very interested in your lesson," she added, trying to sound sincere. This last remark drew snickers from a few of Elizabeth's classmates.

"May I?" Brother Bowers insisted.

Elizabeth slowly unclenched her fist. The crumpled ball of paper lay in the palm of her hand. She held out her hand to the schoolmaster.

Brother Bowers plucked up the paper as if he didn't want to soil his fingers with it. He unraveled it, then smoothed the paper out flat.

Elizabeth watched him stare at the drawing. When he looked up, his eyes were smoldering with anger. "I'm afraid I fail to see the humor in this drawing. As you are the daughter of stalwart, respected parents in our community, Miss Kade, I don't understand your behavior. I will show this to your father and see if he finds it amusing."

Elizabeth sunk down in her seat. Christian would be angry with her for misbehaving in class. "Yes, sir," she replied sullenly.

The schoolmaster fixed Elizabeth with an icy stare, and then slipped the drawing into his vest pocket.

Elizabeth slouched lower on her bench. She heard Sarah Rogers sniggering behind her. She felt like turning around and pinching Sarah. It was Sarah's fault that she had gotten into trouble in the first place. When she was sure Brother Bowers was not looking in her direction, she turned in her seat and stuck out her tongue at Sarah. Sarah merely tossed her head and glanced away.

The rest of the school day dragged by. Elizabeth was relieved when Brother Bowers finally closed his books and dismissed the class. Avoiding his gaze, she filed out of the classroom with the other students. She hurried through the yard, where Sister Bowers' laundry flapped in the brisk autumn breeze like giant birds on the wing. The Bowers' log cabin doubled as a schoolhouse; Brother Bowers had built a one-room addition to serve as the classroom. In cold weather the room was heated by a black pot-bellied stove, and in warmer temperatures the single window was thrown open to admit a breeze. Each student shared his bench and desk with a partner, and the schoolmaster presided from a forbidding desk at the head of the room.

Elizabeth didn't wait for her brother, instead starting up the street alone; James would surely have a critical remark for her concerning the day's incident. In a few minutes' time, she reached the log structure that was the

Kade home. The cabin sat on the lower end of Durphey Street, not many blocks from the river. A split-rail fence surrounded the property, enclosing a barn, smokehouse, a small orchard of peach trees, and a garden. The corn was taller than Elizabeth by this time of year, golden yellow, and ready for harvest. Corn was the staple crop in Nauvoo, and it dominated the Kades' half-acre garden. But the garden that Elizabeth's mother carefully tended also produced potatoes, beans, peas, squash, pumpkins, and melons. The family also kept a cow for milk, butter, and cheese; and chickens for eggs and meat.

The cabin sat on a large city block, fronted by a street wide enough to accommodate foot traffic, horse-drawn wagons and carts, buggies and carriages. Although the log house was rough-looking on the outside, it was comfortable on the inside. Windows with glass panes let in the sunlight, a stone fireplace kept the cabin warm, and the interior walls were brightened with a coat of white-wash. Two rooms comprised the ground floor with two more in the loft above.

When James arrived home a few minutes after she did, Elizabeth managed to avoid conversation with him. James attended to his chores and then left for Dr. Bennett's office.

Elizabeth's father came home a few hours afterward. His expression gave no indication as to whether or not Brother Bowers had shown him the drawing. Nothing of the incident was mentioned at supper. After the supper dishes where washed and put away, Elizabeth went to her room. She was just beginning to think Brother Bowers had changed his mind about informing Christian of the drawing when she heard her father's step on the wooden ladder leading to the loft. He paused at the top rung. As Elizabeth looked over at him, her heart skipped a beat.

"May I come in?" Christian asked her.

"Of course, Papa." Elizabeth shifted uneasily on the bed where she sat, cross-legged, leaning against the wall of the cabin.

Christian pulled a chair close to her bedside. He sat down on it and studied his hands for a moment. Then he raised his eyes to Elizabeth. "Brother Bowers came by the printing office this afternoon to see me," he said in an even voice.

"Oh?" The word came out as a squeak.

"Would you like to tell me about the difficulty you had today in his classroom?"

"It was all a misunderstanding, Papa. This girl named Sarah Rogers drew a mean picture of Brother Bowers and passed it to me to see."

"Yes. He showed me the drawing," Christian replied, nodding his head.

"Brother Bowers thought it was me who drew the picture and I got into trouble for it. And it wasn't my fault at all." To her consternation, Elizabeth felt hot tears spring up behind her eyes. She blinked, forcing them back. She was certainly too old to have her father see her crying.

"So you didn't make the drawing yourself," Christian said.

"That's right. Honestly, I didn't," Elizabeth replied.

Christian was silent for a moment, his face somber. "Even though you didn't draw the picture, Elizabeth, you participated in making sport of Brother Bowers. You behaved disrespectfully toward him. That is what troubles me. Your mother and I have always taught you to be respectful of others, and particularly of your elders and those in authority over you."

"I didn't do anything wrong," Elizabeth repeated with fervor.

Christian laced his fingers together. "What do you think should be done to rectify the situation?"

"I don't know," Elizabeth muttered, staring at the faded quilt that covered her bed.

"Would an apology be in order?"

"An apology for what?" Elizabeth said in a prickly tone. She felt anger rising within her. Her father was siding with the schoolmaster, and it was unfair of him.

"Brother Bowers feels you were offensive and disrespectful. And you caused a disturbance in class. Perhaps an apology from you would smooth things over, even if you feel you weren't entirely at fault."

Elizabeth's face took on a sullen expression. She clenched her hands in her lap.

"What is the right thing to do?" Christian pressed her.

She shrugged her shoulders.

"Whose example should you follow? Perhaps that will help you arrive at the answer."

Elizabeth knew the answer her father wanted from her. It was Christ's example she should follow, of course. But she couldn't bring herself to say it. She didn't want to be led so easily by Christian. She pressed her lips together into a tight line.

"The Savior spoke often of peacemaking and He was the supreme example. Be a peacemaker, Elizabeth. Even if you're unjustly accused, a spirit of peacemaking will always stand you in good stead. Sacrificing one's pride never diminishes character; it only enhances it."

As Christian rose to his feet, Elizabeth stared grudgingly at him.

"I trust you to do what you feel is right," he said, putting a hand on her shoulder. "Good night, Elizabeth. I love you." He bent to kiss her cheek. Elizabeth sat rigid, unresponsive to Christian's show of affection.

When he left the loft room, Elizabeth lay on her bed. She rested her chin on her arms as Christian's words spun in her head. She resented his preaching and prying. He presumed to have the answer for nearly everything, Elizabeth thought with a scowl. Who was he to tell her how she should feel? He didn't know the first thing about how she felt inside. How could he for he wasn't her natural father.

Elizabeth flopped onto her back. This wasn't the first time such thoughts had troubled her. Part of her yearned to accept Christian as her parent without reservation, just as James did; but another part of her wouldn't forget that

Christian was not actually her father. Her father lay buried in the ground of Green County, Illinois.

Memories filled Elizabeth's head. Usually she tried to suppress such reminiscences because they brought unhappy feelings with them. But she let herself dwell on them now. It seemed to give her a certain perverse satisfaction. And, in fact, she wanted to make sure she never forgot the memories of her childhood. She wanted to hold them close, even if they caused her pain.

In her mind she formed a picture of her natural father, Abraham Dawson. She recalled his dark brooding eyes, his black hair and curly beard. His big hands had always symbolized security for her. Even though the family — her father and mother, James and herself — had lived in a small crude cabin in the back woods of Green County, she had experienced a happy childhood. Happy until that day when their neighbor, Mr. Slater, brought the news of her father's death.

Elizabeth shivered with the memory of it. She closed her eyes, experiencing again the pain she had felt as a five-year-old child. She had been devastated by the loss of her father. James had seemed to accept it, but he had been too young to really grasp the significance of their father's death. Her mother had mourned in her own quiet way. She had tried to comfort Elizabeth, but Elizabeth had shut everyone out. She wanted to wrap herself in her own private misery, insulate herself from the pain. No one, not even her mother, could penetrate the cocoon of suffering Elizabeth had spun for herself.

Things might have gotten better, Elizabeth reasoned, if her mother had not made the mistake of selling their farm in Green County and moving to Independence, Missouri. The move proved to be the beginning of a long nightmare for Elizabeth. In Missouri her mother joined the Mormon Church. Because of their religious beliefs, the Mormons in Missouri were hated and persecuted. Elizabeth's family was driven from place to place by lawless mobs who were bent on destroying the Saints. The memory of all they had suffered burned in her mind with blazing clarity. All of the security Elizabeth had felt in Green County was snatched away from her with her father's death. Snatched away and replaced with uncertainty, fear, resentment, and hurt.

Elizabeth groaned aloud. She got to her feet and began pacing the room. These memories tortured her. She knew she shouldn't dwell on them, nurse them, but she felt powerless to control her thoughts. She forced herself to sit down on her bed. The feel of the sturdy homemade quilt helped to quiet her emotions. She rubbed a hand across the worn fabric, made soft by repeated washings. It lent her a measure of reassurance. She was safe now. Safe here in Nauvoo.

Her thoughts returned to the present. Christian's words reverberated in her ears. He wanted her to apologize to the schoolmaster — apologize for something she had not done. The idea rankled her. Something else Christian had said annoyed her, too. It was the part about being a peacemaker. "Be a peacemaker," he had said. "Even if you're unjustly accused, a spirit of peacemaking will always stand you in good stead." Elizabeth grimaced. She knew from personal experience the fallacy of that statement. Hadn't the Saints in Missouri been peacemakers? They had reacted with patience and forbearance to endless mob atrocities. And what had it gained them? Elizabeth could not see that it had stood them in good stead at all. Even though they were innocent of any crime, the Saints had been driven from Missouri just the same as if they had been the most vile of criminals.

That kind of statement was typical of Christian, Elizabeth thought with ire. It was true that he probably believed the words himself. And Elizabeth knew he acted upon the things he believed. But that didn't make him right all the time.

Elizabeth frowned and folded her arms across her chest. She recalled the occasion of meeting Christian for the first time; it was at the Whitmer home where she and her family were staying temporarily. Christian had come there to recuperate after being injured in a fight with one of the mob. At first she had thought him to be pleasant and kind; but when her mother decided to marry him, Elizabeth had taken a dislike to him. It hurt her to see how easily her mother could forget her father, and marry another man. Elizabeth had never voiced her feelings, of course. Her mother was free to marry whomever she chose. But Elizabeth thought her mother had made a big mistake in choosing Christian. The marriage solidified Lydia's involvement in the Church. Both she and Christian were strict about keeping gospel principles, and seeing that their children did likewise. Elizabeth didn't always agree with her parents' ideas. Most of the time she did what they requested, but lately she'd been feeling more adamant about making her own decisions. And this situation with the schoolmaster was a case in point.

Elizabeth set her jaw. She wasn't going to let Christian push her into doing something she didn't wish to do.

CHAPTER FOUR

"**H**ere's a fat one," James said, pinching a slippery worm from the black soil filling the rusted old coffee can and dangling it nose-high for his friend to inspect.

Hayden Cox took the worm and threaded it onto the dull hook attached to a length of clothesline. His fishing pole was nothing more than a crooked stick snapped off from one of the cottonwood trees lining the river bottoms. Hayden wrinkled his nose in concentration as he secured the wriggling worm to the hook. A hunk of brown hair flopped into his eyes, and he blew it aside with a careless puff. The freckles spattered across his nose and cheeks stood out starkly in the autumn afternoon sun. "I'm ready to 'ave at it, James," he said, snapping the pole forward so that the hook and bait plunged into the water with a plopping sound.

James' own pole was already arched over the gliding, gray waters of the Mississippi. "I'll bet we each catch a big old catfish with these juicy worms," he remarked.

"I'll surprise me Mum with one to cook for supper," Hayden said in his clipped, accented English.

James glanced at his friend. He liked the way Hayden's speech sounded snipped into short pieces, without regard for the ending of one word before rushing on to the next. Hayden had been in his adopted country for only three months. The gospel, recently taken to England by members of the Twelve Apostles, had been introduced to Hayden Cox and his family in their home town of Liverpool. Elder John Taylor had baptized them into the Church, and with the encouragement of the missionary Apostles, Hayden's family boarded a ship bound for New York, and from there made the long trip to Nauvoo. James never tired of hearing Hayden recount the story of his exciting ocean journey, especially the part about the storm at sea. Hayden's family had set sail aboard the ship *Rochester* with a company of newly baptized English Saints, and seven of the returning Apostles, on the twenty-first of April, 1841. While at sea the ship encountered a severe storm. High winds and towering waves lashed at the steamer. Hayden confided to James that he'd feared the ship would sink into the chilly blue depths of the Atlantic. But then the Apostles on board gathered together in prayer, asking God to temper the elements. Almost immediately the storm lifted and the waters calmed. Hayden witnessed firsthand the power that flowed from faith and prayer.

The *Rochester* docked in New York harbor after thirty days at sea, and then Hayden's family traveled with Elders Brigham Young, Heber C. Kimball, and John Taylor to Nauvoo, arriving on the first of July.

When James first met the twelve-year-old British boy, he'd had a difficult time understanding Hayden's speech because of his marked English accent. He thought the boy's given name was Aiden until he realized that Hayden didn't enunciate the "h" when it occurred at the beginning of a word. The vowels, too, took on a different sound when Hayden spoke, and he routinely chopped off the final "g" on words ending with the suffix "ing." But James' ear grew accustomed to the peculiar pronunciation as he and Hayden struck up a friendship. Some of the words and phrases Hayden used meant something different than what James was used to, but James seldom misunderstood his friend now. The two of them shared similar interests, fishing being chief among them. They'd selected their own favorite fishing hole, a spot along the river where the bank jutted out into a grassy triangle. Here they met often to fish, talk, and watch the ships glide down the river.

The two of them sat in silence for a time, their eyes fixed to the clothesline dangling from their poles and disappearing into the murky water. "Think you can go fishing again tomorrow after school?" James asked.

"Perhaps. Thomas is sick with the ague, so I 'ave to 'elp with 'is chores until 'e gets better."

James nodded. Thomas was Hayden's older brother. He was fifteen and looked much like Hayden — the same round face and freckled complexion, unruly shaggy hair, and brown eyes — though he was a few inches taller. "Is he feeling any better?" asked James.

Hayden shrugged. "'e still 'as fever and chills, and keeps to 'is bed."

"Maybe your ma should send for Dr. Bennett. He's the best doctor in Nauvoo."

Hayden took his eyes off his pole to glance at James. "Could you ask Dr. Bennett's advice on 'ow to cure the ague when you go to 'is office again? Me folks don't 'ave money for doctorin'."

"I'll do that. I'll ask his advice and let you know what he says." James tried to reply cheerfully, but he felt a chill snake down his spine. He'd seen a patient suffering with the ague come into Bennett's office for treatment. In spite of the potion Bennett prescribed for him, the man had died a few days later. James had heard Dr. Bennett speak dolefully of the ague, as well as measles, mumps, whooping cough, consumption, and diphtheria. Although James didn't understand the nature of these illnesses, the very names filled him with dread.

"Are you still helping your pa in his shop?" James asked, anxious to leave the topic of Thomas' illness behind.

"Yeh, though Thomas 'elps more than I. 'e's the one who cuts out the leather for the shoes and does some of the stitchin'."

"It must take skillful work to make shoes," James commented as he lifted his hook out of the water, inspected it, and dropped it back in again. "Do you want to be a cobbler, too?"

"I suppose so. Me grandfather was a shoemaker and 'is father before 'im." Hayden pawed at a lock of hair in his eyes. "But that was in Liverpool. Now that I'm in America, I might take up a different trade."

"You could be a river boat captain," James suggested as he caught sight of a steamer churning slowly upriver. The boat was a two-tiered side-wheeler, with double stacks spewing black smoke.

"I'd rather be an officer in the Nauvoo Legion," Hayden replied. "Attached to the mounted cohorts. I'd ride a 'andsome black stallion with a flowin' mane, and sit straight and tall in the saddle with me rifle by me side, shoutin' out orders to me men."

"Me, too," James said, latching onto his friend's vision. "We could be commanding officers together. We'd have the best regiment in all of Illinois."

"Can't you just see us in uniform?" Hayden said dreamily. "With a saber in one 'and and a rifle in the other."

In his imagination, James could see the fishing pole in his hand turn into a silver-edged sword. He swept it across the water, the attached length of clothesline slicing through the gray ripples on the river's surface.

"Assemble your troops, Commander!" Hayden cried.

"Mount up, men, for a review of the troops for Major General Cox!" James sang out.

"Forward! Charge!" shouted Hayden, lifting his hook and line clear out of the water in his enthusiasm. To his surprise, a small, shiny, silvery black fish with olive speckles flailed on the line, its shimmering body twisting and arching in an effort to escape the hook. "Oh! Oh!" Hayden stammered in surprise. "I caught one!" He yanked in the line and grasped the struggling fish. "Look at 'im!" he exclaimed. "'e's a beauty."

"He sure is," James agreed. "That's a fine black crappie. Look at his spiny fins."

Hayden held onto the flailing fish with both hands while the boys admired its silvery color and its flat, oval body and notched tail. James ran a finger over the fish's protruding spines along its dorsal fins. Then Hayden removed the hook from the fish's gaping mouth and laid the crappie carefully on the grass next to him. He fished another worm from the can, stabbed it onto his hook, and flung the line and hook out into the water.

James kept a steady hold on his pole. The ripples on the surface of the water glided by, dragging his line with it. He hoped that the next fish swimming past would bite and he could haul in a nice, plump catch.

Hayden interrupted his thoughts. "Will you be goin' to the military parade on Saturday?" he asked.

"I wouldn't miss it. You?"

"Of course. Want to meet at the parade grounds?"

James nodded. The first one of us to get there can save a spot for the other."

"Right-o."

James smiled to himself as he pictured Major General John C. Bennett at the parade, riding at the head of the troops. The only person with a higher rank in the Nauvoo Legion than Bennett was the lieutenant general, Joseph Smith. Though Brother Joseph was in command of the Legion, he left the general operation of the militia to Major General Bennett. Bennett and his staff of officers oversaw the training of the recruits and organized the Legion's public engagements. James never missed an occasion to watch the Legion's scheduled drills and reviews.

The most impressive and solemn occasion in which the militia participated occurred on the sixth of April, five months before, when fourteen companies of the Legion assembled at the temple site for the cornerstone-laying ceremony. The soldiers formed a square, three men deep, inside of which were marshaled the militia officers, the Legion's band and choir, and distinguished guests. A silk American flag stood on display, handsewn by the ladies of Nauvoo, and Elder Sidney Rigdon gave an inspirational address. Then the cornerstones of the temple were laid one by one. It was a remarkable scene, one James wouldn't soon forget. Since that time, the foundation walls of the temple had been constructed and a temporary font for baptisms installed in the basement level.

James was still thinking about the temple cornerstone-laying, and the part the Legion played in the celebration, when he felt a jerk on his line. "I think I've got a bite," he shouted. He scrambled to his feet and tugged at the line.

He felt a resistance at the other end. "I've hooked a fish, all right. And it feels like a big one!"

"Pull it in, James. Pull it in before it gets away," Hayden directed excitedly.

James inched up his pole, still feeling the pressure at the other end of the line. He held his breath as the hook crept closer to the surface. Finally, the gray water churned into a small pool of bubbles and a bluish, smooth-bodied catfish burst through to the surface.

"Look at that Mississippi cat!" James whooped. The fish was a good ten inches long and set up a terrific struggle to free itself of the hook. James hauled back on the pole, and both fish and line swung into an arc over his head.

Hayden threw down his own pole and caught James' line in one hand and the fish in the other. "'e's near a foot long!" Hayden exclaimed, handing over the fish to its captor.

James gripped the stout-bodied fish in his hands, studying the long feelers around its mouth and the sharp, saw-edged spike on its belly and back fins. He glided his hand over the smooth body, from the fish's broad snout to its stiff, forked tail fin. "Now both of our families will be eating fish for supper tonight," he said proudly.

"Right-o." Hayden collected his own fish and pole, then he and James left the river to return to their homes.

James was up with the sun on Saturday to start his chores so that he could meet Hayden at the parade grounds by ten o'clock. He dressed and then rushed outdoors to scatter feed to the chickens, gather eggs from the coop, and collect milk from the cow. Hyacinth, the Kades' black and white Holstein, was in a contrary mood. She wouldn't stand still while James coaxed milk from her full udder into the tin bucket, and she kept swiping James across the head with her bristly tail.

"Hold still, Hyacinth," James complained. He moved the three-legged stool closer to the cow's side and started milking again. The thin jet of milk squirted into the pail with a pinging sound.

At last the bucket was full with a nice froth bubbling on the top. He patted Hyacinth on the rump and headed for the house with the milk pail in hand. Letting himself inside, he found Elizabeth stirring thick mush over the black iron cook stove, and Roxie setting plates on the table. Two-year-old Milly seemed to be underfoot no matter which way she turned, and baby Zachary was squalling in his cradle.

Lydia glanced at James as he set the pail of milk on the table. "Did you get the eggs, too?" she asked him as she removed a pan of golden-brown biscuits from the oven. The aroma from the freshly-baked biscuits filled the room, making James' mouth water.

"Yes, Ma. And fed the chickens."

"Will you quiet the baby while I get breakfast on?" his mother asked, turning her attention back to the biscuits.

James went to the cradle sitting in the corner of the room and peered down at his baby brother. Zachary's round face was pinched and red from crying, and his little fists quivered with rage. "What's the matter, Zach?" James cooed to the baby as he pumped the leg of the rocker with his foot. The cradle swayed with a gentle rhythm and soon Zachary's wrinkled face smoothed and his cries eased into soft whimpers. James kept up the steady pulse with his foot. "Can I go right after breakfast to watch the Legion parade, like you said, Ma?"

Lydia spooned a glob of biscuit batter from the bowl onto the flat baking pan. "Yes," she responded, keeping her eyes on her task.

"Can I go too, Mama?" four-year-old Roxie asked, pausing from her chore at the table.

James' heart missed a beat. If he had to take his little sister along, his plans to watch the parade with Hayden would be spoiled. He held his breath as he waited for his mother's reply. Zachary began fussing again in his cradle, and James stepped up the pace with his foot.

His mother was still dropping mounds of dough onto the baking sheet. She didn't speak until she finished with the last hillock and slipped the pan into the oven. The big hinges on the oven door squeaked and shuttered as she closed it. "You stay with me. We'll all be going to the parade a little later this morning," she said finally.

A few minutes later breakfast was ready and the family sat down together for a blessing on the food. James wolfed down his portion of hot mush, steaming biscuits, and fresh peaches floating in the milk Hyacinth had provided, then tried to keep from squirming in his chair as he waited for the others to finish. Plans were laid for the family to gather for a picnic after the parade.

At last James was excused from the table. He dashed outside and jogged the four or five blocks to the parade grounds near the corner of Main and White Streets. A crowd of onlookers was already gathering, and the air vibrated with excitement. The Nauvoo Legion Brass Band was in the midst of playing a lively military march; the lilting trill of the flute and the brass melodies of the trumpet and cornet, punctuated with the throbbing beat of drums, fired James' patriotic passions.

A loud BOOM! from the cannon announced the arrival of the officers to review the troops. The discharge of cannon propelled James forward. He broke into a run, slicing his way through the throng of spectators. He ducked under the elbow of a portly gentleman wearing a tall, silk hat and dodged out around a young couple strolling arm in arm. Darting through a gap in the crowd, he skidded to a stop, for there before him in full military array were amassed the soldiers of the Nauvoo Legion. James stared at the scene spread before him. The foot soldiers stood at attention in long, straight rows, the morning sun glinting off their rifles. A regiment of horse troops were assembled opposite them, the mounts standing nose to tail, pawing restlessly. Officers on horseback, dressed in splendid uniforms, rode up and down the lines. Flags and banners fluttered in the air. James stood rooted to his spot, absorbing all the pomp and magnificence of the assembled troops.

He was so enthralled by the sights and sounds of the Legion that he nearly forgot to look for Hayden in the crowd. Reluctantly, he tore his eyes away from the soldiers and scanned the throng for his friend; but whenever the cannon roared, or the band struck up a new tune, James' attention snapped back to the soldiers, and the officers riding among them. He moved slowly through the crowd with one eye cocked on the soldiers and the other searching for Hayden.

The ten o'clock parade hadn't yet begun and James hoped to locate Hayden before Lieutenant General Joseph Smith addressed the troops from the wooden platform erected at the head of the field. As James paused to stare at the stately American flag fluttering in the breeze from its place on the stand, he heard his name called. He turned toward the sound and spotted Hayden signaling him from the limb of a tall hickory a few yards away. James waved back, then forced his way through the throng to the base of the tree.

"Climb up, James. It's a perfect view from 'ere," Hayden shouted.

James shimmied up the trunk of the tree, grasped a branch above his head, and hauled himself up. He arrived nearly nose to nose with Hayden, who was sitting comfortably in a notch created by two limbs. Hayden moved to one side so James could join him.

"This is a great spot," James said, grinning at his friend. "How long have you been here?"

"About fifteen minutes. I've been watchin' for you."
Hayden returned James' grin. "You're just in time, too. 'ere
come the brigadier generals."

James stared in the direction Hayden pointed. Two
mounted officers were riding toward the head of the troops,
dressed in matching uniforms — white breeches, royal blue
tailcoats trimmed with gold braid and shoulder epaulets,
and black hats crowned with a feather plume. A red sash
was tied around each of their waists, and at their sides hung
a shining sword. James recognized Wilson Law, brigadier
general of the cavalry, and Charles C. Rich, brigadier
general of the infantry. Brother Rich had only recently
taken the place of former Brigadier General Don Carlos
Smith, the brother of the Prophet, who had died a month
before.

"Don't they look splendid!" Hayden exclaimed.

The band broke into a stately military tune as the two
officers rode to the head of the troops, dismounted, and
climbed the steps to the stand where they stood at attention
beside the flag.

A crash of the cannon signaled the arrival of the
next officer, Major General John C. Bennett. He rode
a magnificent gray stallion, and his uniform was more
elaborately trimmed than those of the two brigadier
generals. His horse pranced like a ballerina to the head of
the troops, where he dismounted and joined the men on the
stand.

James held his breath as he awaited the arrival of the
lieutenant general. The trumpets blared, the trombones

rang, and the drums boomed as the crowd craned their necks for their first glimpse of the commander of the Legion, and their beloved prophet. A thunderous volley from the cannon announced his appearance on the field. James sucked in his breath as Lieutenant General Joseph Smith, astride his fine black horse, rode into view. The crowd sent up a cheer, and another volley of cannon erupted as the lieutenant general made his way across the parade field. James' mouth hung open in wonder. The tall and handsome lieutenant general cut a striking picture from the top of his plumed military hat to the tip of his shining black boots. The double row of gold buttons adorning his coat gleamed in the sunlight.

When the lieutenant general reached the stand, he exchanged salutes with his subordinate officers, and then removed his hat and waved it above the troops. The crowd clapped and cheered as the official review of the troops began.

James and Hayden hung from their bird's-eye perch in the tree, barely exchanging a word as the dramatic spectacle unfolded below them. The first cohort, the horse troops, commanded by Brigadier General Wilson Law, began its maneuvers. Each rider spurred his mount into a series of synchronized movements, the horses stepping smartly and the riders sitting proud and erect in their saddles. Then the foot soldiers, under the command of Brigadier General Rich, began a coordinated march, shouldering their arms in a spectacular display of discipline and precision. Though the officers sported impressive uniforms, the soldiers on horseback and foot were not all dressed in standard military issue. Their makeshift uniforms consisted of different colored coats, paired with either white or blue woolen trousers. The lack of consistency in their costume made no difference to the citizenry. The Legion was one of the finest units of militia in the state; better trained and better equipped than any other local or state unit. There were nearly fifteen hundred men serving in the fourteen companies of the Legion, equipped with muskets, pistols, rifles, and swords. The Legion drilled regularly and held military demonstrations and reviews. They were lauded for the precision of their maneuvers, and their martial spirit. The marshaling of soldiers in a general parade attracted hordes of observers, often bringing visitors from outside Nauvoo.

As James looked down on this imposing sight, his breast swelled with pride. Hayden, too, sat wide-eyed and gaping. The British boy's first view of the Legion on parade had occurred just two days after his arrival in Nauvoo, during the Independence Day celebration when the Legion put on a grand military display. Afterward, he could talk of little else. He was as much enamored of the Legion as James, and watched them drill and parade at every opportunity.

James' gaze roamed over the troops, the officers, the flags floating on the breeze. His eyes settled on the figure of Major General John C. Bennett, astride his gray steed. He knew Bennett had been an officer in the prestigious Illinois militia, the Invincible Dragoons, and as state quartermaster general had been responsible for securing the Nauvoo Legion with arms from the federal armory.

Some military personnel outside Nauvoo complained that Bennett had favored the Nauvoo Legion by allotting them an unequal share of weapons and supplies. James secretly hoped Bennett had, in fact, shown some favoritism to the famed Legion. That act of service glorified the man even more in James' eyes.

With the review of the troops completed, the officers — with Lieutenant General Joseph Smith in the lead — led the soldiers out on parade. The troops began a march up Main Street amid rousing martial music and waving spectators. James and Hayden scurried down from the tree and raced alongside the marching troops, pretending to be proud soldiers themselves serving in the Legion.

CHAPTER FIVE

Elizabeth waited impatiently for her father to finish his sketch of Lieutenant General Joseph Smith leading his troops on parade. Though Elizabeth enjoyed watching the military exercises, she was more caught up in the air of excitement and the crowds of spectators that accompanied the exhibition. She studied a group of teenage boys who were hooting and whistling as the soldiers marched by. One of the boys she recognized — Willy Saunders — who was fifteen, a year older than she. He was thin and lanky, all arms and legs. But some of the boys with him were appealing. As she watched them, the boys broke into a run, dashing forward to keep up with the marching soldiers.

She heaved a sigh, wishing to be free of the restraints imposed on her and run wild and rambunctious, like the boys; instead, she was continually being reminded by her elders to rein in her straining spirits. She glanced at her father. He was still bent over his sketching pad, his dark hair glistening in the rays of the morning sun. Her mother was standing at his side holding Zachary in the crook of one arm and clutching Millicent's hand in hers, watching the progress taking place on the page of Christian's drawing. Roxana stood close by with her doll dangling from her hand.

"Mama, can I go meet my friends now? You let James go with his," Elizabeth pleaded.

Lydia agreed to her request. "But meet us at the bowery for the picnic. Noon, and not a minute later," she instructed.

"I will. I promise I won't be late." Elizabeth pecked her mother's cheek, waved farewell to her father, then plunged into the crowd before her parents had a chance to change their minds. The festive atmosphere seemed to make the air shimmer like glass. She trailed after the Legion band, nodding her head in time to the strains of the spirited music and smiling with satisfaction at the opportunity to roam at will. She hadn't made specific plans to join her friends at the parade grounds, but the half-truth seemed to be a convenient way to get out from beneath her parents' shadow. Shouldering her way through the throng, she breathed in the sights and sounds of the festivities. The militia was parading up Main Street and then it would turn east onto Mulholland, past Hyde and Partridge Streets, and on to the West Grove near the temple site.

She was enjoying the fanfare when she suddenly spied Willy Saunders and his friends up ahead. She hurried to catch up with them and maneuvered herself into their line of sight. It wasn't thirty seconds before she heard Willy call out.

"Hey, Elizabeth!"

She acted as if she hadn't heard him.

"Elizabeth. Over here!" Willy shouted.

She turned slowly and feigned a look of surprise, then sidled over to him and his company of friends. "Hello, William," she said in an indifferent tone.

"How you doin', Elizabeth?" he returned.

Instead of responding to Willy's greeting, she offered a coy smile to one of the boys standing next to him. He was shorter than Willy, but broader in the shoulders. She hoped Willy would introduce him.

Willy motioned for her to step closer. "Come here, I want to show you somethin'," Willy said. He was reaching into his trouser pocket, and a rascally smile hovered on his lips.

"What is it?" Elizabeth asked, moving a few steps closer.

Willy winked slyly at her, and then slowly snaked from his pocket a length of gold chain, pulling it out a link at a time. The grin on his face grew broader with the appearance of each golden link. Elizabeth watched, curious about what was at the end of the chain. When he yanked out the last bit, she gasped in surprise. Attached to the chain was a man's handsome pocketwatch, obviously expensive and finely crafted, with curlicue etching flowing across the casing.

"Is that yours?" Elizabeth asked, spellbound by the sight of the beautiful watch.

"Naw. What would I be doin' with a piece like this?"

"Where did you get it, then?" she asked, wide-eyed.

The boys who were crowded around Willy began to snicker. "He picked it nimbly out of a gentleman's pocket not more than five minutes ago," one of the boys replied. It was the handsome fellow who answered, the one Elizabeth had been eyeing seconds before.

"You stole it?" exclaimed Elizabeth, staring at Willy. "What did you do that for?"

Willy dangled the pocketwatch from its long gold chain. "The boys here," he gouged his elbow into the side of the boy standing nearest him, "said it couldn't be done without the old fellow noticing. So I showed them it could."

At this recitation of the facts, the other boys started laughing and poking each other in the ribs.

Elizabeth's eyes flicked to the stolen timepiece. "Are you going to give it back to the owner?"

"No," Willy answered scornfully, as if insulted by the question.

"Then you're nothing but a thief, Willy Saunders. And the constable will catch you and throw you in jail," Elizabeth said indignantly.

For an instant Willy's face lost some of its color, then his bravado returned. "No constable's gonna catch me. I'm too sly."

"You're not too sly. You're nothing but a stupid boy, and I hope you get nabbed." With those words, Elizabeth turned her back on the group and stalked away.

She was repelled by Willy's audacious act, yet at the same time she admired his nerve — not the act of thievery itself, but the fact that he was brave enough to carry it out. As she strode away from the boys, the beating of her heart seemed to keep time with the distant thumping of the band's drum. She glanced overhead, trying to pinpoint the position of the sun. From the angle of it, she guessed it was nearly noon and time to meet her family for their scheduled picnic in the grove. She had wandered farther than she'd thought before running into Willy and his friends, and now she would have to hurry if she was to meet her family on time.

The crowd seemed to thicken around her as she tried to make her way through. She found herself wondering if the unfortunate fellow who had lost his watch to Willy's thievery had noticed it missing yet. She imagined his consternation on realizing his loss, and then his anger as he deduced what must have happened. She felt a sudden flash of sympathy for the stranger, and briefly considered retracing her steps and demanding Willy to locate the man and restore his watch to him. But she discarded that idea almost as quickly as she thought of it. It was better just to stay out of the thorny situation altogether.

When she reached the West Grove, she located her family sitting beneath the leafy bowery erected to shelter the spectators for the morning's parade and speeches.

Major General John C. Bennett was addressing the crowd. Elizabeth ignored his remarks as she made her way toward her family. Her mother had already set out the picnic lunch, and her brothers and sisters were seated around it.

Elizabeth plopped down onto the ground next to her two younger sisters. She had to scoot to one side to make room for Effie, Roxana's doll, who accompanied her mistress everywhere. James sat holding a squirming Zachary on his lap, but his attention was riveted on the speaker. Elizabeth noticed him watching Brother Bennett with a worshipful gaze.

"You're late," her mother said as she handed Elizabeth a plate of food.

"I'm sorry, Mama. I lost track of the time while I was with my friends." She saw her father raise a brow in disapproval. Incurring her parents' displeasure by being late for lunch paled in comparison to the secret she was harboring. She felt a sudden pang of guilt, and any admiration she'd carried for Willy's deed quickly withered and died. She knew she should tell her father about Willy's thievery, but she was already in enough trouble with Christian over the affair of the drawing at school, and if she told him she'd have to bear another of his lectures. So she decided to say nothing. But all through lunch her knowledge of the deed lay like a stone in her stomach.

Elizabeth bolted awake from another nightmare, sweating and shaking. She'd dreamed she was fleeing from a Missouri mob, and the scene clung to her consciousness in vivid detail. She got up and began to pace the room. The moonlight coming through her window cast long shadows on the walls and floor of the loft. Half frightened by the shadows, she closed the drapery on the window more snugly. The persecutions suffered in Missouri still haunted her memories. Sometimes she had nightmares about when she fled into the cold November night after a mob broke into the Whitmers' home where her family was staying. She remembered how she had sat shaking with cold and fear as she hid in the woods until the mob retreated. Other times she dreamed about the crazed man with the gun who stormed into the shabby cabin on the prairie where her family had sought temporary shelter, and set it on fire. She could still see the blue smoke, and feel it stinging her nostrils as the cabin burned.

As she stood by the cabin window she felt the tenseness ease from her body. She'd discovered that the longer she lived in this quiet riverside town, the safer she felt from the demons pursuing her — demons both real and imagined.

"Elizabeth? What are you doing?" came Roxana's sleepy voice from the bed across the room.

Elizabeth turned to look at her younger sister. Roxana's face was like porcelain in the glowing light flowing from the moon, and her dark hair splashed across her cheeks. Millicent lay sleeping soundly in the narrow bed next to her.

"Shh, you'll wake Milly," whispered Elizabeth. "Go back to sleep." Roxana obediently curled onto her side and closed her eyes.

Elizabeth slipped back into bed and pulled the covers up around her shoulders even though the September night was warm. Her nightmare was fading now and her mind traveled over other terrain as she lay on her back with her eyes open. Perhaps her bad dream had been triggered by the apprehension she felt over Willy Saunders' theft of the watch that afternoon at the military parade. Perhaps she should tell her parents what she knew about the theft, and salve her conscience. She closed her eyes and her breathing grew slower and heavier. Tomorrow she'd make a decision on the matter. Her mind lingered on the subject for a minute more, and then before she realized what was happening, slumber overtook her.

On Sunday Elizabeth attended Sabbath meeting with her family in the West Grove, where the Prophet gave a discourse on the judgments of God. He took his text from 1 Samuel 16:7, ". . . for the Lord seeth not as man seeth; for man looketh on the outward appearance, but the Lord looketh on the heart." He spoke about the judgments of the Lord being true and righteous, and admonished the Saints "to deal justly before God, and with all mankind, then we shall be clear in the day of judgment."

The topic turned Elizabeth's thoughts again to Willy Saunders and his theft of the watch. She wondered if Willy was in attendance at the meeting. She tried to spot him in the crowded congregation seated on the grassy slope next to the temple site, but couldn't find him. As she sat on the soft grass listening to the Prophet, with a gentle breeze cooling her cheeks, she decided to leave Willy Saunders to his own fate, without her interference.

When Elizabeth returned home from school the following day, she was pleased to learn that her mother intended to do some shopping at the mercantile. She helped Lydia load the younger girls and baby Zachary into the wagon and they set off for the business district of town concentrated along the riverfront near Water and Main Streets. It was a hot, humid September day and the heavily starched petticoat Elizabeth wore underneath her cotton dress trapped the heat against her body. Her shoulder-length ringlets drooped in the oppressive heat, and her cheeks reddened from sitting in the hot sun. The heat made her irritable, so when Roxana complained about Elizabeth taking up more than her fair share of room in the wagon, Elizabeth snapped at her in reply.

Lydia reined in the horse in front of the Law brothers' general store on Water Street. Elizabeth eyed the displays in the store window as she climbed down from the wagon and helped her younger sisters out. Inside the mercantile the air was cooler. A customer was conversing with Brother William Law, the proprietor, at the counter. Brother Law, along with his brother, Wilson Law, were successful entrepreneurs who operated a thriving business with their store. William Law was the same age as Elizabeth's father, in his early thirties, and served as the second counselor in the First Presidency of the Church.

While her mother shopped for sugar, flour, and molasses, Elizabeth went directly to the shelves holding colorful bolts of cloth. She ran her hand over a soft, shimmering silk, the color of emeralds. Oh, what she wouldn't give for a party frock made out of that glistening fabric! Then her eye fell on a rose-colored satin. She imagined herself at a fancy cotillion dressed in a flowing gown cut from the rose satin. She could see herself bowing to a handsome partner, taking his hand, and stepping gracefully to the music of the cotillion band.

Her attention shifted to the bonnets and hats displayed on the shelf above the fabrics. Most of them were simple broad-brimmed straw hats with ribbon ties, but one was of elegant design, embellished with ruffles and bows. She carefully lifted the stylish bonnet from the shelf and put it on. The fabric was sapphire blue, and Elizabeth thought the color looked fetching with her blue eyes and her blonde curls spilling out from beneath. She glanced at her mother, hoping Lydia wouldn't notice her trying on the bonnet. Both her mother and father assiduously avoided costly or showy apparel, and encouraged their children to do likewise. Her mother had taught her how to stitch a fine seam, and expected her to sew her own frocks, rather than purchase them. Elizabeth enjoyed sewing for herself, but her own efforts never matched the elegance and style she saw on the store shelves.

Elizabeth removed the bonnet and placed it back on the shelf. She leaned over an open page of *Godey's Lady's Book*, lying on the shelf beside the bonnets for perusal by store customers. *Godey's Lady's Book* showed the latest fashions in clothing, and pictured on this particular page were illustrations of four ladies dressed in gorgeous gowns. The gown that caught Elizabeth's attention featured three tiers of ruffles adorning the full skirt; the runched, snug sleeves fit fashionably at the wrists, and a ruffled collar accented the off-the-shoulder neck. Elizabeth gazed longingly at the colored illustration. Part of the caption below the drawing proclaimed that tight sleeves were now the height of fashion, showing "the beautiful contour of a lady's arm."

Elizabeth glanced at the loose-fitting sleeves of her plain cotton gingham and winced. She yearned to be a lady of fashion, outfitted in the most stylish gowns and bonnets of the day. She knew that would never happen so long as she was under the roof of her strict, conservative parents; as soon as she was old enough to carry out her own decisions, she would dress in the style of her own choosing.

She was still studying the illustrations and dreaming of the beautiful dresses she would someday wear, when she felt a rough jab to her shoulder. She turned to find Willy Saunders standing next to her. She scowled at him. "What do you want?"

"You ain't told anyone about that pocketwatch, have you?" Willy said, keeping his voice low.

Elizabeth detected a trace of apprehension in his eye, and that put her at the advantage. "Maybe," she said, staring coolly at him.

"Well, have you or haven't you?" he said in a harsh whisper.

She tilted her chin. "No. I haven't told anyone that you're a liar and a thief," she retorted. "But I might."

Willy grasped her wrist and squeezed it until she winced. "You better not. If I hear tell of you blabbing about what ain't none of your business, I'll get even with you."

Elizabeth wrenched her hand free. "Don't try threatening me, Willy Saunders. I'm not afraid of you."

Willy glared at her. "I'm warning you. You keep your mouth shut."

"Or what?" she countered.

"You'll be sorry. That's what."

Elizabeth snorted and turned her back on him. She heard him walk away, his boots clicking on the plank wood floor. Glancing over her shoulder as the door to the mercantile slammed shut, she let out her breath in an audible stream of air. Despite her bold front, Willy had frightened her a bit. Just the fact that he was a boy, rowdy and unruly, and older than she, created some cause for alarm. She had no intention of telling on him so she didn't need to worry about his threats, but she sensed that Willy Saunders was not a boy with whom she'd want to tangle.

Elizabeth's mother finished her shopping and joined Elizabeth beside the bolts of cloth. "Shall we pick out a fabric to make you and your sisters each a new dress? Perhaps one to wear for special occasions, or to Sabbath meeting," Lydia suggested, smiling.

"Oh, yes, Mama. I'd like that." Knowing that her mother would never agree to the lovely green silk, or the exquisite rose satin, Elizabeth selected an indigo blue cotton enriched with a delicate feather pattern in lighter blue. Lydia purchased the yardage along with her groceries and then they all climbed into the wagon.

As Elizabeth's mother jiggled the reins, Elizabeth kept a wary eye out for any sign of Willy Saunders lurking about.

CHAPTER SIX

James hurried along Water Street to the small, stone house that served as Dr. Bennett's home and office, and let himself inside the door. The doctor was standing with his back to the entrance, placing a bottle filled with thick, syrupy medicine into the glass-fronted cabinet. He set it on the shelf among a jumble of glass medicine bottles sealed with corks. The door to the inner, private office stood open allowing James to see inside. He spotted a bed, washstand, table, and a few chairs. A window on one side of the room let in a golden stream of sunlight. Through the window James could see a glimpse of the river, winding around the bend.

"Good afternoon, sir," James said hesitantly. He was always unsure of how to address the eminent doctor, which of Bennett's titles he should use — mayor, major general, or doctor. So he'd settled on "sir," which seemed the most appropriate coming from a boy his age. "I hope I'm not disturbing you."

Bennett turned around. In his hand was a hollow wooden cylinder about twelve inches long, bell-shaped at one end. "You're never a bother, my boy," he said. "In fact, if you'd arrived a few moments earlier, you could have had a listen with this." Bennett held out the stethoscope. "My patient is suffering from an acute case of inflammation of the lungs. His lungs rattle with each breath," he added, emphasizing his point by giving the instrument a shake.

James knew the doctor would have placed the flared end of the stethoscope against the patient's chest and put his ear to the opposite end in order to listen to the sounds of the heart and lungs. He watched Bennett set the stethoscope on the top shelf of the cabinet and close the glass doors. "What did you prescribe for him, sir?" James asked.

"I instructed the patient to take a daily draught of strong sassafras tea, and cough lozenges. The lozenges will promote expectoration and expel the disease," replied Bennett briskly.

James' gaze slid to the cabinet where a number of bottles in various sizes and shapes sat clumped in disarray. He could read a few of the labels from where he stood — Swaim's Panacea, Marchant's Gargling Oil, and Swift's Botanic Blood Balm. There were also compounds of arsenic for fever and indigestion; laudanum, an opium-based drug, for pain; and calomel, a mercury compound, for stomach and bowel disorders. The doctor kept powdered medicines to be mixed with water, many of which he ground himself with a pestle and bowl. Cough lozenges were used as a remedy for not only coughs and colds, but for the treatment of consumption and whooping cough. There were restorative bitters, rheumatic liniments, and neutralizing cordials.

The doctor dispensed drugs derived from minerals, as well as medicinal herbs and plants. A prescription and office visit generally cost the patient about a dollar, more if the doctor was required to make a house call, deliver a baby, or perform a surgery. James had been observing the doctor long enough to know that his practice consisted of attending to the usual illnesses, injuries, and ailments. Occasionally, an outbreak of disease in epidemic proportions struck; a yellow fever or cholera epidemic could take hundreds of lives.

James was impressed by the doctor's manner and his medical knowledge. His face must have shown the admiration he felt, for Bennett smiled and said, "If you pay careful attention, boy, I can teach you the physician's art."

"Yes, sir. I want to learn all I can." James' eyes flicked to the wall where a chart depicting the human skeleton was mounted. Alongside it hung another wall chart illustrating the muscles in the body. On the bookcase, which was overflowing with thick volumes, rested a model of a skull. The cavernous holes of the eye sockets stared grotesquely at James.

Bennett seated himself on a chair. "Sit down, boy," he offered, indicating a chair across from his own. "You seem quite sincere about wanting to study medicine. I like that in a lad. It demonstrates initiative and intelligence."

"Yes, sir," James said simply, not knowing how else to respond to such a compliment.

Bennett leaned forward and rested his hands on his knees. "How would you like to apprentice with me? A smart boy like yourself could learn much in a short amount of time."

"Yes, sir," James repeated. His heart sped at hearing Bennett's generous offer.

"I'll speak to your parents about the arrangement," Bennett said, his words moving at a fast clip. "But as I'm unoccupied at present, why don't we begin now?"

James held his breath, as if breathing would shatter this dream coming true for him.

"Let's see," Bennett said, rubbing his lower lip. "Where to start?"

"The ague," James blurted.

"What?"

"The ague. My friend's brother has it, and his family is too poor to see a doctor. I told my friend that perhaps you'd recommend a remedy." James blurted out the sentences in a single breath before his courage failed him for speaking so boldly to the doctor.

"Hmm, the ague, is it?" Bennett said. "What are the boy's symptoms?"

"Fever and chills, sir. And weakness. He can't leave his bed."

"How long has he been exhibiting these symptoms?"

"More than a week."

"Well, now, James. The usual treatment is bed rest and a careful diet, along with a regimen of Dr. Sappington's Pills. And I would prescribe a compound containing antimony as well."

"Antimony?" James repeated, wrinkling his brow.

Bennett didn't pause to elaborate on the drug derived from the metallic mineral, antimony. "August and September are the worst months for the ague, so I'm not surprised to hear that your young friend is suffering with the illness. Tell his mother to fix him a good quantity of sassafras tea, and wash the boy's body with whiskey and water to reduce the fever," he instructed.

"Yes, sir. And about the antimony, sir? Where can he get some?"

Just as Bennett was about to respond, a soft tap came at the office door, and a pretty, young woman stepped inside. James noticed immediately the rich golden color of her hair caught up beneath her close-fitting straw bonnet, and her deep green eyes. She was small and slender, and her bottle-green frock fit snugly at the waist. James saw a spot of color redden her cheeks when she glanced at the doctor.

"Good afternoon, Miss Dixon. What can I do for you?" Bennett asked, promptly rising from his chair. He strode to the young woman's side and took her gloved hand in greeting.

"I've been suffering from a lingering cough. Here, in my chest, doctor," she said. Her voice was light and fluttery. She covered her heart-shaped mouth with her hand and expelled a dainty cough.

Dr. Bennett offered his arm and guided her to the chair he had just vacated. James remained seated, mesmerized by the woman's pretty face and shapely form.

"How long have you been indisposed with this cough, Miss Dixon?" Bennett asked in a voice as soft and smooth as velvet. When James tore his gaze away from the lady long enough to glance at Dr. Bennett, he noticed that the doctor's eyes shone with a curious light. Bennett bent close to the woman, and she rested her gloved hand on his arm as they continued to converse.

The familiarity that seemed to exist between the two of them made James uncomfortable. He began to fidget on his chair.

His movements apparently caught the doctor's attention. "Hand me that listening instrument from the cabinet shelf, James," Dr. Bennett instructed. "And I'll see if I can determine the cause of this young lady's ailment."

James was glad to leave his seat and have a task to perform. He retrieved the stethoscope and handed it to the doctor.

"Thank you, James. That will be all. You can run along now." Bennett set the stethoscope on the table beside him without using it. A smile curled the corners of his mouth as he returned his attention to the woman.

James stood motionless for an instant, surprised that Bennett was dismissing him so suddenly and disappointed that the doctor was not going to discuss a diagnosis of the patient with him, especially now that James was his new apprentice. But most importantly, their conversation concerning a remedy for the ague was left unfinished.

James cleared his throat. "Uh, sir," he said in a voice that sounded more like a squeak than a spoken sentence.

As Bennett glanced at him, a look of annoyance crossed his face. "Yes, James. What is it?"

"The antimony, sir. You were going to tell me where to get some antimony for my friend."

To his embarrassment, the beautiful young patient softly giggled at his words. James flushed, feeling a heat rush from the roots of his hair to the tip of his chin.

Bennett exchanged a brief smile with his lady patient. "We'll discuss that later," Bennett said. "You come back in a day or two."

"Yes, sir," James replied sheepishly. He hung his head in order to avoid the laughing eyes of the young woman and hurriedly exited the office. Before the door closed behind him, he overheard the woman say, "What an adorable boy. Wherever did you find him, John?"

When James arrived home from the doctor's office, he was eager to tell his parents about the apprenticeship, but his father wasn't yet home from the printing house and his mother was absent together with his younger sisters and brother. Only Elizabeth was inside, cutting a piece of fabric at the table.

James sat down at the table across from her. He was bursting to tell someone his good news, but he remembered Elizabeth's negative remarks the last time the subject of doctoring was discussed in front of her. So he bit his tongue and sat feverishly on his chair, trying to still his hands and feet.

"What's wrong with you?" Elizabeth asked, glancing up at him.

"What do you mean?"

"You're dancing in your chair. Can't you sit still? You're jiggling the table and making me cut a jagged line."

"Sorry," James said quickly. He leaned back in his chair and folded his arms tightly across his chest. "What are you making?"

"What does it look like?"

James eyed the length of blue cloth that Elizabeth was carefully cutting with a pair of large-handled scissors. "Another dress?" he said.

"It's not just another dress, James. It's going to be a fancy dress to wear someplace special."

"Where?"

"I don't know yet."

James studied the dark blue cotton, accented with a feather pattern in lighter blue. "It'll be real pretty," he acknowledged.

"Thanks," she mumbled as she concentrated on cutting along the lines of the paper pattern fastened atop the fabric.

James shifted in his chair. "Where's Ma and the others?" he asked.

"Gone visiting a neighbor who is ill," Elizabeth replied without taking her eyes from the blue cloth.

"When will she be back?"

"Soon, I expect. She's been gone about an hour already."

James was too agitated to stay seated on his chair any longer. He popped to his feet and capered up the wooden ladder leading to his room in the loft. He went to the bedside table where his school books lay. The schoolmaster, Brother Bowers, had given his students several after-school assignments, but James wasn't able to harness his attention enough to settle down and read. He was still too excited about Dr. Bennett's offer. Instead, he took from the bureau drawer his peg and hole game and began to shuffle the wooden pegs into the holes. But the game wasn't much fun without an opponent to play against. He soon tired of the distraction and set it aside. A moment later, he heard a horse and buggy enter the yard. He darted to the window and saw his mother, with Zachary on her hip, climbing down from the open buggy, and Milly and Roxie scrambling after her. He sped down the ladder and met his mother at the door.

The next half hour was too hectic to broach the subject on his mind. His sisters jabbered and milled around the cabin while his mother started the evening meal. More clamor ensued when his father arrived home from the newspaper office. All through supper James forced himself to be patient while the usual conversations flowed across the table.

After the meal Christian pulled out the sketches he'd drawn while watching the Nauvoo Legion on parade three days before. Christian was handy with pencil and paper; he enjoyed drawing and often took along his sketching pad to capture on paper an interesting or unusual scene. He'd once drawn a likeness of James' mother, before their marriage, and the drawing now occupied a place of honor on the wall of the cabin.

While the family was still seated at the table together, Christian passed around the sketches. James especially liked the one of Lieutenant General Joseph Smith sitting astride his gallant horse. Christian had drawn the lieutenant general with his arm extended and his sword in hand. James noticed the detail on the Prophet's uniform and the trappings on his handsome steed.

Although Brother Joseph's position required dignity and solemnity, James was well enough acquainted with the man to know that his natural tendencies leaned more toward cheerfulness, warmth, and humor. He wasn't averse to playing tag or a game of marbles with the children, or engaging in a wrestling match or a competition in pulling sticks with the men. James had heard it said that Brother Joseph had rarely been bested in a contest of strength. He was a muscular, handsome man who stood over six feet tall, broad-chested, with a prominent nose, light hair, and striking blue eyes.

But it was during the Prophet's frequent Sabbath discourses that James found him most magnificent. His voice was calm and soft, yet powerful, like the voice of an archangel, James often thought to himself. Sometimes the Prophet's face would seem to glow with light when he was discoursing on some glorious principle of the gospel. It was during times such as these that James' heart would burn inside him and the Spirit would testify to him of the truthfulness of Brother Joseph's words.

James' parents had known Brother Joseph almost since the organization of the Church. In fact, they were acquainted with many of the brethren who held prominent positions in the Church, both in Nauvoo and in Missouri. James knew that some of his parents' friends had abandoned their religion, disillusioned by perceived injustices, or unwilling to keep the commandments as revealed to Brother Joseph from the Lord. James had been only three when he and his mother and sister traveled to Independence from Green County after his natural father was killed in a mining accident. He retained a few clear memories of living in John Whitmer's household and of meeting some of the Church leaders in Missouri who came to the house to converse with Brother Whitmer. Some of those men, including John Whitmer and his brothers, had later apostatized. James wasn't aware of the reasons why these formerly faithful brethren had left the Church, but his parents had taught him to leave judgment to the Lord.

His parents maintained ties with some of their old friends from Missouri, especially Brother William W. Phelps.

Christian had worked with Brother Phelps at the printing office in Independence where the Church's newspaper, *The Evening and the Morning Star* had been published. After the Saints were driven out of Independence and resettled in Far West, Missouri, Brother Phelps had become disaffected from the brethren for a short while. He later reconciled with the Prophet and returned to full activity. James had heard his father often say that there wasn't a more loyal, faithful man than Brother Phelps, or one who loved the Prophet more.

James' thoughts focused again on the sketch of Brother Joseph as he studied it a last time before passing the page on to Elizabeth. His father's other drawings included a sweeping view of the militia standing at attention and a sketch of the horse troops showing the men sitting tall in their saddles while the horses pranced proudly.

It was nearly time for bed before James was able to corner his parents for a private conversation. He told them about Dr. Bennett's invitation and his own eager response to it. His parents seemed pleased with what he had to say and said they'd wait for Bennett to approach them on the matter. James had difficulty falling asleep that night. When he finally drifted into a restless sleep, he dreamed of working alongside Dr. Bennett as his able assistant.

The following day at school James relayed to Hayden all that Dr. Bennett had told him concerning a remedy for the ague, especially with regard to the antimony which James hoped Dr. Bennett would secure for Hayden's brother. Then James recited what Bennett had said concerning the apprenticeship. Hayden listened closely, hanging on every word. Since the two boys sat across the aisle from each other in the cramped one-room schoolhouse, they whispered together on occasion when the teacher's back was turned, and spent every noon recess in one another's company. Hayden usually carried in his pocket a small wooden soldier, which he often brought out and marched across his desk. Once Brother Bowers had caught him playing with the toy soldier when he was supposed to be studying his speller, and took the trinket away from him for the remainder of the week. James thought Hayden fortunate he hadn't gotten his knuckles rapped for the indiscretion. Though James was serious-minded about his studies, Hayden's attitude about his schoolwork was more lax. He was often ill prepared with his assignments, and had difficulty with reading and sums.

At noon recess the two boys wolfed down their lunches, then Hayden found a couple of crooked sticks, which they transformed in their imaginations into gleaming rifles. The two of them marched in unison up and down the school yard, pretending to be soldiers in the Nauvoo Legion.

When school was over for the day, James visited Dr. Bennett's office. Though the doctor was in, he told James that he was too busy to be disturbed. James went again the next day, at Hayden's urging, but this time Bennett was away from the office.

On Friday Hayden was absent from school. James especially missed his company at noon recess. They had enjoyed pretending to be soldiers in the militia for the whole week, but without Hayden, the game wasn't nearly as interesting.

When his afternoon chores were completed, James decided to visit Hayden at his home. It wasn't unusual for Hayden to miss a day of school. Like many of the other students, their presence was occasionally required at home to help in the fields during the seasons of plowing, planting, and harvesting; or assist with the family business; or tend to other chores that took precedence over school. Since Hayden's older brother had been ill, Hayden had missed a few days of school already in order to help his father in the cobbler shop.

Hayden's house sat several blocks away from James' home, closer to the bluffs. The Cox home was a typical English-style wattle, constructed of posts and woven willows, and plastered over with mud. The house was small but snug.

James hurried up Durphey Street, which ran north and then angled onto Mulholland. Between Mulholland and Knight Streets lay the temple site. From the road, James could see the basement walls of the temple taking shape. They stretched heavenward, a tangible reminder of the Saints' strivings to live the gospel and one day return to God's presence.

When James caught sight of the Cox's wattle house, he pulled up short and his breath stalled in his throat. On the door of the house hung a wreath with a black ribbon draped from it. He blinked, then stared at the wreath in disbelief. The black-ribboned wreath could mean only one thing — a member of the household had died. James stood rooted to the spot, his legs shaking. His mind refused to operate clearly. Should he knock on the door and ask for Hayden, or should he slip silently away?

He'd decided on the latter course when the front door suddenly spilled open and Hayden stumbled out. James saw him sit down on the stone doorstep and bury his head in his arms.

James' heart ached for his friend. He'd just started toward Hayden when his foot crunched on a pebble. The sound carried to Hayden's ears, and the boy looked up abruptly. In the glare of sunlight, James clearly saw the tears making muddy tracks down Hayden's cheeks. James dashed to his friend's side without speaking a word. He sat down on the step next to Hayden and put his arm around the boy's shoulder.

Hayden looked at him with a sorrowful expression. "It's me brother, Thomas," he said in a choking voice. His lips quivered and tears started again in his eyes. "'e died early this mornin'."

CHAPTER SEVEN

Elizabeth didn't attend school the following Monday because of Thomas Cox's funeral. Since Thomas' younger brother, Hayden, was James' best friend all of the Kades attended the funeral. Though James held back his tears during the service, Elizabeth saw how white and pinched with emotion his face looked. Elizabeth, too, felt badly, even though she hadn't known the English boy at all. His parents, and his younger brother, Hayden, had been baptized into the Church before the family left England, but Thomas had refused to accept the gospel. After arriving in Nauvoo, however, he experienced a change of heart and was preparing for baptism when he fell ill with the ague. He died before receiving that ordinance.

His parents, distraught over their son's death, gained a measure of peace from knowing that Thomas' baptism could take place by proxy. The Prophet Joseph Smith had begun teaching about proxy baptism the summer before, in August of 1840, when he preached a funeral sermon for his friend, Seymour Brunson. At that time, Brother Joseph announced that the Lord would permit the Saints to be baptized in behalf of deceased relatives. Since then, vicarious baptisms had been carried out in the Mississippi River and in nearby streams. In a revelation the Prophet received at the beginning of the new year, however, the Lord revealed that baptisms for the dead should take place in the temple. The baptismal font was nearing completion and Thomas' parents were eagerly awaiting the proxy baptism of their son within the sacred walls of the temple.

On the day following the funeral, the Kades traveled to Quincy, Illinois, to visit Lydia's two older brothers, both of whom owned farms there. Elizabeth enjoyed the change of scenery and the association with her relatives. When she returned to school a week later, her friend, Sarah Rogers, couldn't wait to relay the latest gossip making the rounds among their classmates. When the girls were alone at noon recess, Sarah began whispering her news.

"Willy Saunders has been going around saying bad things about you," Sarah confided with relish.

"He has?" Elizabeth exclaimed. "What kinds of things?"

"That you stole some old man's pocketwatch. You didn't, did you?" Sarah's eyes bulged in anticipation, as if anxious to hear Elizabeth confirm the rumor.

"No. Of course not!" Elizabeth snorted. "That varmint! Willy is the one who took the watch. He stole it the day the Legion marched on parade and then he showed it to me."

Sarah looked almost disappointed by Elizabeth's answer. "Why would he make up a lie like that?" she asked.

"Because he wants to pass the blame onto me, so he won't get into trouble. I can't believe he'd do such a thing," she fumed.

"Willy says you've been stealing other things, too. A book from the schoolroom, and a pencil belonging to one of the students."

"What?" Elizabeth exploded. "That's a black lie. I'm going to wring Willy's neck." Elizabeth's heart bucked wildly with indignation. She felt her cheeks redden, and the hair on her arms bristled.

"Maybe you'd better do something about it. He's been spreading that stuff around to a lot of people at school."

With Sarah's words came a sudden, terrifying thought. "Has the schoolmaster heard about this?" she asked Sarah.

"Brother Bowers? I don't think so. Why?"

Elizabeth let out a whistling breath. "I'm already in enough trouble with him because of that drawing you passed me. My father got real mad about it when he heard the story."

"That wasn't my fault," Sarah shot back. "You shouldn't have let Brother Bowers see it. I passed it to you when he wasn't looking." Sarah's face hardened like an adobe brick drying in the sun.

"It was too your fault. And I'm the one who got scolded for it," Elizabeth snapped in reply.

"Well, if that's what you think, then you can just find another friend!" Sarah retorted. She turned her back on Elizabeth and stalked away.

Elizabeth felt angry and repentant at the same time. She wouldn't have lashed out at Sarah if she hadn't been so upset over the news of Willy's tales. She considered catching up to her friend and making amends, but she was feeling too thorny to even do that. She glanced away from Sarah's retreating figure and began to search the school yard for Willy. She hadn't noticed him in class before the noon recess, but she hadn't given any thought to him then.

She stood with her hands on her hips, and a scowl on her face, trying to figure out how she should handle Willy's lies. Maybe the best way would be to confront him head on in the presence of the other school children. It would be her word against his, and everyone knew that Willy Saunders was a troublemaker. The only thing holding her back from adopting this plan was Brother Bowers, the schoolmaster. He'd taken a disliking to Elizabeth after the incident with the drawing, and he might side with Willy for that reason. And then Elizabeth would be up to her neck in trouble and her father would surely hear about it. She could expect a ruler across her knuckles from the schoolmaster and a scolding from her father.

While she was contemplating all of this, Brother Bowers rang the bell for the students to return from recess. He stood by the schoolhouse door as she filed in with the other pupils, and she felt his disapproving eye fall upon her as she passed by him. As she sat in class, she was certain Brother Bowers kept glancing at her with a glowering expression, as if he was well aware of the charges against her.

Sarah ignored her after recess and Elizabeth kept feeling as if the other students were glancing furtively at her, aware of the supposed thievery. The only person who didn't seem to be paying any mind to her was James. He sat near the front of the classroom beside his friend, Hayden, his eyes fastened on the open reader lying on his desk.

Elizabeth hunched down in her seat, trying to make herself as inconspicuous as possible, and pretended to study her reader. When Brother Bowers' gaze was turned elsewhere, she glanced behind her to the bench Willy normally occupied. Sure enough, there he was lounging in his seat, his legs sprawled out in front of him, and his hair hanging limp and long over his forehead, staring out the window with a blank expression. A blaze of white hot anger shot through her as she stared at him. Just as she was about to pull away her gaze, his eyes drifted in her direction. In the split second that he made eye contact with her, he pulled an ugly face and glared at her.

Elizabeth whipped back around in her seat. Her blood boiled and her cheeks glowed with heat. A dozen devious plans aimed at seeking revenge on Willy whirled in her head.

"Miss Kade."

Elizabeth jumped at the sound of Brother Bowers' harsh voice. "Yes, sir," she answered loudly.

"Please stand and recite the first stanza of Mr. Bryant's poem."

She gulped. "Which poem would that be, sir?" she asked.

"The one you should have been reading silently along with the rest of the class. You have your reader open to the proper page, I presume?"

Elizabeth swallowed hard. She hadn't been paying attention when Brother Bowers gave the reading assignment after the students came inside from recess. She felt a knot of panic forming in her stomach.

"Come up to the front of the class, Miss Kade, and read the poem aloud."

Elizabeth stood up, her legs feeling as unstable as sand. She grasped her reader and walked to the front of the room with it. She had no idea what page the poem would be found on. She nervously smoothed the skirt of her dress and straightened a straying ringlet. Her eye fell on Sarah Rogers who, despite their argument, had a sympathetic look for her. From the back of the room she saw Willy Saunders smirk, and then he made a cutting motion across his throat. "You're dead," he mouthed to her. She sent him a scorching look.

"You may proceed, Miss Kade," said the schoolmaster.

Just as Elizabeth was about to confess her error, James caught her eye. Keeping his hands close to his desk, and without changing expression, he slowly held up three fingers on one hand and two on the other.

Elizabeth understood his message immediately. She snapped open the reader and turned to page thirty-two. But instead of William Cullen Bryant's poem printed on the page, there was a lengthy passage, obviously an ongoing piece continued from the page before. She held her breath as she flipped back through the pages until she reached page twenty-three. She exhaled slowly, trying to still her pounding heart and feeling a rush of gratitude for her younger brother.

She glanced at Brother Bowers, who wore a stern expression, and then began to recite from the reader:

"When beechen buds begin to swell,
      And woods the blue-bird's warble know,
The yellow violet's modest bell,
      Peeps from the last year's leaves below."

Her voice captured the rhythm and beauty of the words, and the subtle shades of meaning. She put her whole heart into the reading and concluded the poem with a dramatic flourish.

"And when again the genial hour,
　　Awakes the painted tribes of light,
I'll not o'erlook the modest flower,
　　That made the woods of April bright."

When she finished, Brother Bowers stood silently with his arms folded across his chest. "That was well done, Miss Kade," he said finally.

"Thank you, sir."

"You may take your seat."

As Elizabeth passed the row where James sat, she flashed him a grateful smile.

Brother Bowers then called on Hayden Cox to stand and read aloud. Hayden had a difficult time doing so. He stumbled over the words, ran sentences together, and lost his place in the paragraph. His British accent sounded even thicker than usual because he was so nervous. Elizabeth felt sorry for the boy. Apparently, reading didn't come as easily for him as it did for her. Even though she hadn't glanced through the poem beforehand, she was able to read it aloud with expression and feeling. She knew Brother Bowers' response had been a genuine compliment.

As the afternoon wore on, Sarah's attitude toward Elizabeth thawed, and by the time school recessed for the day the two girls had assumed their former friendly relations. As Elizabeth was gathering her school books and lunch pail and preparing to leave the schoolroom, Brother Bowers asked her to approach his desk. Her heart started hammering in her chest. She was sure he was going to

question her about the rumors Willy had been circulating
and was probably going to accuse her of stealing the school
book and pencil. She dragged herself to the schoolmaster's
desk with her chin lowered. She could feel Brother Bowers'
harsh gaze on her.

"You did very well with your oral reading today, Miss
Kade," he said sternly.

She looked up at him in surprise. That wasn't at all
what she was expecting to hear. "Thank you, sir."

"Very well, indeed." The schoolmaster tented his
narrow fingers and tapped them together while he studied
her. "There's to be a city-wide school competition next
month, Miss Kade. One of the categories is Recitation."

"A competition? You mean like a spelling bee?"

What looked like a smile flickered across Brother
Bowers' mouth. "Yes. Spelling will be one of the categories.
Along with Arithmetic and Geography. It should be quite
a contest. In fact, next week we begin in our own little
schoolroom to prepare for the competition. The winner in
each category will go on to the city-wide meet."

Elizabeth didn't know what to say in response. She was
still unsure of his reason for singling her out.

When she made no reply, he continued. "I think you
would make a good candidate for the Recitation portion of
the competition."

"Oh."

"If I'm not mistaken, you could take the lead handily in
our own schoolroom trials. That is, if you put your efforts

into study and practice. Can you do that, Miss Kade?" He eyed her sharply, like an eagle focusing on its prey.

"Yes, sir," she managed to say. "Of course, sir."

"Good. Then I shall expect your best effort. You may be dismissed now."

Elizabeth hurried out of the schoolhouse. She held her breath, afraid Brother Bowers would call her back when he remembered that he meant to reprimand her for some offense. But he didn't. That was all — no mention of the stolen pencil, no talk of the escapade with the drawing. Only an offer to compete in the competition.

Sarah was waiting for her in the school yard. "Did you get into trouble?" she blurted as soon as Elizabeth reached her side.

"No. In fact, you won't believe what he said to me." She went on to relate the conversation between herself and the schoolmaster.

"I'll bet you were surprised," Sarah remarked when Elizabeth finished her recital.

"About as surprised as a chicken meeting a fox in the henhouse," Elizabeth said, grinning.

By this time everyone else had left the school yard, including James, whom she wanted to thank for his help that afternoon in class. She was feeling happy and magnanimous. She would thank James, and she would even forgive Willy Saunders for his slander. She started along the road in company with Sarah, her bundle of schoolbooks bouncing jauntily from the strap thrown over her shoulder.

True to his word, Brother Bowers announced the competition the following week at school. He told the students to begin preparing for participation in their own class competition. Every student would be required to take part in at least one category, and more than one if he so chose. The classroom competition would begin in two weeks, and parents and families of the students were invited to attend.

Elizabeth was looking forward to the challenge, but James was dreading it. He disliked standing before an audience and the thought that both his peers and his parents would be in attendance was especially unnerving. Over the next few days the competition was a topic frequently discussed at the dinner table, always accompanied by a few words of encouragement for James' benefit. James had decided that his best hope for success lay with spelling, and so his parents began a nightly drill of spelling words.

As for herself, Elizabeth put uncharacteristic effort into her preparation for the Recitation portion of the competition. She had chosen a selection entitled *The Wreck of the Hesperus*, written by the popular poet, Henry Wadsworth Longfellow, which she was committing to memory and practicing nearly every afternoon after school. In addition, she began the habit of reciting passages from various works for her family in the evenings to practice her diction, expression, and tone. Her father, who had experience with different works of literature because of his work at the newspaper office, was usually the one to assign her a piece to memorize and then perform for the family. To accustom her to reciting in front of an audience, he occasionally invited friends to the house to listen to her rehearse. Elizabeth found that she enjoyed performing before an audience, and the exposure increased her confidence as well as her ability.

One afternoon only a few days before the class competition was to take place, Elizabeth decided to seek a quiet spot to practice her piece. It was a Saturday and so she was not hindered by school attendance or after-school homework. She decided to stroll down to the river and perhaps find a secluded place at the water's edge to practice. It was a cool and windy day in late October and the fallen autumn leaves crunched underfoot as she made her way down Durphey Street and crossed onto Water Street. From the distance the river's surface looked like smooth, gray marble. She walked along the shoreline, noticing how the sunlight slanted across the water, and watching the ripples glisten and glide. She could see as far as the point, where the mighty Mississippi swept around the bend and disappeared from view.

Plying the waters were all manner of river craft. She watched a river steamer, its twin stacks belching black smoke, churn through the water as it headed for the wharf at the south end of Main Street. Two rowboats, tied to log pilings, bobbed and wobbled as the wake from the steamboat drove against them. The river seemed to have a life of its own, with its never-ending current to the sea and the curious mix of river craft that rode its surface. It had a smell peculiar to itself that fired Elizabeth's imagination. Where the Mississippi rounded the bend and left her sight, she could imagine the waters flowing on through strange lands and exotic scenes.

On the lowlands the Saints had erected scores of houses made of rough split log, along with a few new red brick dwellings. Split rail fencing defined individual plots of ground. Dirt roads were clogged with horse-drawn wagons, carts, buggies, and carriages. The town was growing into a busy, prosperous place and was quickly becoming one of the finest towns in all Illinois.

Elizabeth found a quiet spot where a grove of trees screened the river. She sat down on the grass, tucking her skirt beneath her, and set her book of poetry containing *The Wreck of the Hesperus* beside her. Idly, she watched the riverboat chug closer to shore and finally come to a throbbing halt against the wooden pier. Several passengers disembarked, carrying with them traveling cases and trunks. The steamer was close enough for her to make out the name emblazoned in large fancy letters across the wooden casing of the paddlewheel: *Mississippi Maiden.* She watched the riverboat until all the passengers had gotten off and the boat hands had secured the craft firmly to the landing with ropes. When nothing much else of interest was happening with the steamer, Elizabeth turned her attention to the poem.

She practiced it through once while sitting on the grass, just to be sure the words were fixed in her mind.

Then she stood up under the privacy of the trees and recited it again with all the emotion and expression she had mastered. A soft breeze came up, stirring the withering leaves on the trees and tugging a few from their moorings. A flurry of crimson, rust, and amber leaves tumbled around Elizabeth's shoulders and cartwheeled to the ground. She pulled from her hair a dry leaf that matched the color of her golden curls.

She had just started a third time into the poem when she noticed a lone figure walking toward the *Maiden*. Something about the man looked familiar. She stepped away from the nearest tree to get a better view. She couldn't see his face because he wore a low-fitting cap, but she recognized the swaggering walk — the young man was Willy Saunders. She watched him stride across the pier, up the ramp, and onto the river steamer. Someone aboard the boat stepped out of the shadows and spoke with him, then the two disappeared into the cabin.

Elizabeth stood staring at the boat, wondering why Willy was there. The river steamer appeared to be moored for the night, and no other passengers entered or exited it as far as Elizabeth could tell. She knew that Mississippi riverboats were often havens for thieves and gamblers. The Church newspapers had published several articles denouncing those rogues and scoundrels who plied the Mississippi, disposing of stolen goods and passing counterfeit money, and engaging in robberies, horse-stealing, and murder. She eyed the *Mississippi Maiden* with misgivings, hoping Willy wasn't walking into a dangerous den of thieves.

At length she turned her attention away from the riverfront and back to rehearsing her poem. Though she felt nervous about the upcoming school competition, she looked forward to the challenge. She was prepared with her recitation and possessed the confidence to believe that she was just as good, if not better, than any of the other students.

CHAPTER EIGHT

James' mouth was as dry as a dusty field as he waited nervously for his turn at the spelling bee portion of the school competition. The eight- to ten-year-olds were facing off, and James noticed that the words were getting more difficult. He still didn't feel very confident about his spelling skills, even after all the drills his parents had given him over the last two weeks. The only two students left standing were a nine-year-old girl and a ten-year-old boy. The boy missed the word BROAD, and the class groaned. Teacher, parents, and students leaned forward anxiously in their seats as the girl started spelling the word the boy had missed. "B-R-0-A-D." Applause greeted the girl's efforts as she completed spelling the word correctly.

James swallowed as the schoolmaster called for the eleven- to thirteen-year-olds to line up at the front of the class. He glanced apprehensively at his parents, younger sisters, and brother as he slowly got out of his seat and shuffled to the front of the room with the other students his age. There were six competitors in his age bracket. He hardly had time to draw a breath before Brother Bowers shot off the first word to be spelled.

"Mister Townsend," he barked. "SAMPLE."

The student at the beginning of the line froze. James didn't know if the boy was having a sudden attack of nerves, or if he sincerely didn't know how to spell the simple word. The boy mumbled some letters under his breath, but the letters didn't add up to any word James had ever heard.

"Speak up, Mister Townsend," the schoolmaster said crisply. "I can't hear you."

The boy, who James knew only slightly, colored and his lips quivered. He stood stiff as a rod and nothing came out of his mouth.

"Sit down, Mister Townsend," said Brother Bowers crossly. The boy returned to his chair in disgrace.

The next contestant was a girl and she spelled her word, FAVORITE, without error. James was next in line. He swallowed and licked his parched lips. His glance swept to Elizabeth who was sitting in her normal seat in the school room, but she wasn't paying any attention to him; instead her gaze was fixed outside the window.

"Mister Kade. FRACTIONAL."

James' heart was rattling in his chest, but luckily he knew the spelling of the word, fractional, and somehow he got out the letters in the right order.

"Correct," Brother Bowers barked. "Miss Fife. CONSTRUCTION."

Winnie Fife spelled the word correctly. James sent her a quick smile. Of all the girls in class, James thought she was the nicest and the prettiest.

When the sixth and final contestant had his turn, Brother Bowers started again at the head of the line. Each of the five students still standing spelled his word correctly. James began to relax. The words he'd been given weren't as difficult to spell as he'd feared. He chanced a peek at his parents. Both of them nodded in approval and encouragement at him. The classroom was bulging with parents and family members who had come to watch the competition. James began to feel a ripple of anticipation as he waited for his turn to spell the next word.

This time through, two more competitors misspelled their words and were eliminated from the contest. That left James, Winnie Fife, and another girl who was thirteen, a year older than James. James went first. The word assigned to him was RECEIVE. Suddenly, he felt flustered and confused. He was unsure of the order of the vowels in the middle of the word, if the "e" came first, or the "i." He tried to remember the spelling rule that applied to such situations, but it had totally escaped his memory. He scrunched up his eyes, bit his lip, and made his choice. "R-E-C-E-I-V-E."

"Correct," came Brother Bowers' brisk reply.

James blew out his breath in a sigh of relief.

"Miss Fife. DEFINITION."

Winnie suddenly looked as if she'd swallowed a hot coal. Her eyes grew big and round, and her mouth fell open. She stuttered through the first three letters, then rushed through to the end.

"Incorrect," sang Brother Bowers. "You may take your seat, Miss Fife."

James felt a pang of sympathy for her. Her shoulders slumped and she looked as if she were on the verge of crying as she walked to her seat.

Now there was left standing only James and the older girl. She turned to him and smiled smugly. Her arrogance stirred James' ire. He scowled, determined to snatch victory away from her. Brother Bowers gave her the word ORGANIZATION. She spelled it quickly and easily. James' word was PASSENGERS. He, too, spelled it without difficulty. The words bounced back and forth between the two of them, like a game of kick ball. They'd each spelled three more words correctly when the older girl faltered on the word ESSENTIAL.

A hush gripped the room. All eyes, students and parents alike, were concentrated on the girl as she struggled to spell the word. She kept repeating the first few letters, as if getting a running start at it would carry her through to the end. "E-S-S-E-N-S-I-A-L."

"Incorrect," pronounced Brother Bowers in a clipped tone. "You may take your seat."

The girl slunk away, leaving James standing alone at the head of the classroom.

"Mister Kade. ESSENTIAL."

James swallowed what felt like a wad of cotton in his throat. If he spelled the word correctly, he would win the preliminary round for his age group. If not, the eleven- to thirteen-year-olds would forfeit a place in the contest. He said a quick, silent prayer, asking Heavenly Father for help in spelling the word accurately. "E-S-S-E-N-T-I-A-L," he said slowly.

"Correct," bellowed the schoolmaster.

James could hardly believe his ears. He had won a place in the final round of the spelling bee! He nearly yelped with joy. The audience cheered and clapped, and he heard his father's voice boom above the clamor, "Well done, James."

James took his seat, his chest nearly bursting with pride. Hayden, who sat across from him, poked him in the shoulder and grinned his congratulations. His eye traveled to Winnie Fife. She was staring at him, and she favored him with a timid smile. He smiled back and the feeling of elation he experienced nearly lifted him right off his chair.

The last preliminary round of the spelling bee was for the fourteen- to sixteen-year-old students. There were only two competing. By the time most boys and girls were nearing sixteen, they no longer attended common school. The boys left to farm or take up a trade, or continue with courses through the University of the City of Nauvoo. The girls either married or continued their schooling at the university level. The two boys competing in the fourteen- to sixteen-year-old bracket were both sons of farmers; both had missed a lot of school in the past because of their responsibilities on the farm, and both were poor spellers.

One was stumped by the first word Brother Bowers threw out at him, and the other misspelled the next word.

That concluded the first round of competition in the category of spelling. The winners of each age group would now vie for first place and the opportunity to compete at the city-wide spelling competition. The competitions at James' school had been going on all week. The day before yesterday, Elizabeth had secured first place in the Recitation category. It had hardly been a contest, for no one else approached the level of competence that she exhibited with her recitation of Longfellow's poem. James had been awed by her presentation even though he'd heard her practicing the piece for two weeks. She'd recited the poem with more feeling and emotion than he'd ever heard in her voice before, and she hadn't stumbled over a single word.

James' friend, Hayden, had competed in the Geography category, but he'd lost the round with the first question. The question called for the name of the capital city of Tennessee, an ill-suited subject matter for the British boy who had little basic knowledge of places outside his native England.

Brother Bowers wasted little time in preparing for the second round of trials in the Spelling category. He called for the winners from the four different age groups to take their places at the front of the room. James drew a long, deep breath as he climbed out of his seat and joined the others in line. A hush fell across the classroom as Brother Bowers tossed out the first word directed at the youngest contestant. The level of difficulty would be adjusted according to the age of the competitor to make the contest fair.

The small, wiry, seven-year-old girl spelled the word MIRROR without hesitation. She was the daughter of one of the professors who taught classes for the University of the City of Nauvoo, and she was an outstanding speller, schooled, James suspected, by her father.

The next word went to the ten-year-old boy who stood next to James. James could sense his nervousness. The boy kept flexing his fists as he spelled the word, AUTUMN.

The next word was James'. "APPEARANCE," Brother Bowers bawled at him. James felt the tension and pressure building inside him, but he knew the spelling of the word and offered it correctly. He glanced at the beaming faces of his family, and sent them a quick smile in return.

The last contestant was the second of the two farm boys who had competed in the fourteen- to sixteen-year-old age bracket. Though he'd missed the first word given him in the preliminary contest, he haltingly spelled without error the word Brother Bowers assigned him now, SATISFACTION.

All four participants correctly spelled their next set of words, but the following word caused the sixteen-year-old to falter. He mangled the spelling and hanging his head in shame, took his seat.

The next several words were batted down the line of contestants without any misspellings. The spelling bee was grinding into high gear, and tensions were rising. The seven-year-old girl stumbled over her next word, but righted herself quickly. The ten-year-old boy standing next to James fumbled his word and Brother Bowers eliminated him from the competition. Now there remained only James and the younger girl left to compete.

James started perspiring. He loosened his collar with his finger and wiped his brow with the back of his hand. Outside the window the sky was gray as lead and a swarm of fallen autumn leaves swirled in the stiff breeze. It had been cold that morning when the students entered the classroom, and so Brother Bowers had fed the black pot-bellied stove a breakfast of coal. Now the heat generating from the stove made the room uncomfortably warm. James glanced at the stove, wishing it would digest its lump of coal.

"Mister Kade. MACHINERY." Brother Bowers said the word so loudly that it seemed to reverberate in James' ear. It was the most difficult word yet assigned to him, and he had to consider carefully the spelling of it. He paused, unsure of the correct spelling; he wiped a trail of sweat from his neck.

"Mister Kade?"

The schoolmaster was waiting for his response. In a hoarse voice he spelled, "M-A-C-H-I-N-E-R-Y."

"Correct, Mister Kade."

James' knees nearly buckled with relief. He glanced again at his parents. His mother was kneading her handkerchief, and his father's head was bent as he whispered something to Roxie, who was sitting beside him. James turned to look at Elizabeth, seated on her classroom bench. She felt his gaze, looked up, and gave him a smile of encouragement.

He knew his family was rooting for him, anxious for his success. The burden of their expectations weighed heavily on him. He hadn't expected to win the first round in his age group, and now that he had made it to the second round, with only himself and one other student still standing, his drive to win soared. Then, too, there was a matter of personal pride at stake — his only opponent was a seven-year-old. To lose to the younger girl would be especially humiliating. He straightened his shoulders, sucked in his breath, and waited with trepidation as his opponent spelled the word assigned to her.

"PALACE."

She carried it off nicely, without hesitation or effort. And now it was James' turn again. He shifted from one foot to the other, tense with anticipation.

"MAJESTIC," crowed Brother Bowers.

James started to spell the word. "M-A-" He stopped abruptly. Was the next letter a "j" or a "g," he thought with sudden panic. He started again. "M-A-" The word "magic" kept leapfrogging through his mind and he knew that word was spelled with a "g." But was "majestic" also spelled with a "g?" His blood ran icy cold in his veins as he realized he didn't know the answer. He felt the color leave his face and his hands started to tingle.

He turned wild eyes on Brother Bowers, who stood stonily waiting for an answer, and then his eyes careened around the room in uncontrollable panic. What must have been only a few seconds seemed as long as a winter afternoon when his gaze suddenly alighted on the big silver letters printed across the front of the pot-bellied stove. *MAJESTIC,* read the manufacturer's brand, stamped in silver lettering. James stared at the word, and it was a moment before the realization sunk in. His eyes darted away from the stove, then flicked back to it. MAJESTIC, MAJESTIC, MAJESTIC, the word screamed out at him.

"You must give the spelling now, Mister Kade," he heard the schoolmaster say gruffly.

James' eye sprinted once more to the word displayed on the front of the stove, then he recited in a small voice, "M-A-J-E-S-T-I-C."

"Correct," the schoolmaster croaked.

James felt numb. The next word Brother Bowers assigned to the younger girl didn't even register with him. His senses cleared only when he heard the groan from the audience and realized that she had misspelled her word.

"I'm sorry. That's incorrect," Brother Bowers said with an unexpected tone of sympathy in his voice.

James watched the girl slowly retreat to her seat. He knew she was crying because he could see her shoulders shuddering with silent sobs.

"Congratulations, Mister Kade. You are the winner of our spelling portion of the competition. We'll expect you to represent us well at the school-wide meet next month." Brother Bowers' words evoked a hearty round of applause from the audience, and the school boys whooped and cheered. James forced a smile. He had won the school competition for spelling. He should have been feeling jubilant, but he wasn't. The single act of dishonesty robbed him of all its pleasure.

That night James' family celebrated his success. His mother prepared his favorite meal for supper, and afterward his father surprised him with a special gift — the polished antler-handled pocketknife James had recently been admiring in the Law brothers' store. All though supper James had sat quietly, hardly speaking, and eating only a morsel of the scrumptious chicken and biscuits sopped with gravy that his mother had baked for him. He kept trying to convince himself that he would have spelled the word "majestic" correctly without seeing it printed on the stove. He won the competition fair and square, he reasoned. But if that was true, why was he feeling so miserable? His sense of shame had only grown sharper when his father presented him with the pocketknife.

The next day at school James was the recipient of more praise and a host of congratulatory slaps on the back. It seemed that the only thing his friends wanted to talk about was the outcome of the spelling bee.

"You sure did swell, James," one boy enthusiastically said to him.

"Yeah. You trounced all the other contestants!" another exclaimed.

"I'm glad you didn't let some little girl beat you," a third laughed derisively.

James had accepted all the words of congratulations, but this last remark was too much for him to countenance. "She could have beat me," he said in the girl's defense. "She's real smart and a good speller."

The group of boys gathered around James burst into laughter, as if James had just made the world's most comical remark.

"No, I'm serious," James protested. "She probably should have won. Her words were really hard to spell."

The boys still misinterpreted his meaning. "Sure, James. As if you couldn't beat a seven-year-old."

James fell silent amid all the jeering of his peers. He had planned to say something in the way of sympathetic consolation to the younger girl who had nearly won the contest, hoping it would remove the heavy stone that seemed to have taken up residence in the pit of his stomach, but with the eyes of his friends on him, it didn't seem like such a good idea. He avoided the girl all morning, not having the courage to look her in the eye.

By afternoon recess he'd ceased dwelling on his sham victory. He was playing a game of kick ball with the boys and starting to enjoy his newly-achieved popularity when he caught sight of Winnie Fife walking toward the door of the schoolhouse. On impulse, he left the ball game and caught up with her just as she started into the schoolhouse.

"Hello, Winnie," he said, breathlessly.

She looked surprised to find him at her side.

"I was just heading inside, too," James stammered. Suddenly, he didn't know what to say to her. She'd turned big, blue eyes on him and he'd abruptly lost his train of thought. She stood looking at him, waiting for him to speak.

"How'd you do on this morning's arithmetic quiz?" he asked. It was the first thing that popped into his head. Not particularly brilliant conversation, but at least he hadn't stood there gaping like a monkey at her.

"I got 82% on it. How about you? I'll bet you earned a better score than that."

"No," James said. "My score was only 79%."

"I'm sure you usually do better. You're so bright."

He felt his face redden. "Naw. I'm just average."

"You weren't average yesterday at the spelling bee," she said, peeping up at him with a shy smile. "I was hoping you'd win."

"Thanks." He didn't wish to get mired in that conversation.

Before he could change the topic she added, "You deserved to win that competition. You knew how to spell every word."

Her comment was like a knife twisting into his heart. It pierced him with shame and self-loathing. He ducked his head and mumbled something, then dashed inside the schoolhouse without even saying good-bye to her.

As the afternoon wore on, James began to sag under the weight of his deception. By the end of the day, the stone that had lodged in the pit of his stomach felt like a boulder. He was relieved when Brother Bowers finally dismissed the class. He hastily gathered his books and lunch pail and made a beeline for the door.

"'old up, James," came Hayden's voice from behind him, "and I'll walk with you."

James halted, keeping his eyes lowered while he waited for Hayden to catch up with him. He didn't feel like talking to any of his friends, not even Hayden. While he stood waiting, Elizabeth brushed past him, deep in conversation with Sarah Rogers. He and Elizabeth seldom walked home together any more, but today he would have liked her companionship. He needed to unburden himself of the guilt weighing him down. Elizabeth might ridicule him for his act of deception, but at least she'd help shoulder the load of his guilty secret.

"Where are you goin' in such a 'urry?" Hayden asked, nudging James' elbow.

"I have to get home," James mumbled.

"Want to go fishin' this afternoon?" Hayden suggested. The two boys hadn't been back to their favorite fishing hole on the river since Thomas Cox's death.

"I don't know if I can. I have a lot of chores and things."

The boys left the school yard and started up the broad, dusty road. "You goin' to Dr. Bennett's office, are you?" Hayden asked.

"No. Not today." James glanced at his friend. As irrational as he knew the thought was, James placed part of the blame for Thomas' death on Dr. Bennett. He'd told the doctor about Thomas' illness, yet Bennett had not responded by dispensing the drug that might have acted as a curative. And Dr. Bennett had neglected, as well, to speak to James' parents about the proffered apprenticeship. James harbored some resentment toward the doctor on both counts.

This was the first time since Thomas' death that Hayden had suggested they go fishing. Perhaps an afternoon of fishing would provide solace for Hayden, and take James' mind off his own miserable situation. There would not be many pleasant days for fishing left, for the season was getting late; it was already the end of October.

"Fishing is a good idea," James said, turning to his friend. "I'll hurry with my chores, and you hurry with yours, and we'll meet down at the hole and fish awhile before supper time, all right?"

"Right-o," Hayden responded with a grin.

The two boys parted at the corner of the street, with a promise to meet at the river in an hour.

Fishing turned out to be prosperous and James and his family ate catfish that evening for supper. The next day at school most of his friends had mercifully forgotten about his success at the spelling bee, and it was no longer a topic of conversation. But his stomach clenched every time he looked at Winnie Fife, or the younger girl who rightfully should have won the spelling competition.

The city-wide competition was coming up in ten days, on November eighth, and James' parents kept pressing him to prepare for it with nightly spelling practices. But his heart wasn't in it. As the day drew nearer for the competition, James withdrew into himself. His conscience kept lashing him, especially when his fingers stumbled across the polished pocketknife he kept in his pocket. He hadn't shown the knife that his father had given him to any of his friends because it was a tangible representation of his deception and duplicity. Under normal circumstances, he would have felt great pride in owning such a treasure, and would have enjoyed displaying it to his comrades. But he kept the knife sheathed in his pocket where it continued to torment him.

Four days before the competition was to take place, while his father was drilling him on his spelling, James nearly burst into tears when he couldn't remember the spelling of a particular word. His father set aside the list of words he'd assembled for James to practice, and pulled his chair closer to James'. "Why don't you tell me what's bothering you," he said gently.

"Nothing's bothering me, Pa," James lied. He felt the tears pressing against his lids, like water against a dike.

Christian sat forward in his seat. "It's only natural to be nervous about the competition. You're carrying quite a load on your shoulders, and you're bound to feel the pressure of it."

James nodded without speaking, wanting his father to believe that he'd guessed the reason.

"Is that all that's causing you concern?" his father asked after an uncomfortably long pause.

James nodded again, keeping his eyes to the floor.

"It's perfectly all right if you don't win, son. No one will think the less of you." Christian put his arm around James' shoulder.

The trusting words of his father acted like a fissure in the dike. The barrier collapsed and James poured out a torrent of tears.

"I don't deserve to compete, Pa," he gasped through his tears. His voice sounded high and squeaky like a girl's, but he was powerless to control it. "I cheated when I spelled that last word, and I didn't tell anyone about it."

Christian couldn't disguise the startled expression that sprang to his face.

When James saw his father's look of surprise, the tears flowed even harder. "I know it was wrong of me," he wailed.

"Why don't you tell me exactly what happened," his father said without a trace of condemnation in his voice. He reached in his pocket and handed James his handkerchief.

James wiped his eyes with the cloth and tried to stop sputtering and coughing. He swallowed a lump in his throat that tasted as bitter as caster oil. "It was that last word Brother Bowers gave me to spell. 'Majestic.' I didn't know whether it was spelled with a 'j' or a 'g'," he related with a hiccup. "I didn't know which one it was, Pa."

"Go on."

"Then I happened to spot the name spelled out on the old school stove," James said, tears threatening his eyes again.

"I don't understand," Christian said, leaning forward and placing his hands on his knees.

"Majestic," James whispered. "The brand was stamped on the front of the stove. The brand was Majestic."

Christian said nothing for several agonizing seconds, then he leaned back in his chair and eyed James with a steady, penetrating stare.

"I'm sorry, Pa. You must be real disappointed in me," he stammered with tears rushing to his eyes.

Christian's expression remained unchanged, and his tone sounded neither angry nor accusatory when he finally spoke. "I think the biggest difficulty will come from having to face the disappointment you feel in yourself."

The only response James could muster was a loud sob into the handkerchief.

"I want you to always remember how it feels when you behave dishonestly, whether in word or deed," Christian said quietly.

"Oh, I will, Pa. It feels like some monster is eating a hole in my stomach."

"I suspect you'll be feeling that way for some time to come," replied Christian.

"I won't ever behave dishonestly again," James said, wiping his eyes with the handkerchief.

"What course of action should you take now?" Christian asked him.

James thought about the question. "The Lord said to confess and forsake your sins."

Christian nodded.

"I guess that means I have to tell God about it. And Brother Bowers. Although it will be a whole lot harder confessing to Brother Bowers than to God," James added as an afterthought.

A quick smile crossed Christian's face. "I know you possess the courage to do what's right. We all make mistakes, James; but overcoming our mistakes, and learning from them, is what builds character. That's what you're striving to achieve — to become a man of integrity."

"I'll tell Brother Bowers first thing in the morning at school." He felt better just making that decision, but the thought of facing the stern schoolmaster with such a confession of guilt was nearly overwhelming.

"Would you like me to come with you?" asked Christian.

"No. I carried out the lie on my own, so I guess it's only fitting that I correct it on my own." With sinking heart James guessed what the ramifications would be — strict reprimand from the schoolmaster and agonizing embarrassment in front of his friends when they learned of his deception.

Christian started to get to his feet.

"Wait a minute, Pa." James reached into his trouser pocket and withdrew the antler-handled pocketknife. He held it out to his father. "I guess you'll be wanting this back."

He saw his father hesitate, then take the knife and hold it in his open hand. "I'll look forward to you earning this back," he said simply. He pocketed the knife and left the room, leaving James alone with his thoughts.

CHAPTER NINE

Elizabeth listened to the rain drum against the window of the schoolroom. It had been stormy all morning, and the sky was gray and glowering. Brother Bowers' dreary reading of a passage out of Thomas Paine's *The Age of Reason*, seemed to keep time with the falling rain. The past winter had been cold and wet, and now the spring seemed to be following suit.

Elizabeth forced her attention back to the schoolmaster. He was reading aloud from the book in a droning monotone. She listened with a critical ear to his cadence and intonation, and couldn't help thinking how much more interesting the passage would sound if someone other than the schoolmaster was doing the reading. That thought led her mind back to the day in early November when she'd participated in the city-wide school competition. The competition had been held in an actual schoolhouse located on the bluffs, not in a makeshift room connected to the schoolmaster's cabin where she normally attended school. She'd been nervous about her recitation when she first began it, but after starting into the piece she had relaxed and her words had glided and sparkled like a clear-flowing stream. When she had finished the poem, she knew she'd done a masterful job, and her instincts were confirmed when the judges awarded her first place in the Recitation category.

She recalled the excitement she'd felt about the victory and the accolades she'd received from students and parents. She'd worn her new blue, feather-patterned dress that she'd sewn herself; her yellow hair, falling past her shoulders in long ringlets, had created a striking contrast against the deep blue of the fabric.

But the event had nearly been spoiled when Willy Saunders confronted her on the school steps after the competition and provoked an argument. She was glad Willy was no longer in school. He'd attended sporadically during the winter months, but with the arrival of spring he'd ceased coming altogether in order to help his father plow and plant their family farm. Elizabeth couldn't have been happier about the situation.

Elizabeth's gaze drifted to her brother who was seated near the front of the room; she could tell by his face and by his posture that he was listening with close attention to Bother Bowers' dronings. She studied James for a moment, noticing the way his dark hair curled at the nape of his neck and the square set of his shoulders. She couldn't help but admire him after witnessing the way he'd handled the debacle that followed the spelling competition.

James hadn't been allowed to compete in the school-wide contest because of his act of dishonesty in the preliminary rounds. Elizabeth had been as surprised as everyone else when Brother Bowers announced that James would be disqualified from the city-wide competition, and the first runner-up would take his place. The schoolmaster recited for the class in lurid detail the nature of James' crime. The punishment meted out to him was three sharp whacks on the knuckles with the hickory stick that Brother Bowers kept handy for unruly pupils. Then he'd required James to sit in the corner of the room with his back to the students until noon recess. Elizabeth felt both sympathy for her brother's plight, and pride in the fact that he'd borne his punishment without a whimper or a complaint. She doubted she would have behaved so nobly under the same circumstances.

Elizabeth's gaze returned to the head of the classroom where Brother Bowers was still reading from the passage. School would be out for the summer recess in a month, and Elizabeth could hardly wait for the day. She was bored with classwork and uncomfortable under the watchful and disapproving eye of her schoolmaster. Her achievement in public speaking had somewhat redeemed her in Bowers' estimation, but she had the feeling that the schoolmaster still disliked her. She hoped there would be a new teacher when school started again in the fall.

Elizabeth reluctantly turned to the passage Brother Bowers was reading aloud. She knew he would randomly call on students after he finished to explain or summarize what had been read. She didn't wish to be caught unprepared and be berated in front of her classmates for her inattention. Though she was liked by her schoolmates, Elizabeth didn't have a special best friend with whom she could share her private thoughts and feelings. At one time she had looked to Sarah Rogers to fill that role, but as the school year had worn on, the two girls had drifted apart and now rarely spent time together. Elizabeth squirmed in her seat, struggling to rid her mind of extraneous thoughts and concentrate on the passage Brother Bowers was reading.

Elizabeth scurried home from school that afternoon in a fierce torrent of rain. She burst inside the cabin, water streaming from her clothes and her ringlets hanging limp and stringy around her shoulders. "Get me a towel," she demanded of Roxana, who was sitting cross-legged on the floor drawing a picture.

Roxana scrambled to her feet and hurried into the adjoining room where the bed linens and towels were kept in a chest at the foot of her parents' bed. She handed a worn, faded towel to her sister.

Elizabeth peeled off her dress, stepped out of her shoes, and began toweling herself dry. When Lydia, who had been in the other room rocking baby Zachary to sleep, caught sight of her standing in her petticoat and shivering like a frightened pup, she took control of the towel and vigorously scrubbed Elizabeth with it.

"Go up and change into dry clothes," she said. "Milly's asleep. Don't wake her."

When Elizabeth returned dressed in warm, dry clothing, she saw that her mother had added a log to the fire in the hearth. Elizabeth's clothes had been hung on a line in front of the fire and her damp shoes set nearby to dry. Roxana had returned to her drawing.

Lydia was standing by the door putting on her shawl and bonnet. "If I don't leave now, I'll be late for the meeting," she said, tying the ribbon strings of the bonnet underneath her chin. "The baby is asleep and Milly is napping," she told Elizabeth hurriedly. "James will be home in a hour or so from Dr. Bennett's office."

"You're going to get soaking wet in this weather," Elizabeth warned her mother.

"I'll take the buggy. And I don't have far to travel," she replied. "Roxie, mind your sister," she added, glancing in the girl's direction.

Roxana sprang to her feet and ran to give her mother a hug. "I will, Mama."

Elizabeth cast a glance at the black sky and pounding rain as she shut the door behind her mother's retreating figure. She'd been enlisted to watch her younger siblings while her mother attended a meeting of the Female Relief Society of Nauvoo. Lydia had joined the women's society, organized the month before under the direction of the

Prophet, and was looking forward to her association with the sisters of the Church. The Prophet's wife, Emma Smith, served as the organization's president.

Elizabeth wandered over to Roxana's side. "What are you drawing?" she asked, squinting at the paper on the floor. Roxana was on her knees hunched over the sheet of paper, drawing carefully with a sharpened pencil.

"Our house. See, there's Mama and Papa's room, and upstairs is our room."

Elizabeth studied the drawing. "That's a very good likeness," she said, smiling at her sister. Roxana's fifth birthday had been in December, and she'd received the drawing paper and pencil as a gift from her parents. She used the precious paper sparingly, filling every inch of it with drawings before selecting a new piece. She'd proudly shown Elizabeth her drawings of the cabin; family members; Hyacinth, the milk cow; and even her rag doll, Effie.

"Do you want to sit down and draw with me?" Roxana offered. She glanced up at Elizabeth out of big, brown eyes framed with thick lashes.

Elizabeth shook her head. "I have schoolwork to get started on." She walked over to the fireplace and poked at her wet clothing. Her dress was still damp and Elizabeth noticed a splattering of mud on the hem. She brushed the caked mud off the skirt of the dress, frowning at the spot it would leave.

A sudden clap of thunder rattled the window. Roxana glanced up nervously from her drawing.

"Don't worry. Thunder won't hurt you," Elizabeth said to reassure her.

Roxana returned to her drawing, but the loud peal of thunder had evidently awakened Zachary. He bellowed from his crib in the adjoining room. Elizabeth fussed with her damp clothes drying near the fire, then went to get Zachary from his cradle. When she returned to the outer room, she spied Milly straggling down the loft ladder, dragging her quilt behind her.

Elizabeth sighed. It looked as though she wouldn't be starting her schoolwork anytime soon.

It was still raining when Lydia returned from her ladies' meeting. As Elizabeth helped her mother prepare supper, Lydia told her what had transpired at the meeting and gave her a summary of Sister Emma Smith's remarks. A short time later Christian arrived home from the newspaper office and the family gathered for the evening meal. Conversation at the table revolved around the family's activities of the day, and Christian shared a few lines from an editorial appearing in the Church newspaper, the *Times and Seasons*. The piece, dated Friday, the fifteenth of April, 1842, concerned baptism for the dead.

From the window near the table, Elizabeth could see the temple taking shape on a hill on the bluffs. The walls of the first floor of the temple were rising, and the cut and polished stones glittered in the falling rain. The baptismal font had been completed and dedicated the November before, in 1841. Only a few weeks ago, Elizabeth had attended a Sabbath meeting in the grove near the temple site where the Prophet Joseph Smith had preached about baptisms for the dead.

Proxy baptism wasn't the only topic the Prophet had been diligently teaching the Saints. His translation of the Book of Abraham, an ancient record written on papyrus which had fallen into the Prophet's hands in 1835, had been recently published in the *Times and Seasons.* During that same month of March, Brother Joseph had also published in the Church newspaper a copy of a letter he'd sent to Mr. John Wentworth concerning the origin, progress, and doctrines of the Church. He'd given discourses on a variety of other religious topics such as the resurrection, the salvation of little children, the principles of the priesthood, and the importance of building the temple.

While her father continued to read from the editorial, Elizabeth gazed at the walls of the temple, thinking about their Prophet leader and the many times she'd heard him preach. A reverence for the Prophet was taught at home, and obedience to his teachings was stressed. Occasionally in reporting his sermons, Brother Joseph's words were twisted out of context, embellished or diminished in meaning, and let loose to the four winds by the tongues of evil men. These false doctrines and notions sometimes caused distress among the believing Saints.

The remainder of the evening passed quickly, and as Elizabeth prepared for bed she noticed that she could no longer hear rain pinging on the wooden shingles of the roof. She pulled her cotton nightgown over her head and wriggled her arms through the sleeves, then glanced out the small, square window set in the log wall of the cabin. The rain had stopped, leaving behind muddy puddles on the ground. The night sky was filled with dark clouds, tattered and stringy now that they were relieved of their burden of heavy rain. They floated across the moon and cast eerie shadows on the wooden floor of the loft.

The loft room ran the full length of the cabin, with a window at either end, and was divided in two by a rough-hewn log wall set with a door that separated the girls' room from the boys'. The girls occupied the larger portion above the kitchen and living area; Elizabeth's bed rested against one wall, and Milly and Roxie shared a bed at the opposite wall. The younger girls were already asleep, with moonlight streaming across their faces. Elizabeth brushed her hair, then slid into bed.

Lying on her back, her arms underneath her head, she stared at the golden glow of the full moon outside her window. The moon's light illuminated the few items that filled the girls' room — a maplewood bureau, a traveling trunk used to store shoes, bonnets, and petticoats, and a rockinghorse with real horse hair for the mane and tail. The rockinghorse was constructed of dark, polished wood, and the mane and tail were honey blonde. Christian had contracted with a cabinet-maker in town to construct the toy, and surprised Roxie with it last Christmas. It was her most cherished possession, next to her doll, Effie. She and Effie rode miles together on it every day.

Elizabeth yawned and turned over onto her stomach. The cabin was silent and dark except for the crack of light that shone underneath the door separating the two rooms. James still had his lamp burning, reading one of his schoolbooks, she guessed. She could almost hear the rustle of pages as he turned them one by one. For a boy of twelve, she thought he was entirely too sober and serious-minded. She wished they still shared the closeness that had characterized their relationship since childhood. She missed having James to confide in, and to share in her challenges and triumphs. They had grown apart over the last several months, and she didn't know why or how it had so suddenly happened. She wished they had more interests in common, more of a tie to bind them together. They should be sharing a warm camaraderie, she mused, since they shared the same parents. But that point, too, was dividing them.

James loved and admired Christian, while Elizabeth resented him. She blamed Christian for displacing her father's rightful role in the family. Lydia seldom spoke of her first husband, Abraham Dawson, and she never took Elizabeth and James to visit their Dawson relatives. But even though her mother had apparently forgotten Abraham, Elizabeth had not neglected his memory. She kept her few treasured remembrances of her father clenched close to her heart. She nursed them, cradled them, cherished them; and the more she did so, the more resentful she felt toward her stepfather. She disliked Christian telling her what to do and how to behave, and she took offense at his every suggestion.

She still fumed at the memory of his remarks concerning Sarah Rogers' drawing of the schoolmaster. When Christian had learned of the trouble she'd had with Brother Bowers, he'd encouraged her to apologize to the schoolmaster. She might have done so if Christian hadn't suggested it. But Christian's interference had rankled her, and she'd never made the apology. Christian hadn't brought up the matter since; he probably assumed that she'd done as he directed, and he'd let the matter drop. Elizabeth was glad she'd defied him on that point. It was a small victory, but a victory nonetheless. And it made it easier to evade his instructions the next time he asked her to do something she didn't wish to do.

She was getting all stirred up on the subject when she became aware of an exchange of voices coming from the street. She could hear the rise and fall of two male voices, though she couldn't make out the words through the closed window. She heard enough, however, to know the men were angry and involved in an argument.

Slipping from her bed, she tiptoed to the window. Near the corner of the cabin, hidden in the shadows and away from the street, she saw two men standing close together. One of the men suddenly grabbed the other by the shirt collar, nearly lifting him off his feet. He snarled something in the man's face, then released him with an angry shove.

Surprised by this open display of hostility, Elizabeth's curiosity got the better of her and she quietly pushed open the window, grimacing as the window squeaked on its metal hinges. She glanced hastily at the bed against the opposite wall, hoping neither Roxie nor Milly had heard the grating of the window. Both girls lay placid and still. Elizabeth breathed out a soft sigh of relief; the last thing she needed was two little girls questioning her about what she was doing, and calling attention to herself in earshot of the men outside.

She leaned closer to the open window feeling the cold, damp air against her cheeks. As the men's voices became audible, she was startled to find that one of the voices sounded familiar. She squinted into the darkness, trying to make out the speaker's face.

"I ain't been holdin' back," he said. "I delivered every penny of the money where I was supposed to."

"Then why are we more than fifty bucks short?" growled the other. He was taller and broader than the first man, and more aggressive.

"I'm telling you. I don't know nothin' about it." This time the voice held a trace of fear.

With a start, Elizabeth plucked the voice from her memory — it was fifteen-year-old Willy Saunders cowering under the bigger man's shadow.

Elizabeth drew a quick breath. What was Willy doing out so late at night, and why was he involved in an altercation with someone who sounded ready to whip him?

A sudden creaking from the corner of the room made Elizabeth jump. Her eyes cut to the rockinghorse, which was slowly swaying on its wooden rockers. The chilly night air streaming through the open window stirred the horse's long mane and tail, and set the horse gently rocking. Elizabeth wrapped her arms around her shivering body and turned back to the window.

Her gaze returned to the two figures outside just as the larger man gave Willy a hard shove that sent him reeling backwards. Before Willy could regain his balance the man's fist shot out, connecting solidly with Willy's jaw. Elizabeth heard Willy's startled yelp of pain as he pitched backward and landed with a thump on the muddy ground.

The other man lunged forward and began hammering Willy's face with his fists. Stunned by what she was witnessing, Elizabeth recoiled in horror. In the dim light from the moon, Elizabeth saw the stranger crouched over Willy delivering punch after punch. She could hear the dull thudding of the man's fists and hear Willy's low groans. Willy's feeble efforts to fight off his attacker were no match for the larger, stronger man. Elizabeth was transfixed by the scene going on below her window. Though she wanted to dash for the security of her bed and throw the covers over her head, she couldn't move.

A long, thin, blue cloud glided across the moon, concealing its light. In the absence of moonlight, Elizabeth couldn't see what was happening outside. The two figures scuffling on the ground turned into shadowy animals, clawing and growling at one another. She heard a snarl, and then a grunt, and when the cloud finally drifted on she saw Willy sprawled on the muddy ground and the other man striding quickly away.

Elizabeth stared at the crumpled figure on the ground. Willy wasn't moving and she couldn't hear a sound coming from his lips. Fear reared up inside her. Was Willy lying dead beside the road, murdered by the man who had silently fled? She knew she must take some kind of action, but she was too stunned to determine what it might be. She glanced toward James' room, hoping to enlist his help; but the light under his door had been extinguished, and she could hear his soft snoring.

Her eyes darted back to Willy's still figure. As much as she disliked Willy, she had to help him. If she didn't, he might lie hidden in the shadows until daylight when some passerby spotted him.

She made her decision. Quietly closing the window, she threw on her shawl and soundlessly descended the ladder leading from the loft to the floor below. She paused to listen at the foot of the ladder before crossing the room to the back door of the cabin, then eased away the heavy wooden arm barring the door, careful not to make a sound, and slipped outside. The ground was soggy and slippery from the rain, and mud clung to her bare feet as she ran soundlessly the few yards toward Willy. She found him in the same prone position, his arms flung out in a haphazard angle from his body, and his legs bent at the knees. She kneeled down beside him and whispered urgently, "Willy? Willy, can you hear me?"

He made no sound or movement, but she could see the rise and fall of his chest. Her own breath was coming in short, heaving gasps as she leaned over him, desperate for him to regain consciousness. His face was ghostly white in the moonlight, and blood was trickling from his nose and a jagged gash on his chin. A chill crept down her spine when the moon darkened behind a cloud, turning the night black as pitch. What if the other man returned to the scene, Elizabeth thought suddenly, and found her there with Willy? Her heart pumped wildly and fear shot through her veins. "Willy!" she whispered stridently. "Wake up!"

The sound of her voice must have roused him. He moaned and turned his head. One side of his face was smeared with mud, and mud caked his shirt and trousers. He opened his eyes and stared at her with a vacant look.

"Let me help you up," Elizabeth whispered, glancing over her shoulder.

Willy groggily got to his feet, swaying and stumbling. Elizabeth steadied him with her arm. "What are you doing here?" he mumbled.

"I heard you and that other man arguing."

"Huh?" Willy answered dully, as if he couldn't comprehend what she was saying.

"From my window. I overheard the two of you quarreling. What happened, Willy?"

By this time Willy had finally gotten his wits about him. He stared at Elizabeth as if seeing her for the first time. "Why are you here?" he demanded.

"You're hurt. I want to help you." She started to wipe the blood off his chin, but he shoved her hand away.

"Let me alone," he growled. He glared at her, as if he held her responsible for his injuries.

"What were you fighting about with that man?" she asked, irritated by his lack of appreciation for her help.

"None of your business," Willy snapped. His eyes darted through the darkness, hunting for something. "Where's my cap?" he muttered. Setting off in search of the cap, he finally found it across the road trampled in the muddy ground. He flicked off the worst of the mud and jammed the hat on his head.

"I was only trying to help," Elizabeth sniffed as she watched him wipe the blood from his nose with the back of his hand.

"I don't need your help. Go away."

"You better have that chin looked at by a doctor. You'll probably need stitches."

He didn't reply. Instead, he cast a nervous glance over his shoulder.

"Who was that man?" Elizabeth persisted. "And why was he so angry with you?" She felt that she deserved an explanation since she'd been exposed to some risk herself in coming to his aid.

Willy seemed to be calmer now and more clear-headed. "He thinks I pocketed some money I was supposed to give him."

"Did you?"

"Maybe. Maybe not."

Elizabeth's brows arched in disapproval. "He doesn't seem like the sort of person you'd want to have dealings with."

Willy took another swipe across his bloodied nose. "He's only the errand boy. He's not the boss."

"The boss of what?"

"Never mind. You're too nosy for your own good." He pulled the brim of his cap over his forehead and started to walk away. "You best forget what you saw here tonight," he added, looking back over his shoulder at her.

Elizabeth watched him shuffle out of sight, then she hurried back to the cabin. After wiping the mud off her feet, she let herself in the door. All seemed quiet inside — apparently, no one had detected her absence. She soundlessly climbed the ladder to the loft. Once in bed, she lay awake for a long time thinking about Willy. She wished she knew what had provoked the attack against him.

CHAPTER TEN

By the next afternoon the sun had struggled out from behind the clouds. The ground was still soggy and wet from the morning's rain when James left the house bound for Dr. Bennett's office. Though Bennett had not yet spoken with James' parents about the proffered apprenticeship, James had continued to visit the office regularly to observe the doctor in his practice. Occasionally, Dr. Bennett allowed him to bandage a cut or cleanse a wound. James stepped aside to allow a young lady to pass him on the plank walk. The sidewalk and rutted road were crowded with people going about their business in town. Shop doors were flung open to admit the April breeze, permitting James to hear snatches of conversation from within as he walked by.

He approached a cooper's shop and glanced inside the open door. An assortment of wooden barrels sat stacked against one wall, and wood shavings and sawdust littered the floor. The clean smell of new lumber wafted out into the street. James caught sight of the cooper bent over an oak plank, shaping it with a knife to produce the curve of the stave. In addition to barrels used for storing and shipping, the cooper created a variety of staved products for household use such as wooden tubs, butterchurns, ladles and bowls, and oaken well-buckets.

James crossed the muddy street and continued on, enjoying the feel of the sun on his back and the scent of spring in his nostrils. He paused at the window of a gunsmith where weapons of different kinds were on display. A long saber of the type carried by the Nauvoo Legion occupied a central spot in the window. The Legion was preparing for a grand parade to take place in three weeks, on the 7th of May. There was to be a review of the troops and a mock battle. James never tired of watching the Legion's frequent musters and drills; he and Hayden Cox planned to join the militia as soon as they were old enough.

With thoughts of the Legion whirling in his head, James hurried to Dr. Bennett's office. He opened the door of the stone house and let himself inside. The room was empty, but James could hear the murmured rise and fall of voices through the closed door that led into Bennett's private office. He assumed that Bennett was inside and would return to the outer room when he was finished with his business.

James set to work with his appointed tasks. He had adopted a loose routine under Bennett's direction of tidying up the office, returning medical instruments to their drawers, and replenishing the pitcher with water. While he waited for Bennett to come out of his office, James swept the plank floor and returned a medical book to its place on the shelf. Then he straightened the pair of chairs sitting near the window. On one of them rested a newspaper. He recognized the paper immediately; it was the first issue of the *Wasp*, dated the sixteenth of April, 1842.

James picked up the newspaper and smoothed it out. The *Wasp* was edited by William Smith, the Prophet's brother, and devoted to the arts, sciences, agriculture, commerce, and general news of the day. The paper was ostensibly under the direction of the Church, but unlike the *Times and Seasons*, which the brethren had been publishing in Nauvoo for the past two years, it carried little religious instruction. James' father had helped launch the newspaper, and he worked regularly at the printing house writing articles and assisting Smith and others in the printing and distribution of the paper. James knew his father was proud of this first edition of the news sheet and had heard him express hope that the paper would fill a viable need in the community.

James turned to the second page of the paper. Someone had inserted a handbill on which was printed a cartoon depicting the political squabbling in Washington. The caricature portrayed President Tyler in a tug of war with his Cabinet members. Tugging at one end of a stretched and tearing dollar bill labeled "Bank of the United States" and "land sales" was Tyler, and at the other end were his

Cabinet members, with Henry Clay in the forefront. James knew full well what it implied. Ever since Tyler had come to the presidency, he'd been embroiled in bitter disagreement with his Cabinet and other key political leaders, particularly Clay. It was an accident of nature that Tyler was president at all. In the election of 1840 the Whig candidate William Harrison, with Tyler as his running mate, had won the nomination over Martin Van Buren. James still remembered the election slogans of the heated contest: "Tippecanoe and Tyler too" and "Van, Van, is a used-up man." The symbols of the log cabin and the cider barrel were effective in helping to sweep Harrison into office. Shortly after his inauguration, however, Harrison fell ill and died, and John Tyler of Virginia became president.

James' father, of course, had voted for Harrison. Christian was a staunch supporter of the Whig party. James recalled his father's acrid comments concerning Van Buren and the Democrats. Christian wasn't alone in his sentiments, either, as most of the Saints generally voted in favor of the Whigs. The Democrats had failed dramatically to provide any relief for the Saints in returning them to their homes in Jackson County, Missouri, or in compensating them for their losses.

James glanced a last time at the cartoon before replacing the newspaper on the seat of the chair. He decided that when he was finished for the afternoon at Dr. Bennett's office, he'd walk the few blocks to the newspaper office at the corner of Water and Bain Streets, and congratulate his father again on the publication of the new weekly paper.

James could still hear the hum of voices coming from the inner office. Seeing that there was nothing more for him to do, he stood in front of the window and idly gazed out. The sky was still gray and overcast, threatening more rain. He breathed a puff of air directly onto the pane, then traced circles and long squiggles with the tip of his finger in the cloudy vapor. He continued to amuse himself in this manner for a few minutes more before growing tired of the distraction. Then he began to pace the room, considering whether he should wait for Dr. Bennett, or leave the office and pay a visit to his father at the printing house.

He had just made up his mind to go when he suddenly heard Dr. Bennett's voice flare in anger from behind the closed door. He stiffened in surprise at the harsh tone. He heard another man's voice, placating and soothing, in response. Bennett lowered his tone, but the words were still loud enough for James to easily hear. "I'm telling you this plan will work. No one will ever be the wiser," Bennett said clearly.

The words seized James' attention. He inched closer to the door to listen. The men were talking more quietly now, and James couldn't make out what they were saying. The door to the private office was situated near a bookcase holding Bennett's medical books. Telling himself that he wasn't deliberately eavesdropping on the doctor's conversation, James went to the bookcase, pulled a thick volume from the shelf, and studied one of the pages. From this position, he was able to clearly hear the dialogue going on behind the door. The men's voices ebbed and flowed according to the speaker and the emotion behind the words. James listened for a time without comprehending the meaning of the conversation. He didn't catch the gist of it until he distinctly heard the name "Smith" and then the word "assassination" both in the same sentence.

He froze, thinking surely his ears had deceived him. He dropped all pretense of studying the medical book and instead put his ear to the door, straining to listen. There seemed to be four or five voices coming from within, and none of them sounded friendly.

"If you do exactly as I say, we can make it look like an accident. Confusion on the field during the sham battle. Legionnaires scrambling in every direction. Shots fired. It will be an accident. A tragic accident." James heard the sarcasm in Bennett's voice.

"And what if we get caught? What if someone realizes we have live ammunition in our pistols? You're so smart, Bennett, tell me what happens then?" James heard another man say. The man's voice was unfamiliar.

"There will be too many men scattered in every direction on the field for anyone to pinpoint where the shot came from," a third man responded. "Joseph won't even know what struck him."

James started to shake. The reality of what he was hearing hit him with the force of slamming face-first into a brick wall. His head was reeling, leaving him numb and trembling. He heard the scrape of chairs on the plank floor and realized the men had finished their diabolical conference and were preparing to exit the room, but he couldn't move a muscle. He felt frozen in place, stunned with shock and disbelief. Surely, these men weren't cold-heartedly plotting the Prophet's murder! He refused to believe what he'd overheard. The alternative was too horrific to even imagine.

Without warning, the door to the private office opened and Bennett stepped out. James still held the open medical book, but his hand was shaking so badly that the book nearly fell from his grasp.

Bennett looked surprised to see James standing so near the door, but immediately his expression turned cautious. "What are you doing there?" he asked James gruffly.

James tried to reply, but the words would not materialize.

"Answer me, boy," Bennett demanded, taking a step toward him.

James' ears clanged, and his stomach roiled. "I was just putting away your books, sir," he mumbled. He reached toward the shelf with the book jiggling like jelly in his hand. Somehow he managed to replace it without dropping it, or knocking the adjacent books from their places on the shelf with his palsied hand.

"What's the matter? Are you ill?" Bennett asked. His black eyes bored into James.

James knew his face was as pale as paste. He mutely nodded in response to Bennett's question.

"Then you should go home. Come back another day when you're feeling better."

By this time the other men who had been in the private office with Bennett began filing out, eyeing James suspiciously. "Who is this, Bennett?" asked one of the men testily. James didn't know the man, but now he recognized his voice — it was the same voice that had questioned Bennett about the possibility of getting caught in the crime. James suddenly felt an overwhelming hatred for the stranger.

"He's my young assistant. He's harmless," Bennett answered over his shoulder.

The other men pushed past Bennett, anxious to leave the office. James watched each of them move toward the door, anger, revulsion, and hatred welling inside him for them all. Then he turned his gaze on Bennett. His mind refused to accept the possibility that Bennett could be involved in such a fiendish plot. Surely Bennett must be innocent, his mind kept screaming; innocent, and trying to talk the others out of their devilish plan. He couldn't think clearly with all the feelings churning and burning inside him. This man standing in front of him wasn't a murderous traitor — this was the man he trusted, the man he respected and revered, the man he wanted to model his own life after.

"Go on home, boy. You're pale as death," Bennett said stiffly.

James managed to nod his head. He turned and stumbled toward the door.

Just as his hand was on the knob, Bennett called out to him. "Did you overhear any of my conversation with those men?"

James' hand froze on the knob. "No, sir," he answered in a strangled voice. He twisted the knob, his grip shaky and sweaty, and rushed out the door.

James didn't know how long he wandered the streets before deciding on a course of action. It had started to rain again, a light drizzle that quickly turned into a downpour. His clothes were sodden and his shoes caked with mud by the time he reached the printing house. He burst through the door of the small, frame building, desperate to speak with his father. The structure was a story-and-a-half high with the lower floor housing the printing office, and the upper floor serving as living quarters for a family. James scanned the cramped room. The large, hand-operated press filled nearly the entire area. The Church-owned press was used to print not only the *Times and Seasons* and the *Wasp*, but also other religious publications including a recent third and fourth edition of the Book of Mormon.

Though Joseph Smith had recently taken over the editorial responsibilities for the *Times and Seasons*, he wasn't present at the printing office at the moment — for which James was grateful. He didn't know how he would respond if he met Brother Joseph face to face after what he'd overheard at Bennett's office. James spotted his father bent over a desk, writing with a quill pen. All thoughts about congratulating him on the first issue of the *Wasp* had completely fled his mind. He rushed to Christian's side. "Pa," he whispered urgently.

Christian looked up from his writing. "Hello, son. I didn't see you come in." He set down his pen, giving James his full attention. "It appears that you've been outside in the rain," he said with a smile.

"Pa, I need to talk with you. Right away," James said in a low voice. He glanced over his shoulder at the two men working the printing press. One was positioning a large sheet of blank paper onto the bed of the press, while the other was inking the ball in preparation for transferring ink to the type. James suddenly found himself wary in the presence of the two men. He had no idea how many others might be involved in the plot to take the Prophet's life.

"What's the matter? You look upset," said Christian, leaning forward in his chair.

"I can't talk to you about it here," James returned, making a second hasty glance over his shoulder. "Can you come outside with me?"

Christian arose from his chair and led James out a side door into the alleyway. As soon as they had stepped away from the building he asked, "Is something wrong at home?"

James shook his head. Now that he was free to relate what he'd overheard, he found himself starting to tremble once again. He had to force each word, and when he tried to string the words together into a coherent sentence they came out sounding thick and muddled.

"Wait a minute. I'm not sure I understand what you're saying. You overheard what?" Christian asked, his brow wrinkled in concentration.

"I heard them talking about making it look like an accident. That way, no one would ever know who shot Brother Joseph." James rushed the words together in an effort to expel them from his mouth. The very words scalded his throat and burned his tongue.

Christian's face suddenly lost its color. "What men? Who were they?"

"I didn't recognize them," James said, his voice rising in hysteria. "They were talking with Dr. Bennett. I think they're planning to murder Brother Joseph!" James was shaking like a leaf in a windstorm. His body seemed to have a will of its own, quaking and trembling uncontrollably, independent of what his mind was telling it to do.

"Are you sure about this?"

"Yes, sir," James answered.

Christian's jaw twitched, and his eyes took on a hard look. James saw his father's fists clench at his sides.

"What are we going to do, Pa?"

"We'll take this information directly to Brother Joseph. If there is, in fact, a plot brewing, Joseph needs to be made aware of it."

James nodded in nervous agreement.

"Can you tell Brother Joseph exactly what you've told me?"

James nodded again. His mouth was too dry to utter a reply.

"You've done the right thing by coming to me immediately with this," Christian said.

The expression of confidence buoyed James' spirits. He felt better able to bear the crushing burden of knowledge he had unwittingly inherited.

"I know Brother Joseph isn't planning to come into the printing house this afternoon. Let's see if we can find him at his office," Christian suggested.

James kept stride with his father as the two of them left the alley and started along Water Street, feeling all the while as if he were caught in the throes of some terrible nightmare. They walked the short block to Joseph's new red brick store and let themselves inside. The Prophet's private office was located on the second floor, at the top of the stairs. Above the door was a painted tin sign that read: "Joseph Smith's Office. President of the Church of Jesus Christ of Latter day Saints." The door was open, and James could see the window facing to the south which opened onto a clear view of the Mississippi and the bank on the opposite shore.

Joseph was sitting at his desk and he turned when Christian tapped lightly on the opened door.

"May we interrupt you for a moment, Brother Joseph?" asked Christian. "My son and I have a matter of some urgency to discuss with you."

Joseph arose from his chair and started toward them with his hand extended in greeting. His smile was the kindliest and most welcoming James had seen on any man, and it penetrated to the furthest corners of his face. His eyes, shaded by long, thick lashes, were the color of the sky on a spring morning, and they reflected a keen intellect and a calm disposition. He stood with his back framed against the window, and the sun coming through the pane turned his light brown hair to burnished gold. He greeted each of them with a handshake and an arm around the shoulder, and when he spoke, his voice was soft and mild. James felt as if he were in the presence of an angel.

Brother Joseph listened quietly as James related everything he had overheard. The Prophet didn't seem surprised by the news of the betrayal. Perhaps he already knew — perhaps the Spirit had whispered to him that his life was in jeopardy. With a hammering heart, James volunteered to continue at Dr. Bennett's office as usual and try to learn more about the identity of the traitors, and the details of their plot. At first, Brother Joseph refused his offer, telling him that it would be too dangerous to continue in the company of the conspirators. But James pleaded with him to be allowed to help, and it was only when Christian consented to the plan that Joseph gave his approval. The Prophet instructed James to exercise caution, and if he sensed that Bennett or any of the others might suspect him of spying, he was to leave the premises immediately and not return. James readily agreed to the arrangement. When James and his father finally left the Prophet's office, James' heart felt lighter.

CHAPTER ELEVEN

Unmindful of any troubles beyond her own, Elizabeth joined her mother in preparation for a visit to the Johanssen family who lived across the river in the settlement of Montrose. Elizabeth was acquainted with the three Johanssen girls and their younger brother. An older Johanssen boy named Jens had left home to make his own way before the family came to Montrose.

The sky was overcast when the family climbed in the wagon. James and Christian had work to do and would remain behind, but the two younger girls eagerly looked forward to the outing. Elizabeth held Zachary on her lap while Lydia reined the horse down Durphey Street toward the ferry landing, a loaf of freshly baked bread for the Johanssen family resting on the floor of the wagon.

Sister Johanssen had been a close friend of Lydia's when both families lived in Green County. The Johanssens later joined the Church and moved to Missouri; soon afterward, Lydia and her two children followed them there. Niels and Gerda Johanssen and their five children occupied a cabin on the prairie about twelve miles out of Independence, far enough away that Lydia wasn't often able to see her old friend.

After the Saints were driven out of Missouri, the Johanssens settled in Montrose, across the river from Nauvoo. In 1839, when the Saints were first gathering along both sides of the river, Sister Johanssen had taken ill. Many of the newly arriving Saints were falling sick with fever and chills brought on by living near the unhealthy swamp lands. Through the power of the priesthood, the Prophet had healed a number of the sick Saints on the Illinois side of the river, and then he crossed the Mississippi and administered to the sick there. Elizabeth had heard the story of how Brother Joseph entered the Johanssens' home to find both Niels and Gerda so ill with the fever that they could not leave their beds. He laid his hands on Brother Johanssen's head and gave him a blessing, and immediately the man arose and left his bed. As the Prophet prepared to give a blessing of healing to Sister Johanssen, the Spirit restrained him, whispering that she had been appointed to death. Joseph then pronounced a blessing of comfort and peace upon her. Gerda Johanssen died two days later and when Lydia learned of her friend's death, she'd been brokenhearted.

Since then, the Johanssen family had never been far from Lydia's thoughts, or beyond the boundaries of her charity. She often visited Brother Johanssen and his children and always took along a bundle of fresh vegetables from her garden, or a freshly baked loaf of bread, or a basket of eggs for them. One time when the eldest daughter, Johanna, had taken sick, Lydia stayed three days at the Johanssen home to nurse the girl back to health.

When they reached the ferry landing, the ferryman guided the horse and wagon onto the flat-bottomed boat for the two-mile trip across the river. As they neared the opposite shore, Elizabeth caught sight of a group of seven or eight Indians walking toward the trading post located across from the ferry landing. She stared at them in fascination as the flatboat bumped against the pier and then came to rest alongside it. Still toting Zachary in her arms, Elizabeth stepped off the ferry and stood waiting on shore for the ferryman to bring the horse and wagon. The Indians were now just across the street from where she stood — five sun-bronzed braves, a squaw, and a young Indian who looked close to her own age.

From beneath lowered lashes she stared at them, fascinated by their appearance. The men wore leather leggings and moccasins, and the woman was clothed in a buckskin dress decorated with colorful glass beads. The woman's skin looked weathered and her braided hair was streaked with gray. The men wore their hair straight and loose to their shoulders; but the young Indian brave's hair was shorn on both sides of his head, leaving only a stiff crest along the top that continued down the back of his head and fell in a long tail past his shoulders. A single yellow feather was tucked into his hair. The Indians silently passed by without lifting their eyes from the ground, but just as the group started to enter the door of the log hut that served as a trading post, Elizabeth saw the young brave turn back and glance at her. His stony face remained impassive, but his dark brown eyes narrowed into slits as he gave her a quick, fierce glare.

The unexpected contact filled her with sudden terror. All her life she'd heard stories about the ferocity and brutality of the Indians, and the frightening glare she'd received from the young buck seemed to confirm those tales. She clutched Zachary tighter in her arms as she waited to climb into the safety of the wagon. She didn't dare glance in the direction of the trading post again.

Soon they were all nestled inside the wagon, much to Elizabeth's relief, and on their way to the Johanssens' log home, which sat only a short distance away, along the river front. Kirstine answered their knock at the door. Of the three Johanssen girls, Elizabeth liked Kirstine the best. She was seventeen years old and Elizabeth thought she was the prettiest of the sisters. Her silky yellow hair fell to the middle of her back and her eyes were the color of bluebonnets.

Kirstine invited them inside and then fetched the rest of the family. When Inger entered the room, Elizabeth gave her a quick smile. Inger was taller than her two sisters, and her flaxen hair trailed down her back in one long braid.

Elizabeth retained a few vague memories of Inger from when the two of them were children in Green County, and enjoyed renewing their acquaintance in Montrose. Although Inger was a year younger than Elizabeth, the two girls got along well together.

Elizabeth turned and smiled at Johanna, who had come into the room with Lars a step behind her. Lars was the youngest of the children, eleven or so, and like his sisters he possessed yellow hair and bright blue eyes.

"It's good to see you again, Elizabeth," said Johanna. "You look so pretty in that calico."

Elizabeth was surprised by the girl's compliment. She didn't think that Johanna was interested in anything as frivolous as fashion. Johanna was plain-faced and stout, and wore her hair arranged into a braid ringing her head; her dress was a rumpled checked gingham. At nineteen, she already looked the part of a spinster.

"Did James come with you?" Lars wanted to know.

"Not this time," answered Lydia. "He and his father were up to their elbows in chores when we left."

"Tell him I said hello," replied Lars.

"I will. This is for your family," Lydia said, handing Johanna the loaf of bread. "Now tell me what's been happening with all of you."

Johanna set the bread on the table and thanked Lydia for it. "We're fine, Sister Kade. Inger and Lars are doing well in school . . ."

"Inger's doing well," Lars interrupted. "I'm having a world of trouble with arithmetic."

Lydia treated him to a warm smile and a pat on the back.

"Kirstine and I are taking in washing to earn a little money. Inger helps us, too, when she has time from her studies," Johanna continued as if there hadn't been a ripple in the conversation.

"Your mother would be very proud of all of you," Lydia responded. "I can just hear her saying, 'These are fine girls. And strong boys.'" Lydia pronounced the words with a lilting Scandinavian accent.

Johanna smiled. "We miss Mama. There's not a day that goes by we don't speak of her."

"Always remember your mother. She was a wonderful person. Strong in the gospel of Jesus Christ. And she was a great friend to me."

Elizabeth saw Kirstine's eyes suddenly fill with tears.

"Papa used to lift me up on his shoulders and carry me about the room," Lars related. "Mama would tell him to put me down before I fell, and he'd pretend to drop me. Then Mama would put her hands on her hips and scold him." Lars laughed at the happy memory.

"Yes, and Mother could bake the best sweetcake in the whole world," Kirstine added.

"Remember how Jens used to love her sweetcake?" Inger said with a grin. "He'd always eat more than his share and Mama would chide him for it."

Elizabeth noticed a chilly silence fall upon the group. Johanna pursed her lips, and Kirstine's gaze dropped to the floor. Lars was the only one who seemed to be unruffled by Inger's comment.

"I like sweetcake," Roxana suddenly blurted.

Her innocent remark restored the warmth to the conversation. Kirstine laughed and Johanna smiled at Roxie.

"I wish we had some sweetcake for you right now," Inger said to her. "We don't have sweetcake, but we do have some nice raisin pudding. How would you like a bowl of that, Roxie?"

"Yes, please."

"I'll have some too, Inger," said Lars, jumping up from his chair.

"I knew *you* would," replied his sister. She rumpled Lars' hair as she walked past him to the cupboard.

All of them ate a dish of raisin pudding, which tasted better than Elizabeth thought it would. Afterward, Inger invited Elizabeth to accompany her while she collected eggs for supper from the henhouse. The Mississippi flowed past the Johanssens' back door. A screen of tall trees hid the river from sight, but Elizabeth could hear its gray waters gurgling softly. In the yard, half a dozen chickens clucked and strutted. They gathered around Inger's legs and followed her like puppies.

"I'll be glad when school is out for the summer months," Inger said. "Won't you?"

"Yes. I'm tired of it."

"Kirstine isn't going back to school. She has a beau," Inger said, lowering her voice in a confidential tone.

"She does?" Elizabeth's interest was piqued. "What's his name?"

"Peder Madsen. He's a convert to the Church from Scandinavia."

"How did she meet him?"

"At school. He hasn't lived in Montrose long. He doesn't go to school now, though, because he's helping his father farm."

Elizabeth kicked aside a pebble in her path. "What does he look like?"

"Oh, he's very handsome," Inger said, giggling. "Tall and blonde. And his eyes twinkle when he smiles."

Elizabeth tried to picture the young man. "Do you think Peder and Kirstine will get married?"

Inger nodded. "I think he's already asked Papa for permission. I overheard the two of them talking out in the barn just the day before yesterday."

A breeze came up from the river, stirring Inger's long yellow braid. With the sunlight playing on her face, Elizabeth thought she looked nearly as pretty as her older sister, Kirstine. "If Kirstine gets married, will your brother, Jens, come home for the wedding?" Elizabeth asked cautiously. She wondered about the uncomfortable silence that had ensued back at the house when Jens' name had been brought up in conversation.

Inger kept to her course without missing a stride. "We don't know where Jens is. I don't think even Papa does. The last time we got a letter from him, he was still living in Missouri."

"In Far West?"

Inger tucked her hands in her apron pockets. Elizabeth could see her hesitate before answering. "Papa is real angry with Jens. I doubt he'd speak to him even if he did come for the wedding."

"Really? Why is that?"

"Jens got into some trouble with the law in Far West. But worse than that, he joined the mob there in persecuting the Saints."

Elizabeth's eyes bulged with this piece of information. She built a picture of Jens Johanssen in her mind's eye. Although she couldn't remember his face, she imagined him to look like Lars, only older and taller. She envisioned a gun gleaming in his hand, his mouth in a cruel sneer, and his eyes cold and hard. The image made her shiver.

"Papa and Johanna are real angry with him, and won't speak to him. Kirstine keeps her feelings to herself."

"And what about you?" Elizabeth asked after a pause.

Inger shrugged. "He's my brother. I don't like what he did, but I don't hate him for it. I hope he'll change his ways and come home."

They'd reached the chicken coop now, and the hens tangling themselves in Inger's feet squawked more clamorously. A fat, red rooster was perched on the top rail of the nearby fence, his chest puffed out with self-importance and his black eyes taking in every detail that went on in his domain.

"Do you want to come inside while I gather the eggs?" Inger asked.

"I'll wait for you here."

Inger ducked through the narrow opening that served as a door and disappeared inside. The flock of chickens scurried after her, hopeful for a meal.

Elizabeth turned her attention to the river. From here she could see the sunlight reflecting off its surface, making the waters glisten. She stood watching the water glide downstream, thinking about what Inger had told her concerning Kirstine and Jens. While she stood staring at the water, the big rooster on the fence suddenly let out a loud squawk, flapped its wings, and darted toward her. Instinctively, she covered her face with her arms, bracing for the bird's attack. She felt the rush of air as the rooster flew past her and landed on the ground a few feet away from the henhouse.

"You nasty old bird," she scolded. The rooster stretched its neck and screeched. It took a moment before Elizabeth realized that the rooster's beady, black eye was not fixed on her. She felt a chill snake down her spine as she sensed that she was not alone in the yard. She whirled around and a silent scream rose in her throat when she saw an Indian crouched behind the trees not more than a couple of yards away.

Her first inclination was to run, but as soon as the Indian knew he'd been sighted, he sprang from his hiding place and bounded into the open as quick as a deer. He stood there glaring at her. She was paralyzed with fear; her feet refused to budge from the spot. As they stared at one another — he with haughtiness, and she with terror —

it dawned on her that this was the Indian youth she'd seen outside the trading post when she'd gotten off the ferry. His eyes were the color of coal, and his hair was as black and glistening as a raven's wing. He was dressed in fringed leather leggings and a loose-fitting deer-skin shirt, and around his neck he wore a necklace of beads. A yellow feather was tied into his hair with a strip of leather. He began to stealthily move toward her, his footsteps soundless in his moccasined feet. She backed away and started to scream for help, but a choking croak was the only sound that came out of her throat. She watched the Indian reach toward the waistband of his leather breeches and slowly pull out a huge knife. He waved it at her as he slowly advanced.

Elizabeth thought she was going to faint from fear. Her legs began to give way and darkness gathered at the corners of her eyes. She stumbled backward until her spine was up against the henhouse. The Indian continued to creep toward her.

Just as she began sinking down the wall of the chicken coop, covering her face with her hands, she heard Inger's raised voice from behind her. "Yellow Feather! Put that knife away. You'll frighten Elizabeth to death."

Elizabeth opened her eyes and peeped out between her fingers. The Indian youth stopped in his tracks. Then he said something to Inger in a language Elizabeth couldn't understand, and waved his knife angrily in the air.

The display of hostility didn't seem to frighten Inger. She confidently strode toward the youth until she was only a few feet away from him. "Tell me with signs what you want," she said to him.

The Indian turned to glare once again at Elizabeth. She shrank back against the wall of the coop, in fear now for Inger's life as well as her own. She couldn't understand why Inger wasn't crying out for help.

The Indian youth returned his gaze to Inger, and the hardness left his eyes. He talked in an animated stream of gibberish, pointing and gesturing as he spoke. At one point he slashed the air with his knife, his face twisted into a scowl.

When he was finally through with his tirade, Inger started to chuckle. Elizabeth was stunned — instead of laughing, Inger should be screaming for someone to rescue them.

Inger made a gesture to the Indian which clearly meant, "Wait here," and then she hurried over to Elizabeth and helped her to her feet. "It's all right," she said. "Yellow Feather is very sorry he frightened you."

"What?" Elizabeth mumbled, holding on to Inger's arm for support.

Inger smiled, and Elizabeth realized she was trying to smother another chuckle. "Yellow Feather was impressed by the golden color of your hair. He wanted a piece of it for his amulet. Sort of a good luck charm," Inger concluded, still striving to keep a sober face.

"What?" Elizabeth shrieked. "I thought he was going to murder me!"

"Oh no," Inger said quickly. "He just wanted a lock of your hair."

Elizabeth's eyes jerked from Inger to the Indian. He stood with a somewhat contrite look on his broad, bronzed face. "He came at me with that knife!" she exclaimed, still not convinced by Inger's explanation.

"I know. I'm afraid he has rather bad manners."

Elizabeth stared at the other girl in disbelief and then shook off her steadying hand, feeling suddenly very foolish and indignant.

"Yellow Feather and his tribe have been camping for a few weeks near the river bank before they leave to go back to the reserve. He's a Sauk and Fox Indian, and he knows some English. But he likes to pretend that he doesn't." Inger glanced over her shoulder at the youth as she finished explaining this to Elizabeth. The Indian looked away as if his attention was fixed on something else, and not on what Inger was saying.

As Elizabeth took a moment to study the Indian — now that she knew her life was not in jeopardy — she saw that he was not any older than herself. His body was lithe and strong, but hadn't reached full maturity. He had thin lips, a broad nose, and deep-seated black, piercing eyes. His skin was the color of chestnuts. His head was clean shaven except at the top where his crest of black hair stood up straight and stiff, and glistening with grease.

"His name isn't really Yellow Feather," Inger went on. "That's just what I call him because of the yellow feather he always wears in his hair. His actual name is Kis-ku-kosh."

"How do you know all of this?" Elizabeth asked, keeping one eye trained on the Indian.

"Yellow Feather and I are friends. I met him when he and some other members of his tribe came to our door asking for food. Johanna wanted to shoo them away, but I persuaded her to let them have some cornmeal and a couple of apples. The next day, Yellow Feather came back to the house and hid outside until I happened to come out. Then he asked me for another apple. He really likes apples." Inger turned her head and nodded toward the Indian. "Don't you, Kis-ku-kosh?"

The Indian sniffed, and with a haughty look turned away. Elizabeth breathed easier when she saw him replace his knife in his waistband.

"We started talking, using sign language, and it was awhile before I discovered that he knew some English. Once in awhile he'll speak to me in English, but not very often. It's as if he's too proud to stoop to the use of English."

"How do you dare trust him?" Elizabeth whispered. "He's a wild, savage Indian."

Inger's lip twitched with a smile. "I doubt Yellow Feather would intentionally hurt a fly."

The Indian was starting to become impatient now with the girls' conversation. He said something to Inger in a guttural growl and began to stride quickly toward them. Elizabeth ducked behind Inger's shoulder. When he reached them, the Indian again pulled out his knife and gestured at Elizabeth with it. She cowered behind Inger.

"It's all right, Elizabeth, really," Inger said, trying to draw Elizabeth out from behind her. "He's wondering if he might have a strand or two of your hair."

"Absolutely not," Elizabeth said.

The Indian moved a pace closer and pointed the knife at Elizabeth's throat. He was so near that she could smell the animal grease in his hair.

Elizabeth's lips felt as dry and parched as dead leaves. She wet them with her tongue. "Why doesn't he just ask me for it?" she squeaked.

"He's a little backward when it comes to strangers," Inger replied. "Why don't you let him have a strand? I gave him a bit of mine because he liked the color. He won't hurt you."

Elizabeth was quavering from head to toe as she came out from behind Inger's shoulder. "All right," she said in a quivering voice. "Just one strand. Tell him that."

Inger gestured to the Indian and held up one finger. Quick as lightning, Yellow Feather sliced his knife across the bottom part of one of Elizabeth's curls and a hunk of ringlet fell into his brown hand.

Elizabeth hadn't even had time to brace herself for the act before it was accomplished. She stared in horror at the inch-long chunk of hair Yellow Feather clutched in his dirt-stained hand. The Indian spouted something in his language which didn't sound very flattering, and then he spun around and stalked off.

"You said he was going to take only one strand," Elizabeth cried, whirling on Inger. She was close to tears, and frightened and humiliated by what the Indian had done.

Inger put an arm around Elizabeth's shoulders. "I think he was a little annoyed that it took so long to get your permission."

Elizabeth blinked in bewilderment.

Inger patted her shoulder. "I'll finish getting the eggs from the coop."

"I'll come with you," said Elizabeth hastily.

CHAPTER TWELVE

James raced Hayden out of the school yard to see who could get to the road first. In spite of Hayden's shorter, heavier size, he beat James by several paces. James excused himself by saying that he had to dodge a group of girls. One of the girls in the group was Winnie Fife. He would have liked to stop and talk with her for a moment, but he didn't want to drop out of the foot race. Winnie had been friendlier than usual to him over the recent months, ever since the mayhem resulting from the spelling competition. When his dishonesty had come to light in the classroom, he assumed Winnie would never speak to him again, and so he was pleasantly surprised when she made it a habit to seek him out and exchange a few words.

"You're as slow as a mule," Hayden said good-naturedly when James reached his side.

"You got a head start on me," James protested.

"Not a chance, mate. I'm just faster than you," Hayden said with a laugh. He brushed a tangle of brown hair off his forehead, exposing a soft, pudgy face full of brown freckles. He was a bit flabby and squat, and his clothes fit poorly. His rumpled shirt refused to stay tucked in his trousers, and his wrinkled britches were too short for his legs, exposing his bare ankles.

The two of them started up the road, continuing their friendly banter as they walked. The road was scarred with more ruts and lumps than usual after the past two weeks of sporadic rainfall. Though yesterday the sun had shone in full force, this afternoon black clouds were again rolling across the sky. James was tired of the dreary weather. He wanted to sit along the bank of the river with his fishing pole in hand, and feel the warm spring sunshine on his back.

"Want to come to me 'ouse for a game of marbles?" asked Hayden.

"I wish I could, but I have to go to Dr. Bennett's for the afternoon." A nervous frown creased James' brow. He'd been to Bennett's office several times over the course of the past ten days trying to ferret out more information concerning the supposed plot, but he hadn't been able to uncover another single detail. While James was present at the office, he'd seen only one of the traitors come in to talk with Bennett. And that had been a brief visit. Bennett and the man had sequestered themselves in the back office, but before James could overhear much of anything, the man came out again and left the office without so much as a glance in James' direction. James was beginning to doubt his earlier impression of a plot brewing against the Prophet. Maybe he'd been wrong about what he'd overheard that day. Perhaps there was no plot at all, and he'd sullied the reputation of innocent men. That thought brought out a line of perspiration along his forehead.

"You've been to Dr. Bennett's office nearly every day," Hayden complained. "Take an afternoon off and we'll play a game of circles. I'll let you use me big gray-eye."

James seriously considered the invitation. Hayden's gray-eye was as large as a fifty-cent piece and made of smooth clay fired to a rock-hard texture. The marble was a mottled gray with a black center that resembled the pupil of an eye. It was Hayden's favorite marble because of its appearance, and because it rolled the furthest and the straightest when shot from the fingers. "I can't," James answered regrettably. "Maybe tomorrow."

The boys were approaching the corner where they would part company, with Hayden turning one way in the direction of his house and James the other. Just as they reached the corner, they caught sight of a small contingent of militiamen marching toward them on the road.

"Blimey! It's a unit of the Nauvoo Legion!" whispered Hayden excitedly. "Where do you think they're 'eaded?"

"I don't know."

James and Hayden watched the soldiers march in synchronized step along the road. There were about fifteen of them, dressed in full uniform. James didn't recognize the commander in the lead. The unit continued up the road past the spot where the two boys stood staring at them.

"Let's follow 'em," Hayden said, nudging James in the ribs.

"What?"

"Come on. Let's see where they're goin'."

Before James could respond, Hayden was off like an arrow shot from a bow, sprinting after the soldiers. James galloped after him. They followed the unit of militia, lagging at a safe distance, all the way into the center of town. Hayden was dancing on his toes in excitement as they trailed after the troop of soldiers. The commander barked out an order and the militiamen came to an abrupt halt in front of a tavern on Main Street. Hayden wheeled to a stop, and James rammed into the back of his shoulder with a grunt.

"Look. The commander is goin' inside," Hayden said out of the corner of his mouth.

James peered over Hayden's shoulder. Sure enough, the lieutenant had disappeared behind the door of the saloon. The soldiers waiting in the street stood at attention. James and Hayden held their breaths, wondering what was taking place inside the grog shop. A moment later the lieutenant reappeared, accompanied by an angry, florid-faced man. The commander had in his hand a folded sheet of paper which he smoothed out and then tacked onto the outside of the door. The beefy man, who James presumed was the owner of the saloon, gestured angrily at the paper fastened onto the door of his business and directed a few unsavory remarks at the lieutenant. The man had shoulders like a bull, and his body was stocky and heavy-set. He glared at the assembly of soldiers and then huffed back inside the saloon. The appearance of the Legion, and the exchange of hot words, had collected a small crowd of onlookers. The commander of the militia barked out an order and the troop began moving back up the street in the same direction from which they had come.

After the militiamen had rounded the corner and disappeared from sight, and the spectators had drifted away, James' attention turned to the paper tacked onto the door of the grog shop. "Let's go see what it says," he suggested to Hayden.

The two of them crept cautiously to the door of the shop, glancing over their shoulders to see if anyone was watching. No one seemed to pay them any mind. That fact didn't lessen James' feeling of growing guilt. He'd been taught to strictly avoid the few saloons taking up residence in town. Even approaching the door of such an establishment was in violation of the bounds his parents had set. At the moment, however, his curiosity overruled his desire to be obedient and he and Hayden inched up to the door of the grog shop.

James carefully read the words of the notice posted on the door:

THIS ESTABLISHMENT HAS BEEN DECLARED A PUBLIC NUISANCE AND IS HEREBY CLOSED BY ORDER OF THE MAYOR AND CITY COUNCIL.

The words were printed in big, bold, black letters, and the sentence nearly leaped out from the page. The forceful tone made James cower. The mayor had probably anticipated trouble from the owner of the saloon and directed the unit of militia to carry out the order.

As James stood reading the notice through a second time, the door of the grog shop suddenly flew open and the owner stood in the doorway like a snorting bull. "Hey! What are you two doing? Get out of here," he bellowed, charging at them.

Startled, James stumbled backward, lost his balance, and fell on his rump on the hard, dirt-packed road. "Yes, sir," he croaked, scrambling to his feet. He and Hayden took off at a run and didn't stop running until they were a dozen yards away.

"Whew, that was close. We nearly got our ears boxed!" Hayden exclaimed.

James looked at his friend. Hayden's brown eyes were sparkling with excitement and his freckles stood out vividly against his pale cheeks.

"That cranky shopkeeper couldn't stand up to the militia," Hayden went on. "Did you see 'ow brave and bold that commander was? That's just 'ow I'll be — fearless as a tiger."

James knocked the dust off the seat of his britches.

"I can't wait to be old enough to join the Legion!" Hayden said. "We'll be the best soldiers ever, 'ey, mate?"

James glanced at his friend without replying. He no longer shared Hayden's enthusiasm for the job. Just knowing that there were wicked men in the Legion plotting to kill the Prophet tarnished the whole business for him.

"Won't we look splendid in our uniforms?" Hayden said, nudging James with his elbow. He started strutting along the side of the road with an imaginary rifle tucked under his arm. "Come on, James. Fall in step."

James stared at him, saying nothing.

Hayden took a few more high-stepping turns along the road and then came to a stop in front of James. "What's the matter? You're not marchin'," he said with a confused look on his face.

"Naw. I have to get going. I'm supposed to be at Dr. Bennett's office."

"Is everythin' aright with you, mate?" Hayden asked. "You've been a bit jumpy of late."

James bit his lip to keep from spilling the secret he was carrying. He longed to tell Hayden about the plot against the Prophet, but he couldn't drag Hayden into the web of intrigue being spun by the conspirators. He'd promised his parents that he would tell no one about what he'd overheard, except as the Prophet directed.

"Want me to come and give you a 'and at the doctor's office?" asked Hayden.

"No," James answered hurriedly. "I won't be there long. Maybe I can stop by your house afterward for a quick game of circles."

"Right-o."

The two parted and James headed for Dr. Bennett's office. Black clouds were scudding across the sky before a brisk wind. The wind tore at James' clothes and whipped his hair into a tousled mess. He bent into the stiff breeze and hurried along the street.

When he arrived at the doctor's door, he saw that Bennett had put out the sign marked CLOSED. Yet when he put his ear against the door, he heard voices coming from within. The curtains on the front window were closed, so he couldn't see inside. He stood uncertainly beside the door for a moment, then decided to go around to the side of the house where a window opened onto Bennett's private office. He felt self-conscious about sneaking around the corner of the house, but he had a feeling that the conspirators might be inside. Hopefully, the curtain on the side window wouldn't be drawn.

The wind was growing stronger and the sky darker as he made his way to the side of the stone house. The wind snatched at his shirt as if trying to lift it off his back. He had to step over a hedge of knee-high bushes, and go out around a thick-trunked elm tree in order to get to the window, but his efforts were rewarded when he reached the window and found the curtain loosely drawn. There was enough space left open where the two halves met for him to get a partial view into the room.

He took a step closer to the window and angled himself in such a way as to make the best use of his vantage point, taking precautions to keep low and out of sight to anyone who might be within. As he cautiously raised his eyes to the window, he held his breath. What he caught in that first glimpse confirmed his suspicions — a group of men sat with their chairs pulled together in a tight circle, deep in conversation. He ducked down below the window sill. The group was seated close to the window; the nearest man sat with his back toward the pane only inches away from where James crouched outside. James could barely make out their conversation through the glass.

James let out his breath slowly. He was stooped over in a cramped position, but he didn't dare move a muscle. The men inside the house would be able to see his movements as easily as he was able to see theirs. He crouched, motionless, hardly daring to draw another breath. He could hear Bennett's voice rise and fall, and another deeper voice answering in reply. With only the window between them James could hear the men, but he had trouble making out their words. James had been the one to shut the window yesterday afternoon when the sky threatened rain. Now he wished he'd left it open a crack.

He drew a deep breath and held it as he ventured another peek through the glass. His eyes darted around the group, straining to place each face. He recognized them only as the same men he'd seen the first time in Bennett's office. Aside from Dr. Bennett, he could not put a name to any of the faces.

The wind was picking up in intensity, and James felt a drop of rain splash against his cheek. He glanced up at the darkening sky and groaned. A cloudburst was threatening. Steeling himself against the coming rain, he rose up on one knee to peer through the corner of the window. As he did so, a sudden, painful cramp attacked his leg. He kneaded the spot with his fist, but the pain wouldn't stop unless he stretched out his leg. He had no choice but to shift position.

As he changed position, his foot brushed up against a bush and a twig snapped off with a loud, sharp crack. The sound seemed thunderous in his ears. He froze in horror. He flattened himself against the wall of the house, hoping, praying, that none of the men inside had heard the noise. The cold, rough stone wall scraped his elbows. He thought he heard the sound of a chair leg scraping against the floor, and then from the corner of his eye he caught a quick pulling aside of the curtain. He cringed, gluing himself to the wall. As he kneeled there shaking and shivering, as much from the cold as from fright, the sky opened up and rain began falling in sheets. James didn't dare risk raising a hand to wipe away the water running down his face.

He sat there in the pouring rain for what seemed an eternity. Rain slashed against his face and pelted his bare arms. Thunder rumbled in the distance. With the rain beating against the window and hammering the ground, there was little chance of James being able to hear anything of what was going on inside the room. But he was determined to stay his ground and accomplish his task — discover some tidbit of information to pass on to Brother Joseph. And the only way to do that was to wait and watch and listen at the window.

Shivering from the rain and the cold, wet wind, James again slowly and cautiously raised his head to the window. Whoever had moved the curtain aside had left the drapery wide open. Whether it was from the falling rain, or from the sound of the twig cracking, James could see that the men inside the room had grown restless. The one who had been seated with his back to the window, now stood leaning against the pane. He was a tall, thin man with a thick tuft of black hair. A second, louder, clap of thunder caused him to turn toward the window, stoop, and peer outside. In the streak of white lightning that followed, James and the man stood eyeball to eyeball through the glass.

James gasped. He was still crouched against the wall of the house and when he straightened in order to sprint away, the cramp in his leg returned with a double intensity of pain. He yelped and started to drag himself off, but the man at the window was quicker. He threw open the window, reached out, and grasped James by the collar. "Hold on, there," he growled. "What are you doing sneaking around here?"

As James struggled to free himself from the man's iron grip, another man dashed out the door of the house, rounded the corner, and confronted James. "Who are you?" the man demanded.

Before James could reply, the man grabbed James' shirtfront and shoved his face in James'. "Answer me, boy, before I take a willow to you."

"Take it easy, Meiers. I know the boy. Bring him inside," came Dr. Bennett's voice from the room.

Now that the man outside had James cornered, the one inside released his grip. The man named Meiers jerked James to his feet and steered him toward the house. James' heart was pounding with fear, and his mind was traveling a dozen different directions at once. Part of him desperately wanted to flee, yet another part was glad for the opportunity to finally face the conspirators and identify them. When they reached the door of the house, Meiers roughly hauled him inside.

James found himself standing in front of half a dozen glaring pairs of eyes. Bennett walked slowly over to him, a false smile spread on his face. "Hello, James. Do you want to tell me what you were doing outside the window?"

For an instant James considered whether to boldly tell Bennett the truth — that he knew about the plot and Bennett's implication in it — or try to lie his way out of what was fast becoming a dangerous situation.

"I came by, like usual, to spend the afternoon at the office," James said evenly. It was a half-truth, and James tried to sound convincing. "I saw the CLOSED sign on the door, but then I heard voices inside. So I came around to the window to see if I could find you inside."

Bennett's hard, piercing eyes narrowed as he considered James' response. The other men remained silent, and all James could hear was his own strident breathing. He rubbed the rain off his face with a jerky motion of his hand.

"The boy's a liar."

James' eyes cut toward the speaker, the same man who had dragged him inside. He had a stocky, bulky frame, long sideburns and a narrow band of beard running underneath his chin. His face was grim, and his eyes were cold and heartless.

"Let me handle this, Meiers," Bennett shot back. "The boy's probably telling the truth. He works as my assistant."

James' eyes returned to Bennett's scowling face. There was no pretense of a smile on it now. "What did you overhear, James, while you were standing at the window? I want the truth from you."

"Nothing, sir." James answered too quickly — he knew it as soon as the words left his mouth. Bennett knew it, too.

"Sit down, James. You're getting water all over my floor," Bennett said in a tired voice.

"I can come back later," James stuttered. "When you're not busy."

Bennett pushed him into a chair. "I don't think so."

"What are you going to do about him?" one of the other men asked Bennett.

James glanced at the speaker from beneath lowered eyes. The man's face was puffy and pale, and one eye was plagued with a nervous tic.

"I'm not sure yet," answered Bennett.

"We're going to have to get rid of him if he knows about our plans," the man named Meiers said hotly.

"I told you to shut up," Bennett shouted, whirling to face the man. "The boy's parents know he's here, you idiot."

Meiers' face took on a sullen look under Bennett's reprimand. James could see that he wasn't satisfied with Bennett's answer, however. If any of the men present were going to threaten James with harm, he guessed it would be this one.

"Meiers is right, John. We can't set the boy loose now. Let me take him into the woods and dispose of him there. His parents will never know what happened to him," said the tall, reedy man who had grabbed James from inside the window. The man ran a restless hand through his thicket of dark hair.

James' heart nearly stopped beating on hearing these words. From the look on the man's face, James knew he wasn't trying to scare him. He meant every word he said.

"I agree," Meiers said. "We can't run the risk of getting caught because of some nosy kid."

James glanced imploringly at Bennett. Surely Dr. Bennett wouldn't allow these villains to harm him. To his consternation, however, Bennett's expression was as hard as stone. "I'm asking you one last time, James. Tell me exactly what you overheard."

James knew he had a decision to make. He could either burst into frightened tears and beg for his release — which was definitely his preferred choice — or admit what he knew and stand up to these traitors with courage and resolve, no matter the consequences. He knew what his answer to Bennett must be; he knew it and he dreaded facing it more than anything he'd ever had to face before. His tongue felt thick and his mouth was dry. He clutched at his rain-soaked clothes, wishing he could sink through the floorboards.

"I won't ask you again, James." Bennett's voice was as hard as nails.

"I overheard some of what you said two weeks ago, Dr. Bennett," said James in a trembling voice. "You and these men talked about murdering the Prophet!"

Meiers jumped up from his chair and grabbed James by the shirtfront. "You little . . . ." The foul words he spat out were drowned by the ringing in James' ears. He probably would have twisted James' neck right then and there if Bennett hadn't prevented him.

"Stop it, Meiers," Bennett said behind gritted teeth. Bennett pried the man's hands off of James. "Give me a minute to think about this."

Meiers glared at James, his mouth twisted into an almost unrecognizable form.

The other men glanced at one another nervously. The one who had threatened James with destruction began to pace the room, grimacing and baring his teeth. The others looked as if they were at a loss to do anything about the drama unfolding around them.

James was quaking in his boots, but at the same time he felt proud of what he'd done — even if it cost him his life. He'd never tell these criminals, however, that Brother Joseph already knew about their plot. He wouldn't give them that satisfaction. James could feel the hatred directed against him; the room bristled with it.

Bennett bent down to stare him full in the face. "I'll tell you what I'm going to do, James. I'll let you go . . ." The man named Meiers groaned in exasperation. Bennett shot him a dark look. "I'll let you go on the condition that you keep your mouth shut about what you overheard. No one is going to harm Brother Joseph. It was just a lot of idle talk. I love the Prophet like my own brother."

James wondered how Bennett could say those words without choking on them.

"However, I can't be responsible for what these others may do if you don't cooperate," Bennett said, gesturing toward Meiers and the puffy-faced man with the nervous tic. "They don't know you like I do. I know you're a trustworthy young man, one who knows how to keep a secret between friends."

You're no friend of mine, James wanted to blurt out, *or Brother Joseph's.* But he remained silent, staring unflinchingly into Bennett's cold eyes.

"You promise me that you won't say anything about what went on here today, or whatever mistaken notion you think you overheard, and I'll be happy to let you leave unharmed."

Before James could even think about how to reply, Meiers swooped down on him like a hawk seizing its prey. His nose practically touched James'. James could smell the stench of tobacco on his breath. "If you tell a single soul about what you saw or heard here, I'll rip your scrawny throat out. Do you understand me? I'll slip into your bedroom one night while you're sleeping and slit your throat."

James' chest tightened in fear, and his breathing took on a wheezing sound.

"You heard him," said Bennett calmly. Bennett gestured with his hands as if he was powerless to stop it. "I won't be able to help you."

"Now get out of here, you miserable little sneak," Meiers said. He grabbed James roughly by the shirt collar and shoved him toward the door.

James hastily let himself out, and dashed away the moment his feet hit the doorstep. The sky was weeping rain and in seconds he was drenched, and shivering with fear and cold. He didn't stop running until he reached the door of his house.

Late that night as James lay in bed, he replayed the scene at Dr. Bennett's over and over in his mind. None of the conspirators had thought to inquire if he'd already reported their plans, and in their haste to be rid of him, they'd neglected to extract a promise from him not to tell anyone. James wouldn't have given his word anyway, even if they'd demanded it. Upon arriving home, he'd gone immediately to his parents with the story. His mother had reacted with horror, and his father's face had turned ashen and grim-looking.

James turned over onto his side to stare out the small, square window above his bed. The skies had cleared and stars shimmered like bits of crystal. The window was high off the ground, situated as it was in the loft, but that didn't prevent James from thinking about Meiers' dreadful threat.

He climbed out of bed and padded quietly to the window to make sure it was firmly shut and securely latched. Then he checked it a second time. Satisfied that no one could enter without breaking the glass and alerting the entire household, he crawled back to the warmth and security of his bed. He could hear his sisters' gentle breathing in the next room, and the sound of it comforted him. He pulled the quilts up to his chin and willed his body to relax. He was exhausted from the trauma he'd experienced, but it took a long while before he finally tumbled into sleep.

CHAPTER THIRTEEN

As Elizabeth stepped off the ferry onto the Montrose side of the river, with James at her side, her gaze flicked to the trading post across the street. She hadn't told her mother about the encounter with Yellow Feather. That incident had happened a week ago, and since that time she had progressed from feeling violated and angry with Yellow Feather to a curiosity about the Indian and an interest in seeing him again — although from a safe distance this time. James was accompanying her as far as the Montrose shore, and then he'd ride the ferry back to the Illinois side.

"Thanks, James," she said to her brother. "I can walk the distance to the Johanssens' place by myself."

"You sure? I can go with you and then come back to the ferry," he responded as he handed her the traveling bag. "Pa wanted me to make sure you got there safely."

"I don't need Christian's protection, or his permission," Elizabeth answered flippantly. Lately, she'd taken to calling him "Christian" rather than "Papa" behind his back, even when talking about him to James.

"Why are you so angry with Pa?" asked James. He stood on the bank of the river, frowning against the glare of the afternoon sun.

"He's not my pa. And he's not yours, either. I wish you'd quit referring to him as if he was," Elizabeth answered crossly.

She gripped the handle of the traveling bag and set off down the road that hugged the river front, turning once to wave to James. It was only a few blocks to the Johanssens' log house, and James would be able to keep her in sight from the ferry. She'd made plans with Inger to spend the night at the Johanssens' home, and as she walked her traveling bag bumped against her thigh.

She turned one last time to glance back at James. He was still standing on the dock, watching her progress. As she looked over her shoulder, she spotted the walls of the temple on the opposite shore. They stood straight and tall, like a sentinel guarding the city. From this perspective on the far side of the river, the temple walls were angled in such a way that they took on a slightly different appearance from what she was used to seeing.

Soon she had the Johanssens' house in sight. She walked up the stone-lined path and knocked on the door. Inger welcomed her inside, and immediately Elizabeth was enveloped in the warmth and hospitality of the Johanssen household. Peder Madsen was there visiting with Kirstine, and he was exactly as Inger had described him — tow-headed, blue-eyed, and kind-hearted. As Elizabeth passed part of the afternoon in the couple's company, she came to appreciate Peder's qualities. He was witty and clever, and possessed a jovial disposition. Kirstine confided that the two had plans to wed in the summer, and that Peder had already started work on a small log cabin for the couple to occupy after they married.

Brother Johanssen came in from his work in the fields at supper time. He was a quiet man who kept his thoughts to himself. His hair was gray and balding, and his eyes seemed to droop with some eternal sadness, but he welcomed Elizabeth to his home with simple graciousness.

After supper, Inger's sisters occupied themselves with their own interests, and her father and her younger brother, Lars, returned to their work in the fields to take advantage of the last few hours of daylight. Inger and Elizabeth sat at the supper table talking together.

"Peder seems really nice," Elizabeth said, her chin resting in her hand.

"Oh, he is. I adore him practically as much as Kirstine does," Inger giggled.

Elizabeth grinned, too. "How old is he?"

"Eighteen. A year older than Kirstine. He'll turn nineteen just before they're married."

"Would your mother have approved of the match?" Elizabeth asked after thinking about the question.

"I'm sure she would. She would have loved Peder."

"I bet your father misses her very much."

"Yes, he does. He's grown more solemn since her death. It breaks my heart to see him unhappy."

Elizabeth nodded. She thought about her own father who had died when she was only five. Losing a loved one was something you never got over, she decided.

"How is James?" Inger asked, glancing away to avoid Elizabeth's eyes.

"James? He's fine. Annoying, as ever." It wasn't until she'd replied to Inger's seemingly innocent question that she noticed the girl's cheeks were tinged with red. "Why, Inger Johanssen, you're not sweet on James, are you?" she asked incredulously.

Inger flushed a bright pink. "I think he's very nice."

Elizabeth chortled in delight. "You *are* sweet on him! I never would have imagined that."

Inger looked a bit embarrassed, but still she pursued the topic. "I'll bet he has a girlfriend, doesn't he?"

"He's too young to have a girlfriend. And too caught up in his books to even notice if a girl liked him," she snorted. "Well, except for maybe Winnie Fife."

"Winnie Fife?"

"She's a girl who goes to school with us. I've seen James talk to her a time or two."

Inger let out a long sigh. "I wish I was Winnie Fife."

"You've got to be joking," Elizabeth said. "James couldn't be any more ordinary and boring."

"Oh, that's not true. James is the kindest, most considerate boy I've ever met."

Uninterested in discussing her younger brother's qualities, Elizabeth turned to the subject she'd been wanting to broach with Inger ever since her arrival. "Have you seen Yellow Feather again since I was here last?"

Inger's eyes lost their dreamy sheen. "Once. A couple of days ago. He told me that his band is getting ready to leave the area. He wanted to say good bye."

"Do you think they've gone already?"

"I don't know. I haven't seen him for a few days."

"Oh," Elizabeth said, disappointed.

"But we could find out."

"We could?"

A mischievous gleam danced in Inger's eye. "The band has been camped for several weeks only a mile or two downstream. We could go and see if they're still there."

"You're not serious? Actually walk right into their camp?" Elizabeth said.

"Not into their camp, but close by it. We could walk down there and see if they've left. If they haven't, maybe we can find Yellow Feather."

"Do you know exactly where the camp is located?" Elizabeth asked, stalling for time to mull over this daring plan.

"Not exactly, but Yellow Feather told me where it is. I'm sure we could find it without much trouble. Do you want to try?"

Elizabeth swallowed hard. Tangling with Yellow Feather was frightening enough, but the thought of encountering adult Indian braves was sufficient to make her swoon.

"Come on, let's go. It'll be exciting," Inger said with mounting enthusiasm. She got up from her chair and gestured for Elizabeth to follow suit.

Elizabeth reluctantly trailed Inger out the door. They trotted along a dirt path beside the river, under cover of a canopy of leafy trees. When they ran out of breath, they slowed to a brisk walk with Inger leading the way.

"Peder has told me about the Sauk and Fox," Inger said, breathing hard. "He knows a lot about the different Indian tribes."

Elizabeth glanced at her without responding, concentrating on keeping up with the younger girl's quick stride.

"He said that the Sauk Indians were known as the yellow earth people, and the Fox as the people of the red earth. The two tribes came together and lived along the Rock River where it flowed into the Mississippi, a place the Great Spirit had prepared for their people. They built lodges to live in, and the women tilled the ground while the men hunted in the forests and plains."

"Uh huh," Elizabeth said, caught up in Inger's tale of the Indian tribe.

"Black Hawk was a great Sauk warrior who was angry with the whites for taking his ancestors' tribal lands. He led a group of Sauk and Fox Indians against the whites in an effort to regain his people's lands, but the Indians were massacred on the shores of the Bad Axe River."

Elizabeth had learned in school about the Black Hawk War that ended with the Indians' defeat in 1832. "What happened to Black Hawk?" she asked Inger.

"He died and his peoples' lands were sold. Now Yellow Feather and his clan of Sauk and Fox live on a reservation, except when they come down to the river to trade at the trading post."

Elizabeth was listening so intently that she tripped over a root and nearly fell. Inger waited for her a moment, then the two of them continued walking over the uneven ground while Inger went on with her description of the tribal way of life.

"Yellow Feather told me that his people believe in the Great Spirit, and that everything has its own *manito*, or guardian spirit, which comes from the Great Spirit. As a younger boy, he stayed by himself in the forest for several days seeking guidance and strength from the Great Spirit, and learning the ways of Mother Earth and Father Sky."

They tramped through the woods, keeping close to the river and talking between themselves. After they'd gone quite some distance, Elizabeth began to have second thoughts about the expedition. What if they walked all that way and the Indians had already left the area? Or worse, what if the Indians were still there and caught the girls spying on their camp? She could only imagine the horrible tortures they'd put Inger and her through once they captured them.

"Maybe this isn't such a good idea, Inger. Maybe we ought to turn back," Elizabeth whispered.

"We're almost there now. I'm sure of it. Aren't you curious to see an Indian wigwam?"

"Yes, but what if the Indians spot us? There's no telling what they'll do to us," Elizabeth replied nervously.

"We'll just tell them we're acquainted with Yellow Feather. That we're friends of his."

Elizabeth frowned. "How are you going to do that when you can't speak the Indian language?"

Inger didn't seem to have an answer for that question. They padded through the forest the rest of the way in silence. Suddenly, from up ahead they saw a clearing, and in the clearing were scattered over a dozen round huts. Inger pulled up short, and Elizabeth nearly bumped into her.

"Shh," Inger whispered, putting a finger to her lips.

Both girls ducked behind a tree, then cautiously peeked out around it. The Indian camp was still a good distance off, but they had a clear view of it. From their hiding place, Elizabeth could see that the oval-shaped houses were constructed of saplings covered with woven mats made from dried river rushes. She could smell the wood smoke curling from the domed tops of the huts as it was carried away on the breeze. Dogs roamed loose throughout the camp, and a dozen horses were corralled in a common area near a stream. She caught sight of a group of Indian braves riding through the camp on their ponies, an Indian woman gathering sticks for her fire, and bronze-skinned children making a zigzag dash as they chased each other. Off to one side Elizabeth spotted what looked like a woman tanning hides. She had the skins spread out and pegged to the ground, and was scraping one with a sharp instrument.

Elizabeth and Inger stared in fascination at the jumbled scene. Inger silently pointed to a group of young Indian boys who were playing fetch the stick with a big yellow dog. The boys wore only leggings and moccasins, and their long hair streamed down their bare backs. Nearby, Elizabeth saw a woman wrapped in a bright-colored woven blanket carrying her papoose, strapped to a cradleboard, on her back. Four young children were gathered around her — a boy with shaggy, unkempt hair, and three bare-footed girls with their black hair loosely braided. Not far away, a woman sat cross-legged on the ground weaving a basket. A bark canoe was pulled ashore on the river bank, loaded with animal pelts. The pelts would be traded for guns, whiskey, and tobacco at the trading post, Elizabeth guessed. The Indians' guttural speech, soaring up from the camp, sounded like a cacophony to Elizabeth's ears, all discordance and dissonance. It played a haunting accompaniment to the scenes spread before her eyes.

Elizabeth was mesmerized by the sights, smells, and sounds of the Indian encampment. She had no idea how long she and Inger had been watching from behind the tree when she suddenly heard the soft rustling of brush and the snapping of a twig, and then an old Indian woman carrying a basket of washing stepped into view. In that first instant, she looked as startled to see Elizabeth and Inger as they were to see her. Before the girls could even think how to respond, the old Indian woman let out a piercing, high-pitched wail." "Eeeee! Eeeee!" she screeched, alerting the other members of her tribe.

The terrifying noise frightened the girls more than the appearance of the woman herself. They leaped from their hiding place and bolted away, sprinting through the forest at breakneck speed. Elizabeth's heart pounded as she followed Inger over the rough ground. She bounded over roots and rocks in her path, her heart feeling as if it would fly from her chest. She was crying and praying all at the same instant, certain that a band of warriors on horseback were in hot pursuit. She didn't dare risk turning around to see if she could spot her pursuers; their horses' hoofbeats seemed to thunder in her ears. The woman's cry of alarm seemed to ring endlessly on the wind.

The girls must have run for over a mile before they were forced to stop and catch their breath. Elizabeth bent over, her hands on her knees, gulping for air. "Do you think they're still after us?" she wheezed.

Inger shook her head, too much out of breath to answer.

Elizabeth chanced a quick glance behind her. She didn't see any warriors or hear any sound of horses crashing through the brush giving chase. "Maybe they didn't follow us," she said hopefully, still wheezing and huffing for breath.

Inger shot a wide-eyed glance over her shoulder. "Let's keep going," she sputtered.

The two of them started off again at a run, skirting the path that edged the riverside. Elizabeth's side started to ache with the rugged pace, and she clutched at it with both hands as she stumbled after Inger. They didn't stop running until they had the house in sight. They burst through the back door and collapsed in a heap on the floor.

Kirstine and Peder, who were sitting at the table, started in surprise. "For goodness sake! What's gotten into you girls?" Kirstine asked.

"We're . . . we're . . ." Inger struggled to get the words out through labored breaths. "We're being chased by Indians!"

"What?" both Peder and Kirstine exclaimed. Peder bolted from his chair and dashed outside to see if the cabin was under attack. Kirstine helped the girls to their feet.

"There's no one out there," Peder reported on coming inside a few moments later. "Tell me exactly what happened."

The girls related their experience in jumbled sentences, each one interrupting the other to add details.

Peder and Kirstine listened closely, and then a smile started at the corners of Peder's mouth. "That's quite a tale, all right," he said, trying to keep a straight face. "But I doubt you were ever in any danger. They're just a small band of Sauk and Fox Indians camped upriver, and they've traveled back and forth to town for several weeks. They're a peaceful people."

"How do you know that for sure?" Elizabeth replied in consternation. "We could have been captured and skinned alive."

"And no one would have ever known what happened to us," Inger added, her blue eyes wide with apprehension.

Peder chuckled. "Then it's a good thing you girls escaped."

"You're safe now," Kirstine said, giving her fiancé a sharp look. She wasn't as amused by the girls' escapade as Peder seemed to be. She put an arm around her younger sister. "No one's going to hurt you."

After Kirstine was certain the girls were calm, she and Peder left them to themselves and went into the next room. Inger bolted the cabin door. It was nearly dark, and the girls weren't entirely satisfied with Peder's perfunctory search outside the cabin. As they settled in for the evening, Elizabeth kept one eye on the door.

That night she dreamed she was being chased through the woods by a band of Indians. But midway through the pursuit, the Indians changed into a mob of angry Missourians carrying rifles and shouting threats. Elizabeth awoke with a start. Her heart was pounding and her mouth felt dry. As she struggled to calm her emotions, she saw the first early rays of sunlight slanting through the windows of the Johanssens' cabin and heard Inger's soft breathing beside her in the bed. She lay awake until the sun burst over the prairie, burning away the early morning mists and the last traces of her dream with its brilliant, hot light. To Elizabeth's relief, her nightmares were occurring less frequently and with less intensity. Elizabeth hoped that one day soon they would cease tormenting her altogether.

Elizabeth had been invited to participate in a special program held by the ladies of the Female Relief Society of Nauvoo. The event was to take place in Joseph Smith's new red brick store, and Elizabeth was slated to give a recitation in the presence of about fifty ladies. There was also to be a second dramatic reading, a vocal number, and a musical selection. As Elizabeth accompanied her mother to the mercantile, she didn't feel particularly nervous about her performance; since winning the school competition she'd participated in a number of similar events. Once again, she was prepared to recite *The Wreck of the Hesperus*.

Elizabeth had been inside Joseph Smith's new store several times since it opened for business the previous January. It was a large and handsome place with shelves and drawers bulging with goods — flour, sugar, molasses, raisins, salt, nails, glass, yardage, thread, needles, combs, hairbrushes, razors, and all manner of merchandise. The less expensive woods used to construct the counters, drawers, and pillars were painted to resemble oak, mahogany, and marble.

The impressive two-story building had been constructed about a block west of the Prophet's log home on Water Street, and across the road from the Law brothers' general store. Brother Joseph often tended the counter himself, but he'd recently hired another to manage the store because of his own heavy responsibilities in religious and community affairs. Elizabeth glanced at the counter as she entered the store. Someone other than Brother Joseph was helping customers behind the long counter. She and her mother climbed the back stairs to the second story, which led to a spacious room. The upper floor of the store was often used as a place to host social, civic, and religious activities such as theatrical presentations, debates, and lectures; it was also the meeting place for the Female Relief Society, priesthood councils, municipal officials, and staff of the Nauvoo Legion. It was the largest assembly room in all Nauvoo and a center of activity.

The room was filling up with ladies dressed in their finery; many had brought along their daughters or young children. The meeting was called to order by the president of the organization, Sister Emma Smith. She and her counselors, Sister Elizabeth Ann Whitney and Sister Sarah M. Cleveland, and the secretary, Sister Eliza R. Snow, had organized this event for "the betterment of the mind, and the enjoyment of the sweet bonds of sisterhood."

Elizabeth gave her attention to Sister Smith, who stood at the head of the room behind a table brightened by a vase of spring flowers. The Prophet's wife was tall and regal looking, with large dark eyes and black shining hair. She had a lovely soprano voice Elizabeth had enjoyed hearing at a recent choral performance. This particular afternoon as she stood before the sisters, she outlined the program and introduced the participants. Elizabeth was scheduled to perform after the vocal solo.

Elizabeth wasn't personally acquainted with the woman who stood up to sing. She was a short, plump lady, round as a peach, and her brown eyes were lined and deeply-set like two wrinkled peach pits. She sang a patriotic piece in a droning alto voice that sounded more like a dirge than a song of pride. Elizabeth didn't care much for the rendition, but when the soloist finished the last sonorous note, the ladies gave her an enthusiastic round of applause.

It was Elizabeth's turn to perform next. Her heart started racing as she rose from her chair and stepped to the front of the room. Seated before her were a field of bonneted faces. For an instant, the ladies' oval-shaped bonnets reminded her of the wigwams at the Indian encampment. The memory made her heart hammer even harder. She struggled to slow her hurried breathing before starting into the piece she had memorized.

> "It was the schooner *Hesperus*,
>   That sailed the wintry sea;
> And the skipper had taken his little daughter,
>   To bear him company.
>
> "Blue were her eyes as the fairy-flax,
>   Her cheeks like the dawn of day,
> And her bosom white as the hawthorn buds,
>   That ope in the month of May."

Now that she was under way, she felt calmer. She used added expression and emotion as she recited the words of the poem, and employed her hands in gesture. Before she had completed very many more lines, she knew she had the ladies enthralled.

"Colder and louder blew the wind,
    A gale from the Northeast,
The snow fell hissing in the brine,
    And the billows frothed like yeast.

"Down came the storm, and smote amain
    The vessel in its strength;
She shuddered and paused, like a frighted steed,
    Then leaped her cable's length."

She continued on without forgetting a single line or stumbling over a single word, and concluded the tragic tale of the captain and his daughter with a flourish of expression of both hand and voice.

"At daybreak, on the bleak sea-beach,
    A fisherman stood aghast,
To see the form of a maiden fair,
    Lashed close to a drifting mast.

"The salt sea was frozen on her breast,
    The salt tears in her eyes;
And he saw her hair, like the brown seaweed,
    On the billows fall and rise.

"Such was the wreck of the *Hesperus,*
In the midnight and the snow!
Christ save us all from a death like this,
On the reef of Norman's Woe!"

The audience burst into applause, and Elizabeth smiled and curtsied graciously. When she returned to her seat, her mother reached over and squeezed her hand. "You did a marvelous job with that, Elizabeth."

Elizabeth felt an intense sense of pride, almost a smugness, over how well she had performed. She basked in the glory of the beaming smiles and approving glances from the ladies. As she settled back in her chair, she could feel the sun on her shoulders from where she sat at the end of the front row of chairs, next to the tall, rectangular windows that faced the street below. She imagined herself bathed in a golden glow, her yellow hair like an angel's halo. She smiled at the fanciful image of herself. Perhaps she might take her talents abroad, out of the small, provincial town of Nauvoo and perform her recitations in the big Eastern cities, or before queens and kings of Europe. In a matter of moments she had built up in her mind a picture of herself as a sought-after entertainer, with the whole world recognizing her name.

It was several moments before she realized that the next performer had stepped to the front of the room and was in the midst of playing a soaring melody on the violin. Elizabeth recognized the piece as a favorite Latter-day Saint hymn from the Church's hymnbook. The sweet strains of music filled the assembly room with warmth and peace. Elizabeth saw several women nodding their heads in time to the slow, smooth rhythm.

The last performer gave a humorous reading taken from a current popular play. It was a charming piece, and the audience chuckled throughout it. Elizabeth had to concede that the woman showed talent and ability. The woman's performance took some of the shine off of Elizabeth's vision of personal success.

When the entertainment was over, Sister Emma Smith again took her place at the head of the room to address the sisters. Elizabeth sat forward with interest to hear her remarks. Sister Smith began with a statement of the purpose of the Female Relief Society, whose object, she said, "is the relief of the poor, the destitute, the widow and the orphan, and for the exercise of all benevolent purposes." She then went on to outline a number of opportunities that were at present available for the sisters to exercise their charitable ministrations. She brought forward for the ladies' consideration the names of individuals who needed their assistance, and a number of projects that required their aid.

As Sister Smith discussed the specifics of each case, Elizabeth's attention began to wander. She studied the attractive coal-oil lamps hanging from the ceiling, and the simulated mahogany wood trim around the windows and doors. Her gaze came to rest outside the window where she idly watched people passing by on foot and in horse-drawn vehicles. Against the side of the building someone had carefully planted a colorful array of flowers, blooming in all their spring glory. Probably Sister Smith's handiwork, Elizabeth thought. She returned her attention to the Prophet's wife and listened as the woman concluded her remarks.

After all the acclamations were extended, and the good byes completed, Elizabeth and her mother left the red brick store. As they started down Water Street, Lydia paused in front of Sidney Rigdon's two-story frame home, which also served as the post office. Brother Rigdon was the city postmaster.

"I'm going inside the post office to pick up our mail," she said. "Do you want to come along?"

"No. I'll wait out here."

Elizabeth watched her mother disappear inside the house, then her gaze turned to the passersby on the street. The plank walk was crowded with people. This was a busy section of town where the merchants and tradesmen had set up their shops. The commercial district consisted of about six blocks along Water and Main Streets; a second business sector was located on the bluff near the temple. The city was growing rapidly, and all manner of commerce flourished in the burgeoning town.

As Elizabeth stood eyeing people pass by on the street, she caught sight of Willy Saunders. He was striding in her direction with long, purposeful steps, the brim of his cap pulled over his forehead, and his shirtsleeves rolled up to his elbows. He would have passed right by without noticing her if she hadn't called out his name.

He ground to a halt in front of her. "Hello, Elizabeth," he said without any show of emotion.

"What are you up to, Willy?" she greeted him. She noticed that his shirt was stained and his rumpled cotton trousers sported a tear in one knee. There was a white scar on his chin where he'd been hurt in the fistfight that night two weeks ago near her home.

"Just workin'. You?" he returned, regarding her with heavy-lidded eyes.

"I just finished giving a recitation for a group of ladies."

"Yeah?"

"That's right. How about yourself? Are you still helping your father farm?"

"Naw. I got myself a real good job. Pays a lot."

"Is that so?" She had trouble believing that statement considering the way he was dressed. "Doing what?"

"I'm workin' for a steamboat captain, down on the dock. It pays real good wages." As if to verify his words, Willy snaked a hand into his trouser pocket and pulled out a shiny five-dollar gold piece. He flipped the coin up in the air in front of Elizabeth's nose, and caught it again in his grime-caked fist.

"You don't say," Elizabeth returned dryly. Her first thought was that Willy had stolen the gold piece, just like he had the pocketwatch that time at the parade grounds. "What do you do at the docks to earn that kind of money?"

"Anything the captain asks me to do," he said smugly. He tossed the coin into the air again, and caught it with one hand. "Besides loading wood onto the steamboat for the boilers and giving a hand with repairs," he added, almost as an afterthought.

His words brought to mind the afternoon she'd seen Willy from her secluded spot near the river while she'd been practicing her recitation for the school competition. He'd swaggered aboard the steamship, *Mississippi Maiden,* and disappeared inside the cabin. She'd wondered then what he was doing aboard a boat reputedly infested with gamblers and thieves.

"You still goin' to school?"

She nodded. "Only three weeks more until I'm out for the summer."

"Yeah. I bet you'll be glad about that." He flipped the gold piece skyward again. Elizabeth watched the coin shimmer and sparkle in the sunlight before he caught it and stuffed it back into his pocket.

She didn't bother to respond to his remark. She'd had only a few brief conversations with Willy since the night of the altercation outside her bedroom window. On those occasions, he'd treated her in a civil manner. Today's conversation seemed to be flowing along those same lines. They'd developed a tentative, uneasy friendship, stemming from the aid she'd rendered on the night of the quarrel.

"Did you do good on your reading?" Willy asked her, shifting his weight from one leg to the other. The scar on his chin flashed with a glossy sheen when the sunlight struck it.

"Yes, as a matter of fact. The ladies loved it."

"Since you enjoy that stuff, maybe you'd like to go with me to the theatrical production tomorrow night," Willy said, slurring the word "theatrical" into an almost unrecognizable sound.

Elizabeth's eyes widened in surprise. "Are you inviting me to keep company with you?"

"Yeah, I guess that's what it is," he replied sheepishly.

Elizabeth burst into laughter. "You can't be serious. Do you think I'd actually agree to be courted by you?"

Willy didn't seem to be offended by her stinging refusal. He shrugged his shoulders and shoved his hands in his pockets. Then muttering a farewell, he brushed past her and walked away.

Elizabeth watched him saunter down the street. She could hardly believe her mixed fortune. This was the first time a boy had asked to share the pleasure of her company for an evening — something she had looked forward to with eager anticipation — and the boy turned out to be that scoundrel, Willy Saunders.

CHAPTER FOURTEEN

James and Hayden stood at the front of the crowd watching the preparations for the sham battle between the two cohorts of the Nauvoo Legion. The grassy square where the proceedings were to occur was crowded with spectators. Citizens of Nauvoo and visitors from outside the city had gathered to watch the Legion parade and then assemble for the mock battle.

Hayden could hardly stand still. He kept gesturing and jabbering as he waited for the battle to begin. James watched the scene with trepidation. He neither shared in Hayden's excitement, nor joined in his anticipation of the event. He kept his gaze fixed on the Prophet. If today's drill was to be the setting for the assassination attempt on Brother Joseph, then he hoped the Prophet would keep his mounted guards close and that he would avoid coming in contact with his major general, John C. Bennett.

James held his breath as the two cohorts lined up on opposite sides of the field with Lieutenant General Joseph Smith, his staff, and guard positioned at the head. Sister Emma Smith and the wives of some of the officers sat on horseback beside their husbands. Sister Smith was wearing a black riding habit and a bonnet with a feather plume, and carrying a riding crop in her hand. The Legion Band, playing a brisk military march, was situated next to the officers and their ladies, and Major General Bennett and his staff were assembled nearby.

"Blimey! If this isn't the most excitin' day of me life," Hayden exclaimed.

James didn't trust himself to respond. He stood beside Hayden, wringing his hands with worry over the Prophet's safety.

"Don't those soldiers look splendid!" Hayden continued. He was so enamored with the sight before him, that he didn't notice James' absence of enthusiasm.

A loud volley from the cannon, like a sudden thunderclap, signaled the commencement of the battle. The first cohort of cavalry, under the direction of Brigadier General Wilson Law, surged forward onto the field to engage the second cohort commanded by Brigadier General Charles C. Rich. Hayden squealed as the two cohorts came together in a clash of arms. James moved his lips in silent pleading for Brother Joseph to remain where he was, safely removed from the center of the confrontation.

The mock battle, designed as a training exercise for the troops as well as for the enjoyment of the spectators, progressed into a lively conflict. The riflemen engaged their opponents with first one side gaining the advantage and then the other, and the field was festooned with colorful uniforms and prancing horses. The spring weather was fine and clear, ideal for a display of the Legion's proficiency. The noise of the crowd cheering, hooting, and clapping as they witnessed the performance of the militiamen clanged in James' ears. The artillery was situated at the foot of the field, and every so often a cannon would boom and the crowd would roar its approval. The sham battle took on an almost festive atmosphere, like a garish carnival, but James couldn't relax or enjoy the military display. All he could do was fret over the Prophet's safety, and pray that Brother Joseph wouldn't be left unprotected or drawn into the confusion on the field where he could fall prey to an assassin's bullet.

Brother Joseph had joined the rank of soldiers now, but James noticed that he'd selected a secure position, and kept his horse guards by his side. James gnawed at his knuckles as he watched the exercises. At his side, Hayden was shouting out encouragement and instructions to the troops on the field.

"Engage those soldiers to the rear!" Hayden shouted, leaping in the air. "Bring up that unit of mounted riflemen!"

James spared a glance at his friend. Hayden's freckled, round face was glistening with sweat, and his hair fell across his eyes. The back of his shirttail had come loose, and his cotton trousers were rumpled. He kept jumping up and throwing his fist above his head in excitement. James envied his friend's naïve enthusiasm. Hayden had no inkling of the dark undertow flowing beneath the surface of the exhibition.

After nearly an hour of maneuvering on the field, the military exercise came to a close. No one was happier to see its conclusion than James. The Prophet rode off the field safe and sound, with his sword at his side. Afterward, Brother Joseph gave a brief address expressing his satisfaction with the day's events, and giving an account of the growth of the Legion. He remarked that one year ago the Legion consisted of six companies; today it comprised twenty-six companies totaling over two thousand troops. At half-past four in the afternoon, the regiments were dismissed and the crowd began to drift away.

Hayden wanted to stay until the last soldier had left the grounds. His admiration for the militiamen was at a fever pitch, and glowing praises rolled off his tongue as thick and syrupy as molasses. James listened to him with one ear as he led the way from the square, dodging between clumps of straggling spectators. As he circled out around one such group, he accidentally bumped into a soldier striding across the grounds.

"Pardon me," James said automatically. When his eyes met those of the militiaman's, he froze in sudden fear.

It took a moment for the soldier to recognize him, but when he did the man's expression changed from simple annoyance to open malice. The soldier grabbed James by the shirtfront and glared into his face. "You! What do you think you're doing?"

James' face paled as he stood nose to nose with the man, Meiers.

Meiers' eyes narrowed and his mouth twisted into an ugly gash. "Do you think you can play games with me?" Meiers whispered harshly. His face was jammed so closely to James' that James could smell the stink of tobacco on his breath.

"I'm . . . I'm . . . sorry," James choked. "It was an accident. I didn't see you."

There was surprising power and strength in Meiers' fist as he tightened his grip on James' shirtfront. Meiers was stocky, and his bulk was squeezed into the white woolen breeches and blue coat of his Legion uniform. He smelled of sweat and grime, and his long sideburns and narrow beard glistened with perspiration.

"You little snake," Meiers spat out. "You better remember what I said about keeping your trap shut. Now get out of here." He tossed James aside as if he were a rag doll, and strode away.

Hayden, who had been standing close by and heard the whole exchange, stared at James. "What was that all about?"

James swallowed hard and tried to stop his voice from shaking. "It was nothing. The man was annoyed because I rammed into him. That's all."

"Then why do you look as if you've seen a ghost?" Hayden asked, staring at his friend.

"I'm fine," James said, trying to shake off his fear. "Let's go." He started off at a quick pace, but his legs felt as wobbly as two wooden stilts. Hayden trailed behind him wearing a puzzled look on his face.

In the days that followed, James learned that Bennett had, in fact, tried to manipulate Joseph's position on the field during the course of the sham battle. The assassination attempt sickened James, and he did not go back to Bennett's office again.

Ten days after the mock battle, John C. Bennett resigned his position as mayor of Nauvoo. Shortly thereafter, Bennett left the city. Information began to surface concerning the man's true character; some people reported that Bennett had been openly critical of the Prophet Joseph, and worse, that Bennett had engaged in improper relations with one of the young women in town. In the latter part of June, the Nauvoo papers printed a complete disclosure of Bennett's misdeeds, along with the news that he had been stripped of his rank and membership in the Nauvoo Legion, ousted from the Masonic Lodge, dismissed as chancellor of the city university, and excommunicated from the Church.

Bennett's treachery created a flood of difficulties for the Church. Several individuals who had been influenced by Bennett were found guilty of unvirtuous conduct and lost their membership in the Church. Rumors circulated concerning a plot instigated by Bennett to stir up the Missourians to mob action against the Saints in Nauvoo, to destroy their property and drive them from their homes, and to capture and kill the Prophet Joseph. Bennett also had a hand in initiating legal proceedings against the Prophet with regard to the shooting of Wilburn W. Boggs.

On May sixth, former Missouri governor Boggs had been shot and wounded at his home by an unknown assailant. Newspapers outside of Nauvoo were publishing accounts of the deed, and insinuating that it had been perpetrated by Joseph Smith himself, or at least was carried out under the Prophet's direction, because former Governor Boggs had issued the extermination order and driven the Saints from Missouri resulting in loss of life and property. Based on false claims set forth by Bennett, the Prophet was arrested in August, and ordered to return to Missouri to face charges of assault with the intent to kill. Knowing his life would be in jeopardy if he returned to Missouri, Joseph instead went into hiding. Church leaders were doing all they could to turn the tide of malice and misunderstanding away from the Saints. No one knew how long Brother Joseph would remain in seclusion or when they might see their beloved Prophet again.

The whole series of events affected James more than he wanted to admit. He had admired and trusted Dr. Bennett almost as much as his own father. He had believed the man to be a faithful, honest Latter-day Saint dedicated to serving others. To find out that Bennett was none of these things was a devastating blow. Because of Bennett's example, the whole idea of doctoring became distasteful to him, smacking of treachery, disillusionment, and disappointment. Not only had Bennett sullied his own reputation as a physician, but he had destroyed James' dream to become a doctor as well.

James and his family exited the ferry on the Iowa side of the river. The August sun was hot, and James felt uncomfortably warm and cramped in his stiff new trousers and crisp white shirt and collar. His hair was smoothed back and slicked down with a dose of his father's hair tonic, and it felt unnatural plastered as it was to his head. He walked carefully along the dirt road adjacent to the river, careful not to wrinkle his clothes or rumple his hair. It was the afternoon of Kirstine Johanssen's marriage to Peder Madsen, and the Kades had been invited to the wedding. Elizabeth was dressed in a green and yellow plaid, with a wide lace collar and cord trim along the edge of the skirt. Roxana's dress was cut from the same checkered fabric as Elizabeth's, but was of simpler design. A bit of the same cloth draped the rag doll Roxie gripped in her hand.

"Will Kirstine be dressed in her pretty wedding gown?" Roxie wanted to know.

"Uh huh," James answered absently. He wiggled a finger in back of his tight-fitting collar, trying to loosen it a bit.

"I'll bet she looks pretty as a rose," Roxana went on. "That's what Mama said."

James glanced down at his younger sister. Her dark curls glistened in the summer sun and her blue eyes sparkled. She'd be six in December, old enough to start common school. James felt a swell of tender feeling for his little sister. She seemed so slight and small, with delicate hands and dainty feet. When she started school, he knew he would willingly play the role of her champion and protector.

Christian carried fourteen-month-old Zachary in his arms while Lydia held Millicent's hand. Milly was four and growing a crop of carrot-red hair. She was never still and twittered like a songbird. Her movements were like a bird's, too, quick and darting. She looked like a little red robin, constantly bobbing, hopping, and chirping.

Before long, the Kades arrived at the Johanssens' log home. A crowd of people had already gathered, and the house was filled with laughter and merriment. In the center of the crowd James caught a glimpse of Kirstine, red-cheeked and glowing. Her intended stood beside her, tall, slender, and handsome.

James spotted Lars Johanssen standing across the room, and not far from him stood his two older sisters, Inger and Johanna. Johanna's hair was done up in a braided circlet on the top of her head. She'd tucked a small sprig of flowers into the braid, but the flowers did little to soften her stern features. Inger's hair was plaited into one long golden braid trailing down her back, with a half a dozen violets woven into the braid. James noticed that the violets matched the color of her eyes.

He was about to cross the room and speak with Lars and his sisters when Brother Johanssen invited the guests to take their seats. James reached his chair just as the bishop of the Montrose ward came to the head of the room and invited the young couple to join him. Kirstine, shy and smiling sweetly, took her place beside Peder. The groom's smile was unrestrained — James had never seen anyone with such a beaming countenance. Peder cast a loving glance at his bride-to-be and squeezed her hand.

The crowd seemed to collectively hold its breath as the bishop began his remarks. James stared at the bride and groom. Kirstine was wearing a white cotton gown, and her hair was crowned with a wreath of fresh flowers. She carried a bouquet of wildflowers in her hand. Peder was dressed in black trousers and tailcoat, and held his tall silk hat under one arm. As the bishop performed the marriage ceremony, James glanced at his mother. She was dabbing at her eyes with a handkerchief. James guessed that she was thinking about Sister Johanssen, who had passed away when the Johanssen family first came to Montrose.

James didn't remember the Danish woman very clearly for he had been younger than Milly when the Johanssens moved from Green County. But he knew that it was Sister Johanssen who had brought Parley P. Pratt to the family cabin that cold winter afternoon when James, suffering from serious illness, lay near death. His mother had recounted the story to him — how Sister Johanssen exercised the faith to ask Brother Pratt to come and administer to James, how his mother had at first questioned Elder Pratt's motives, and how Elder Pratt had placed his hands on James' small head and pronounced a priesthood blessing on him. James didn't personally remember any of that, of course, but he'd heard the story so many times that it seemed as if every detail burned brightly in his memory. He'd started to recover from his illness that very evening, and by the next day his fever had broken. That experience had profoundly affected his mother. Lydia read the Book of Mormon that Elder Pratt left her, and a testimony of the gospel of Jesus Christ began to grow in her heart. It was a combination of the power of the priesthood, which she had witnessed firsthand, and the testimony of the prophets in the Book of Mormon, that had converted her to the gospel. Her testimony never wavered after that, even during the difficult days in Missouri.

It was through the Johanssens that his mother had been introduced to the gospel; consequently, the Johanssen family was very dear to her heart. She had tender feelings for the Johanssen children, not only because they had lost their mother, but because she wished to repay Sister Johanssen in some way for her act of faith and kindness on that wintry day ten years earlier.

James' attention returned to the ceremony taking place. After a few concluding remarks, the couple exchanged their first kiss as husband and wife, and then the bishop introduced Mr. and Mrs. Peder Madsen to the guests for their pleasure and approval. The guests clapped enthusiastically, and some of the men whistled and hooted. Then the couple stood hand in hand while the guests surged forward to offer their congratulations.

After James joined his family in congratulating the married couple, he began hunting for Lars. The ensuing celebration didn't hold much interest for him, and he wanted to show Lars his new pocketknife. He spotted the younger boy in the press of people. The Johanssens' two-room cabin seemed to be bulging at the seams, and James hoped he and Lars could step outside into the open air and sunlight.

He threaded his way over to Lars and the two of them slipped out the back door of the cabin and walked down to the riverside. Lars picked up a round, smooth stone and sent it sailing across the water. "Did you watch the Nauvoo Legion parade last month on Independence Day?" Lars asked conversationally.

"Yeah, I did," answered James. He and Hayden had joined in the Fourth of July celebrations held in town, which included viewing the Legion march on the parade grounds. As usual, Hayden had been mesmerized at the first appearance of the militiamen, but since the conspiracy against the Prophet by a few treacherous members of the Legion, James had lost his taste for soldiering. Those men who had plotted to take the Prophet's life had been identified and expelled from the Legion, and the militia continued to be a symbol of pride and patriotism.

"So did I. Pa let us all go into Nauvoo to watch the Legion. We stayed for the fireworks, too."

"It was good, wasn't it," James said, choosing a small, flat stone to skim across the surface of the water.

"I'll say it was! It lit up the sky so bright that we could have seen it from here."

James glanced across the river to Nauvoo. He could see trees and houses on the opposite shore, and had a clear view all the way to the temple being built on the bluff. The stonemasons had started their work on the base of the building, and the cut blocks of limestone glittered in the sun.

"Pa let us each have a nickel to spend in celebration of the Fourth. I bought a marble. Want to see it?"

"Sure."

Lars reached into his trouser pocket and withdrew a shiny green marble. It was one solid color, with no bands or speckles of contrasting hue. Lars held it out in the palm of his hand for James to admire. It was handsome, but not as fine as Hayden's polished gray-eye. Lars held his marble up to catch the sunlight.

James was itching to bring out his pocketknife. He fished into his pocket and caressed the deer-antler handle. "I don't have any marbles with me, but I brought this to show you," he said, pulling out the knife for Lars to see.

Lars let out a whistle. "That's a beauty! Where'd you get it?"

"My pa gave it to me."

"For your birthday?" Lars asked, his eyes fastened on the knife.

"No, my birthday's not for another month. It's kind of an early birthday present, I guess."

He wasn't able to tell Lars the whole reason why he'd received such a gift. After the incident at Dr. Bennett's office when he'd been caught eavesdropping, Christian had told James how proud he was of him for his courage in standing up to the conspirators. Then he'd presented James with the pocketknife — the same one he'd given James after the school spelling competition. James had been stunned to see the beautiful knife again. He thought his father had returned it to the general store where he'd purchased it; but Christian had been saving it for him all along, waiting for an appropriate occasion to restore it to him. "You've earned this pocketknife, James," his father had told him, "through your persistence in doing right." James had been thrilled with the gift, as well as the words of praise.

"That's about the prettiest pocketknife I've ever seen," Lars said.

"Here, you can try it out." James held the knife out to his friend.

The younger boy carefully opened the blade and then turned the edge to catch the sunlight. The blade glistened and sparkled in the sun. "It's a beauty," said Lars.

"It's real sharp, too."

The two boys stood together admiring the pocketknife. James had just returned the knife to his pocket when Elizabeth and Inger strolled into view. The girls spotted them and sauntered over.

"Hello, James," said Inger softly. "How did you like the wedding?"

"It was fine. Kirstine looked real pretty."

"Didn't she? I thought it all was so lovely."

Elizabeth nodded in agreement. "And Peder looked as handsome as a prince."

James' eye strayed to the Johanssen girl. He noticed her large blue eyes, milky complexion, and flaxen hair. She smiled shyly at James, and he smiled back.

"Did you catch a glimpse of that new big boat steaming upriver the other day?" Lars asked, turning to James. "It was the largest steamboat I ever saw. It looked like a floating village, crowded with people and goods."

"No. I missed seeing it. There seem to be more steamers on the river every day," James replied. His eyes flicked to Inger as a slight breeze came up, stirring her long yellow braid. The sight made his heart beat a bit faster. He wanted to smile at her again, but she had looked away.

"I want to be a riverboat captain when I grow up," Lars went on, "and steam up all the big rivers. A steamboat captain can make a lot of money delivering goods to the riverside towns."

"He can also get himself killed," observed Elizabeth dryly. "You hear all too often about a steamboat exploding or hitting an obstacle in the river and sinking."

Lars ignored her negative comment. "Just think of the view you'd have from the river during the Fourth of July fireworks show."

"We were in Nauvoo on Independence Day," Inger said. "It's too bad we didn't get to see one another." Her gaze took in both Elizabeth and James.

James suddenly felt his face getting hot and red. He cast a furtive glance at Inger, and decided she was even prettier than Winnie Fife.

"We saw a group of Indians at the celebration," she added.

"You did? Was Yellow Feather with them?" Elizabeth asked with sudden interest.

"No. I didn't see Yellow Feather."

"Who's Yellow Feather?" James wanted to know.

"He's an Indian that Inger made friends with," Lars said.

"How did you get to be friends with an Indian?" James asked. His admiration for Inger increased tenfold with this disclosure.

Before Inger could reply, Elizabeth piped up. "Not only is she friends with him, James, but she and I sneaked down to his camp and spied on his people. We got caught, too, by an old Indian woman. But we escaped. If those Indians had captured us, they would have kept us captive and no one would have ever seen us again," Elizabeth concluded dramatically.

Lars started to chuckle.

"What's so funny?" Elizabeth demanded, her brows rushing together in a scowl.

"Peder says that the Sauk and Fox Indians are friendly with the whites. You were never in any danger."

"That's not true," Elizabeth said, straightening her back in indignation. "Haven't you heard all those stories about Indians abducting white woman and keeping them captive for years and years. Sometimes they even make them marry Indian braves from the tribe."

"Not the Sauk and Fox. They never captured any white women."

"You don't know that," Elizabeth retorted.

James wanted to defuse the argument. "Did you tell Ma about spying on the Indian camp?" he asked Elizabeth.

"No, and you'd better not tell her, either. She'd take a willow to me for doing something like that."

"It's over and done with now," Inger cut in, trying to restore peace. "Nothing happened to us. And it was my fault anyway because it was my idea to spy on the camp."

James glanced at the girl, thinking that it was a very brave and daring act, even though a foolhardy one.

Elizabeth stuck out her chin, as if she felt insulted to have it known that the spying wasn't her own idea.

They drifted into other topics of conversation, and it wasn't long before Christian came looking for James and Elizabeth to tell them it was time to leave for home. The friends exchanged farewells, then Elizabeth and James and the rest of their family walked down the dirt road toward the river where they'd board the ferry for Nauvoo.

"Did you know that Inger is sweet on you?" Elizabeth asked her brother as they trailed their parents to the ferry landing.

"What?"

"It's true. Didn't you notice how nervous and quiet she was around you? She likes you." Elizabeth poked her brother in the ribs.

"Cut it out," he said, pushing her hand away. He hoped she wouldn't notice the color rushing to his cheeks. His feelings about Inger were the last things he wanted to discuss with his sister.

Elizabeth dug her elbow into his ribs again and grinned.

CHAPTER FIFTEEN

Elizabeth sat on the grass in the West Grove near the temple site listening to William Law's sermon. Brother Law, a counselor in the First Presidency, was speaking about remaining firm in the gospel of Christ, despite persecution. "Let none suppose that God is angry with His Saints because He suffers the hand of persecution to come upon them. He chasteneth those whom He loveth, and trieth and proveth every son and daughter, that they may be as gold seven times purified. Be zealous in the cause of truth, in building up the kingdom of Christ upon the earth, in rearing up the Temple of God at Nauvoo, and in all works of righteousness," he was saying.

Zachary squirmed in her lap. She held him closer to quiet him. His soft brown hair brushed her cheek, and his clean-scrubbed little body smelled faintly of lye soap.

"Be virtuous, be just, be honorable, be full of faith, love and charity; pray much and be patient. . ." Brother Law continued.

"Keep still, Zachary," Elizabeth whispered in his ear. Lydia, who was sitting beside them, cast a quick glance at fourteen-month-old Zachary. Millicent and Roxana sat close by, along with James and Christian.

Elizabeth sighed. It was a splendid summer morning, this August of 1842, making it difficult for her to sit quietly listening to a sermon. Elizabeth gazed restlessly around her. To the east rose the temple, built now to the first floor, with sills set in some of the windows and stones laid up to a height of ten or twelve feet. Construction on the temple had slowed because of the difficulties arising from the apostasy of John C. Bennett, the shooting of former Governor Boggs, and the attempts to arrest the Prophet Joseph. Across from her on the grassy lot she caught a glimpse of Brother Bowers, her schoolmaster. She winced as she recalled the trouble she'd had with Brother Bowers during the school year. On more than one occasion, she'd been reprimanded for not paying attention in class. Consequently, she was relieved when school recessed for the summer. The leisurely days of summer had passed all too quickly, however, and Elizabeth was not eager to return to the monotony of schoolwork. She was weary of studying arithmetic, history, science, and religion. None of those subjects held much interest for her. Her father, though, was adamant about education. Not only did he want her to complete common school and then continue to take classes through the University of the

City of Nauvoo, but he also encouraged her to attend public lectures, debates, and literary club meetings.

Zachary began to fuss. As he twisted and turned restlessly in Elizabeth's lap, Lydia darted another look at the boy, then she held out her arms and Zachary crawled into them. Free of the weight of his little body in her lap, Elizabeth smoothed out her skirt; it was rumpled and damp from where Zachary had been sitting. She sighed once again. Brother Law's preaching seemed to be endless, but she tried to pay attention knowing her parents would conduct a discussion on points from the sermons they'd heard that Sunday morning.

Because of these family conversations reinforcing what she'd heard at meeting, Elizabeth was well versed in the principles of the gospel of Jesus Christ. She was acquainted with the numerous revelations Brother Joseph had received from the Lord and taught to the Saints. Many of the doctrines were new and novel ideas, contrary to established theology. Such tenets as the character of the Godhead, the eternal nature of man, and the doctrine of free agency were revolutionary. These teachings rejected the commonly held views of predestination and man's inherent evil.

Because the minds of the Saints had been opened to such teachings, it was all the more distressing now to be deprived of their leader and prophet. Brother Law and the other leaders of the Church were fine preachers, but everyone missed the Prophet Joseph, who was still in seclusion.

The August sun beat down on Elizabeth's back. She wiped away a trickle of perspiration from her forehead. She glanced at Zachary, sucking his thumb in his mother's lap while Lydia focused her attention on Brother Law. At length the speaker said, "Amen," and returned to his seat. Hyrum Smith, the Prophet's brother and Church Patriarch, then addressed the congregation. Hyrum spoke about the persecutions the Saints had suffered because of the treachery of John C. Bennett. Not only had Bennett been unfaithful to his covenants, but he'd played a role in urging ex-governor Boggs to file the complaint against Brother Joseph. He spoke vehemently about the nature of Bennett's character, his hypocrisy, his iniquity, and his apostasy. Elizabeth stole a glance at her brother as the Patriarch spoke of Bennett's indiscretions. James' head was bowed, but Elizabeth could see the tight white line of his mouth. She knew James had been deeply wounded by Bennett's deceptiveness.

She turned away, thinking about the many discourses she'd heard preached in the grove. She believed the gospel of Jesus Christ to be true, but it was hard to practice its precepts every day. How nice it would be, she mused, to do just as she pleased on a sunny Sunday morning rather than attend several hours of meeting. She let her imagination play and summoned up an image of a handsome dark-haired young man who came riding into the grove on a glistening black stallion. He spied her in the congregation, immediately fell in love with her, and swept her up into his saddle. Together they rode off while everyone sitting in meeting at the grove watched in astonishment. She smiled at the romantic flight of fancy she allowed herself. She continued to daydream until the conclusion of Brother Hyrum's remarks. Afterward, the congregation sang a hymn, and then a benediction was delivered by Brother Newel K. Whitney. Elizabeth and her family left the grove and leisurely walked down Durphey Street to their log home.

Later in the day Elizabeth sought out James in private. She'd noticed that he'd come away from the Sabbath meeting looking solemn and downcast, and he'd remained in his room for most of the evening. She found him there now, sitting at his desk with a book in his hands. "May I come in, James?" she asked, standing in the open doorway of his room.

"Of course," he answered, closing his book.

"What are you reading?" she asked conversationally. She sat down on the corner of his bed.

"*The Green Mountain Boys.* Pa had it on his bookshelf."

"Is it good?"

"Yeah, it is." He looked at her with one raised brow. "Did you come here to discuss books with me?"

She gave a short laugh. "No. I actually came to ask why you're so glum."

"I'm not glum," he shot back.

She crossed her feet at the ankles and stared at him without speaking. When he didn't say anything else, she cleared her throat. "I just thought you might want to talk.

But if you don't . . ." She left the sentence hanging, hoping he would pick up on it. When he remained silent, she started to get to her feet.

"Wait a minute, Elizabeth," he said finally.

She sat back down on the bed.

He ran his fingers over the cover of the book saying nothing for several seconds. Elizabeth knew he was having a difficult time putting into words whatever was on his mind. She decided to help him out.

"You're upset by the remarks made about Dr. Bennett today at meeting, aren't you?" she asked. She could see that her arrow had hit the mark. James' face lost some of its color.

"It's not just that," he said slowly. He stared down at his hands. "Ever since this whole sordid affair with Bennett has come to light, I've found myself struggling with doubts about the truthfulness of the gospel and Joseph Smith's role as a prophet." He swallowed hard, then looked up for her reaction.

His response wasn't at all what Elizabeth had expected to hear. "What do you mean?"

James raked a hand through his hair. "It's been bothering me how Bennett could dupe so many people and get away with it."

"He didn't get away with it. He was caught and punished for his lies."

"Yes, but look how much trouble he's caused and how many people he's hurt by betraying his trust. Why would

God let him get away with that?" A pained look flickered across James' face.

Elizabeth sat silently, not knowing what to say in reply.

James stared at her with a tortured look in his eye. "Do you know why?"

She slowly shook her head.

He dropped his gaze and Elizabeth could not read his expression.

Elizabeth wanted to help so she said the only thing she could think of. "Well, the whole thing's over now. Bennett's no longer in Nauvoo to trouble the Saints, and everyone knows his true character." She could see by the look on his face that her answer had not satisfied him, but she had done her best. She got up from the bed. "I'm sure you're just upset at the moment, and it will pass."

He didn't say anything else as his eyes followed her out of the room.

On Thursday afternoon, Elizabeth watched her younger sisters and brother while Lydia attended a meeting of the Female Relief Society. Since James was no longer at Dr. Bennett's office, he'd spent the summer working on a neighbor's farm outside the city. Each morning the neighbor stopped by in his hay wagon to collect James for a day of labor on the farm, and each evening the farmer brought him home again. But now that school was about to begin again for the fall term, James' work at the farm was drawing to a close.

As Elizabeth spoon fed Zachary a bowl of thin porridge, her thoughts lingered on James and the private conversation the two of them had the previous Sunday after the meeting at the Grove. She'd always thought of James as being steadfast, impregnable and unyielding as a rock on the ocean shoreline with the waves battering against it. The fact that he might waver in his testimony had never occurred to her. She assumed that James would sort it out in his mind and come to terms with his dilemma.

Zachary clamped his teeth over the spoon and wouldn't release it. Elizabeth tugged on the handle. "Let go, Zachary, and I'll give you some more cereal." Zachary slapped her hand away and grunted, his mouth still firmly clenched around the spoon.

Elizabeth sighed with exasperation as she watched Zachary take the spoon from his mouth and wave it in the air, flinging wet, sticky porridge onto the table and floor. "Stop it, Zachary. You're making a mess." She snatched the spoon out of his hand and Zachary began to wail in protest.

"What's wrong with the baby?" Roxana asked from across the room. Roxie was sitting cross-legged on the floor, carefully drawing a figure on a sheet of paper. She didn't look up from her page as she asked the question, but kept her attention centered on the paper. Her brow was wrinkled in concentration. Elizabeth noticed that it was the same look Christian wore when he was focused on a thought. She looked like Christian, too, with her dark hair and dark brows.

Millicent was astride the wooden rockinghorse, riding it at a gallop. She seemed unperturbed at Zachary's fussing. If Roxie looked like her father, Milly was growing into the picture of her mother; she had Lydia's same red hair, slender face, and deep blue eyes. Elizabeth glanced at the drawing of her mother framed and hanging on the wall of the back room of the cabin where her parents slept. Christian had drawn the likeness before he and Lydia were married, and while the two of them were living in Independence. Elizabeth knew that her mother cherished that drawing, not because it was a sketch of herself, but because it represented Christian's affection for her. As Elizabeth gazed at the drawing, she easily identified the features that Milly shared with her mother.

Elizabeth wiped off Zachary's hands and face and lifted him from the stool. When she set him on the ground, he tottered over to Milly and began to whine and hold out his arms. "Put him on the rockinghorse with you, Milly," Elizabeth instructed her younger sister.

Milly helped her little brother onto the horse and together they seesawed back and forth contentedly.

Elizabeth cleaned up the spilled cereal and rinsed out Zachary's bowl and spoon, then she wandered over to look at Roxie's drawing. Six straggly stick figures filled almost the whole page, and Roxie was patiently working on a seventh. "Who are those people?" Elizabeth asked her sister.

Roxie carefully set down her pencil. "That's Papa, Mama, you, James, Milly, and me," she said, pointing to each figure. "And now I'm drawing Zachary."

"What are you going to do with the drawing once you get it all done?" Elizabeth asked with little real interest.

"Take it to school with me so I won't be lonely without my family while I'm there," Roxie said, picking up her pencil again and bending over the paper.

Elizabeth placed a finger on the figure that represented Roxie. "What's that?" she asked of the scribbly mark in the center of the stick figure.

"That's Effie."

"You can't take Effie to school with you, you know."

Roxana looked up in alarm. "Why not?"

"Because the other students will think you're a baby if you bring your doll."

"But I can't leave Effie home. She goes with me everywhere."

"Not to school, she doesn't," Elizabeth said.

Big tears welled in Roxie's eyes. "But I have to take Effie with me. I need her."

"You don't need your doll. James and I will be there with you. You'll be fine, Roxie. You're going to like school."

The tears dribbled down Roxie's cheeks as she stared at the scribble cuddled in the stick figure's arms.

Elizabeth let out a sigh. Roxie was by nature timid and shy — Elizabeth wondered how well her little sister was going to cope with the new experience of going off to school.

The following week the fall term of school began. On the first morning of school, Roxie left the cabin with mixed feelings of anticipation and anxiety in the company of Elizabeth and James. She bravely set forth without Effie under her arm, but Elizabeth knew that she yearned for the security of her doll. As they trudged the short distance to the schoolhouse, Roxie clung to James' hand.

Elizabeth exchanged greetings with a couple of girls who were also on their way to school. She would have liked to fall in step with them, but she'd promised Roxie that she'd stay close. As the two girls walked up ahead, Elizabeth critically scrutinized their dresses and their hair styles. Both girls wore their hair in braids, but Elizabeth had pulled hers back at the sides and let it fall into a sunny cascade of ringlets down her back, held in place by a big yellow bow that matched the yellow in her dress.

Roxie balked when they reached the school yard and refused to enter the gate. James bent down to offer her encouragement. "Elizabeth and I are right here with you. We're not going to leave your side."

Roxie's eyes filled with tears. "I don't want to go to school," she whispered, her lip trembling.

"You have to go to school, Roxie," replied Elizabeth firmly. "Don't you want to learn to read and write like everyone else?"

"No," Roxie wailed. "I want to go home."

"Come with us to school just this one day," James bargained with her, "and then if you don't like it, we can tell Ma that you want to stay at home."

The logic seemed to make sense. Roxie grudgingly wiped away her tears.

"Are you ready to go inside now?" James asked her.

She nodded wordlessly, and sniffled.

James adjusted the strap of the knapsack Roxie carried on her back which held her slate and pencil. Lydia had sewn new knapsacks for all three of them to carry their books and school supplies in. "You're all set," he said to Roxie. He led her by the hand into the schoolhouse while Elizabeth lingered on the step to visit with her classmates.

When Elizabeth entered the classroom, she was disappointed to see Brother Bowers standing at the head of the room with his arms folded sternly across his chest and his face wearing a scowl. She'd been hoping for a new schoolmaster — preferably a young, handsome one — to enliven the school year. She gloomily slumped into her assigned seat. James sat at the desk next to hers, with Roxie seated between them. The schoolroom was outfitted in exactly the same way as in previous years, except Brother Bowers had tacked to one wall a new mathematics poster. The heading on the poster read, *The Mechanics of Arithmetic*; colorful illustrations of fruits and vegetables depicted the mechanics of addition, subtraction, multiplication, and division. A volume of *McGuffey's Eclectic Reader*, along with a ragged copy of a textbook on ancient history, sat neatly stacked in the center of Elizabeth's desk.

Elizabeth reached into her knapsack for her slate and her wooden box of slate pencils, and placed them on the desk beside the books. An inkwell and quill pen rested on every desk. Elizabeth's desk was scratched and scarred from years of repeated use, and a previous student had carved what were probably his initials into one corner of it.

She turned her attention to Roxie with the intent of helping her organize her school supplies onto the desk, but James had already seen to it. Roxie sat behind the desk looking small and scared, with a pile of books almost hiding her face. "Look at your new school books, Roxie," she said encouragingly. "Soon you'll be able to read them all on your own."

Roxie's eyes widened with worry.

Elizabeth picked up Roxie's primer and thumbed through it. On the first page was an illustration of a single red, shiny, apple with the caption below it reading: *A is for Apple.* She replaced the book and glanced again at her younger sister. Roxie was leaning against James' shoulder and clutching his arm. She leaned over and whispered in Roxie's ear, "Don't be nervous. Everything will be fine."

Roxie continued to hug James' arm without even a sideways glance at Elizabeth. The little girl sat with her shoulders hunched, and her eyes wide and unblinking, staring at the schoolmaster.

Brother Bowers rapped his hickory stick on the corner of his desk to gain the students' attention. It was time to begin lessons for the day. Elizabeth slouched even lower in her seat, reluctantly settling in for what she knew would be another long and tedious school year.

CHAPTER SIXTEEN

James leaned into his shovel, scooped out a full load of dirt, and then dumped it into the wheelbarrow at his side. He wiped his brow with the sleeve of his shirt and then bent to the work again. He wanted to fill the wheelbarrow several times over before Brother Pratt returned from his errands in town. The day was cool and overcast, with a mild breeze, but his exertions caused him to perspire nonetheless.

He'd been helping Brother Parley P. Pratt dig the foundation for his new house for the past few afternoons after school. It was the last part of May, 1843, and school would soon be in recess for the summer months. Brother Pratt had recently returned from a three-and-a-half year mission to England where he served as the editor and publisher of a monthly periodical for the British Saints called *The Latter-day Saints Millennial Star.* Upon his return to Nauvoo, he started construction on a red brick, two-story home and general store, and hired James to help him with the excavation. Pratt's lot was located on the corner of Wells and Young Streets, one block north of the temple, and several blocks up the road from the Kades' own new two-story brick house.

James' family had moved into their red brick home only the month before. Like many of the other new homes in Nauvoo, it was built in the Federalist style with lintels above the windows, and a chimney at either end. A capital letter "K," fashioned of iron, was nailed on the front of the house near the door. The inside consisted of three bedrooms upstairs, and a parlor and kitchen on the ground floor. James had helped his father erect the new house on Durphey Street, which sat just through the block from their old log home. Their place was situated on an acre of ground with a garden and an orchard of fruit trees behind it, and a barn and chicken coop.

Nauvoo had grown into one of the largest and most impressive cities in all of Illinois, boasting wide straight streets bordered by shade trees. Farming and manufacturing was thriving. James could count dozens of new private and public buildings under construction, including the Joseph Smith Mansion House, a two-story frame home and hotel with twenty-two rooms. The gray stone walls of the temple were rising majestically on a hill overlooking the city. Positioned on the highest point, the temple would be the crowning jewel of the City Beautiful.

James filled the wheelbarrow with dirt, then wheeled it up out of the hole and dumped it. As he picked up his shovel again, he caught sight of his father striding up the road toward him.

"Afternoon, son," Christian hailed him. He reached James' side and eyed the progress of the excavation. "How is the work coming along?"

"Good. We should have the cellar completely dug out within the next day or two."

"I know Brother Pratt appreciates the help you're giving him. He stopped by the printing office this morning and mentioned how hard you've been working."

James glowed at the compliment. He was glad Brother Pratt was pleased with his efforts. "Are you on your way back to the printing house?" he asked his father.

"Yes. I just finished a few hours' work at the temple site."

Christian had been helping with the temple construction whenever he could break away from his job at the newspaper office. The walls of the temple were steadily stretching heavenward, and stonemasons were capping the first-floor windows. A conference had been held in the partially built structure the month before, at which James had attended.

Christian stuffed his hands into his pockets. "Will you be taking some time off tomorrow to watch the Legion drill?"

"I'd like to."

"I'm sure the occasion will be grand enough to elicit comments from the anti-Mormon press," Christian said with a wry smile.

"I don't understand why non-Mormons are so jealous of the Legion." James leaned his chin on the handle of his shovel and frowned.

"I think some are critical of the Legion because it's a city militia commanded by the mayor, who has their allegiance, rather than a county militia who is directly responsible to the state. Some people see that as a threat. Then, too, there are those who complain about the so-called 'showy trappings' of the Legion, and its supposed intent to stockpile weapons."

James straightened his shoulders. "Why can't people see that the Nauvoo Legion is a symbol of our patriotism, instead of twisting the truth all out of shape."

"People's ideas are formed by what they hear and what they read. That's one reason why it's so important to conduct honest newspaper reporting," said Christian.

"Like that printed in the *Nauvoo Neighbor.*"

"Yes," Christian replied with a smile. "The *Nauvoo Neighbor* and the *Times and Seasons.*"

"I guess Brother Taylor feels that responsibility as editor of the paper," James said after a moment's thought.

"Yes, he does. He spoke with us this morning about some articles we're preparing for the *Nauvoo Neighbor.* Thomas Sharp has been renewing his vitriol, and Brother Taylor wants us to exercise temperance in dealing with it."

James shook his head. "I'm sorry Mr. Sharp is making so much trouble for the Saints."

"I understand he's still lobbying for repeal of the city's charter, even though that question was put to rest last December in the state assembly. That man doesn't give up," Christian sighed.

James knew the history behind his father's comments. Thomas C. Sharp was the editor and publisher of a newspaper in the neighboring town of Warsaw called the *Warsaw Signal*. For months now, he'd been printing abusive articles about the Saints and their religious doctrines. The Prophet's brother, Apostle William Smith, had founded the *Wasp* in part to refute Sharp's vicious attacks. The *Wasp* had grown increasingly acerbic as the newspaper traded personal and political barbs with the *Signal*. Bad feelings between Smith and Thomas Sharp intensified when William Smith ran for election in 1842 against Sharp for a seat in the state House of Representatives. The Apostle won the seat, which further aggravated Sharp's hostility. Brother Joseph became uncomfortable with his brother's zealous rebuttals in the pages of the *Wasp* and persuaded William to resign as editor. That had taken place just the month before, in April. John Taylor succeeded Brother Smith as editor and renamed the newspaper the *Nauvoo Neighbor.* The very name of the paper was designed to reflect a more conciliatory attitude. Christian, who had been with the paper from its inception, was pleased with the changes. The newspaper now took a gentler approach and supported a nonpartisan political and editorial stance.

"Do you think the Whigs and the Democrats will ever come into agreement, Pa?" asked James.

"I doubt it, son. Politics has always been a volatile business. Most people in the state believe Mormons vote as a block, and so they view us as a political asset or a political liability, depending on their point of view and their party affiliations." Christian rubbed his chin thoughtfully. "I wish we had a political candidate who was not identified with either party."

"Why don't you run for office, Pa?" James asked. "You could create your own new political party."

Christian chuckled. "No, not me. There's trouble enough. But I'd like to see one of the brethren campaign for high political office. This country needs moral, honest men in government. Someone who will protect the rights of all citizens — political as well as religious rights."

"Maybe one of the Twelve Apostles should campaign for President of the United States in the next election," James suggested.

"Yes, or perhaps even the Prophet himself." Christian rumpled James' hair. "Here I am discussing politics with you when you're supposed to be working."

James grasped his shovel. "I'm glad you came by, Pa."

"So am I. I'll see you at home for supper." He smiled, then started down the broad, dusty road.

James returned to his work. He shoveled another heap of dirt and threw it into the wheelbarrow. While his body toiled, his mind dwelled on the conversation he'd had with his father. He would miss their discussions together.

Christian had received a call to preach the gospel in the eastern states and would be leaving for his mission in a few months. He was happy about this call to serve the Lord, extended to him by the Prophet Joseph Smith. James thought about the Prophet. Brother Joseph had spent nearly five months in seclusion, coming out only occasionally to address the Saints. At the beginning of the new year he returned home, at last acquitted of the charge of complicity in the shooting of ex-Governor Boggs, and with the threat of arrest and extradition to Missouri behind him. But it was rumored that John C. Bennett was trying to obtain a new indictment against the Prophet on numerous charges.

James' feelings were still raw concerning Dr. Bennett. Because of Bennett, James' testimony of the gospel had been shaken and he was still struggling to regain his faith. He knew of some members who had abandoned their beliefs and left the Church because of Bennett's duplicity; others had become disaffected because they believed Bennett's charges against the Prophet. Even now, a year later, the whole episode was like a sore that wouldn't heal.

His thoughts were interrupted by the arrival of Brother Parley P. Pratt. Pratt removed his topcoat, rolled up his shirtsleeves, and grasped a second shovel. "You've been here all afternoon," said Pratt. "I don't want you neglecting your schooling, James. Your studies come first."

"Yes, sir. I'm keeping up on my schoolwork and should be able to help you nearly every day after school."

"I appreciate that," Pratt said, surveying the elongated hole the two of them had been digging out. Pratt had contracted the work for laying the foundation of the house, as well as the framing and brickwork, but he and James were doing the backbreaking job of digging the basement. Pratt scooped out a heaping mound of dirt and deposited it in the wheelbarrow.

James set to his task again, keeping pace with the older man. There was little talk between them as they both strained and sweated over their shovels.

"You work as hard as any man I've seen," Pratt said, hauling away another load of dirt. "How old are you now, James?"

"I'll be fourteen in a few months, sir," James replied without breaking stride in his work.

"Fourteen," Pratt mused. "When I was just past fourteen I left my father's household to labor on a gentleman's farm some distance away. I was with the man and his family for eight months. During the following winter, I boarded with my father's sister. I spent the winter attending common school, and it was the last opportunity I had of improving my education in a formal setting. When spring returned, I commenced again in agricultural pursuits."

Pratt paused to wipe his brow with his handkerchief. "Have you given any consideration to a vocation, decided on a profession or a trade? Perhaps farming?"

"I don't think I'd make a very good farmer," James replied, smiling. He thought about the time he'd spent the previous summer helping a neighboring farmer harvest his crops. He hadn't particularly enjoyed the work.

"If you put your mind to the task, you'd be successful," Pratt advised.

"Yes, sir."

They labored side by side in silence for another few minutes, then Pratt continued. "If you're not attracted to farming, then what trade have you contemplated?"

James' mind toyed with the old idea of doctoring. Even though he knew Dr. Bennett's duplicity had nothing to do with practicing medicine, still it had spoiled the dream for James. "I have a friend whose father is a cobbler. Maybe I'll take up shoemaking. Or perhaps become a newspaper man like my father."

"Both admirable professions," Pratt responded.

"Yes, sir."

Pratt didn't say anything more for a moment and James thought his answer had satisfied the man. James dug deeply into the soil with his shovel and tossed the dirt into the wheelbarrow.

"However, you need not follow the course taken by your companion's father, or your own," Pratt went on. "Perhaps you should take into account the talents and abilities God has given to you."

James was startled by Elder Pratt's comment. "There is something I once thought about pursuing," he admitted hesitantly.

Pratt leaned on his shovel and looked James directly in the eye. "What would that be?"

"Medicine," James said, feeling almost sheepish about his answer. "I wanted to become a physician."

"I suspected you had aspirations of your own."

"Yes, sir. I guess so."

"And you've changed your mind about doctoring?" Pratt asked, still gazing intently at him.

James rubbed his thumb over the handle of the shovel. He knew what Pratt's next question would be. He nodded his head.

"What made you change your plans?"

James drew a deep breath. "It was because of Dr. Bennett. I don't want to be anything like him."

"I see." Brother Pratt stroked his chin as he considered James' answer. "And you think that becoming a doctor somehow puts you in the same category as Bennett, is that right?"

James slowly nodded again.

"Let me tell you of a particular experience I had," Pratt began, putting aside his shovel. "I visited your home one wintry afternoon when your family lived in Green County. Your father was away, and your mother was alone caring for you and your sister. You were a young child and desperately ill. I remember the great faith your mother exhibited on that occasion and her belief in the healing power of the priesthood of God, even though she was not fully acquainted with the gospel. She allowed me to give you a priesthood blessing, and the Lord answered her pleas for your recovery because of her trust in Him."

James felt a warmth begin to build in his chest as he listened to the Apostle's narrative. He knew this story well for his mother had repeated it to him many times, but hearing Brother Pratt's account of it stirred his emotions.

"I believe the Lord spared your life because of your mother's prayers, but also because He had a path marked out for you. Find that path, James, and follow it. Your heart and mind, enlightened by the Holy Spirit, will lead you to it. Listen to the Spirit and do the work God has marked out for you."

James' heart felt on fire. He listened, spellbound, to the Apostle's words.

"God has blessed you with the talents and abilities necessary to carry out your tasks in mortality. Don't be afraid of what men may say or do, but lean on the Lord and on your own good judgment." Pratt gazed at him a moment longer, then he reached for his shovel.

James stood motionless, digesting Pratt's counsel. He decided that he would pray about the subject and ask for Heavenly Father's guidance in choosing the course he should take in life. He glanced at Brother Pratt. The man's dark, penetrating eyes were bridged by thick brows, and his expression was firm in purpose. He was in his mid-thirties, strong-bodied, articulate, and intelligent. James knew he was a righteous man, called to the Apostleship by God.

James took hold of his shovel and began to dig. The two worked together throughout the remainder of the afternoon, and the task seemed lighter and easier to do with Brother Pratt alongside him.

James continued at his labors until suppertime. He was satisfied with the amount of work he'd accomplished that afternoon. He put his hands in his pockets as he walked along the dirt road toward home. The rough lining of the pockets irritated the blisters on his hands earned from his day's work of digging out the cellar, but he ignored the pain. When he reached the door of his family's brick home, he set down his shovel, dusted the dirt off himself, and went inside. The hearty smell of bubbling stew permeated the house. It made him acutely aware of the rumblings in his stomach. He took his seat at the maplewood plank table, made white with repeated scrubbings, just as his mother called the family to supper.

The next day at school James was glad to see Hayden Cox in his seat. Hayden's attendance had been spotty during the year because his father needed his help in the shoemaking shop. But today Hayden was enthusiastic about being in the classroom, and during the noon recess he organized a game of rounders for the boys to play.

Rounders was a popular British game, played with a wooden paddle or bat, and a ball; the new American game of baseball was loosely patterned after its British counterpart. Baseball had been introduced to the country only a few years before and become a popular sport among school-age boys, especially after a young man named Abner Doubleday established rules for the game. Doubleday had incorporated a playing field with eleven players in set positions, and fixed the rules of play. But this afternoon the boys were playing a good old-fashioned game of rounders, and Hayden was the best hitter. When his turn came to bat, Hayden smacked the ball clear out of the school grounds. One of the younger boys set off in pursuit of it while Hayden trotted effortlessly around the circular track and started back to home place.

While James was waiting for the ball to be put back into play, he noticed Winnie Fife and a group of her friends watching the boys play ball. Winnie's eyes were fixed on Hayden and a smile danced on her face. The girls with Winnie pointed and squealed as Hayden arrived back at the point where he'd started and then pranced around the spot with his arms raised in triumph. When he spotted the girls standing nearby he swooshed off his cap and swept it across his chest, and offered them a gallant bow. James watched Winnie's smile grow as bright as a rainbow.

The exchange between Hayden and Winnie sent a swift stab of jealousy to his heart. During the school year Winnie had mysteriously blossomed into a slender-waisted, rosy-cheeked young woman. She even wore her hair differently than the year before when James had first taken notice of her. Instead of pulling it back into two tight braids, she wore it loose and falling down her shoulders. James had taken a liking to her the previous year, and his feelings for her during this school year were the same as last. He suspected that Hayden knew of his sentiments, and to see his best friend deliberately flirting with her raised James' hackles.

When Brother Bowers rang the school bell to signal the end of recess, James left the playing field without waiting for Hayden. He stomped inside the schoolhouse and thumped down into his seat. He couldn't even manage a smile when his younger sister, Roxie, slid onto the bench beside him and affectionately rested her head on his shoulder. He averted his gaze when Hayden plopped down onto his seat. From the corner of his eye he could see Hayden impatiently drum his fingers on his desk.

Hayden wasn't any more of a scholar this year than he was last. Brother Bowers' lessons bored him and he seldom completed his home assignments. Because of his many absences, he'd fallen behind in his studies. Playing ball with the boys at recess, grouping his collection of toy soldiers into a mock battle, and shooting a game of marbles occupied his attention at school. James heard him rustling at his desk, fussing with his papers and books.

"What a game, 'ey, James?" whispered Hayden, leaning across the narrow aisle that separated them.

Brother Bowers was giving an assignment, and James was listening to his instructions. "Yeah," he answered without glancing at his friend. Giving his attention to the schoolmaster let him off the hook from having to engage in conversation with Hayden, at least until his ruffled feelings had soothed.

Hayden tapped James' shoulder and leaned closer. "Did you see 'ow far I whacked that old ball?" he whispered.

James nodded.

"That was some game, wasn't it, mate?" Hayden said, bobbing his head in satisfaction.

James didn't answer. Instead he pretended to be busy writing down the assignment Brother Bowers was giving the class. He could hear Hayden start thrumming his fingers on the desk again, and knew his friend's mind was still on the ball game.

Brother Bowers instructed the class to open their readers and begin studying. James turned to the assigned page and started to scan the lines. He willed his mind to focus on the page, instead of the hurt he was harboring over Hayden's disloyalty. After he'd forced himself to read a paragraph or two, he became interested in the passage. He hadn't been reading long, however, when he felt a nudge on the back of his shoulder. He glanced at the student seated behind him and was surprised to see the boy stealthily hand him a folded slip of paper. On the front of the note was the single word, "Hayden."

His eyes swept the room as he tried to determine who had authored the note to Hayden, but nearly every student's head was buried in his textbook; except for Hayden who was gazing out the window, his book lying untouched on his desk. James tapped Hayden's arm and passed him the note. Hayden looked surprised to receive it. His eyebrows shot up in silent question as to who had written the note. James shrugged his shoulders.

As Hayden unfolded the small piece of paper, James kept his eyes on his schoolbook. He allowed himself a brief glance, however; enough to determine that the delicately drawn letters were printed in a feminine hand.

Hayden quickly read the note, and then grinning, passed it to James.

James glanced up at Brother Bowers first to make sure the schoolmaster wasn't looking in his direction, then his eyes hurriedly traveled over the words handwritten on the page: *HAYDEN, I THINK YOU'RE THE BEST BALL PLAYER OF ANY OF THE BOYS. WINNIE.*

The paper suddenly seemed to scorch James' fingers. He hastily returned it to Hayden, mumbling some remark. Hayden's whole face was set in a grin. His brown freckles stood out starkly against his pasty skin, making his smile seem all the more obnoxious. He folded his arms against his chest and leaned back on the bench, the smile clinging to his face.

James returned to his text, but the words swam in front of his eyes like fish in a pond. He tried to figure out exactly when Winnie Fife had transferred her affections from him to Hayden. Maybe she'd never had feelings for him at all. Maybe he'd only imagined that she did because he was attracted to her, and wanted to believe that she returned his affections. Even though he wanted to, he couldn't be angry with Winnie; she was one of the nicest girls he'd ever known, friendly and kind to everyone. She'd been the first to approach him after the disastrous outcome with the spelling bee. Perhaps he'd misinterpreted her kindness for affection. Even so, the realization that she was attracted to Hayden stung him.

He had a difficult time keeping his mind on his studies throughout the remainder of the school day. When Brother Bowers finally dismissed the class he made a beeline for the door, keeping his eyes to the ground so he wouldn't encounter Winnie and be cornered into having a conversation with her.

He was taking long, quick strides when he heard Hayden calling his name. "'ey, James, 'old up."

James' heart sank. He had wanted to avoid Hayden until his feelings leveled, but he had no choice now except to wait for Hayden to catch up with him.

"I 'ave a terrific idea," Hayden said, loping to his side. He didn't pause for James to respond. "Let's organize two teams among the lads at school, and start a rounders tournament. You and I can be the captains of one team, and we'll choose a couple of the boys to be the captains of the other. I figure we can call our team the Pathfinders. What do you think?"

"Sure. It sounds great," James said, starting off again at a quick stride.

"I thought so, too. I've been thinkin' about it all afternoon. We can 'ave a regular competition between the two teams, and the losers 'ave to treat the winners to a sack full of licorice from the mercantile."

James genuinely liked the idea and was fast abandoning his animosity toward Hayden as he got caught up in the plans. "I think we should choose Zeb Tanner for our team. He can run faster than just about anybody."

"Right-o. And Nathaniel Brown is a strong batter."

"We can play every day during noon recess."

"Yeh, and after school too," Hayden said eagerly.

"Right," James said, forgetting all about his earlier wounded feelings.

"And the girls can watch us play if they want to." Hayden was bouncing on his feet with excitement.

"Uh huh."

"Say, mate, what do you think of Winnie Fife?" Hayden asked after a pause.

James slowed his stride. "What do you mean?"

"Do you think she's nice? For a girl, I mean."

"Yeah. Why?" he asked suspiciously.

"If I tell you a secret, will you keep it to yourself?"

"Sure."

"You promise?"

James crossed his heart.

"I kissed Winnie under the big old 'ickory tree in the school yard."

"You did?" James gasped.

Hayden nodded. "Day before yesterday."

James was so astonished by this news that he didn't even mind the fact that the girl being kissed was Winnie Fife. He'd personally never kissed a girl before, other than a peck on his sisters' cheeks, which didn't count when it came to kissing. James was impressed by his friend's bold act.

"Remember, you swore you wouldn't tell," Hayden said, frowning. "The other lads would make terrible fun of me if they knew I'd kissed a girl."

"No, I won't say anything," James promised. He wanted to ask Hayden how it felt to kiss Winnie, but he didn't dare. Hayden might suspect that he was interested in Winnie, and that could lead to all kinds of problems. Just knowing that Hayden was sweet on her changed the way he felt about Winnie. And that left him feeling a little sad.

The next day at school Hayden organized two teams of boys for the first competition game of rounders. Hayden was the captain of his team and James served as assistant captain. Hayden knew which boys would be the most valuable players, and when the choosing of team members was completed, the Pathfinders had a definite edge over the opposing team.

The boys gobbled their lunches and started a game at the noon recess. It was James' turn to bat just as Brother Bowers rang the school bell to return to class. James had to wait until the following day to take up his position with the bat, and the wait seemed impossible to bear.

The boys played a game of rounders every day in the school yard for the rest of the week. The competition between the two teams grew intense. On Friday, the score was tied. Every member of the Pathfinders was on edge; their team had won the last three games and they didn't want to lose to the Deerslayers and ruin their winning streak. The boys on James' team breathed a little easier when it was Hayden's turn to bat. He was easily the best batter on the team and a fast runner.

"Come on, Hayden!" yelled James from his position at the edge of the school yard.

Hayden heaved the bat in a practice swing. He dug in his heels and squinted at the pitcher. Everyone on both teams knew that Hayden would likely score a point with his strong hitting. Hayden brushed the hair out of his eyes and hunched into position. The pitcher threw the ball. It came sailing toward Hayden, straight and sure. Hayden walloped it with a terrific blow. James let out a whoop as Hayden threw down the bat and started racing along the first leg of the circle; but then James' eyes were drawn to the ball which was flying high in the air. The hard whack the ball had sustained had sent it spinning out of control. James watched it arch sideways across the school yard, and then to his horror, he saw the ball smash right through the glass windowpane of the schoolhouse.

In an instant, the boys' joyous shouts turned to horrified silence as all eyes focused on the shattered pane. James was so stunned by what had happened that he couldn't move from his spot. An instant later Brother Bowers came charging out of the schoolhouse, his face as red and hard as an apple. The boys on both teams hung their heads as the schoolmaster berated them for their carelessness and their stupidity.

That was the last game of rounders the boys would play for the rest of the school year. Brother Bowers forbid them from playing rounders ever again in the school yard.

After school recessed for the summer months, James didn't have the opportunity to spend as much time as usual with Hayden. The British boy was busy working in his father's shoemaking shop, and James was occupied with helping Brother Pratt erect his brick house and store. Brother Pratt had allowed him to assist the carpenters with the finish work, a trade that James enjoyed learning. By the end of the summer, Pratt's handsome, two-story house was complete and he was tending the counter in his store. James had given a lot of thought to his conversation with Brother Pratt concerning a future occupation, and he'd spent some time on his knees praying about it. But he hadn't received an answer — at least not one he could recognize.

The summer wore on without anything out of the ordinary to mark its passing, and soon James was preparing for another school year. He was looking forward to renewing his friendship with the other boys, and hoping that Brother Bowers had forgotten about his ban on the game of rounders. Some of the neighboring boys had gotten together a few times over the summer to practice their skills with the ball and the bat, but the former rivalry between the two teams had waned. As James walked to school on the first day of the fall term there was a chill in the air, which seemed to be a portent of the cold days ahead.

CHAPTER SEVENTEEN

A lively tune played by Captain Pitt's Quadrille Band set Elizabeth's toe tapping. The voice of trumpets, cornets, piccolos, and a throbbing bass drum resounded throughout the social hall where scores of young people were gathered. The Harvest Social of 1843 was the biggest event of the year. Young men and women from all ten of the wards in Nauvoo were invited, and for weeks Elizabeth had been giddy with excitement.

Elizabeth stood at one end of the large room above Joseph Smith's general store to catch her breath and talk for a moment with her friend, Sarah Rogers. Sarah's cheeks were flushed from dancing, and her brown eyes glistened like two polished chestnuts. As they chatted together Elizabeth noted the cut and style of the pale blue muslin Sarah wore. The dress had lace cuffs and was embellished with a square lace collar, at the base of which Sarah had pinned a beautiful blue cameo brooch.

Elizabeth's own dress of striped navy and powder blue gingham was fitted with straight sleeves and a frilled collar. Elizabeth had made it herself, staying after hours at the tailoring shop where she worked three afternoons a week. She had a quick hand with the needle and enjoyed sewing for herself and others.

A crash of cymbals from the band brought Elizabeth's attention back to the music and the dancing. She smiled at Willy Saunders, who was slouched against the wall a few feet away from her. He grinned in return, then poked an elbow into the ribs of a young man standing next to him. Elizabeth had been eyeing the comely young man ever since he walked into the room with Willy. Willy wasn't much to look at. He'd grown thin and lanky, and his mouse-colored hair spilled over his forehead into his eyes. But this man standing next to Willy she'd never seen before, and she'd been intrigued by him the moment she spied him.

She smiled again at Willy. Why didn't he come over to speak with her and bring his friend along? She'd been surrounded by young men all evening, but Willy and his companion had kept their distance. Almost before she'd completed the thought, Willy began sauntering toward her, with his companion a few steps behind. Elizabeth ran a hand over her yellow curls to smooth them into place, then turned her face and assumed a nonchalant pose.

"Hello, Elizabeth," Willy Saunders said, idling up to her side.

"Oh. Hello, Willy."

"Having a good time?"

"Yes. Are you?" Her eyes drifted to the conspicuous scar on his chin.

Willy nodded in answer to her question and then said, "I don't think you've met my cousin, Alexander Scott. He's visiting with us for a few weeks."

Elizabeth turned her full attention on Willy's cousin. He was much more handsome at close range. His hair was dark and curly, brushed stylishly forward in front of the ears, and his eyes were the color of slate. He had a strong square jaw and full mouth. He gave her a lazy smile.

"How do you do, Brother Scott," Elizabeth said in an even voice.

"Please," Scott replied, holding up his hands in mock horror. "This habit you people have of referring to one another is a bit unnerving."

"Alexander isn't a member of the Church," Willy explained with a smirk. "He's still getting used to our ways."

"Oh. How do you like Nauvoo, Mr. Scott?"

"Alexander, please. Curious. I find Nauvoo quite curious. What did you say your name was?"

"I didn't. But if you wish to know, it's Elizabeth Kade," she replied.

"Well, Elizabeth Kade, I'm very pleased to make your acquaintance. Have you lived in Nauvoo long?"

"A little over three years now. We're originally from Green County. What about you?"

"Wisconsin. There aren't many Mormons in Wisconsin Territory," Alexander remarked, the corners of his mouth curling up.

"I don't imagine there are," answered Elizabeth. She felt her cheeks growing pink. Alexander was boldly staring at her, and not with the usual decorum accorded ladies by most Mormon boys.

Willy was talking to Sarah Rogers, and began introducing Alexander to her. Alexander's blue-gray eyes kept flicking back to Elizabeth's face, and with every glance Elizabeth felt more attracted to him.

Willy asked Sarah to dance. She nodded and they joined the dancers gathering for the next quadrille. Alexander watched them go, then turned his gaze on Elizabeth.

"So, tell me what a pretty girl like you does in Nauvoo?" he asked. His tone was a peculiar mixture of curiosity and sarcasm.

"The same as most sixteen-year-old girls. I go to school, and in the afternoons I work at one of the dress shops in town."

"Did you make that pretty gown you're wearing?" His eyes roved over the ankle-length gingham, but Elizabeth was sure he was not looking at the dress.

She blushed deeply in spite of her best efforts not to. "Yes, I made it. Do you like it?" she added with a toss of her honey curls.

A slow smile spread across his ample mouth. "Very much. Very much, indeed. Would you care to dance, Elizabeth?"

She walked with him to the center of the dance floor where couples were in position to dance an English reel. It took only a few seconds for her movements to match his in perfect synchronization. Alexander led her through the steps confidently as they moved with the music. Though he couldn't have been more than three or four years older than she, he was far more mature and self-assured than any of the boys with whom she was used to associating. He looked princely in his white shirt, silk floral waistcoat, black coat, and trousers. His cravat was elaborately knotted at his neck and pinned with a slender gold stickpin. His attire epitomized the peak of fashion, right down to his square-toed boots which were spotlessly polished.

When the reel ended, Alexander steered her to a deserted spot near the wall. "Do you live here in town with your family?" he asked casually.

"Yes, with my mother, my mother's husband, two younger brothers, and two sisters. What about yourself? What does a fellow like you do in Wisconsin?" she returned, giving him a saucy smile.

"I work at a lumber mill owned by my father. It's fairly interesting and pays well. Why do you refer to your father as your mother's husband?" he asked with the same lazy smile she was beginning to find quite irresistible.

"Because he's not my father. My real father died when I was just a child."

"Do you remember him?"

"Of course. I'll never forget Papa. I loved him so."

"But you don't particularly care for your mother's husband," Alexander finished for her.

"We don't get on well together. He's too opinionated to suit me."

"To suit you?" Alexander laughed. The sound of it was not very pleasant. It made Elizabeth feel as if he were sneering at her.

"I think we've talked enough about me," she said stiffly. "What about your family? Do you have brothers and sisters back in Wisconsin?"

Alexander leaned against the wall and folded his arms across his chest. "Two sisters, no brothers. My sisters are sweet but incredibly dull. They don't resemble you in the least, Miss Kade." He smiled down at her and Elizabeth's breathing quickened.

"The bishop is watching us and scowling something fierce," Elizabeth informed him with a nervous giggle.

"What?"

"Over there. That man with the side whiskers is our bishop. He watches over our temporal welfare."

Alexander looked in the direction Elizabeth pointed, grinned, and smugly waved a hand at the bishop.

"Oh, that will infuriate him," Elizabeth whispered.

"Does everyone do just as the bishop says?"

"Almost everyone."

"I know for a fact my cousin, Willy, doesn't. I've seen him take a snort from the cider barrel a time or two," Alexander grinned.

Elizabeth tried to cover her surprise at this by deliberately taking a confident tone. "You can bet he won't try that tonight. The brethren aren't taking their eyes off us."

"That one over there looks like the Grim Reaper waiting impatiently for his harvest," Alexander said, indicating one of the brethren chaperoning the young people's dance.

Elizabeth giggled uneasily. Alexander Scott was unlike anyone she had ever met. He was outspoken and shockingly irreverent.

Alexander bent his head closer to hers. She smiled up at him. "You know," he said, "I think I'm going to like Nauvoo."

"Elizabeth, would you please come here and get Zachary? I'm in the middle of pinning up the hem on this dress for your sister," Lydia called in a harried tone.

Elizabeth trotted down the stairs from her room to find her two-year-old brother happily dumping out the contents of Lydia's sewing box.

"Hold still, Milly. I'll never get this hem right if you keep wiggling," Lydia said. Milly stood on a chair while her mother worked at shortening the dress Roxana had outgrown so it would fit her younger sister.

Elizabeth gathered up the scattered thimbles and thread and put them back into the sewing box, then she scooped Zachary off the floor. He protested by kicking his legs and squirming to get free of her arms. "Nooo, Elsbuff," he whined.

"Turn around now and let me get the back," Lydia directed. When Milly had made a half turn, Lydia took a pin from several she held between her lips and thrust it through the hem. Then she stood back to eye her handiwork.

"Ooh, I like this dress," five-year-old Milly said, dancing on her toes.

Lydia rearranged a couple of the pins rimming the bottom of the skirt. "I'm just about finished with it. Stand still now, Milly."

That was asking the impossible, Elizabeth thought. Milly couldn't stand still for more than a minute. She was always in motion and chattering like a squirrel. Her braided red hair swished in the air as she twisted and turned, trying to gauge the progress her mother was making on the dress.

"I hope you can finish it, Mama. I told Becky I was going to wear a new dress this Sunday to meeting and she said that she bet I wouldn't."

Lydia eyed the hem of the dress critically. "All right, I'm through. Elizabeth, please help your sister change clothes and then tell Roxie to come help me with supper." She took Zachary from Elizabeth's arms. He put his thumb in his mouth and laid his head on Lydia's shoulder.

"Mama, you haven't forgotten that Alexander is coming for supper tonight? I told him to be here at five o'clock," Elizabeth said.

A frown creased Lydia's brow. "I think you're seeing entirely too much of that young man, Elizabeth."

"I'm not. Really I'm not. Only one evening a week."

Elizabeth intentionally concealed from her mother the numerous afternoons she'd spent with Alexander over the past few weeks. If her mother found out just how often she enjoyed Alexander's company, she would have forbidden Elizabeth from seeing him again. She felt an uncomfortable stab of conscience thinking about the deceit she was perpetuating, but she wanted to be with Alexander more than anything else in the world. Her mother probably wouldn't understand that, so it was better if she didn't know, Elizabeth had rationalized. Alexander wanted to be with her, too. He had already twice put off his return to Wisconsin. Eventually he would have to leave Nauvoo, but she didn't permit herself to think about that.

"No later than eight-thirty tonight, Elizabeth. Is that agreed without argument?" Lydia asked, still frowning.

"Yes, Mama. I promise."

"All right. Don't forget to tell Roxana to come downstairs."

Elizabeth helped her younger sister slip off the frock and replace it with the day dress she'd been wearing earlier. Then she trudged up the staircase to get Roxana.

Roxie was in the cozy room she shared with her sisters. The room still smelled of new lumber and fresh paint. Elizabeth had chosen the sunny yellow color for the walls, and the braided rag rug covering the wooden floor. On one wall hung a painting of a young girl in a billowing sky blue dress walking through a meadow of flowers. Roxie was across the room, standing before a rippling old mirror fastened to the girls' dresser drawers. She jerked when she saw Elizabeth's sudden reflection in the glass.

"You scared me. I thought it was Ma."

"You should be scared," Elizabeth answered. "She'd take a willow to you if she saw you like that."

Roxie looked sheepishly at her reflection. Her cheeks were rouged ruby red and her lips were the same vivid color. She quickly scrubbed off the rouge with her hand.

"Now look at your hands," Elizabeth directed. They were streaked with red. "You better get that off fast. Mama wants you downstairs to help with supper."

"You won't tell her I've been in her rouge box, will you? I can't wait until I'm old enough to wear it. I bet you'll get to wear color on your cheeks when you get a little older."

"No, I won't and neither will you. Here, use this to wipe your hands." Elizabeth dampened a cloth with water from the pitcher sitting in a basin on a table beside the bed.

Roxie scoured her hands with the cloth. Elizabeth smiled to herself as she watched her. Roxie was in such a hurry to grow up; when she matured, she was going to be a beauty. Elizabeth admired her sister's thick dark hair, blue eyes, and long curling lashes. She reminded Elizabeth of a beautiful princess she had once seen pictured in a storybook.

Elizabeth glanced at her own face in the mirror. Her complexion was ruddy and her nose a bit too sharp. She would have liked larger, wider eyes. Elizabeth's most attractive feature was her hair, which was a rich shade of yellow and curled gently down her shoulders. Alexander said it was the prettiest hair he'd ever seen. She didn't quite believe him, but she relished the compliment anyway.

When five o'clock arrived, Elizabeth answered Alexander Scott's knock at the door. He pulled her into the shadows of the porch and gave her a quick kiss, then followed her to the supper table where the family had assembled to eat. James sat across from Alexander and the two of them spoke politely, but their conversation was strained. James had privately told Elizabeth that he did not think much of her choice in companions.

Millicent was her usual boisterous self. She asked Alexander a dozen questions and would have chatted on if Elizabeth hadn't sent her a sharp look. Alexander rather liked Milly and called her "Miss Piebald" because of her red hair and generous supply of freckles. Milly didn't seem to mind the unflattering term.

Roxana was less vocal. She said very little to Alexander, but she watched him intently, enthralled with his every move. When he smiled at her, or made a teasing remark at her expense, she blushed from the roots of her dark hair down to her toes.

After supper Elizabeth and Alexander sat in the parlor. Milly peeked at them from behind the parlor door until Elizabeth lost patience and spoke rudely to her.

"Why don't we go for a buggy ride?" Alexander suggested with a grin.

"I'd love to, but Mama won't allow it. She doesn't believe young people should be left unescorted for a minute."

"We could tuck Milly in the seat between us."

"Very funny," Elizabeth said, making a wry face.

"How else am I going to get you alone, Elizabeth Kade?" Alexander put his arm around Elizabeth, drew her close, and kissed her.

Elizabeth's heart pumped wildly. When Alexander released her, she glanced toward the door half afraid of finding Milly there stealing a peek at them. She let out a sigh of relief to see the doorway unoccupied.

"Willy says I should stay here in Nauvoo," Alexander remarked, settling back into the couch and folding his arms across his chest.

"Does he?" Elizabeth answered coyly. "What else does Willy say?"

Alexander favored her with a lazy grin. "He says I should stay in Nauvoo and go into business with him."

"Business? Since when did Willy go into 'business'?" she asked with a snide edge to her voice.

"He works down at the docks."

"I know that. He told me that he loads firewood onto the steamers."

A sarcastic smile started across Alexander's face. "He did, did he?"

Elizabeth nodded. "In fact, I saw him once down at the pier at the end of Main Street. He was boarding the *Mississippi Maiden.*

The unpleasant grin stayed on Alexander's face. "To load firewood?"

"I assume so." Elizabeth twisted in her seat to look at him. "What are you smirking about?"

"Your naiveté. It's pleasantly refreshing."

"What am I so naïve about?" Elizabeth asked, stiffening. She hated it when Alexander made sport of her.

"If I promise to tell you, will you meet me for a midnight tryst?" Alexander's mocking eyes nettled Elizabeth.

"Then don't tell me. I'm sure I don't care what your cousin does."

Alexander laughed. The sound of it was harsh and grating on Elizabeth's ears. "I'll tell you, my sweet Elizabeth, though you must keep it to yourself. No telling Papa."

Elizabeth lifted her nose in the air and sniffed.

"Willy is working at the docks, but he's not loading firewood. He has an arrangement with the captain of the particular riverboat you mentioned. He's passing counterfeit money for the captain."

"What?" Elizabeth sat forward to stare at him. "You can't be serious."

"As serious as a weasel in a henhouse. He's been doing it for months. He's none too careful about flashing around his wages, either." A frown flickered across Alexander's brow.

"That's insane," Elizabeth responded. "Why would he get involved in something so dishonest? And so dangerous."

Alexander shrugged his shoulders. "Opportunity opened its door to him and he stepped through. The *Mississippi Maiden* is a gambling boat, and the captain has his own operation on the side. With lucrative returns, I might add."

"You're not thinking about joining him?" Elizabeth asked quickly.

"I can't say that the money's not attractive. But, no, I wouldn't be that foolish."

"I'm certainly glad to hear that." Elizabeth relaxed her shoulders and leaned back in the couch. "Isn't Willy afraid of getting caught?"

"He's too stupid to be afraid. He's going around town bragging to his friends about how much money he's making," Alexander said scornfully. "And he's already been warned once to shut up about his activities."

Elizabeth chewed her lip in thought. "I'll bet that was the reason for the quarrel that night on the street outside my house."

"What are you talking about?"

"Several months ago, late at night, I overheard an argument in the street beneath my bedroom window. When I looked out, I saw Willy and some other man involved in a disagreement. And then the man attacked Willy."

"You saw all that?"

"Yes. I even went to help Willy after the man left. He was beaten senseless and left lying on the roadside."

"Willy told me that the captain accused him of pocketing some of the cash instead of delivering it to the party he was supposed to, and sent one of the crew to talk to him about it. He didn't tell me that the crewman had roughed him up." Alexander frowned.

"So Willy is involved in a counterfeiting ring — that's hard to believe," Elizabeth said, shaking her head. "After all the accusations Church leaders have had to combat, and then to learn Willy is doing that very thing . . ." Her voice trailed off without finishing the thought.

"Church leaders? Why do you say that?" Alexander sounded annoyed that he even had to ask the question.

"The Church newspaper that my father writes for has published several articles denying the false accusations directed against Latter-day Saints of stealing, gambling, and making and passing counterfeit money."

"Are you really so surprised to learn that members of your Church might be involved in illegal activities? Come, come, Elizabeth. Those rumors aren't circulating because they have no basis in fact."

"What do you mean?"

"Your Church leaders preach one thing and do another."

"I have no idea what you're talking about, Alexander."

Alexander glanced over at the parlor door and lowered his voice. "I've heard it said that your Church leaders sanction, and in fact encourage, their membership in the theft of property and livestock from those who are not affiliated with your faith."

Elizabeth's mouth dropped open. "That's pure nonsense," she sputtered.

"Maybe. Maybe not."

"Why do you pay heed to such lies, Alexander? Those falsehoods are spread by vile men who want to bring down the Church and disgrace the Prophet."

"I wouldn't be so sure about that if I were you. There's plenty of talk going around in the city. Including whispers about your Prophet secretly engaging in robbery, horse stealing, and murder."

Elizabeth laughed. "I've never heard of anything so ridiculous. Really, Alexander, who's the naïve one now?"

Alexander's gray eyes hardened. "Maybe you shouldn't be so quick to laugh. Your so-called Prophet has set up his own private theocracy here in Nauvoo, and wields absolute power over the people. That ought to frighten you, Elizabeth, not amuse you."

"You've been listening much too closely to Willy. Your cousin professes to be a Latter-day Saint, but obviously isn't one in practice. Forget what Willy's told you. He doesn't know what he's talking about." Elizabeth dismissed the whole topic with a wave of her hand. "The only good thing I've heard about Willy is his suggestion that you stay in Nauvoo awhile longer. Might you?"

Alexander was still miffed with Elizabeth for dispelling his arguments against the Church. He sat stiff-backed on the couch. "I doubt it. I need to be getting back home."

Elizabeth rested a placating hand on his arm. "A few more days won't hurt anything, will it? I might even consider that tryst you were suggesting earlier," she said half in jest.

Alexander drew his arm away. "No, you won't. Not if Mormon Joe says not to," he said disagreeably.

Elizabeth ignored his response. At the moment, the most important thing on her mind was to persuade Alexander to extend his stay in Nauvoo.

CHAPTER EIGHTEEN

"That's one of the prettiest Christmas trees I've ever seen," Inger Johanssen said to James. She stood staring at the decorated fir set in the parlor of the Kades' new home. The tree was festooned with strands of colored popcorn and berries, velvet bows, and sprigs of holly; and the boughs twinkled with lighted candles. The gleaming candles cast a soft sheen around the tree, like a halo. Inger stood with her hands on her hips admiring the effect.

"It's kind of nice, isn't it," James agreed.

"Oh, it's absolutely lovely."

James gave Inger a furtive glance. The golden glow from the candles heightened the color of Inger's yellow hair. The sight of her standing beside the tree with sparkling eyes made his heart beat a little faster.

The Johanssens, along with Kirstine and her husband, Peder Madsen, were among the guests invited to the Kades' home for a festive Christmas Eve party. The parlor was glistening not only candlelight, but with warm camaraderie and merry laughter. The guests had enjoyed a Christmas dinner of berry-glazed ham, creamy potatoes, sweet corn, and carrot pudding. The delectable smells from supper still lingered in the room, making James feel hungry again even though his stomach was filled to bursting. He felt relaxed and contented from the big meal, and from the cozy fire crackling in the hearth. Outside the window snow was silently falling, piling up in soft white pillows against the porch of the house.

"Did you help dress the tree?" Inger asked, turning to James.

He nodded, his eyes traveling over the decorations snuggled in the boughs.

"The tree at our house is smaller, but it's lovely. Kirstine and Peder helped with the ornaments."

James nodded again without speaking. Like the Kades, the Johanssens had recently moved into a new house. James hadn't seen it yet, but Lars had described it to him. It was a one-story frame with the roof edged in blue tiles in the Scandinavian tradition, and it sat on the road skirting the river, a stone's throw from the water.

"Is Peder and Kirstine's house near yours?" James asked.

"Yes, they built a small cabin in Montrose only a few blocks away from ours. Kirstine visits often, and I'm glad she does. I miss her."

James spied the couple on the other side of the parlor, visiting with his mother and some of the other guests. Lydia had been the one who suggested giving a party, and she had drawn up the guest list. It seemed as if all of his parents' oldest and dearest friends were in attendance — Brother William W. Phelps and his wife, Elder Parley P. Pratt and his family, and the Johanssens were just a few among the many guests crowded into the parlor of the Kades' new home on Durphey Street. From the window James could see the small, snug, log cabin his family had vacated, shrouded now in snow. His father had sold the cabin to a convert to the Church who had only recently arrived from Europe.

"There you are, Inger. I've been looking for you." James' older sister glided in a welter of billowing skirts to Inger's side. "The dancing is about to begin."

James turned to study his sister. She was wearing a new frock the color of India ink that she'd sewn herself while working after hours at the tailoring shop. Her cheeks were pink with excitement. She didn't pay any heed to James or even acknowledge him standing there beside Inger.

"The fiddler is getting ready to start," Elizabeth eagerly told Inger. Candlelight reflected from her eyes, lending them an extra sparkle.

Inger glanced at James.

"Go on," he said, grinning. "Before my sister wears a hole in the floor from pacing with anticipation."

Inger smiled. "All right. I'll talk with you again later."

James watched the two girls bustle away. For Elizabeth, the dancing was the highlight of the evening. James saw his father and some of the other men start to move the tables and chairs against the walls, and then the sound of the fiddle swelled the parlor with melody. James saw Christian bow gracefully to Lydia, take her hand and lead her into the center of the room. For the first few moments they were the only couple stepping to the music, with their eyes shining like candlelight and their lips curled into smiles as cheery as Christmas bows, while the other guests looked on with pleasure.

Then the parlor began to fill with dancers. James watched the couples form into a circle to dance a Virginia reel. He grinned when he saw Lars Johanssen squiring seven-year-old Roxana onto the makeshift dance floor. He watched Lars lead Roxie in the intricate steps of the reel, and saw them laughing and joking together, enjoying the company and good cheer of the holiday season. Soon Elizabeth and Inger joined the parade of dancers, their partners part of the group of close family friends. James leaned against the wall, crossing one foot in front of the other, and studied the dancers as they moved through the fancy stepping.

"Not dancing, my young friend?"

James turned to see Elder Parley P. Pratt standing close by. The Apostle held a cup of sparkling apple wassail in his hand.

James straightened and smiled at the older man. "Hello, Brother Pratt. Are you enjoying yourself this evening?"

"It's a fine party, James. Why aren't you dancing with one of these pretty young ladies?" Pratt gestured to the guests assembled in the parlor.

"I'd rather be a spectator than a participant when it comes to dancing," he replied with a sheepish smile.

"A sober-minded lad, are you?"

"I'm afraid so. My sister, Elizabeth, says I'm much too serious, which makes me dull company."

Brother Pratt smiled, then took a sip of his wassail. "If you don't take pleasure in the dance, then what pastimes do you enjoy pursuing?"

James shrugged his shoulders. "I like to fish. And to read."

"Ah, a man after my own heart," Pratt said. "I always loved a good book. From the days of my youth, a book has been in my hand at every leisure moment."

"Yes, sir. It's the same with me."

Pratt took another sip from his cup. "From an early age, my mother encouraged me in reading from the scriptures. I loved the stories of Joseph in Egypt, David and Goliath, Saul and Samuel, Samson and the Philistines. All of them made a deep impression on my young heart and inspired me with the noblest sentiments."

James nodded.

Elder Pratt went on, describing how he had felt as he read of Jesus and his Apostles. "How I longed to serve my Savior and Redeemer and partake of His gospel! How my mind was drawn out on the things of God and of eternity! I had a firm belief in Christ and wished with all my heart to serve Him."

James listened attentively.

The Apostle paused and when he spoke again, his tone was quiet and thoughtful. "With my mind dwelling so heavily on things of a spiritual nature, imagine my astonishment and my great joy when I learned of the Book of Mormon, the contents of which contained the fullness of the gospel. Upon reading the book I knew that it was true, just as surely as I knew that men exist, for the spirit of the Lord testified of such to me. This discovery filled my heart with joy. The Book of Mormon is worth more to me than all the riches of the earth."

"And so it was then that you were baptized into the Church?"

"Yes, on the first day of September, 1830, by the hand of Oliver Cowdery."

James silently considered what the Apostle said about his conversion, and his baptism by Oliver Cowdery. Cowdery had held positions of leadership in the Church, and been a close friend of James' father. But Cowdery had subsequently lost his testimony and separated himself from the Church. He remained apart when the body of the Saints migrated to Illinois and established Nauvoo. James had heard his father lament the loss of friendship and fellowship with Oliver Cowdery, as well as his friend, John Whitmer, and the Whitmer brothers.

James felt a sudden chill wiggle down his spine as he recognized that his own testimony had dwindled after witnessing the fall of Dr. John C. Bennett. For the past year he'd wrestled with doubt concerning the truthfulness of the Church; he'd even questioned Joseph Smith's role in restoring the gospel. He felt at times as if he were trying to keep his balance on a teetering plank of wood placed atop a barrel. He was constantly shifting his weight from one side of the plank to the other in order to stay upright. Pratt's recital of his conversion and his testimony of the gospel soothed James' heart, but it didn't heal it.

While he was pondering these thoughts, he didn't notice Pratt's scrutiny of him. With a start, he realized that Pratt was staring steadily at him. He quickly arranged a smile on his face. "And afterward you traveled to the British Isles to preach."

"The Lord called me to labor in the British Isles, young James, through the inspiration of His prophet, Joseph Smith," Elder Pratt corrected him.

James guessed that the Apostle had gazed into his heart and discerned his true feelings concerning the gospel and Brother Joseph. He averted his eyes, pretending to take an interest in the dancers on the floor. "I think I might take a turn at dancing like you suggested, Brother Pratt," he said, keeping his gaze away from the Apostle's face. "It was nice talking with you," he added.

"And you. Have a pleasant holiday, James, and may your deepest desires come to fruition during the new year."

"Thank you, Brother Pratt." He hurriedly left Pratt's side and slipped through the crowd gathered in the parlor. He knew, however, that he had to make good on his word to Elder Pratt and invite some young lady to dance with him.

He spotted Inger Johanssen standing by herself and entertained the thought of asking her to dance. He wouldn't have considered the proposition if Elizabeth were with her. In his mind's eye he could see Elizabeth wiggling her brows meaningfully at him, insinuating that he was sweet on Inger. The very thought of that picture drove him to abandon the idea of asking Inger to dance. He wheeled around and headed for the opposite side of the room, looking for a girl less intimidating with whom to share a dance.

His eyes roamed the parlor until they fastened on five-year-old Millicent. Perfect. He snaked through the crowd to his sister's side. "Having a good time, Milly?" he asked.

She looked up at him with shining eyes. "Uh huh, the best."

"Want to dance with your big brother?"

Her freckled face broke out into a broad grin.

"Come on, then." James scooped her up into his arms and carried her to a spot where there was room to perform their own personal dance. He willed his clumsy feet to keep time with the music, and holding Milly in his arms dipped and whirled with her.

Milly shrieked with glee as James twirled her around and around. Her gleaming red hair was parted in the middle and swept back into two smooth braids, each ending with a big bright yellow bow. She had on a yellow frock and white pinafore, and long white cotton stockings. She looked like a bit of summer sunshine, come to brighten the winter eve.

Despite his reservations, James found himself enjoying the dance with his partner. He got caught up in Milly's enthusiasm, and the more she giggled and squealed, the more flair he put into his performance. When the fiddler sawed his bow over the singing strings for the last note, James was perspiring from his exertions.

The fiddler introduced the next number, a jaunty reel. Couples began to form into a circle in preparation for the group dance.

"I'm pooped, Milly. Let's sit this one out," James said, setting his little sister on her feet.

"Can we dance some more later?" Milly wanted to know.

"Of course."

"You're the bestest big brother in the whole world," Milly said, giving him a squeeze.

James grinned as he watched her scamper off.

"I couldn't help noticing what a good dancer you are, James."

James whirled around. There stood Inger Johanssen with a teasing smile on her face. His cheeks flushed a deep red. "I was just fooling around with Milly. Making it fun for her," he stuttered. He was embarrassed to know that Inger had been watching him.

"Are you going to dance this next reel?" she asked.

"Naw. I don't know the steps."

Inger inclined her head to one side, regarding him with a steady eye. "I can teach you the steps."

His cheeks burned even hotter than before. He tried to think of an excuse to offer her, but his tongue got tripped up in his mouth.

She laughed softly. "It's easy, James. You'll catch on fast."

Before he could collect his wits enough to reply, she reached for his hand and gently pulled him into the circle of dancers taking their places for the reel. The fiddler signaled the start of the Scottish round dance, with its lively and fancy stepping. James held Inger's hands as she led him through the fancy footwork. He was not totally unfamiliar with the steps, but his feet were not used to the routine. He let Inger guide him through the dance. She was a year older than he, and yielding to her lead seemed appropriate in the present circumstances. Her hands felt soft and delicate as he held them lightly in his own work-roughened ones. Her flaxen hair, wound into a single braid tumbling down her back, smelled sweetly of rose water. He could see her black high-buttoned shoes peeping from her skirts as he watched her feet perform the intricate steps.

"Now a little kick forward and back with your right foot," she said to him with a smile.

He performed the maneuver awkwardly, nearly tripping over his own feet.

Her smile broadened. "Now three steps forward, then three steps back, and cross," she said as they went through the motions together. Still keeping hold of his hands, she crossed in front of him and passed to his opposite side.

He smiled to himself. Now that he was getting the hang of the dance, he was starting to enjoy it. Inger was a good teacher — patient and forgiving of his mistakes.

"Now change, and change again," she murmured as she glided beside him.

His right hand engaged hers at chest height, and his left skirted the back of her shoulders to clasp her left hand. Poised in the position of the dance, he concentrated on memorizing the pattern of the steps. The rhythm was lively and quick, and when his feet fumbled while executing an intricate step, she laughed good-naturedly.

"You're doing fine, James. You're going to be an excellent dancer in no time at all."

"I find that difficult to believe," he returned, grinning at her.

The next portion of the round dance required the ladies to step forward and take the hand of the partner in front of them. As Inger reached for her new partner's hand, she glanced over her shoulder at James and gave him an encouraging smile. James grinned back at her.

James' new partner was the matronly looking wife of one of his parents' friends. She was short and plump, and her hands felt pudgy and sluggish in his. She greeted him by name and the two of them performed the required steps together before she moved on to her next partner.

Soon all the ladies in the round had opportunity to exchange a few steps with James, including his sister,

Elizabeth, who made sport of his poor skills. He was relieved when Inger returned to his side. Taking her hands, he kidded with her. "I was afraid I'd never see you again."

"No, I'll always be here for you, James," she said. "Just out of sight until you need me."

Something about her smile, and the way her eyes held his, made his heart flutter. His throat felt dry, and he found himself suddenly out of breath. The dance ended at that moment and James abruptly let go of his partner's hands. "I think I'll get a cup of punch," he said quickly. Then remembering his manners, he inquired if she would like one, too.

"Yes, thank you."

They walked together to the punch bowl sitting on the parlor table. His mother had prepared a Christmas cinnamon apple wassail, sweet, yet tart at the same time. The liquid cooled James' throat as he swallowed a mouthful of it from his cup.

The two stood beside the punch bowl, with James feeling uncommonly awkward and shy. He chanced a quick, nervous glance at Inger. She was wearing a peach-colored dress with a ruffle starting at each shoulder and meeting in a point at the waist. The dress shimmered in the glow of candlelight filling the room. It reminded him of peaches ripening in the summer sun. Her gaze was focused on the scene outside the parlor window.

"Oh, look, James," she said suddenly. "It's stopped snowing."

His eyes moved to the window. The snow lay glistening under the light of the full moon, covering the rooftops, roads, and fields like a cozy down comforter.

Inger pressed her nose against the window pane. "Let's go outside on the porch where we can get a better view," she suggested.

She followed James through the parlor and down the short hallway to the front door. The two of them stepped outside onto the covered porch, and James shut the door behind them. The air was cold and his breath escaped in plumes of vapor.

"Listen to the silence," Inger said in wonder. "It's as if the snow has muffled every sound."

James cocked an ear. They were alone on the porch, and there was no clatter of carriage and horse in the streets or people passing by on foot. The road stretching away from the house was perfectly still and serene. When he glanced at Inger, he saw her face was luminous in the moon's light. He watched her furtively as she leaned against one of the red brick pillars stretching from the porch to the roof, and stared up at the round, butter moon.

James' heart began beating faster. He'd never seen Inger look as pretty as she did now, standing in the wash of moonlight. He felt a sudden, unexpected impulse to kiss her. The thought terrified him, yet at the same time it filled him with excitement. Perhaps she wouldn't mind a single, quick kiss. Hadn't Elizabeth mentioned that Inger had feelings for him? If that was true, then maybe Inger wouldn't take unkindly to a kiss from him. His heart sped with the thought of it, until it was bounding in his chest like some caged animal. He hugged his arms to his chest to keep from trembling, from the cold as well as from fear. Just as he was gathering his courage, Inger abruptly turned to look at him. He saw golden moonlight reflected in her eyes.

James leaned forward with a jerky motion, squeezed his eyes shut in trepidation, and bestowed on Inger a wobbly kiss. It was over and done with before he even realized it had happened.

He held his breath, waiting for Inger's reaction. Would she be angry with him for his brashness, or pleased? For an instant, Inger's expression remained unchanged. Then a smile slowly started to build on her face. She lowered her eyes and looked away, smiling without speaking.

It was only after they had gone back inside the house and parted company that James felt the thrill set in from his first kiss.

The ice on the Mississippi was uneven and lumpy, but thick enough for skating. James strapped on the new skates he'd received that morning as a Christmas gift from his parents; the silver metal skates had been an unexpected surprise and James was thrilled with them. The skates fastened onto his boots with a leather strap. He tied the strap securely and stood up to test the blade on the ice. The thin blade came an inch or so past the toe of his boot and curved upward, like the runner on a sleigh. He slid his feet forward and back, checking the sharpness of the blade.

"Wait for me, James," said his sister. Roxana was seated on the bank of the river, fitting a pair of old skates Elizabeth had outgrown onto her shoes. Elizabeth was supposed to be at the river, too. The three of them had planned to spend the afternoon together skating on the frozen Mississippi, but on the way to the river Elizabeth had abruptly veered off in a different direction, telling James that she'd meet him and Roxie in a few minutes. James scanned the shoreline, searching for his older sister. The bare branches of the trees growing along the river bank were glazed with ice, giving them the appearance of delicate crystal. It was so cold that James' chest ached with each drawn breath, but the bitter cold didn't dampen his enthusiasm for the afternoon of skating before him.

"Will you tie these straps for me, James? My fingers are frozen already," Roxana said.

James took his sister's mittened hands between his own and rubbed them briskly. "That should warm your hands some," he said. Then he bent down to tie the straps of her skates onto her shoes.

"Thanks," she said, shivering. Her nose was red and already running from the cold. She wiped it with her mitten.

"You'll warm up once you start skating. I wonder where Elizabeth is," he added under his breath. Not finding her anywhere in sight, he took Roxie's hand and led her out onto the ice. She wobbled and would have fallen had he not had a tight grip on her hand. "Get your balance, Roxie," he told her.

She put out her arms to stabilize herself, and then cautiously put one foot in front of the other and shuffled forward.

James had to stay right with her to prevent her from losing her balance and taking a tumble on the ragged ice. He was itching to break in his new skates — see how quickly and how smoothly they could skim across the ice — but he couldn't leave Roxie's side. Where was Elizabeth? he grumbled. Elizabeth was usually content to skate hand in hand with their younger sister. Though Elizabeth was a good skater, she didn't enjoy the sport as much as James did.

"Come on, Roxie. Come out a little further on the ice where you have some room to skate. I won't let you fall."

"You promise?" Her words sounded thick, as if they were frozen to her tongue.

"Of course. Watch me." He temporarily let go of her hand and demonstrated his skill in skating forward and backward. He skidded to a stop at her side, digging the blade of his skate into the ice. A shower of icy spray spit from his skate. He nodded in satisfaction. The new skates worked beautifully. He could hardly wait to tear across the ice at breakneck speed. "Now you try it," he said to his sister, striving to rein in his impatience.

Roxie tentatively scooted one foot forward, and then dragged the other to meet it.

"That's right. Do it again."

This time she moved two steps forward, and soon she'd found confidence enough to venture forth without James' assistance. "Don't skate too far away from me," she told her brother.

"I won't." James skated in a tight circle around her, crouching low to the ice and keeping his arms close to his side. Then he sped out a short distance and back again to Roxie's side. "Are you getting warm now?" he asked her as she painstakingly plodded across the ice.

She nodded, too focused on her task to answer with words.

"This is supposed to be fun. Are you having fun?" James asked, laughing.

"I'm having fun," she retorted, as if she were offended by the question.

"Good." James sped off across the ice, swinging his arms as he raced over the choppy surface of the frozen river. There were about a dozen other young people skating on this same stretch of the river. James zipped past an acquaintance and turned to wave hello. As he did so, his feet tangled underneath him. Unused to the new skates, he tripped over one curved front blade and fell onto his hip on the hard ice. He heard a muffled creaking underneath him; then he saw a zigzag crack appear under the surface of the ice. He was more surprised than frightened by the splinter in the ice. The weather was so cold that he'd assumed the river would be frozen solid. He hadn't taken into consideration the fact that there might be some areas where the ice was not as thick as in other places.

He got to his feet and started to skate back towar
Roxie to warn her about possible patches of thin ice whe
he caught sight of Elizabeth on the snow-covered roa
leading to the river. He was startled to see that she wasn'
alone. He recognized the swaggering gait of her new beau
Alexander Scott, as he walked with Elizabeth to the river'
edge. Alexander had a pair of skates flung over his shoulder
and was carrying Elizabeth's skates in one hand and holdin
her hand with his other.

A surge of irritation welled up in his chest as he realize
that Elizabeth had invited Alexander to join them for th
afternoon of skating. He'd only met Alexander twice, an
he hadn't been particularly impressed with him on eithe
occasion. And he knew that his mother had no idea tha
Alexander would be joining the skating party. That though
rankled him even more than his own displeasure at havin
to bear Alexander's company.

"James!" Elizabeth called on spotting him out on th
ice. She waved, and motioned for him to come join her. H
grumbled under his breath as he grabbed Roxana's han
and toted her along to the spot where the road met th
frozen river.

"How's the ice?" Alexander asked, hefting the skate
from off his shoulder.

"Fine," James mumbled. He turned to his older sister
"This is why you took so long getting here?" he asked
nodding toward Alexander.

"Oh, don't be such an old grump," Elizabeth said. "
ran into Alexander along the way and he decided to joi

us." She glanced up at the young man beside her and smiled slyly.

"That's right. And I just happened to be carrying my skates with me," he said with a mocking face.

Elizabeth thrust an elbow into his ribs. "If you tell James that, he'll carry the tale straight to my mother."

Alexander gazed evenly at James. His slate-blue eyes were the color of the cold winter sky.

James was about to make a sharp reply when he felt Roxana tugging on his arm. "I'm cold. Let's go home, James."

James glanced at his younger sister. Her nose was bright red and her lips were turning a bluish color. "We just got here, Roxie. I've hardly had a chance to try out my new skates."

"James received a pair of skates for Christmas," Elizabeth informed her beau.

"Good for you," Alexander remarked to James without any evidence of sincerity.

Roxie pulled on James' arm again. He brushed her hand aside. "Elizabeth is here now. She'll skate with you for awhile, then I'll take you home." He wasn't so much annoyed with Roxie, as he was with Elizabeth for bringing Alexander along and for being late. He turned and skated off without another word, and it was only after he'd covered a fair distance that he remembered he'd intended to warn Roxie about the thin ice. He dug the edges of his skates into the ice to slow himself, and turned around to glance back at his sisters. Roxie was patiently waiting for Elizabeth and

Alexander to fasten on their skates. She was beating her arms against her body to ward off the cold, and stamping on one foot and then the other. James felt a twang of conscience. His little sister was cold and he should accompany her home now rather than make her wait; but it was Elizabeth's fault that Roxie had to wait, not his. Elizabeth shouldn't have taken so long to get here.

He ignored the bite of conscience. He'd keep an eye on his sisters to make sure they didn't venture out too far on the ice. And Alexander was with them; both Alexander and Elizabeth could help Roxie if she fell down on the rough ice. With that thought in mind he set off at a brisk pace, skating as fast as he could go. The new skates had a sharp, smooth blade that propelled him across the ice with minimum effort. He crouched into a racer's stance and sped across the frozen river.

He was having such a good time that he completely forgot about his promise to Roxie. Sometime later when he spotted the three of them — Roxie, Elizabeth and Alexander — skating out in the center of the icebound river, he felt guilty about enjoying himself on the ice for so long. He started toward the trio, intending to curtail his own pleasure and walk Roxie home if she still wanted to go. As he skated closer to them, Roxie caught sight of him, waved, and started toward him. In a moment's time she was separated from Elizabeth and Alexander and well out into the middle of the frozen river — right in the spot where James had earlier felt the ice crack beneath him.

"Stop, Roxie!" he yelled. "Stay right there." His heart leaped into his throat and his blood pounded against his temples. "Stay where you are. I'll come and get you."

The words were no sooner out of his mouth when he saw Roxie's hands fly into the air and an expression of horror cross her face as one foot suddenly broke through the ice and she went down on her knees. James didn't know whether the scream came from her throat or his. He flew across the ice toward her, tearing off his coat and muffler as he went. He saw Roxana's legs crash through the ice, leaving her on her belly and clawing at the slick surface with her fingers to keep from falling into the water flowing beneath the crust of ice.

James didn't wait for assistance even though there were other skaters nearer to Roxana than he. When he got within a few feet of her, he threw himself chest first on the ice; then keeping hold of one coat sleeve, he flung the garment toward Roxana. "Grab the sleeve, Roxie!" he cried. "Grab it!"

"I ca . . . ca . . . can't," she stuttered, numb with shock and cold.

James didn't hesitate an instant. He started across the ice toward her, arms and legs splayed out flat, and scooting along on his stomach. He could see Roxie's body slipping into the jagged hole in the ice. She couldn't keep a grip on the slippery surface. She kept snatching at the ice, her red mittens a stark contrast against the brilliant whiteness, and her eyes bulging in desperation.

When he'd gotten to within a foot of her, he heard the ice begin to crack beneath his chest. The creaking thundered in his ears, drowning out all other sounds — his older sister's shrill screams, the gasps and shouts of the other skaters crowding around, and his own hoarse breathing. "Roxie, try to grab the coat sleeve," he repeated, scooting the coat toward her.

This time the only answer he received was the look of mute terror in her eyes. James lunged forward just as Roxie's hands slid out from under her, and her head went under the water.

With a cry, James grasped her flailing hands before they disappeared into the icy, gray river. He was vaguely aware of strong hands grabbing onto him and tugging him backward from the yawning hole. He clenched his fingers around Roxie's wrists and concentrated all his energy on holding fast to her. Roxie's upturned face broke the surface of the water. She sputtered, and coughed, and let out a terrified cry.

Then without warning, a chunk of ice beneath James' chest broke away and splashed into the water. Both he and Roxie would have spilled into the river if some of the other skaters had not been hanging onto his legs. They pulled both James and Roxie away from the crumbling edges of the hole.

As soon as they were clear of the thinning ice, James scrambled to his knees and began ripping off Roxie's soaking coat and mittens. Once again, hands reached out to help. Roxie's lips were blue and her whole body was shaking violently. As James wrapped his coat around her, Roxie lapsed into unconsciousness.

James shut out the sound of Elizabeth sobbing over his shoulder, and Alexander barking out advice and directions. He disregarded the drawn countenances of the other skaters and bystanders, and concentrated only on bundling up Roxie as warmly as he could in his own coat and muffler, and getting her home. He tore off his skates, and then carried Roxie off the ice and up the snow-clogged road toward their house with Elizabeth keeping pace at his side. The whole way home, trudging through the deep wet snow with his precious burden, he kept praying that Roxana would be all right.

James lay awake in his bed with the covers pulled up to his chin. He was shivering and his teeth were chattering, more from a delayed reaction to the horror of Roxana's mishap on the ice, than from the cold. He could hear Elizabeth and Milly talking quietly together in the next room. Roxana was spending the night downstairs beside the hearth where a fire would be kept burning, and where her parents were close by. The doctor had been to the house to examine her, and his face was grave when he left an hour later. Roxana had suffered a chill from the shock of the cold water, and tonight a harsh cough had set in. James could hear her now, coughing sharply in her makeshift bed beside the fire.

In spite of the trembling that had taken over his body, James slipped out of bed and sank to his knees. He bowed his head and pressed his eyes tightly shut, offering another in a long series of petitions to his Heavenly Father. He pleaded with God to help his sister get well and not suffer any more from the ill effects of the accident. He begged God to forgive him for being selfish and thoughtless that afternoon when Roxana had wanted to go home. Tears welled in his eyes and spilled down his cheeks as he sought forgiveness for all his weaknesses, especially the doubts he'd harbored over the last year and a half concerning the truthfulness of the gospel.

Now, in the midst of a crisis, he needed to know that God was there, listening to his prayer. He prayed for the Holy Spirit to attend him — to speak peace to his heart and his mind. He needed to know for himself that the religious principles he'd been taught since his childhood were true and correct, and that God would give heed to his anguished prayers. For how could he ask God to help Roxana, if he didn't truly believe that God answered prayers?

He stayed on his knees for a long time, shivering with cold and emotion. When he finally climbed back into bed, he fell into a fitful sleep, still yearning for an answer to his pleas.

CHAPTER NINETEEN

Elizabeth handed her younger sister a cup of hot broth to sip. Roxana took several swallows and then set the cup down. "That's all for now," she said.

Elizabeth propped the pillow under Roxie's head and tucked the blanket snugly around her shoulders. "Are you warm enough, Roxie?"

"Yes, you can stop fussing over me." The words ended in a fit of harsh coughing. Roxie held a handkerchief to her mouth as the hard coughs racked her body. Since her accident two days before, a congestion in her lungs had set in, along with fever and chills.

"The doctor said to stay warm and get lots of rest. Shall I put another log on the fire?"

Roxie shook her head. "I'm plenty warm." She snuggled under the blanket and closed her eyes, hugging her doll, Effie, in the crook of her arm.

The doctor had come by again this morning to check on Roxie, and his tone was grave as he conversed with Christian and Lydia in the hallway before leaving. Elizabeth hadn't heard what he said, but she didn't like the worried look in his eyes.

"Is James home?" Roxana asked, her eyes fluttering open. "I need to talk to him."

"Yes. He's in the barn milking Hyacinth. When he comes inside, I'll tell him you want to see him."

Roxana nodded. She pressed the handkerchief against her lips to stifle another cough.

"I think James has been more upset than anyone about your accident. He tries not to show it, but I know he's been worried about you."

"I wish he wouldn't fret so."

Elizabeth had found her brother on his knees in prayer that morning when she'd gone upstairs to tell him breakfast was ready. She'd quietly shut the door without disturbing him and waited for him to finish. When he came out of his room his face was pinched and pale, and Elizabeth was afraid that he, too, had taken ill from the effects of the cold two days before. He had carried Roxana home from the river without coat or hat, and sat beside her bed until their mother insisted that he go upstairs to rest. It was a brave thing he'd done in rescuing Roxie. While everyone else stood wringing their hands and trying to get their wits about them, James had sprung into action and saved Roxana from drowning.

Elizabeth tried to recall what Alexander's reaction had been to the emergency. She hadn't paid him much heed at the time of the crisis, but thinking back on it now, she wondered why Alexander hadn't been among the first to give James a hand. Alexander was nearer to Roxie when she fell through the ice than anyone else, yet he seemed to be the slowest to react. Elizabeth shrugged her shoulders. She hadn't been a bundle of help, either. All she could remember doing was screaming hysterically. Alexander had parted company with them once they left the riverbank. She hoped he would come calling this evening.

Ever since she'd begun keeping company with him after the Harvest Social, more than two months ago, not a day had gone by that she hadn't thought about him. Alexander had escorted her to a play held on the upper floor of Joseph Smith's red brick store, and a few weeks later to a lyceum discussion where Apostle Orson Pratt had presented a lecture on astronomy. Brother Pratt had woven gospel beliefs into the scientific presentation, which Elizabeth discovered afterward had rankled Alexander. Her beau wasn't a member of the Church, and the better Elizabeth came to know him, the more she realized that he was antagonistic to the Church and its leaders. The two of them had gotten into an argument later that evening over some principle of the gospel. Elizabeth couldn't remember now what the disagreement was about, but she'd come home unsettled by the argument and the views Alexander held. Alexander's stay with his cousin, Willy Saunders, was drawing to a close, and Elizabeth was anxious to spend as much time as possible with him before he returned to Wisconsin. Because of her feelings for him, and the fact that he would soon be leaving Nauvoo, she'd continued to secretly meet him without her mother's knowledge or her permission. Her parents had taken a disliking to Alexander and were pressing Elizabeth to put an end to the relationship. A case in point occurred the day before yesterday. Alexander wanted to see her on Christmas Day; he had a gift for her, he'd said. Knowing her parents would never let her spend the holiday in Alexander's company, she had privately arranged to meet him near the river where the two of them would join James and Roxie in skating. The afternoon with Alexander had been interrupted by Roxie's accident. She hadn't seen him since and hoped tonight he would call for her at the house.

A few minutes later James came inside carrying a pail full of frothy, white milk. Elizabeth delivered her sister's message, and then followed James into the parlor and sat down near the hearth.

"How are you feeling this afternoon?" James asked, stroking his sister's dark curls.

"Much better." She drew James' hand into hers. "Thank you for saving me from drowning in that icy hole," she said earnestly.

"I'm glad I was close by." He kissed the top of Roxana's head.

Elizabeth sat silently, watching the exchange between her brother and sister. Though she and James were full-blooded siblings, she knew that James enjoyed a closer relationship with Roxana than he did with her. Generally that kind of thought would have bothered her, but today she was just glad to have James near.

"And how is Effie doing?" James took the doll from Roxie's arms. "She looks a little pale."

Roxie giggled as James pretended to examine the doll as if he were a doctor.

"I'm going to prescribe bed rest for this young lady," he said, nodding toward the doll. "And plenty of liquids. Will you see that my instructions are carried out exactly as I've ordered," he said, turning to Roxana with a mock look of sternness.

"Yes, I will, doctor," she said, smothering a chuckle. James handed Effie back and she tucked the doll into bed beside her.

Elizabeth watched the two of them interact. She'd noticed before that James had a knack for putting people at ease, especially those who were ill or injured. She'd seen him nurse her younger sisters and brother on more than one occasion. James seemed to have a way about him that inspired trust and confidence. In reality, he would make a good doctor, she mused. She knew he had ambitions in that direction at one time, but she hadn't heard him talk about practicing medicine for quite awhile. The three of them were soon joined by Milly and two-year-old Zachary. They sat chatting beside the hearth until Lydia summoned them all to supper.

Shortly after supper, Alexander called at the house. Elizabeth's father invited him in only as far as the hallway, where he explained that Elizabeth was not taking visitors that evening. Elizabeth was furious with her father for handing down that decision. She had waited all day to see Alexander, and now she wasn't even allowed to say hello to him. After she heard the front door close, she sped on tiptoe to the rear door of the house and quietly let herself out. Snow was falling, and a full moon illuminated the barren trees and shrubbery bordering the house.

"Alexander!" she called in a loud whisper.

He paused, and turned around.

"Over here," she said, stepping from the shadow of the house and beckoning to him to follow her. She could see his square, angled face in the light of the moon, gleaming like alabaster. His head was bare, but he wore a stylish knee-length overcoat.

"Elizabeth? What are you doing out here?"

When he was within reach, she grasped his arm. "I heard my father tell you that I'm not taking visitors this evening. Well, he's wrong. I am," she said with a defiant toss of her head.

Alexander stood looking at her, an amused smile playing over his face.

"Aren't you going to say anything?" she asked impatiently.

"What do you want me to say?" The infuriating smile spread further across his face.

"That you're glad to see me."

"I am glad to see you. But a little surprised, too. I didn't think a young lady of your breeding would go sneaking behind her father's back."

Elizabeth felt her face flush. "If that's all you have to say, then I'll go back inside."

She turned and started back the way she'd come. She'd only taken a few steps when Alexander caught her by the hand. "I didn't say that I disapproved. In fact, I admire your spunk." He chuckled openly.

"Shh. Be quiet or my parents will hear you," Elizabeth hissed with a frown. She pulled him into the shadows of the house.

"Umm. This is much better than visiting you in your parlor," he said, lowering his head to give her a kiss.

She pulled away, annoyed by his sardonic tone. "I didn't come out here to have you kiss me."

"Then what did you come out here for?"

"To make arrangements to see you."

"Oh, I see." His eyes still held a trace of amusement in them.

"I can get away tomorrow afternoon, if you like."

"Perfect. My cousin, Willy, is sweet on some girl in town and wants us to accompany him on an outing with her."

Elizabeth felt a twinge of disappointment. She preferred to be alone with Alexander, especially now when their time together was short. "What kind of outing?"

"Dinner at one of the new hotels on the bluff."

Elizabeth bit her lip. She was afraid someone might spot her with Alexander at such a public place, and mention it to her parents. "All right," she said reluctantly. "What time tomorrow?"

"Five o'clock."

"Isn't that a bit late? I thought we might spend the afternoon together." Elizabeth shivered. She had dashed outside without a coat and the cold December night air bit through her thin frock.

"That's what Willy wants. You and I can get together earlier if you like."

"If we're going to be gone most of the evening, then I can't get away much earlier than five or Mama will suspect that something is going on."

Alexander snaked an arm around her waist and pulled her to him. "Something is going on, isn't it?" He closed his eyes and bent to kiss her. This time she let him do it. She wanted him to kiss her again, but he drew back and removed his arm from her waist.

"You'd better get back inside before your parents discover you're gone," he said evenly.

"All right." She turned to go.

"Wait. I almost forgot," Alexander said. "I brought you this." He withdrew from his coat pocket a small wrapped gift tied with a fancy red ribbon, and held it out to her.

"This is for me?"

"Merry Christmas," replied Alexander. He surprised her with another kiss and then turned and strode away.

She noticed the moonlight splash across his broad shoulders, and the snow sparkle in his dark hair. She sighed with the pleasure of watching him, then she started for the rear door of the house. She soundlessly let herself inside and slipped up the stairs to her room. Luckily, Milly was still downstairs with Roxana. She sat down on the bed with her gift and removed the ribbon and colored wrapping paper. Then she lifted the lid of the small box. A cry of pleasure escaped her when she saw its contents. Lying inside was a cameo locket affixed to a deep blue velvet ribbon. The ivory-colored cameo was carved with the profiles of a man and woman gazing at one another. It was the most exquisite piece of jewelry Elizabeth had ever set eyes on. She carefully lifted the necklace out of the box and tied the ends of the velvet ribbon around her throat. Then she stood in front of the oval mirror mounted on her bureau and admired her reflection.

She gathered her hair in one hand and pulled it up onto the crown of her head, letting a few ringlets cascade down the back of her neck, then turned this way and that in front of the mirror, noting how pretty the choker looked on her neck. She giggled out loud and let her fair fall back into place at her shoulders.

"I love you, Alexander Scott," she whispered into the mirror.

"So who is this girl that Willy likes?" asked Elizabeth, stroking the raised carving on her new cameo necklace. "Have you met her?"

"No, but Willy seems taken with her." With his finger, Alexander traced the same path over the cameo's polished surface as Elizabeth had, then he cupped his hand over hers. The two of them were seated at a small sewing table in the dress shop where Elizabeth worked. Elizabeth had been given her own key to the shop, and she'd employed it this evening for her after-hours rendezvous with Alexander. Alexander brought Elizabeth's hand to his lips and kissed it.

Elizabeth's cheeks warmed with his kiss. She was aware of how attractive she looked in her favorite blue cotton dress and matching bonnet. The new choker accentuated the outfit, and the touch of pink that Alexander's kiss brought to her cheeks was not uncomplimentary. She knew Alexander thought she looked enchanting for he hadn't been able to keep his eyes off her from the moment he entered the shop.

Elizabeth had told her parents that she was going to the dress shop to work on a frock that needed to be finished by the next day. They'd sent James to accompany her to the shop, and as soon as he'd driven away in the buggy, she met Alexander at the back door and let him inside.

"How much time do we have until we're supposed to meet Willy and his girl?" Elizabeth asked, removing her hands from Alexander's clasp. Not wanting Alexander to know how smitten she was with him, she tried to maintain a cool demeanor. She smoothed the skirt of her dress and retied the ribbon streamers of her bonnet into a smooth bow under her chin.

Alexander reached for the timepiece he kept in his vest pocket. "It's past five now. Willy and his lady friend should be arriving any moment. He told me that he had to make a quick stop at the dock first to speak to someone about loading supplies on the riverboat."

"You really mean to conduct his business with the counterfeiters, don't you?" Elizabeth said, giving Alexander a sideways glance. "I'm appalled that Willy would be involved with such scoundrels."

Alexander laughed. "Apparently, it's not such a bad life. Willy's pockets are always full of greenbacks."

"You condone Willy's actions?" Elizabeth asked incredulously.

"No, I don't condone them. My cousin is keeping dangerous company. I've encouraged him to find other employment."

"I should think so."

"I believe he's going to talk to the captain of the *Maiden* about it tonight."

Elizabeth stared out the window as though straining to spot Willy all the way down at the dock. Snow was falling, laying down a white carpet along the streets and yards. A sudden chill passed through her.

Alexander saw her shiver. He leaned over and wrapped his arms around her. "Are you cold?" he asked softly.

No, but I like the warmth of your arms anyway," she said, snuggling against him.

"You know how I feel about you," Alexander whispered. "I can't stop thinking about you."

"I can't stop thinking about you, either," Elizabeth murmured. Her cool demeanor was fast crumbling.

"Why don't you come with me back to Wisconsin?" Alexander said, his mouth seeking hers.

"Umm. That would be nice."

He pulled away and looked into her face. "I'm serious."

"You are?"

He nodded.

"My parents would never let me go, Alexander."

He pushed aside her hair to stroke the soft velvet ribbon fastened around her neck. "Then here's your chance to get out from under your stepfather's thumb," he purred in her ear.

For an instant, she considered his proposal.

"You'd like it in Wisconsin. You could stay with my family and we could be together every day." He rubbed his finger over the polished surface of the ivory cameo. "My father's lumber business is turning a good profit. I'd like nothing better than to dress you in the fancy clothes and fine jewelry that a beautiful girl like yourself deserves."

She twisted in her seat to look at him. She couldn't tell if he was serious or only toying with her for his words were often mocking. Yet his invitation was tempting. Her gaze took in the stylish cut of his waistcoat and trousers, and his handsome boots which were polished to a high luster. His hair was brushed forward in front of his ears, with every strand in place and glistening with hair tonic. She knew that he could provide her with an equally fashionable living.

"What do you think?" he asked, nestling his lips against her cheek.

She wanted to believe him, but every instinct warned her to be cautious. "You'd buy me silk dresses and stylish bonnets?" she asked, arching her brow.

"A half dozen of them." He kissed her cheek.

"And fancy shoes?"

"You can have more shoes than any girl in Wisconsin Territory."

"But then I'd turn the head of every boy in town, and you wouldn't like that," she said.

He laughed. "No, I wouldn't. I want the prize all to myself." He leaned back in his chair, his face a smirking grin.

His sarcastic tone annoyed Elizabeth. She had half believed his offer. She berated herself for letting Alexander make her feel foolish. "If I had said yes, then what would you have done?" she said petulantly.

"Then I would have swept you up on my horse and carried you away," he said, the smirk still clinging to his face.

That remark nettled her even more. She stood up abruptly. "I think this conversation has gone far enough. Perhaps you should leave."

"Now why should I do that? You don't want me to leave any more than I want to." He took her by the arm and pulled her back down on the chair.

She frowned up at him, trying to maintain her indignation.

Alexander slipped an arm around her and leaned close. Every unpleasant thought fled from mind as Elizabeth closed her eyes in anticipation of his kiss.

Elizabeth and Alexander waited for over an hour for Willy to meet them, then deciding that Willy must have changed his plans without notifying them, they left the dress shop and went alone to dine at the hotel. Elizabeth was back at the shop in time for James to meet her at the pre-arranged hour and take her home.

When she entered the house, she spotted Lydia in the parlor. Her mother stood up from her chair as Elizabeth came down the hallway.

"Hello, Mama. Have you been waiting up for me?"

"Yes, I have. Have you been at the tailoring shop all this time?"

She froze. She knew immediately that trouble was imminent. Her mother's usually placid face was drawn into a hard knot. "Yes. James took me there and picked me back up." She held her breath.

"Yes, I know he did. But that's not what I asked you. Have you been at the shop all evening?"

"Yes," she said slowly and cautiously.

"I came by about seven o'clock to give you a hand with the sewing so you wouldn't have to stay so late."

Elizabeth felt as if someone had delivered a punch to her stomach. She couldn't catch her breath and her throat went dry. "I did step out for a minute, Mama. Yes, it was probably about that time." She nearly choked on the lie.

"Why don't you sit down, Elizabeth, while you and I have a talk. Your father is still at the printing office or he'd be here to join us."

Elizabeth knew she'd become entangled in the lies she'd just spun.

Lydia sat down in the chair opposite her and stared at her for a long moment without speaking. Then she folded her hands in her lap. "Why don't you tell me where you really went?"

Elizabeth cleared her throat, trying to think of something her mother might believe. "I ran out of blue thread for the dress I was sewing, Mama. So I had to go to the owner's house to see if she had any more. She rents a small room behind the shop. So I didn't go far." The excuse sounded plausible. Elizabeth chewed her lip, hoping her mother would believe the story.

Lydia looked at her with a pained expression. "Oh, Elizabeth. One lie is bad enough. You only make the situation worse by compounding them."

Tears rushed to Elizabeth's eyes. "I'm sorry I lied to you, Mama. It's just that I thought you wouldn't understand if I told you the truth." She swiped at her eyes before the tears started rolling down her cheeks.

"And what is the truth?"

She gulped before plunging into her story. "I was with Alexander. He'd invited me to supper, and I couldn't get out of the invitation because he'd already made plans with his cousin to come along, too."

"And so you deliberately lied to me in order to be with Alexander. Has this happened before?"

Elizabeth wanted to say no, but she couldn't face her mother's gaze. So she just sat wordlessly, staring at the floor.

"I see." Lydia shifted in her chair. "Well, it seems that deception has become a habit with you."

Elizabeth glanced at her mother's face and then quickly dropped her eyes again.

"I'm very disappointed in you, Elizabeth. And shocked by your behavior. I can only hope that your actions have been influenced by the company you keep and is not a reflection of your true character."

Elizabeth realized she was boxed into a corner. If she agreed with her mother, then she was admitting that Alexander was poor company and she shouldn't be associating with him. If she disagreed, then she was acknowledging that the fault lay with herself. She didn't know what to say to best protect herself, and so she remained silent.

"Haven't you anything to say?"

"You've already accused and condemned me," she said quietly.

"You've convicted yourself, Elizabeth. You have no one to blame but yourself for the consequences of your actions."

Elizabeth felt a stirring of indignation rise within her. "Alexander is going back to Wisconsin soon. If I don't see him now, I may never get to see him again."

"And that is reason enough to barter your integrity?"

The offense she had felt at her mother's words shriveled to a nub. She remembered other falsehoods she'd told her parents — her lie about having plans to meet her friends at the grounds to watch the Legion parade, her deception when she'd invited Alexander along to join her in skating on the river with James and Roxie. She laid deceitful plans every time she'd secretly met Alexander for a stolen afternoon visit. She thought of the cameo necklace hidden in her bureau drawer. That, too, represented a lie. The gravity of her actions suddenly rushed upon her, snatching her breath away. What she had considered to be harmless white lies now burst upon her mind in all their scarlet character. She felt her face burn with shame.

"Oh, Elizabeth, haven't you yet learned that disobedience cankers the soul?" Lydia said softly. "That lying, deceit, and envy are all god-children to pride and disobedience? Don't you realize that your actions shape the person you are becoming and carry in them the seeds of their own consequences?"

Her mother's questions filled her with remorse, but she couldn't bring herself to outwardly acknowledge them or ask for forgiveness. She sat rigid in her chair with her eyes glued to the floor. She heard Lydia expel a sigh.

"Elizabeth, I want you to know that I admire your strengths and your abilities. You're intelligent, ambitious, talented, and accomplished. But your willfulness has overruled your good judgment. If you can't discern for yourself the kind of influence Alexander is having on you, then I will make the choice in this matter. From this moment, you are not to associate with Alexander again."

Elizabeth's heart lunged in her chest. "But, Mama, he's leaving Nauvoo in a few weeks. Please let me keep seeing him until then," she begged. She felt overwhelmed by this edict her mother had pronounced on her.

Lydia shook her head. "You're just sixteen, Elizabeth, and not experienced enough yet in the ways of the world to recognize cunningness and craftiness when you meet it. Alexander is not the kind of companion who will encourage you in keeping your values and standards, and assist you in developing Christlike attributes."

"That's not true," Elizabeth cried, frantic to reverse her mother's decision. "You hardly know Alexander."

"I know his character. I know the effect he has on my daughter. You're not to see him again, Elizabeth." She stood up from her chair, her face set like stone.

Elizabeth knew it was useless to argue with her mother. Once Lydia had made up her mind about something, there was no turning her aside. Elizabeth arose from her chair, sulking and feeling wronged. Without another word she left the parlor, leaving her mother to gaze after her.

After school the next afternoon, Elizabeth went to the dress shop to work on the frock she was sewing for a customer. The woman had ordered a length of plain blue muslin fabric to be made into a simple frock. Elizabeth was hemming the cuffs of the dress when Alexander barged through the door of the shop. He reached her side at the sewing table in three quick strides.

"I wasn't expecting you," Elizabeth said with a nervous smile. His appearance wasn't a total surprise for Alexander often stopped at the shop for a quick hello, or to make plans to meet her after she finished work for the day. But she wasn't prepared to face him yet with the news of her mother's ultimatum. She'd agonized over it all night, and vacillated between defying her mother's directive and submitting to it. Now that Alexander was here, standing in front of her, she shrank from having to make any decision about it at all.

"I have to talk to you. Now," he said brusquely. He took hold of her arm and nearly lifted her off the chair.

"All right, Alexander. Just let me put down my sewing."

He waited impatiently while she laid her needle and thread aside. Explaining to her employer that she'd return in a moment, she followed Alexander outside into the snow-glutted street.

"You mustn't come charging into the shop and whisk me away like that," she scolded him. "My employer frowns on it and we have customers to help."

"Never mind your employer or your customers," Alexander said quickly. His eyes darted up the street and then back to Elizabeth's face. "I have something urgent to tell you. My cousin, Willy, was found dead at the dockyard early this morning. Stabbed in the chest."

"Oh!" Elizabeth's hands flew to her mouth. "Oh, no! Please tell me you're not serious."

"I wish I could. I just came from his house."

"This can't be true," Elizabeth wheezed. She sagged against Alexander's chest, fighting off a wave of nausea.

"Willy was a fool," Alexander said, anger flashing in his eyes. "His greediness got him killed."

Elizabeth's body trembled. "Was it someone from the riverboat, do you think?"

"Of course. Willy was double-dealing with the captain's money. I'm sure it was the captain who orchestrated Willy's murder."

"Then you'll tell the authorities that."

"No. And neither will you."

"Why not?" Elizabeth exclaimed.

"Because we're not getting involved in this," Alexander scowled. "The riverfront is infested with thieves, counterfeiters, and murderers. Everyone knows that. The Nauvoo police will assume that Willy was just some unlucky victim."

"But you have to tell the police what you know," Elizabeth objected.

"Let them figure it out. We're staying out of it."

This news about Willy, coming on the heels of her mother's demands to sever her association with Alexander, upset her nearly to tears. She cradled her head against Alexander's chest, seeking his comfort and protection.

"Perhaps you should go back inside now."

"When will I see you again?" she asked, still clinging to him.

"Tonight. I'll come by at dusk and walk you home."

"Do you promise?"

Alexander bent to kiss her. "Leave the shop door open for me. I'll be there."

Elizabeth attended Willy Saunders' funeral two days later, with James as her escort. Throughout the service, images of Willy flickered across her mind. She remembered the incident at the parade grounds when Willy showed her the pocketwatch he'd stolen, the times in the schoolroom when he'd taunted her, and the night of the altercation in the street outside her window. Although she had never been on particularly good terms with Willy, his murder negated all the bad feelings she'd harbored for him.

The service wasn't anything like the one she'd attended for Thomas Cox. Willy's family weren't actively involved in the Church, and there was no mention of spiritual comforts to ease his family's sorrow. Among the mourners were a group of rough-looking men from the docks, seedy characters who looked as if they felt uncomfortable in the bright glare of daylight.

She'd had to avoid Alexander while in James' company, which pained her. She could see from Alexander's furtive glances that he was annoyed with her for ignoring him. She had told him the evening before about the conversation with her mother, and he had reacted as badly as she feared he would.

A few days after the funeral, Alexander told Elizabeth that he would be leaving Nauvoo as soon as the river was free of ice to return to his home in Wisconsin. Elizabeth was nearly inconsolable about his impending departure. Though he promised to write frequently, and return to Nauvoo as soon as his work at the lumber mill would permit, she feared that she would never see him again. At the first thaw in late February, Alexander boarded a steamer bound for Wisconsin. Through the cold, rainy months of the new year, Elizabeth continued to attend school in Brother Bowers' one-room schoolhouse and work in the dress shop in the afternoons. Though she tried to keep her mind and hands busy, she missed Alexander almost more than she could bear.

CHAPTER TWENTY

James gripped the book he was carrying and leaped across a large mud puddle in the middle of the road. It had been a wet spring with snow and rain, and now the roads were beds of mud and nearly impassable to traffic. A cold, blustery rainstorm had blown in during the night, bringing with it chilly temperatures. James drew his coat tighter around his body as he picked his way across the muddy street and emerged on the opposite side. He stamped the mud off his feet and continued down Main Street to his destination. A flock of wild geese came soaring overhead, dotting the dark sky. James paused to watch them pass, listening to their discordant honking and the beating of their long, white, muscular wings. They soared above his head from the direction of the river on their flight northward. The

Mississippi was swollen and running high this spring, higher than James had ever seen it since arriving in Nauvoo.

James was glad to reach the cobbler shop and get out of the windy and rainy weather. He tucked the book he was carrying under his arm and opened the shop door. The pleasant smell of new shoe leather greeted him as soon as he entered the small shop. Two pairs of men's boots, and a dainty pair of ladies' slippers sat on display on the wide sill beneath the window. On the wall behind the rough counter was a shelf holding strips of shoe leather. James spied his friend, Hayden, sitting on a stool working a piece of tough black leather. He looked up as James approached.

"'ello, mate," he said, giving James a smile.

"How are you doing, Hayden?" James pulled over a chair and sat down on it. There was no one else in the shop. Hayden's father had either stepped out or gone home for the day.

Hayden set down the hunk of leather he'd been working. "Through with school for the day, are you?"

James nodded. Hayden had been at school the past term only a handful of days. Brother Bowers had eventually dropped his name from the roll. Hayden was needed at his father's shoe shop, and his formal education had apparently come to an end. That was why James had brought the book. He held it out to Hayden. "I brought this for you to read."

Hayden wiped his hands on his cobbler's apron and took the book from James. He looked at the title. *"Two Years Before the Mast.* What's it about?"

"It's the account of a young man's passage aboard a sailing ship bound for California. His voyage is filled with adventure and danger on the high seas. Since you came to America on a ship, I thought you might like reading it."

Hayden thumbed through the pages. "Thanks, mate. I will like it." He set the book on the counter behind him. "Where'd you get it?"

"My father sent it to me from New York."

"'ow's your father doin'?"

"Fine. He writes as often as he can and occasionally sends us a package, like this book." James nodded toward the book on the counter. Christian had left on a proselyting mission for the Church at the beginning of the new year, 1844. He'd been gone three months now and had already sent the family several letters about his work in New York City. James missed his company and the frequent talks he and his father shared together.

"'ow are things at school? 'ave you organized a team to play rounders?"

"Naw. It's not the same without you. You're our best player."

Hayden nodded, frankly accepting the fact of James' statement.

"Brother Bowers is as strict as ever," James said, trying to provide Hayden with a reason why he should be happy to be out of school. "Yesterday he walloped Benjamin Ivins across the knuckles with the yardstick because Ben was talking out of turn."

Hayden responded with a whistle. "Glad I'm not there. I was gettin' in trouble all the time for not bein' prepared with me studies."

"Are you keeping up on your studies at home?"

"Some. Me mum tries to teach me letters and sums, but she didn't 'ave much schoolin' 'erself back 'ome in Liverpool."

"Maybe I can bring you my school books to study on the weekends. That way, you can keep up with the class."

"That's a fine idea, mate, but I'm not sure when I'd get the time to read 'em. I'm 'ere at the shop every day but the Sabbath."

"I'll bring them by on Friday afternoons and pick them up on Sunday. That way, if you get any free time, you can glance through them."

Hayden nodded again, but he didn't look very enthusiastic about the arrangement.

A customer entered the shop and began to browse at the shoes on display. Hayden went over to help him. The man asked a few questions, but then left without placing an order for shoes or purchasing any of the shoes on display. Hayden returned to his seat beside James.

"Is business pretty good?" James asked hopefully.

"Yeh. It's been slow this afternoon, but usually we're quite busy. Father says 'e thinks we have more business now than when he first opened the shop and Thomas was 'elpin' 'im."

A mental picture of Hayden's older brother flashed across James' mind. Thomas' death had occurred over two years ago, but Hayden still spoke of his brother as if he'd just left for supper and would be back momentarily. James had recently received a clipping from a New York City newspaper that his father sent him describing the work of a Dr. John Sappington who was experimenting with quinine for the treatment of ague. Using quinine to cure the ague, or malaria, as Dr. Sappington termed it, was proving hugely successful. Quinine was a substance easily procured, and perhaps a dose of it might have saved Thomas Cox's life. But that wasn't something James wanted to bring up with Hayden.

James knew that his father had sent the article in part because he thought James would be interested in reading it, but also to encourage James' lagging interest in a career in medicine. James had never put into actual words for his father the real reason he'd abruptly discarded his interest in doctoring, but he guessed that Christian suspected the cause of it. Sending the newspaper clipping about Dr. Sappington's studies was his way of quietly prompting James to take up his interest in medicine.

What his father didn't know, however, was that James had been praying about that very thing. Along with his fervent pleas to gain a surer testimony of the gospel, James had been asking God about which direction he should take with his life. He would turn fifteen in the fall, old enough to be seriously contemplating the future course of his life, and making some decisions toward it. His discussions with Apostle Parley P. Pratt had initiated serious reflection on James' part. Elder Pratt had advised James to identify the talents and gifts with which Heavenly Father had blessed him. The recent near-tragedy with Roxana had stimulated that search for self-discovery. He was grateful for Roxana's recovery and realized that he'd derived satisfaction from taking part in nursing her back to health. He guessed that this was an answer of sorts to his prayers. Only yesterday he had made up his mind to send a letter of inquiry to the school of medicine located in Philadelphia. He wasn't completely committed to the idea of a future in medicine, but he'd decided that it would do no harm to investigate the possibilities.

James' thoughts returned to Hayden, and his friend's work at the boot shop. "You must be good at shoemaking to attract so much business, Hayden," he said. "Do you think you might take up the profession for yourself?"

Hayden pushed out his bottom lip as he pondered the idea. "Father wants me to, of course. But I 'ad me 'eart set on bein' a soldier."

"You can work as a shoemaker and join the Legion, too."

"I suppose so. What about you? Are you still wantin' to be a solider?"

"I never did enjoy pretending to be a soldier as much as you did," James smiled.

Hayden grinned back at him. "We 'ad a good time marchin' up and down the school yard, though, 'ey?"

"Do you still have that toy soldier you used to carry in your pocket all the time?" James asked, chuckling.

"Yeh. It's in me bureau drawer."

"Maybe that's where you should keep it," James said partly in jest. "Real soldiering is serious business. Have you been following in the papers what's happening in Texas?"

"The last I 'eard was that Mexican President Santa Ana will be startin' a war if America tries to grab the Republic of Texas," Hayden said.

James had picked up the habit from his father of scrutinizing the Nauvoo newspapers. In reading the columns of the news sheets, he'd gained a good understanding of what was happening in the country. He knew that President Tyler wanted to make Texas a state, and that former President Andrew Jackson supported the idea. But there were some in the government who opposed annexation.

"I wouldn't be afraid to fight those old Mexicans for control of Texas," Hayden went on. "I wish I'd been at the Alamo with Davy Crockett and James Bowie."

"Then you would have been dead," James said sensibly. "Those soldiers were braver than any I've ever heard about. But I guess bravery doesn't always equate with victory."

"You're forgettin' about what 'appened next. The Texas army boldly attacked Mexico's troops and captured Santa Ana," Hayden recounted, swinging his fists in the air. "Then they forced 'im to surrender 'is forces and acknowledge the independence of Texas. I would 'ave liked to 'ave been there for that!"

James chuckled at his friend's enthusiasm. "You're right. Those soldiers paved the way for Texas to become independent."

"Yeh. And it's not over yet. Brave soldiers will still make the difference when it comes time to stand up to Santa Ana again."

"I guess it will take brave soldiers and wise leaders working together to make it possible for Texas to be admitted to the Union."

"If the Prophet Joseph Smith wins the presidential election, 'e'll make it 'appen for Texas," said Hayden confidently.

James nodded in agreement. The campaign for the presidential election of 1844 was gaining momentum, and both Whigs and Democrats had been courting Mormon favor. Neither political party, however, had done anything to address the wrongs inflicted on the Saints. Consequently, Joseph Smith had allowed his name to be put forward as a candidate for the president of the United States. James had seen the pamphlet containing Joseph's platform, *Views on the Powers and Policy of the Government of the United States*. Joseph Smith's candidacy gave the Saints an opportunity to cast a vote for the rights and protection of all citizens regardless of their religious affiliations, and at the same time deliver them from the wrath of political leaders by aligning with neither political party.

"That wouldn't be the only good reason for the Prophet to win. If he were United States president, he would see to it that the Saints get treated fairly. And it would help to settle opposition here in Nauvoo," James said.

"I know. The apostates are stirrin' up all kinds of trouble for us. Father said that Dr. Bennett is still bent on discreditin' the Church and destroyin' the Prophet's reputation."

James winced at the mention of Bennett's name. He was familiar with the evil Bennett was perpetuating. Bennett had attacked the Church through newspaper articles and public speeches. He'd even published a book entitled *The History of the Saints; or an Exposé of Joe Smith and Mormonism*, in which he accused the Prophet and other Church leaders of immorality, secret murders, and designs to overthrow the government. He was still encouraging the Prophet's arrest on charges stemming from the attempted murder of former Missouri governor, Lilburn Boggs. And rumor had it that he was conspiring with Missourians for the Prophet's death.

A shiver slithered down James' spine as he recalled his own experiences with Bennett. The leaders of the Church were doing all they could to counteract Bennett's scandalous claims. The Prophet published an account of the events that led up to Bennett's fall, and he dispatched missionaries to correct the false perceptions. Brother Parley P. Pratt had told James in one of their conversations together that Bennett's motivation was to seek revenge on those who had exposed his evil doing.

"And it's not just Bennett who is causin' dissension," Hayden continued, lowering his voice. "Me father said that some of the Church leaders are callin' Brother Joseph a fallen prophet, and rejectin' 'is revelations. Father thinks some 'eads will roll at the conference next week."

The talk of apostasy among Church officials made James shiver. He'd worked hard to bolster his own testimony by spending countless hours on his knees in prayer and reading from the scriptures. He hadn't received a witness of the truth yet, but he continued to exercise faith and hold fast to gospel principles. The experiences that his father related from his mission helped to shore up James' faith, and his parents' unwavering devotion to the Prophet was a rod of iron on which he could grasp as well.

"Maybe we'll see one another at the conference," James said. "Perhaps we can sit together." He was anxious to leave the topic of betrayal, apostasy, and discordance behind.

"Right-o. And thanks for the book," Hayden added.

"I'll bring you the schoolbooks on Friday, like I promised," James said, getting up from his seat.

"Give Brother Bowers a big 'ug from me," Hayden joked.

"I'll do that."

James left the cobbler shop and hurried toward home. A cold wind was blowing from the river, driving icy needles of rain before it. He bent into the wind as it buffeted him relentlessly.

That night the wind increased in fury. Thunder and lightning cracked through the sky. The high winds and driving rain lashed the city throughout the night, and in the early morning hours a hailstorm descended, rattling the windowpanes on the Kades' new brick home on Durphey Street.

The General Conference of the Church lasted five days, from April fifth through the ninth. James and Hayden sat together for the Sunday afternoon session where the Prophet Joseph Smith delivered a discourse on the nature of God, the relationship of man to God, and a number of other topics. The Prophet concluded his remarks by saying that he held no enmity against any man, and that his voice was always for peace. "When I am called by the trump of the archangel and weighed in the balance," he said, "you will all know me then."

There had been thousands of Saints in attendance at the meeting, the largest gathering in Nauvoo that James had ever witnessed. Hayden's prediction that the alleged apostates would be exposed and censured by the Prophet did not come to pass. Joseph had said in his opening address on the first day of the conference that "those who feel desirous of sowing the seeds of discord will be disappointed on this occasion. It is our purpose to build up and establish the principles of righteousness, and not to break down and destroy." The conference had gone forward with an outpouring of the Spirit felt by every person assembled who was honest in heart. James had come away from the meeting with his testimony strengthened.

The weather warmed and cleared during the first weeks of April. James commenced work with one of the farmers in town, helping him to plow and seed his five-acre farm in wheat and barley. He would continue his labors throughout the spring and summer until the harvest was in. The wages that he earned he gave to his mother to help with the expenses of running the household. Money was in short supply with Christian away serving his mission; Lydia was trying to support her husband financially on his mission as well as provide for the family at home.

As he was returning home from an afternoon of plowing, he spied Elizabeth on the road. He fell in step with her. "How's your work going at the dress shop?" he asked her.

"We received three new orders for frocks just this week to fill."

"That's good."

"My employer says I have a good sense of style, and a knack for putting colors and fabrics together well," Elizabeth commented.

"I'm not surprised to hear that."

The two of them turned off of Mulholland Street onto Durphey Street where the road curved and sloped down toward the flats. "What about you?" asked Elizabeth. "How's the plowing coming along?"

"Slow. We're hoping the good weather will hold." James glanced up at the sky. He could see dark clouds scudding along the horizon.

"Mama wants me to go over to Montrose tomorrow after school to take some flower seeds to the Johanssens. Do you want to come with me?"

"I wish I could, but I promised to help with the plowing again tomorrow after school. I'd like to see Lars, though." *And Inger,* he thought impulsively. The memory of their Christmas Eve kiss brought a warmth to his cheeks.

"Lars is busy with work and school, I suppose, just as you are. Thank goodness this will be my last year in Bowers' classroom. I'm not going back in the fall."

"But you'll enroll in classes through the University of the City of Nauvoo, won't you?"

Elizabeth pulled a face. "No. Not if I have anything to say about it."

James was surprised to hear this. "But you know that Pa wants us to continue our education."

"Well, *Pa* is not here now, is he?" she said in a snide tone. "And I'm old enough to decide whether I'll attend school or not."

James kept silent. Risking a rebuttal would only increase Elizabeth's hostility. The two walked along for a time in silence.

"Are you going to continue school after you turn sixteen just because Christian wants you too?" Elizabeth asked.

The fact that she'd used the term "Christian" instead of "Father" irked James. He knew full well how she felt about their stepfather. She'd made no secret of it to him, though she'd kept her feelings hidden for the most part from both her parents. "Why do you continue to refer to Pa by his given name?" James asked irritably. He knew the answer, of course, but he couldn't stop himself from asking the question anyway.

"You know why. Christian isn't our real father. Why should I refer to him as if he were?"

James abruptly stopped in his tracks. He stood under the blossoming branches of an apple tree with his hands on his hips. The fruit trees were in full bloom, giving the city the appearance of a lush garden. "Elizabeth, you're a fool. Pa's tender care and love for us is no different from what he feels for Roxie, Milly, or Zachary. He has no preferences when it comes to his children."

Elizabeth paused, too, and turned to face James. "I agree with you, but that doesn't change the fact that he's not our real father. Or the fact that he's unbending in his opinions."

"What do you mean by that?" James asked in surprise.

"You know as well as I do that he won't countenance any opinion that goes against his own."

"That's got to be the craziest thing I've ever heard you say. Pa's always been encouraging and supportive of us in anything we wish to accomplish."

Elizabeth wagged her finger in front of James' nose. "So long as it coincided with his beliefs."

"That's ridiculous," James countered. "Are you and I talking about the same man?"

"And besides," Elizabeth said, backing off from her position under the heat of James' angry glare. "He's taken over our natural father's place in the family."

"Our natural father is dead, Elizabeth. That's all there is to it."

"That's not all there is," she protested. "Mama should retain some loyalty and affection for her first husband. Who, by the way, is also the father of two of her children. I think it's appalling how she never speaks of him, or carries his memory in her heart."

James was annoyed and perplexed by his sister's ranting. "How do you know that she doesn't keep his memory in her heart? Has she told you so?"

"Not in words, exactly," Elizabeth hedged. "But I can tell. She's let Christian sway her. She does everything he says."

"Such as?" James challenged her.

"Such as everything. Including her activity in the Church," she added sullenly.

James clearly understood Elizabeth's reference. Nine days after the conclusion of the General Conference, William and Wilson Law, along with three others, were cut off from the Church for apostasy, and their names published in the Church newspaper, the *Times and Seasons.* The apostasy of the second counselor in the First Presidency, and his brother, the major general in the Nauvoo Legion, had come as a shock to many of the Saints in Nauvoo, and caused tension and unrest. Since their excommunication from the Church, the Law brothers had done everything they could to destroy the Prophet's reputation.

"Are you suggesting that Ma is remaining faithful to the gospel only because Pa wants her to?" James said, glaring at his sister. "Has it ever occurred to you that Ma's desires coincide with Pa's and aren't dictated by him? Come on, Elizabeth, you're completely off the mark with all of this."

James shook his head in frustration as he started off again along the road. With a huffy sigh, Elizabeth reluctantly followed after him.

CHAPTER TWENTY-ONE

During the night a thunderstorm swept in bringing with it a downpour of rain. The storm pounced on the city like a jungle cat, keeping Elizabeth awake with its roars of thunder and its claws making scratches of lightning across the sky. Heavy rain continued all the next day. The small creeks overflowed their banks and rushing water swept away fences and inundated farmland. Because of the foul weather, Elizabeth was unable to make the trip into Montrose to visit the Johanssens. She stayed indoors, watching the rain stream down the windows in rivulets. It was the wettest April that Elizabeth could remember, and the gloomiest.

To seek respite from the dreary weather, in early May Elizabeth accompanied her mother and younger sisters to a dramatic performance held at the newly built Masonic

Hall. The Masonic Hall, or Cultural Hall, was one of the most handsome buildings in all Nauvoo. Constructed on the corner of Main and White Streets, it stretched three stories high and was designed in the elegant Federalist style. For Elizabeth, it represented the beauty and prosperity of the growing city.

Elizabeth was sorry she couldn't wear her cameo necklace to the play; she'd been keeping it hidden in a corner of her bureau drawer so her mother wouldn't see it and ask her where she got it. If Lydia had known that it was Alexander who gave her the exquisite piece of jewelry, she would have required Elizabeth to return it to him. So the necklace remained out of sight, except for when Elizabeth secretly took it from the drawer to try it on.

There were two plays being performed that evening at the Cultural Hall, "Damon and Pythias" and "The Idiot Witness." Elizabeth enjoyed them both. The Prophet Joseph Smith and his wife attended the same performance, and afterward Lydia spoke with Emma Smith for a few moments while Elizabeth and her sisters waited. Elizabeth overheard some men talking with Brother Joseph, encouraging him in his bid for the United States President in the upcoming election. Elizabeth hadn't paid much attention to the political rhetoric making its way into print and over the pulpit other than to briefly touch on it in her letters to Alexander.

On the tenth of May, a prospectus for a new newspaper, to be called the *Nauvoo Expositor,* made its appearance in the city. The prospectus was published and distributed by the group of apostates who had recently been cut off from the Church, and its purpose was to promote the ruin of the Prophet Joseph Smith and other Church leaders, and to discredit the Church. Elizabeth barely gave the news sheet a glance when James brought home a copy of it. Her brother was indignant over the fact that such a spurious newspaper should be printed and have a place in Nauvoo. It was bad enough, he said, that the Saints had to put up with Thomas Sharp's vicious rhetoric in the *Warsaw Signal.*

It was the latter part of May before Elizabeth was able to visit the Johanssens. She delivered the flower seeds and basket of food Lydia had prepared, and returned to Nauvoo the same afternoon. As she exited the ferry and started up the road, she saw a group of forty or so Indians gathered in the yard of the Prophet's home. From their appearance, she guessed they were from the Sauk and Fox tribe. Indians rarely made an appearance in Nauvoo. Following the Black Hawk War, the last of the Sauk and Fox had been forced off their lands in Illinois to settle on a small reservation in Iowa. Occasionally, a small band of Indians returned to the area to trade or conduct pow wows with white settlers.

Elizabeth paused under the shade of a plum tree not far from the Mansion House to watch the Indians. All of them were men, and four or five were mounted on horseback outside the front gate. They were dressed in leather breeches, moccasins, and skin shirts. A few hugged colorful blankets around their shoulders. The old men wore their hair straight and hanging over their shoulders, or in braids. Most of the young men's heads were shorn except for the tall, stiff strip of hair at the center of their heads.

Elizabeth overheard a passerby, who with his companion was also staring at the Indians, say that one of them was Black Hawk's brother, Kis-kish-kee.

Elizabeth's interest in the Indians heightened with this bit of information. She edged closer to the house, scrutinizing their faces to see if she could determine which of the older men might be the chief's brother. As she was trying to get a clear view of one of the men a younger brave stepped into view, gesturing and talking in a loud voice. Elizabeth's gaze was immediately drawn to the young man. He was tall and lithe, and his muscular shoulders stood out prominently under his fringed leather shirt. As she studied the broad, bronze face with its narrow nose and deeply set eyes, she had the impression that he looked faintly familiar. Both sides of his head were shaven and the center hair bristled up stiff and tall, snaking in one long black braid down his back. When he turned slightly, she saw that the braid was decorated with a single yellow feather.

Elizabeth gasped out loud. The two men who had been walking by and talking between themselves glanced back at her. She lowered her eyes to avoid their curious gaze. After they'd passed on their way, she glanced up again at the young Indian who was still speaking shrilly in a strident tone. She felt a ripple of excitement shoot through her. If this Indian actually was Yellow Feather, the young brave she'd encountered at the Johanssens' place two years earlier, then she wanted to get a closer look at him.

She inched her way up the road until she was only a few yards from the fence surrounding the yard of the Mansion

House. She could see now that the Indians were conversing with Brother Joseph, who was explaining something in response to the young Indian's outburst. Elizabeth studied the young brave more closely. He sported a cluster of dangling, beaded earrings fastened in the top of each ear, a heavy necklace of colorful beads, and a beaded belt. This Indian looked older, and more hardened in the face than she remembered Yellow Feather to be, but the facial features were the same. Elizabeth drew a shaky breath. She felt sure this was Yellow Feather, talking boldly with the Prophet.

She strained to hear the conversation the two were having together, trying not to appear as though she were eavesdropping. People were pausing in the street to stare at the Indians. Elizabeth noticed one young mother hurry her small children down the plank walk, and glance nervously over her shoulder at the Indians gathered in the yard of the Mansion House.

Elizabeth returned her attention to the young man she assumed was Yellow Feather. He was speaking in broken English to the Prophet and Elizabeth could make out some of the words.

"When our fathers came to this land, there were no white men to trespass the sacred ground the Great Spirit had given us. Then came the Spanish, and then the French. After that, the English and Americans. Now there are no red men left, only white." Yellow Feather's voice was rising and he gestured sharply with one hand. "We have been robbed of our lands by the whites, and the Great Spirit is angry."

Elizabeth stepped a pace closer to hear the Prophet's reply. He told Yellow Feather and the others with him that he knew their people had been wronged, but that they should cultivate peace among the whites and among each other, and that the Great Spirit wanted them to live in peace.

Yellow Feather protested, as did many of the other young men assembled around the Prophet, but Brother Joseph calmed them with soothing words, calling them his red brethren and friends. Elizabeth heard the Prophet tell them about a book that the Great Spirit had enabled him to uncover, a book which told about their forefathers. The book would do both the red man and the pale face good, he said.

Mesmerized by the scene taking place before her, Elizabeth barely noticed the other passersby who were gathering to listen to the Prophet's exchange with the Indians. Elizabeth heard the Prophet go on to explain how many hundreds of moons ago when the red men's ancestors lived in peace upon the land, the Great Spirit spoke with them, and gave much knowledge to their wise men. They wrote these words in a book made of plates of gold, along with their history, and this book was kept for many generations. The red men had peace one with another. They had much corn and many buildings, and were content.

Elizabeth found herself edging closer to the fenced yard, not wanting to miss a single word that fell from the Prophet's lips as he conversed with the Indians. She listened closely as he went on to tell them how their forefathers became wicked, killing one another, and destroying their great cities. The Great Spirit was angry with them and would speak no more to their warriors and medicine men. The Great Spirit told their wise men, Mormon and Moroni, to seal the book in the earth so that it would be kept safe until it would be revealed to the pale faces who would inhabit the land. Now this book is made known again to the red men, to help them regain the favor of the Great Spirit. And if the red men will obey the words in this book, written by their forefathers, they will again become a proud and peaceful nation.

The Prophet then went into his house and returned a moment later with a copy of the Book of Mormon. He walked past Yellow Feather and through the group of Indians who parted to make way for him, opened the gate of the fence, and offered the book to an elderly Indian sitting astride his horse on the road just outside the fence. The old man, and the few others mounted on horses beside him, had been listening so quietly through Joseph's whole explanation that Elizabeth had nearly forgotten they were there. She watched the elderly Indian eye the book without any change in expression. Then he slowly dismounted, stood before the Prophet, and took the proffered book from his hand.

Though the old man's face was wrinkled from many seasons of sun and snow, his dark eyes were proud and unflinching. His appearance in dress was no different from any of the other Indians gathered there. He wore a red blanket about his shoulders and feathers in his gray hair at the crown of his head, but because of the deference Joseph paid to him, Elizabeth knew this must be Black Hawk's brother, Kis-kish-kee. She watched him as he placed one hand on the cover of the book. Then she heard him speak.

"We feel thankful to our white friend for telling us this news concerning the book of our forefathers; it makes us glad in here." The old Indian pointed to his heart. "Our wigwams are poor, but we will build a council house and meet together and you shall read to us and teach us more concerning the book of our fathers and the will of the Great Spirit."

Joseph replied that he would. The Prophet stood outside the gate as the Indians filed out of his yard and started down the road toward the river. The group passed directly in front of the spot where Elizabeth stood watching. She saw Yellow Feather approach, his face set in a scowl, and made a decision on the spur of the moment. In a voice barely above a whisper, she called out his name.

For an instant he kept walking, his head lowered and his brows set like steel. Then he paused suddenly, with his back still toward her.

"Yellow Feather," she said again more loudly.

The Indian whirled around and his black eyes swiftly found Elizabeth. Now that she had his attention, she had no idea what to say to him. She backed up against the trunk of a tree and pressed herself against it. The Indian suddenly began to stride toward her and reached her in a few quick steps, and glared at her. There was no light of recognition in his dark, stormy eyes.

"Hello," Elizabeth sputtered. "Do you remember me? I'm a friend of Inger Johanssen, from Montrose." She nodded toward the river, her body rigid against the comparative safety of the tree.

For an instant, Yellow Feather's stern gaze faltered. Then he scowled fiercely.

Elizabeth was wearing a broad-brimmed bonnet which hid most of her hair. With shaking fingers, she reached up and tugged on one blonde curl that was peeping out from underneath the bottom of her bonnet. Yellow Feather watched her without any change of expression. If Elizabeth herself had changed as much as Yellow Feather had over the intervening years, she doubted he would recognize her.

He stared at her an instant longer, and then the lines in his forehead smoothed. "Yellow hair," he grunted. His mouth formed into a smirk and he gave a short, harsh laugh. "Yellow hair with the shrieking voice."

"Well, I'm not afraid of you today," Elizabeth retorted. Where she summoned the courage to say such a thing to an Indian, she had no idea.

Yellow Feather's insolent grin dissolved into the semblance of a friendly smile. He suddenly looked like a shy teenager.

"What are you and your people doing here in Nauvoo?" Elizabeth asked. She couldn't think of anything else to say to him.

"We came to speak with your wise man."

"The Prophet?"

He gave her a quick, short nod. "He gave wise counsel to the red man," he said.

"Yes. I overheard some of his conversation."

A light flickered in the depths of Yellow Feather's eyes. "Have you read the book concerning our fathers?" he asked.

"Yes. Some of it."

"Do you have this book? You give it to Yellow Feather. I read it."

Elizabeth shook her head regrettably. "The only one I have belongs to my family."

Yellow Feather glanced down the road where the other members of his tribe were retreating. Then his eyes came to rest again on Elizabeth. "You believe the words written in this book?"

Elizabeth hesitated. She could see that the Indian was sincere in his question. She wanted to tell him that she did believe it, every word. But she wasn't convinced herself that the book came from God for she had never taken the opportunity to pray and inquire about it.

"Your eyes betray you," Yellow Feather said sharply. "It is not a book brought forth by the power of the Great Spirit."

Though his expression was stern, Elizabeth could read the disappointment in his eyes. He turned abruptly away without a parting word and started down the road to join the other members of his tribe.

"Yellow Feather, wait!" Elizabeth cried out.

The Indian didn't pause or turn back around. He kept walking with a swift pace and his head held high.

Instead of leaving the city immediately, the Indians gathered by the river not far from Joseph Smith's former log home and began a ceremonial dance. The beating of drums and the chanting of voices floated over the waters of the Mississippi. The dance drew a number of spectators. Elizabeth watched the dancing for awhile, regretting her response to Yellow Feather's question about the Book of Mormon. It occurred to her that she'd lost an opportunity to share the gospel because she was not prepared herself to bear testimony of its truthfulness. Perhaps Yellow Feather would never again have a chance to hear about the Book of Mormon, and an encouraging word from her might have helped to plant the gospel seed in his heart.

When some kind citizens of Nauvoo approached her about taking up a collection of food and clothing for the Indians, she hurried home to gather some of her own things to give. But the contribution of clothing did little to salve her conscience.

Elizabeth tapped her pencil against the paper as she considered what to write in her letter to Alexander. He'd left Nauvoo in February of the new year of 1844, more than three months ago, to return to Wisconsin. He had written Elizabeth numerous letters since then, expressing his affection for her. In his last letter he'd written of his efforts to persuade his father to construct a lumber mill in Nauvoo; Alexander liked Nauvoo and felt the business would prosper there. Elizabeth hoped he could obtain his father's financial and personal endorsement for such a project because it meant Alexander would return to Nauvoo permanently to operate the mill.

She got up to close the window. It was starting to rain again. It had been a wet spring and was still chilly even though it was now the first week in June. She sat down and began writing. She didn't mention anything about the tensions that seemed to be escalating in Nauvoo; instead she told Alexander of her desires to be with him and her eager anticipation of his return to the city. She deliberately omitted, as well, the fact that her mother's feelings concerning Alexander had not softened.

As she was writing, she heard James enter the house. The sound of his heavy boots crossing the wood floor told Elizabeth he was headed for the parlor where their mother sat sewing in her rockingchair. She hurriedly finished her letter to Alexander, slipped it into an envelope, and sealed it.

When Elizabeth came downstairs a few minutes later, she found her mother and James seated in the parlor with a copy of the *Nauvoo Expositor* between them. James had brought home the first edition of the newspaper, edited by the Law brothers and their apostate associates, under the date of June seventh, 1844, to show to Lydia.

"I'm surprised at the viciousness of these men," Lydia said, shaking her head.

"What did you expect, Ma?" replied James heatedly. "These men will stoop to any level to discredit the Church and the Prophet."

"To print something as slanderous and offensive as this is inexcusable," Lydia said as she scanned the columns of the paper.

Elizabeth bent over her mother's shoulder to get a look at the newspaper, her eyes darting across the words printed on the open page.

"It's nothing but pure libel," James fumed. "The mayor should send a unit of militiamen to close the printing office. I saw the Legion shut down a tavern in town because it was a public nuisance — the same should be done with that newspaper office. Get rid of both the press and office. That would put an end to the rubbish being printed there."

Elizabeth straightened. "I don't know why we have to do anything. Let the scoundrels say what they want about us. What harm can they do?"

"The citizens of Hancock and the surrounding counties are already prejudiced against us," James said sharply to her. "All they need is for the battle cry to be sounded, and they'll fall on us like thieves in a treasure house. The *Expositor* is just the trump they are awaiting."

Elizabeth felt a shiver crawl across her skin. James' words stirred up a cold dread inside her. She glanced at the newspaper, wishing he'd never brought it home.

"James is right. There's no measuring the harm done by scurrilous words, both written and spoken," Lydia was saying. "Not only has the *Expositor* caused problems in that respect, but it may also prove to be a weapon of another sort in the hands of our enemies. They'd like nothing better than to provoke us into acting hastily. If we take unwise or unlawful action, they'll surely use it as a pretext for retaliation against us."

Elizabeth didn't fully understand all the ramifications with regard to the appearance of the *Expositor*, but she sensed a confrontation was coming. And she feared being swept into the swirling maelstrom.

CHAPTER TWENTY-TWO

Nauvoo was a city in mourning. There was a hush about the streets and the unfinished temple on the hill stood silent and forlorn. In the darkness of his room James lay upon his bed, his eyes closed against the thin stream of moonlight coming in through the glass-paned window. Even bright sunlight could not have dispelled the gloom and despair from his soul. Tears squeezed out beneath his closed lids and trickled down his cheeks. He made no effort to wipe them away. The sorrow he felt could not be so easily assuaged.

In his mind he went over again for the hundredth time the details he had both heard and seen that day, details of the awful scene which culminated in the murders of the Prophet Joseph Smith and his beloved brother, Hyrum. They had fallen to a mob so saturated with hatred and jealousy that nothing short of the brothers' innocent blood would satisfy them. A tremor passed over James' body, and his forehead broke out in perspiration. He covered his eyes with his hands and moaned. He couldn't stop the terrible chain of thoughts that echoed through his mind — the steps which had led to the Prophet's martyrdom.

The tragic epilogue had been put in motion with the appearance of the *Nauvoo Expositor* three weeks before. Declaring the newspaper a public nuisance, the city council ordered the *Expositor* press destroyed as well as all the publications issuing from it. After the order had been carried out, the retaliation from the Church's enemies was swift. The publishers of the paper obtained an arrest warrant against the mayor, Joseph Smith, and members of the city council on a charge of riot. Anti-Mormon newspapers in Hancock County urged immediate retribution; protest meetings sprang up at Warsaw and Carthage. Mob violence threatened. Joseph Smith mobilized the Nauvoo Legion and put the city under martial law. After negotiations with Governor Ford, the Prophet and members of the city council went to Carthage to appear before a justice of the peace. The city council members were bound over on bail to appear at the next term of the circuit court and released, but Joseph and Hyrum were detained and committed to the Carthage jail.

James turned over onto his side, staring into the darkness. The events that happened next he'd heard from the lips of Brother Willard Richards, who addressed the people of Nauvoo that afternoon. Brother Richards, who was at the jail with the Prophet and Hyrum, recounted how a mob with blackened faces stormed the prison. Shots were exchanged. Some of the mob rushed up the stairway to the second floor where the prisoners were held, while others remained outside the building firing their weapons through the windows. Hyrum was the first to fall. Struck by a ball in the face and one in the back, he died almost instantly. Joseph, along with his comrades John Taylor and Willard Richards, fought off the attack as best they could. As he tried to leap through the window, Joseph was shot and killed.

With his own ears, James had heard the rumble of wheels on the dirt road as two wagons carrying the bodies of the slain leaders wound their way into Nauvoo. A hush fell upon the crowd thronging the streets as the wagons approached, and then the anguished moaning and weeping of the Saints rent the air as the wagons lumbered past toward their destination at the Mansion House. James had caught a glimpse of each still figure in the wagon bed, shielded with branches to protect the body from the hot sun.

As James recalled the image of the two wagons, his chest tightened until he could scarcely draw a breath. Joseph and Hyrum had been cut down by assassins, murdered in cold blood. Never again would he hear the Prophet address the Saints in powerful testimony, or come to their aid with words of comfort and encouragement. A cheerful word, a kindly act, a blessing called down from heaven — all was stilled now.

The Church leaders in Nauvoo were urging the Saints to remain calm and leave vengeance to God. On the morrow, the bodies of the slain brothers would lay in state at the Mansion House. James, along with thousands of other mourning Saints, would file past the caskets to pay his final respects and take a last look at his beloved leaders.

James rose from his bed, shaking himself in an attempt to dispel the ugly visions from his head. The night air was muggy and close. James went to the window, opened it, and leaned out. There was not a breath of cool air to soothe his tired body. The promise of another hot June day was already on the whisper of the breeze. James returned to his bed and tried to sleep, but sleep eluded him. Later, in the night, he heard muffled sobs from the bedroom across the hall, and knew his mother was crying.

At the time of the Prophet's martyrdom, all of the Twelve Apostles except for Willard Richards and John Taylor were away from Nauvoo serving missions. Both Brothers Richards and Taylor had been at Carthage when Joseph and Hyrum were murdered, and Brother Taylor had sustained serious injuries in the attack, which kept him bedfast for more than a month afterward. Until the rest of the Twelve returned, Brother William W. Phelps and other local leaders helped to comfort the Saints and direct the work of the Church. Brother Phelps had been the main speaker at the funeral services for Joseph and Hyrum. After the funeral, the caskets had been buried in the Nauvoo Cemetery. Brother Phelps labored to maintain peace and calm in the stricken city, and discourage the Saints from seeking reprisal against the murderers of Joseph and Hyrum.

Apostle Parley P. Pratt was the first of the Twelve to return to the city. Later, James had an opportunity to talk with Brother Pratt about his feelings concerning the Prophet. Brother Pratt related to James how he had been prompted by the Spirit to cut short his stay in New York and start for Nauvoo. On the day of the martyrdom, without being aware of what had transpired at Carthage, he suddenly felt overwhelmed with sorrow. He was so burdened with grief, he told James, that he could scarcely speak. He'd remarked to his brother, who was traveling with him aboard a canal boat, that this was a dark day and the hour of triumph for the powers of darkness. He went on to tell James of his love for the Prophet and how he had associated with Joseph in public and in private, in travels and at home, in joy and sorrow, and in adversities of every kind — and he knew Brother Joseph to be an honorable, virtuous man and a prophet of God. James had been profoundly affected by the Apostle's words for the Spirit had borne witness to him of their truthfulness. His testimony of Joseph Smith's role as a prophet was strengthened, along with his conviction of the divine restoration of the gospel. That testimony was like a beam of light in a dark tunnel of gloom.

Shortly before the martyrdom, Joseph had sent out a call to the Apostles who were serving missions to return immediately to Nauvoo, and likewise to all the traveling elders. Christian arrived home from his mission grief-stricken over the Prophet's death. His presence, however, was a strength to James who felt a measure of peace return to their home with Christian there to assume leadership of the family once more.

James looked to his father for guidance and example during the difficult weeks and months that followed the Prophet's death. In addition to the Saints' grief over the loss of their leaders, there arose the troubling question of who should succeed Joseph as president and prophet of the Church. Sidney Rigdon, as a member of the First Presidency, suggested that he act as a guardian for the Church until God called a new prophet. But Brigham Young taught a different principle. He stated that upon the President's death, the First Presidency was dissolved and the governing power of the Church rested with the Quorum of the Twelve Apostles until a new Presidency should be called through revelation and the sustaining vote of the Saints.

James and his father attended a meeting held in the West Grove on August eighth at which the question of succession was addressed. Brigham Young was the speaker for the afternoon meeting, Sidney Rigdon having already pressed his claims for leadership of the Church at the morning session. As Brigham Young spoke about the nature of Church government, and the keys of the kingdom resting with the Twelve Apostles, James was astonished to see a subtle change come over the Apostle's countenance. Brother Young seemed to take on the appearance of the

Prophet Joseph Smith. His face assumed the form of Joseph's, and his voice was Joseph's. James stared in wonder and awe as he beheld this miraculous manifestation. When he felt a stir of astonishment ripple through the crowd, James realized that many others in the congregation witnessed the transformation of Brother Young as well. As he left the Grove that afternoon, James carried with him a confirmation of the truthfulness of the gospel restored by Joseph Smith, together with an affirmation from Heaven testifying that Brigham Young and the Twelve were the rightful ones to lead the Church.

By the time fall arrived, James was striving to put aside his grief and help build up and beautify the city of Nauvoo. The Saints were engaged in every facet of industry. Commerce increased, and manufacture and trade flourished. Homes and public buildings were erected, among them the new two-story Seventies Hall. Work on the temple was accelerated in a push to bring it to completion. The walls were built to the level of the second story and the stones set in place, including some of the decorative sun stones. Before his mission, James' father had donated his time in labor tithing, working one day in ten on the temple. Now, he like many others, put in two or more days in ten on the edifice. James spent part of his after school hours working on a neighbor's farm outside the city, and the rest laboring with his father and the other men in building the temple.

Although James enjoyed the work he was doing, his desire was to pursue a study of medicine. He'd received a reply from the school of medicine in Philadelphia in response to his letter of inquiry, and was eager to accept the school's invitation for enrollment in the future. He'd prayed earnestly about this decision and felt like he'd received an answer. Since settling on this course, he felt more at peace than he had in a long while.

Elizabeth, however, was not attending school and had no desire to further her studies through university classes. She was content to work at the dress shop five days a week. She'd recently turned seventeen and was more preoccupied with fashion and society than with pursuing an education.

The allure of wealth and fashionable society had been making front-page news lately in the nation's newspapers. During the summer, United States President John Tyler had married a young woman by the name of Julia Gardiner. The Eastern papers had reported every pre-nuptial party, ball, and formal dinner in rich detail. Even after the marriage, the many social engagements in which the couple participated continued to draw widespread attention. Elizabeth was fascinated by the glitter and glamour that accompanied the couple's every move.

Along with the coverage of the President and his lady, there continued to be news of the 1844 presidential campaign. Since Joseph Smith's death, the Saints' enthusiasm for the coming election had flagged. The former Congressman, James K. Polk, with his "54-40 or Fight" campaign slogan seemed favored to win over the Whig candidate Senator

Henry Clay. Polk's platform included a pledge to secure a treaty with Britain setting Oregon's northern boundary. Polk's popularity seemed to be reflecting the nation's appetite for broadening its borders. Polk advocated not only the procurement of the British-controlled Oregon Country, but also the acquisition of Spanish California, and the annexation of Texas.

The cool October breeze felt good on James' face as he left the blacksmith shop where he had dropped off an order for his father for a new wagon wheel. Before going home, he wanted to stop at the city library, newly housed on the second floor of the Seventies Hall, to see if the library was open to patrons yet. In order to reach the library, however, he had to first pass near Alexander Scott's lumber mill. James frowned as he considered that thought. Alexander had recently returned to Nauvoo and established a thriving business with his mill. He was ingratiating himself with the wealthier, more influential non-Mormons in the area. Although Alexander was civil to James whenever the two chanced to meet, there was a mutual undertone of dislike between them. James knew that his older sister and Alexander were keeping company despite Lydia's strong objections. On that score, James couldn't agree more with his mother.

The desire to visit the library overrode his distaste for a possible encounter with Alexander. He hurried ahead, anxious to arrive at his destination. As he approached the lumber mill, he saw Alexander in the yard conducting business with some customers. James hoped he could slip past without Alexander noticing him, but his heart sank when he heard the other man call out.

"James, come here a minute, will you? I'd like you to settle a difference of opinion between these gentlemen and myself."

James pushed a nervous hand through his hair and started toward Alexander. Alexander's hands were shoved inside the pockets of his trousers, and his shirt was open at the throat. He grinned laconically as James approached.

"How fortunate for us, gentlemen, that Mr. Kade has come by. I suggest we let him decide the matter. I know the Kades to be honest in word and deed."

James suspected that Alexander was mocking him, but it was too late to back out of the situation now. The others, whom James recognized but knew only slightly, were smirking as well. All of the men were five or six years older than himself. "I'm in a hurry, Alexander. What is it?" James asked, mustering a confident tone.

"This won't take but a minute of your time, James. Mr. McCullough, here, says he found this five-dollar piece in the stream bed on my property."

The man referred to as McCullough opened his fist a few inches from James' nose. Sitting in his palm was a shiny, gold coin.

"I say the money belongs to me because it was found on my ground," continued Alexander, "but Mr. McCullough disagrees. He believes the coin should be his since he's the one who found it. What do you think, James?"

James stared at the coin gleaming in McCullough's hand. He wasn't sure if Alexander really wanted his opinion, or if the older man was toying with him. He hesitated, trying to size up the situation. "Where did you say Mr. McCullough found the money?" he asked.

"Right over here," Alexander replied, taking James by the arm and escorting him toward the stream. Alexander stood on the bank of the stream and pointed at the sluggish water. "There. Take a look for yourself, James."

As James leaned forward to see the spot Alexander indicated, someone from behind gave him a hard shove sending him toppling into the stream. The water was icy cold and James gasped and sputtered as he struggled to catch his breath. Alexander and the other men on shore burst into laughter. James scrambled to his feet, the water running off his clothes and dripping down his face.

James was incensed. He started slogging toward the bank when one foot slid against a slippery rock in the stream bed and he fell backward with a loud splash. Alexander and the others howled with laughter. When James finally managed to gain his footing, Alexander extended a hand and helped him out of the stream. James glared at him.

"Don't be sore, James," Alexander said, with a grin twitching on his face. "We were just having a little fun with you. No hard feelings?"

James brushed past him without a word, the water dripping off his clothes and leaving little spatters of mud puddles on the ground. He heard the men hooting as he stomped down the road. One of them called out after him.

"What's the matter? Can't you Mormon boys take a little joke?"

James was more angry with himself than he was with Alexander. He felt humiliated for allowing himself to be made into a fool. All thought of going to the city library was abandoned now. He slowed his pace as he tried to wring the water from his clothing. The air was brisk and soon his teeth were chattering with cold. When he reached the house, he slipped in the side door, embarrassed to have anyone see him.

That evening, James confided to his father what had happened. "Maybe I took offense too easily, Pa," James explained. "I guess Alexander and the others were just enjoying a joke at my expense."

Christian pursed his lips. "No, I don't believe so. I think Alexander's prank is indicative of the feeling that abounds among non-Mormons."

"But they haven't any reason to be angry with us. They've already accomplished their evil ends by murdering Joseph and Hyrum."

"Even the Prophet's blood isn't enough to satisfy our enemies. No, James, the people are provoked with us because of our beliefs, and envious of our prosperity. They can see the Church continues to prosper despite the Prophet's death, and that enrages them."

"Why can't they just leave us alone?" James muttered.

"Because evil always does, and always will, strive against righteousness — until the Lord comes to personally reign over his Saints and send evil and darkness fleeing before Him."

James felt comforted by his father's words. He reached over and gave him a hug. "I love you, Pa."

"I love you, too, son." Christian rose from his chair. "You're a good boy, James. How old are you now?" he asked with a smile.

"Fifteen," James answered, drawing himself up to his full height.

"Fifteen. Not much older than the Prophet Joseph was when he prayed in the grove and saw the Father and the Son."

"Yes, Pa."

"Always remember Brother Joseph, son. Remember the things he taught and the example he was to the Saints."

"Yes, Pa, I will."

"I'm proud of you, James. You've grown into a fine man. Now, let's go downstairs to supper before your mother clears away the dishes and we get nothing to eat."

James strode along the street with his hands in his pockets. Hidden from sight was the antler-handled pocketknife he carried and a short piece of wood. James was part of Nauvoo's "whistling and whittling brigade," an organized group of young men and boys whose task was to harass any stranger who behaved suspiciously by following him around town whistling, and whittling at a piece of wood, until the stranger felt intimidated and left the city.

James was proud to be a part of the city's effort to protect her citizens. In January of the new year, 1845, Nauvoo's city charter had been revoked through the triumphant efforts of the Saints' enemies. This meant that the City of Joseph — as it was now called in honor of the slain Prophet — was without a system of city government or the protection of a militia. With the disbandment of the Nauvoo Legion, the city was nearly defenseless against mob attack and other crimes.

James walked along the dirt road in the twilight, his eyes alert for any sign of disturbance. The past summer had been a troubled one for the Saints. The presence of lawless elements in the city had drawn fire from the Church's enemies, subjecting the Saints to renewed attacks from the press. County newspapers, under the leadership of the vituperative Thomas Sharp, were again voicing their opposition to the Mormons. At a meeting of Quincy citizens on the twenty-second of September, 1845, a formal request had been made for the Saints to leave Illinois.

James let out his breath slowly, watching it turn to vapor in the cool October air. He pushed his hands deeper into his pockets until his knuckles wedged against the cold steel of the pocketknife. He thought about his family and his friends in Nauvoo. Most of them had accepted with stalwart courage the Apostles' call to prepare to leave the city for a destination in the West. A few of the members, of course, lost faith and fell away from the Church under the burden of this newest trial. But James' parents had heeded the counsel of Brigham Young and were endeavoring to sell their home and property and leave with the body of the Saints as soon as spring came. In preparation for the move, wagon shops sprang up all over the city. The burring of saws and the thwack of hammers echoed from every corner of the City of Joseph as craftsmen turned all their efforts toward wagon building. Nearly every member was engaged in securing articles needed for the trek west.

In the midst of all these preparations, work went forward at an accelerated pace on the temple. The edifice was nearly finished now. The capstone had been laid on the twenty-fourth of May amid much rejoicing, and the finishing work on the interior was quickly coming to completion. James had attended the October conference held in the temple. It was a spiritual occasion where counsel was given with regard to the Saints' removal from Illinois.

As James walked along the quiet street, he pondered the things he'd heard at the conference in the temple. He'd been especially impressed with a sermon given by Parley Pratt. Brother Pratt had posed the question: why is it that we have been at all this outlay and expense, and then are called to leave it? Because, he explained in answer, the people of God have always been required to make sacrifices, and if we have a sacrifice to make, it should be worthy of a godly people. "The Lord designs to lead us to a wider field of action, where there will be more room for the Saints to grow and increase, and where there will be no one to say we crowd them, and where we can enjoy the pure principles of liberty and equal rights," Brother Pratt had pronounced.

The words moved James as he recalled them to mind. They were stirring, prophetic words. James felt eager to take up the march with his fellow Saints to a place in the West where they would be free to enjoy the liberties and bounties of life, unmolested by mobocracy. But the sacrifices Brother Pratt had spoken about were, indeed, difficult ones. James squinted in concentrated thought as he trudged along the road. The people were sacrificing not only the comfort of their homes, but also all their labors in building up the city. James, himself, had spent many long hours cultivating the ground, erecting homes and public buildings, and investing his hopes and dreams in the future of Nauvoo.

Then, too, moving away to the West would of necessity cancel his plans to attend medical college. His disappointment on this point was keen. Christian had suggested he stay behind to attend the school in Philadelphia as planned, but James wouldn't consider it. The family needed his help on the long trail west; but more importantly, Brigham Young and the Twelve had counseled the Saints to move. James firmly believed Young was a prophet of God, and that settled any question of his remaining behind. James was of the opinion that a man who is not willing to sacrifice his all for the Lord is not worthy to be numbered among His people. So he would swallow his disappointment about attending medical school, and trust to the Lord to provide the way and means for him to accomplish his dreams.

James reached the door to his family's two-story brick home. Although it was getting late, lights still burned in the parlor and in the upstairs bedrooms. His sisters were probably in their room, finishing up their studies for the night, he thought. And four-year-old Zachary would be getting ready for bed.

James let himself inside the house.

"Is that you, son?" his mother called from the parlor.

"Yes, Ma. I'm home." He walked into the lighted room where Lydia was sitting beside the lamp, darning holes in a pair of socks. James put an arm around his mother's shoulders.

"How was your evening," she asked. "Uneventful, I hope."

"Yes, it was. The boys and I just strolled about town a bit. All seems quiet."

"That's good. We can use some peace and quiet."

James took a seat on the chair opposite his mother. He watched her in silence for a moment as she worked. A clump of stockings lay in a basket at her feet, waiting for the needle's attention. He picked up a copy of a newspaper his father had left lying on the parlor table and scanned the page. Recently elected president James K. Polk was still lobbying for the annexation of Texas. James read a few sentences printed from an address President Polk delivered to Congress advocating statehood for Texas. Florida had recently joined the Union as a slave state, and Iowa was soon to be admitted as a free state. It seemed to make sense that Texas would follow suit.

James turned to another section of the paper. There was an article on Captain John C. Fremont and his explorations during his third expedition to the West. The year before, the Captain had published a popular account of his journey across the Rocky Mountains on his way to California. James read the piece with interest.

Before folding up the paper and replacing it on the table, he glanced at an item about the formation of a baseball club in New York City, called the Knickerbockers. The story about the ball club brought to mind his friend, Hayden Cox. Though Hayden hadn't returned to public school over the last year and a half, James had continued to loan Hayden his schoolbooks to study. Hayden and his family would be leaving Nauvoo with the rest of the Saints in the spring. After that, James was uncertain if he'd ever see his friend again. His thoughts dwelled on the impending exodus from Nauvoo, and the sacrifices his family would be required to make.

His glance fell on the sampler Roxie was sewing, sitting on the window sill. She'd completed stitching the letters of the alphabet around the edges, and a picture of the Nauvoo temple in the center. Just as it was exemplified on the sampler, the temple was the center of their lives, James mused. Beside the sampler sat Roxie's old doll, Effie. The doll was worn and faded, and the place where James had long ago repaired the heel was frayed. Roxie had lovingly placed the doll on the window sill, facing the temple. She'd confided to James that she intended to leave Effie there on the sill when the family left Nauvoo where the doll could gaze out over the city and the temple. Effie wanted to remain in the City of Joseph, Roxie had said, her voice quivering.

James' gaze moved to the rockinghorse sitting idle in the corner of the parlor. Christian had given the horse to Roxie with fatherly pride and pleasure, and ownership had been passed down to Milly, and then to Zachary; James knew there would be no room in the wagon for the rockinghorse and it would have to stay behind. He sighed softly and returned the newspaper to the table.

Lydia glanced up from her darning. "Is anything wrong?"

"No. I was just thinking, that's all."

"Thinking about what?" She put aside her needle and gave James her full attention.

"I was remembering some of the things Brother Pratt said at the conference in the temple. Somehow it makes it easier to leave Nauvoo after listening to him."

Lydia patted his hand. "Everything will work out for us, James. God will lead us to a place where we can enjoy peace and rest, unmolested by our enemies."

"I know," James nodded. "I believe that."

"Mama?"

Both James and Lydia looked up at the sound of Elizabeth's voice. She was standing in the doorway of the parlor.

"You're not ready for bed yet, Elizabeth?" her mother asked.

Elizabeth shifted her weight from one foot to the other, her gaze fixed on the floor. James' stomach tightened. He knew whatever Elizabeth had in mind to say wasn't going to sit well with their mother; he could see that from his sister's tense expression.

"Elizabeth?" repeated Lydia.

Elizabeth drew an audible breath. "I overheard what you and James were talking about. I'm not going, Mama."

Lydia stared at her blankly. "What?"

"I'm not going with you out West. Alexander has asked me to marry him. We're staying here."

James was as startled as his mother by this announcement. Lydia rose from her chair with a stunned look on her face. "You're not serious," she gasped.

Before Elizabeth had a chance to answer, Christian entered the parlor.

Lydia stumbled to his side. "Elizabeth just said she's planning to marry Alexander Scott and stay in Nauvoo." Lydia's voice was shaking.

"Is this true?" Christian asked, his brows lifting in surprise.

"Yes. Alexander and I are going to be married, Papa."

"Now wait just a minute . . ." Christian began.

"No, Papa. You listen to me. I'm eighteen and grown up now. I have my own life to lead." Elizabeth paused, and when she spoke again her voice quavered. "Alexander and I don't believe Brigham Young is God's spokesman, and we won't follow him to some wild place in the mountains."

James slumped in his chair. He should have guessed this was coming. Alexander's blatant scorn for the Church and its members had finally infected Elizabeth.

"You don't realize the implications of this decision," Christian told her in a quiet voice.

"Yes, I do, Papa. I've thought about this for a long time."

"If you think your mother and I will agree to you marrying Alexander Scott, you've been misled, Elizabeth. The man has earned himself an odious reputation."

"You dislike Alexander solely because he's not a member of the Church," Elizabeth lashed back. "Don't try to pretend there's any other reason."

"That's not true, although we had hopes you'd marry a man strong in the faith. Choosing this course is a mistake, Elizabeth, a mistake that could ruin your life," Christian said softly.

"Ruin my life?" Elizabeth sputtered. "How in heaven's name can you presume to know that?"

"Elizabeth, that will be enough," cautioned Lydia. "I won't have you taking that tone with your father."

"Oh, no. Here comes the volley," James mumbled under his breath. He straightened his shoulders as if to deflect the strike he knew was imminent.

"He's not my father!" Elizabeth cried. "My father is lying in the cold ground of Green County. I have no father!"

Lydia's cheeks suddenly lost their color. She put a hand on Christian's arm to steady herself. Christian stood silently for some seconds. Then in a controlled voice he offered, "Perhaps we should save this discussion for later, when our tempers have cooled."

Elizabeth glared at him. For an instant James feared his sister would refuse to let the matter rest, but then she spun around and stomped out of the room.

James left his chair and went to his parents' side. "I could have told you this was going to happen. Elizabeth has been like a cannon ready for the match," he said quietly.

Lydia stared, ashen-faced, at him. "Has she spoken of this to you?"

"Not directly, at least not the part about marrying Alexander. But I've known for some time how she's felt about Pa," he answered, giving Christian an apologetic look.

"Why didn't you say something about it to us?" demanded his mother.

James shrugged his shoulders. "It wouldn't have made any difference."

"We could have reasoned with her," Lydia returned, her voice rising with emotion.

Christian put a gentle arm around her shoulder. "I should have known how Elizabeth was feeling. Been more sensitive to her needs." He hugged Lydia close. "I'll talk to her again in the morning."

James eyed his parents' despairing countenances. He hoped his father could find the right words to change Elizabeth's mind.

CHAPTER TWENTY-THREE

Elizabeth sat on a chair in her bedroom while her mother pushed another hair pin into place to hold fast Elizabeth's gleaming tresses. It was the day of her wedding to Alexander, and Lydia had offered to dress her hair for the ceremony. She had lovingly pinned up the long yellow locks into a cluster of curls at the top of Elizabeth's head, and now she was nearly through and Elizabeth was eager to get a view of the finished product. "How does it look, Mama?" she asked.

"You look absolutely beautiful," Lydia said.

Elizabeth reached for her mother's hand. "Thank you, Mama, for doing my hair. And for allowing me to wear your lovely wedding gown. It means more to me than you can guess."

Lydia squeezed her daughter's hand. "You look prettier in that dress than I did when I married your father, Abraham," she said, smiling.

Elizabeth sent her mother a tender glance. Lydia had unpacked the wedding dress from the old trunk, cleaned it, pressed it with the heavy black iron, and presented it to Elizabeth to wear. Elizabeth suspected she had done so in part as a peace offering to soothe Elizabeth's ruffled feelings concerning her natural father. The white silk dress fit perfectly after Lydia had made a few tucks and adjustments, and she felt exquisite in it.

Lydia bent down and kissed Elizabeth's cheek. "You look like an angel with that halo of golden hair," she said.

A quick smile settled on Elizabeth's face. Her hair was her crowning glory. She'd always been proud of its amber color and thick texture. And she knew that Alexander thought it was attractive, too.

"Now for the flowers," Lydia said. She selected a delicate pink-petaled blossom from the bouquet of wildflowers Roxana and Millicent had picked that morning for Elizabeth. She tucked the stem of the flower into one of the curls crowning Elizabeth's head and eyed the result appreciatively. Then she chose a sunny yellow bloom and placed it carefully. She continued tucking flowers in Elizabeth's hair until she had a garden of fragrant, colorful petals entwined through the curls. "There. I think I'm finished." She handed Elizabeth the hand mirror. "What do you think?"

When Elizabeth saw her reflection, she caught her breath. "Oh, Mama. It looks gorgeous. Thank you so much." She twisted in her chair to give her mother a hug, smelling the familiar fresh scent of homemade soap that clung to Lydia's clothing, and the sweet fragrance of her hair. A swell of emotion swept over her. "I'm going to miss you so much, Mama!"

"Shh, darling," Lydia said, rocking her gently against her breast. "Let's not speak of that now. I want you to have nothing but happiness today."

Lydia's words were sincere and heartfelt, but tinged with sadness. Elizabeth's family would be leaving for the West in a week's time, and the impending separation wrenched the hearts of both mother and daughter.

"Come on, now, or you won't be ready for Alexander. He's been waiting to come upstairs to see you for quite a spell now. I believe he has a wedding gift for you."

Elizabeth appreciated her mother's show of support. Her parents' feelings for Alexander had not changed in the weeks since her engagement, but both of them had put their disappointment and concern aside in order to provide Elizabeth with a joyous wedding day.

Elizabeth stood up from her chair and smoothed the skirt of her silk wedding dress. The silk had yellowed slightly with age, but she thought the slight discoloring was worth the price paid in order to wear the dress. The bodice fit snugly at her small waist and the full skirt billowed out like a wedding bell. Elizabeth studied herself in the mirror, pleased with her appearance. "All right, I think I'm ready to see Alexander," she giggled.

She felt a surge of excitement at the thought of becoming his wife. Within the hour she would be Mrs. Alexander Scott. The title brought another giddy rush of pleasure. She anticipated the joy of their life together. Alexander had promised to build them a fine brick house in Nauvoo and fill it with lovely furniture. He'd already showered her with presents — a lustrous pearl necklace, a silk parasol, a pair of kid riding gloves. She looked forward to all the lovely things with which Alexander would provide her in the future. Spread before her was a path of sunny happiness. She hugged her mother exuberantly. "Please ask Alexander to come up," she said, beaming.

She admired herself in the glass while she waited for Alexander to appear. She saw his reflection when he entered the doorway. Holding her breath in anticipation, she slowly turned around so he could obtain a full view of her.

He stood staring at her, a smile curling the corners of his mouth. He was already dressed in his wedding finery, black trousers and tailcoat. His dark hair was combed scrupulously into place. She waited breathlessly for his compliments.

"So," he said at last. "What do we have here?"

She twirled slowly in a circle before him so he could appreciate the whole effect.

"You look enchanting, my sweet," he said with little emotion. His eyes came to rest on her hair.

A twinge of disappointment fluttered through her when she realized that his expression had not changed since he'd entered the room; she had expected him to be stunned by her beauty. It took a moment before she realized he was not satisfied with something about her. "What is it, Alexander? Is something wrong?" She looked down at her dress to see if there were some stain or tear she had missed seeing earlier.

"Your hair," he said simply. "You know I like it falling in curls down your back."

"Yes, but I thought I might pin it up to look especially pretty for today."

He approached her and placed a kiss on her cheek. "Loosen it, my sweet," he whispered, his lips caressing her cheek. "For me."

"What?"

"Loosen your hair," he said, stepping back a pace. "I prefer it gathered at the back in long curls."

She was shocked by his request. "But, Alexander, my mother dressed it for me."

A gleam of anger suddenly flared in his eye, and then just as quickly disappeared. "You're to be my wife," he said in a smooth voice. "Your place is to please me."

She pulled away from him. "Surely you're not asking me to do this. It would hurt my mother's feelings, and I fancy my hair as it is. If this is your idea of a joke, Alexander, it's a cruel one." Her heart was throbbing in her chest. She felt betrayed by his insensitive demand.

His mouth still curved with a smile, but his eyes were hard. "I assure you that I am in earnest."

She thought perhaps he was trifling with her, mocking her as was often his custom, but as she stared into his face she realized that he was not.

He smiled, and kissed her again. "I expect to see you looking as lovely as always for the ceremony," he said evenly. "And I brought you this as a token of my affection." He handed her a small, beautifully wrapped box. He kissed her forehead and then walked from the room.

Elizabeth felt dazed. She stood staring at the empty doorway, with the gift in her hand. Her thoughts seemed to stagnate in her head. She sat down on her bed and with numb fingers unwrapped the present. Inside the box lay a gleaming blue brooch fitted in a silver setting. She stared at it, feeling no sense of pleasure or pride in its acquisition. After a moment she set aside the box with the brooch still inside and walked over to the mirror fastened to her bureau. She stared at the elaborate swirl of curls adorning her head. The wildflowers strewn in her hair glimmered in the sunlight streaming through the bedroom window.

She slowly sat down on the chair in front of the mirror and carefully removed one of the flowers from her hair. She held the blossom gently in the palm of her hand and studied it. The bloom reminded her of the bouquet of wildflowers which Kirstine Johanssen cradled in her arms on the day of her marriage to Peder. Kirstine had been glowing with happiness and Peder had watched her every move with a worshipful gaze; the Johanssen home had been filled with warmth and laughter. She had anticipated her own wedding day to be as joyous.

She let the petal fall to the floor, then plucked another flower from her hair. Downstairs her parents waited, unhappy with her choice in a mate. James would be sitting across from Alexander in the parlor, regarding him with a critical eye. Most of her family's friends had already left Nauvoo to take up their journey west. There would be few guests in attendance at her wedding today. And soon she would be separated from her family, perhaps never to see them again. Tears welled in her eyes.

She removed the rest of the flowers from her hair, dropping them one by one onto the floor to join the first in a sad little heap. She thought of the conversation at the Johanssens' home the day she had accompanied her mother and sisters there for a visit. When Jens Johanssen's name was mentioned, the conversation had grown cold. She, too, would be estranged from her family. Would they turn away in sadness when her name was introduced in conversation? Would there be regret in their words, and sorrow in their eyes?

Her fingers fumbled to find a hair pin, then she quickly pulled it out. A lock of hair fell across her cheek, growing damp from the tears that were starting to flow. Her thoughts turned to Christian and the numerous times she had defied him and lied to him in order to get her own way. She realized that the offense she had so easily taken with him was caused by her own pride and stubbornness. She didn't know how to rectify it now — the time was long past for patching prior mistakes with Christian.

She withdrew another of the pins Lydia had so carefully tucked in her hair. The pin seemed to represent her vanity in her appearance, her envy of others, her ambition for worldly acclaim. She flung the hair pin aside.

In quick succession she removed the next few pins, then stared at her reflection in the glass as her hair loosened and tumbled down around her face. Through the blur of tears, her hair took on the color of fool's gold. She remembered Alexander's words from an earlier conversation when he had referred to her as his prize. "I want the prize all to myself," he'd said. Was that all she was to him? A prize to be won? A possession to be acquired and paraded as a symbol of his wealth and attainments? Had she mistaken his greed for love? His selfishness for tenderness?

The tears slid down her cheeks as she removed the last pin and let her hair fall around her shoulders in a tangle of rebellious curls. She had wanted to marry Alexander because she thought she loved him. But had she been too influenced by his promises of pretty clothes, sparkling jewelry, and social prominence? Had her own pride brought her to this precipice? Had she sold her soul for the things of the world? Elizabeth covered her face with her hands and wept bitterly.

The sounds of guests arriving at the house for the wedding jolted Elizabeth back to the present. Soon everyone's eyes would be on her, expecting Elizabeth to glow with radiance as the happy, new bride. Not wanting to admit her doubts about marrying Alexander, Elizabeth straightened her shoulders and wiped away her tears. She was determined to find happiness with Alexander.

CHAPTER TWENTY-FOUR

Nauvoo was rapidly turning into a town on wheels. Every day wagons filled with families and goods crossed the Mississippi in preparation for their long trek west. Tomorrow James and his family would join them, leaving their beloved city and magnificent temple behind.

James' thoughts were melancholy as he gazed at the wagon standing in the yard. It was a stout, sturdy vehicle, painted bright blue with a white canvas top and shiny red wheels. A team of oxen silently waited in the barn, feeding on the last of the sweet hay they would enjoy for many months. From now on they would have to survive on the tall grass of the prairie and the bit of grain Christian held in reserve for them.

The wagon was nearly full, piled to the top of the canvas cover with clothing, blankets, tents, dry goods, seeds, nails, and the family's personal belongings. Tied to the outside of the wagon were barrels of flour and beans, a plow, hoe, and sickle. It was impossible to make room for everything. His parents had chosen carefully what must remain behind. His father had to leave most of his books, taking only a few of his prized ones, along with a newly acquired copy of John C. Fremont's *Journal to Oregon and California*. Most of the Saints had sold their homes and properties for a fraction of their value. One of the new settlers in town had offered four hundred dollars for the Kades' handsome two-story brick home. The amount was ludicrous in view of the home's worth, but James knew his father would accept the offer. It would likely be the only one he'd receive for time was running out. The first wave of Saints had crossed the Mississippi on the fourth of February, 1846, and were setting up a temporary camp on Sugar Creek in Iowa.

James turned the collar of his coat up around his ears. The February wind blew raw and bitter, chilling him through. The Saints had planned to leave Nauvoo in the spring, when prairie grass would be plentiful for the stock, but their enemies had forced them into an early and ill-prepared departure in the biting cold of winter. James repositioned an iron cooking pot to make room for the last of the household items his mother had given him to pack in the bed of the wagon. He placed each item carefully, arranging it to take up as little space as possible. Every nook and cranny was filled, except for the wagon seat where Christian would sit to drive the oxen. Lydia and the children would take turns sitting next to him on the seat, but for the most part the family would be walking the distance to the Rocky Mountains.

All of the family, that is, except Elizabeth. She and Alexander Scott had married the week before. Even though his parents disliked Alexander because of his unscrupulous character and his proud heart, once Elizabeth determined to go through with the marriage, they gave her their support. Before Elizabeth left with her new husband, Lydia bequeathed her as a parting gift the pencil drawing Christian had sketched of Lydia before they were married, and which Lydia had always treasured.

James already missed his sister more than he was willing to admit. And he felt genuine sorrow over her decision to remain in Nauvoo, alienated both physically and spiritually from the Saints. He had hoped up to the last minute that she would change her mind and travel to the Great Basin with them. Now that she was married, it was out of the question. Alexander would never leave his thriving lumber business to go west. At every opportunity he openly displayed his antagonism and disdain for the Church. No, Elizabeth would never come west now. The family would be pulling out of Nauvoo at first light. He wouldn't see Elizabeth again for a very long time. Perhaps never again.

James bowed his head and offered a silent prayer. He asked God to watch over Elizabeth and Alexander, and bless them with peace and safety. He prayed for the other members of his family as well, asking for protection as they crossed the vast plains on their journey west. He petitioned

God's blessing upon all the Saints who had suffered endless trials and heartache. And he thanked God for the blessings he enjoyed in such rich abundance. He prayed for several minutes, his lips moving soundlessly with the deep desires of his heart.

When he said, "Amen," he lifted his eyes to the hill crowning the City of Joseph. The temple on the crest of the hill rose before him in all its beauty and majesty, gleaming in the winter sunlight. James' breath caught in his throat. The sight of the temple filled him with awe. His eyes traced the lines of its stately tower resting atop a limestone structure of perfect symmetry. Thirty pilasters ringed the outside of the edifice, the base of each slender column resting on blocks of stone sculpted into moons, and the tops crowned with sun stones. Above these were engravings of stars. A gilded angel weather vane fluttered in the cold wind. The Saints had completed their building of the Lord's house; sacred ordinances for many hundreds of members had been performed within it walls, including James' own parents, who had been endowed by Apostle Parley P. Pratt. For James, the temple symbolized in a physical, tangible form, his faith in the Lord Jesus Christ and his commitment to the gospel.

James stood for a long time gazing at the temple. Its noble bearing defined the city's skyline. The temple on the hill could be seen from many miles around and would be the last landmark his eye would behold when leaving the City of Joseph. As James stood beside the wagon, with the wind howling around him and the sky threatening snow, his soul felt at peace.

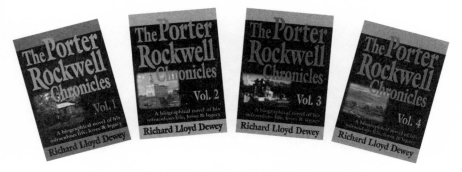

The Porter Rockwell Chronicles
by Richard Lloyd Dewey

This best-selling, historically accurate biographical novel series renders Porter's life in riveting story form, bringing it alive for adults and teens alike.

Volume 1 begins with his childhood years in New York where he becomes best friends with the future Mormon prophet Joseph Smith. The story continues through Porter's settlement with the Mormons in Missouri, where he fights against mobs and falls in love with and marries Luana Beebe.

Volume 2 covers the turbulent first four years in Nauvoo, where he continues to fight mobs and becomes Joseph Smith's bodyguard.

The Nauvoo period of his life draws to a close in Volume 3 as his best friend Joseph is murdered and his wife Luana leaves him and remarries, taking his beloved daughter Emily with her. Porter must bid a heartbroken farewell as he and the Mormons are driven from Nauvoo and flee west.

Volume 4 continues with his first ten years in Utah, where he is joyously reunited with his daughter Emily, takes on the U.S. Army in a guerilla war, and enters a new phase of adventures as U.S. Deputy Marshal.

Volume 1 (ISBN: 0-9616024-6-5)	Hardcover, $23.88
Volume 2 (ISBN: 0-9616024-7-3)	Hardcover, $23.88
Volume 3 (ISBN: 0-9616024-8-1)	Hardcover, $23.88
Volume 4 (ISBN: 0-9616024-9-X)	Hardcover, $24.88

Look for them in your favorite bookstore,
or see last page for ordering info.

Porter Rockwell: A Biography

by Richard Lloyd Dewey

The epic biography that traces Porter Rockwell from turbulent Eastern beginnings to battles with Midwestern mobs to extraordinary gunfights on the American frontier. Quotes hundreds of journals, letters, and court records. Illustrated by western artist, Clark Kelley Price.

Hardcover, $22.95   ISBN: 0-9616024-0-6

*Look for it in your favorite bookstore,
or see last page for ordering info.*

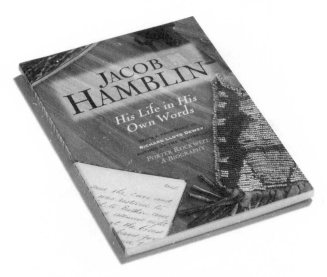

Jacob Hamblin:
His Life in His Own Words

Foreword by Richard Lloyd Dewey

Far from the gun-toting reputation of super-lawman Porter Rockwell, Jacob Hamblin was known in early Western history as the supreme peacemaker.

No less exciting than Porter's account, Jacob's adventures encountered apparent Divine intervention at every turn, a reward seemingly bestowed to certain souls given to absolute faith. And in his faith, like Porter, Jacob Hamblin was one of those incredibly rare warriors who are *absolutely fearless.*

His migrations from Ohio to Utah with life-and-death adventures at every turn keep the reader spellbound in this unabridged, autobiographical account of the Old West's most unusual adventurer among Native Americans.

In his own words, Jacob Hamblin bares his soul with no pretense, unveiling an eye-witness journal of pioneer attempts to co-exist peacefully with Native brothers, among whom he traveled unarmed, showing his faith in God that he would not be harmed.

Easily considered the most successful — and bravest — diplomat to venture into hostile territory single-handedly, Hamblin takes the reader into hearts of darkness and hearts of light.

Softcover, $10.95   ISBN: 0-9616024-5-7

Look for it in your favorite bookstore,
or see last page for ordering info.

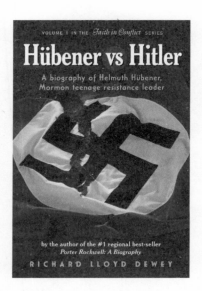

Hübener vs Hitler

A Biography of Helmuth Hübener,
Mormon Teenage Resistance Leader

REVISED, SECOND EDITION

by Richard Lloyd Dewey

Nobel Laureate author Günther Grass said Hübener's life should be held up as a role model to every teen in the world. Regional best-selling author Richard Lloyd Dewey (*Porter Rockwell: A Biography*) holds up Hübener's life as a light not only to all teens, but to adults as well.

As an active Latter-day Saint, young Hübener recruited his best friends from church and work and established a sophisticated resistance group that baffled the Gestapo, infuriated the Nazi leadership, frustrated the highest judges in the land, and convinced the SS hierarchy that hundreds of adults—not just a handful of determined teens—were involved!

While other books have told the story of the group of freedom fighters Hübener founded, this is the first biography of Hübener himself—the astounding young man who led and animated the group. The inspiring, spell-binding, true story of the youngest resistance leader in Nazi Germany.

Hardcover, $27.95   ISBN: 0-929753-13-5

Look for it in your favorite bookstore,
or see last page for ordering info.

When Truth Was Treason

by Karl-Heinz Schnibbe, Blair R. Holmes, and Alan F. Keele

This riveting, autobiographical account of Karl-Heinz Schnibbe is documented with hundreds of notes and dozens of original documents by professors Holmes and Keele, including all pertinent Nazi government documents and a fine collection of photographs and illustrations.

Published recently by the University of Illinois Press, this volume is highly recommended as a companion volume to *Hübener vs. Hitler*.

All rights to *When Truth Was Treason* have more recently been acquired by Academic Research Foundation. The last remaining copies are available for sale through Stratford Books, Inc.

Academic Research Foundation plans to republish the book under the title of *Schnibbe vs. Hitler* in 2005 as Volume 2 in the *Faith in Conflict* series.

Hardback, 467 pages.
$29.95

New ISBN number
for remaining copies:
0-929753-14-3

Note to LDS readers: This book has several passages of harsh language
that will be removed when the book is republished.

See last page for ordering info.

New Evidences of Christ in Ancient America

by Blaine M. Yorgason, Bruce W. Warren, and Harold Brown

In 1947 California lawyer Tom Ferguson threw a shovel over his shoulder and marched into the jungles of southern Mexico. Teamed with world-class scholar Bruce Warren, they found a mountain of evidence supporting *Book of Mormon* claims. Now the reader can follow their adventure as they unearth amazing archaeological discoveries and ancient writings, all of which shut the mouths of critics who say such evidences do not exist. In this volume, the newest archaeological evidences are also presented.

Endorsed by Hugh Nibley.

Hardcover, $24.95   ISBN: 0-929753-01-1

Look for it in your favorite bookstore,
or see last page for ordering info.

Porter Rockwell Limited Edition Prints and Commissioned Paintings

Porter's Ranch at Point of the Mountain
by Clark Kelley Price

Limited-edition art prints of this oil painting, which is featured on the dust jacket of Volume 4 of *The Porter Rockwell Chronicles*, are available at $75 each plus $1 shipping and handling. (See order form on last page.) The edition consists of 880 11" × 14" prints on canvas, signed and numbered by the artist.

Mr. Price's work, found in private collections worldwide, sells in exclusive art galleries and has often been featured on covers of *The Ensign* magazine. A longtime friend of the author, Mr. Price was among the first to inspire Richard Lloyd Dewey about the life of Porter Rockwell. He did the illustrations and back cover painting for Dewey's *Porter Rockwell: A Biography*.

Mr. Price is willing to paint, by commission, additional scenes from Rockwell's life (or any subject that appeals to him) at a minimum size of 24" × 36" (or any dimension of at least 864 square inches) for interested patrons. Commissioned oil paintings are priced at $10 per square inch ($8640 for 24" × 36"). Contact the artist at (307) 883-2322, or P.O. Box 211, Thayne, Wyoming 83127.

The artist requests a lead time of one year. A down payment of 33% is required on the commission. Paintings come on canvas, unframed, and patron pays for shipping.

Nauvoo, Illinois, mid-1840s
by Dan Thornton

Art prints of *Nauvoo, Illinois, mid-1840s*, depicted on the dust jacket of this book, are available from the publisher.

- **Limited Edition** signed and numbered, large size (28.5"w × 19"h) $135.00 each, plus $15.00 shipping & handling (add $1.00 shipping & handling for each additional print sent to same address)

- **Artist's Proof** (same size) $200.00 each, plus $15.00 shipping & handling (add $1.00 shipping & handling for each additional print sent to same address)

- **Greeting Card Packs** unsigned, 10 cards and envelopes $25.00 per pack, plus $3.00 shipping & handling (add $1.00 for each additional pack sent to same address)

As the 860 Limited Edition art prints sell out, the collectors' value may substantially increase.

Heber C. Kimball Home, Nauvoo
by Al Rounds

Full-color, 25" × 15" signed-and-numbered, limited-edition art prints of *Heber C. Kimball Home, Nauvoo*, depicted on the dust jacket of Volume 3 of *The Porter Rockwell Chronicles*, are available from the publisher at the price of $150.00 each plus shipping and handling.

Shipping and handling charges are $15.00 for the first print, plus $1.00 additional shipping and handling for each additional print ordered at the same time and shipped to the same address.

As the 700 limited-edition art prints sell out, the collectors' value may substantially increase.

ORDERING INFORMATION

The Porter Rockwell Chronicles, Vol. 1   (Reg. $27.50) $23.88
by Richard Lloyd Dewey. Hardcover, 490 pp.
ISBN: 0-9616024-6-5

The Porter Rockwell Chronicles, Vol. 2   (Reg. $27.50) $23.88
by Richard Lloyd Dewey. Hardcover, 452 pp.
ISBN: 0-9616024-7-3

The Porter Rockwell Chronicles, Vol. 3   (Reg. $27.95) $23.88
by Richard Lloyd Dewey. Hardcover, 527 pp.
ISBN: 0-9616024-8-1

The Porter Rockwell Chronicles, Vol. 4   (Reg. $27.95) $24.88
by Richard Lloyd Dewey. Hardcover, 568 pp.
ISBN: 0-9616024-9-X

Porter Rockwell: A Biography $22.95
by Richard Lloyd Dewey. Hardcover, 612 pp. ISBN: 0-9616024-0-6

Jacob Hamblin: His Life in His Own Words $10.95
Foreword by Richard Lloyd Dewey. Softcover, 128 pp.
ISBN: 0-9616024-5-7

Hübener vs Hitler *(Revised, Second Edition)* $27.95
A biography of Helmuth Hübener, Mormon teenage resistance leader,
by Richard Lloyd Dewey. Hardcover, 594 pp. ISBN: 0-929753-13-5

When Truth Was Treason $29.95
by Blair R. Holmes, Alan F. Keele, and Karl-Heinz Schnibbe.
Hardcover, 454 pp. ISBN: 0-929753-14-3

New Evidences of Christ in Ancient America $24.95
by Blaine M. Yorgason, Bruce W. Warren, and Harold Brown.
Hardcover, 430 pp. ISBN: 0-929753-01-1

Porter's Ranch at Point of the Mountain $24.95
by Clark Kelley Price.
Signed and numbered, limited-edition print, 11" x 14"

Utah residents, add 6.25% sales tax (before shipping & handling).

SHIPPING & HANDLING:
Add $1.00 for each book or Clark Kelley Price art print.

Send check or money order to:
Stratford Books
P.O. Box 1371, Provo, Utah 84603-1371

Or order online at:
www.stratfordbooks.com

Prices subject to change.